only ever you

Center Point
Large Print

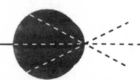

**This Large Print Book carries the
Seal of Approval of N.A.V.H.**

only
ever
you

Rebecca
Drake

CENTER POINT LARGE PRINT
THORNDIKE, MAINE

The text of this Large Print edition is unabridged.
In other aspects, this book may vary from
the original edition.
Printed in the United States of America
on permanent paper.
Set in 16-point Times New Roman type.

ISBN: 978-1-68324-029-7

Library of Congress Cataloging-in-Publication Data

Names: Drake, Rebecca, author.
Title: Only ever you / Rebecca Drake.
Description: Center Point Large Print edition. | Thorndike, Maine :
Center Point Large Print, 2016. | ©2016
Identifiers: LCCN 2016014676 | ISBN 9781683240297
    (hardcover : alk. paper)
Subjects: LCSH: Missing children—Investigation—Fiction. | Mothers
and daughters—Fiction. | Large type books. | GSAFD: Mystery fiction. |
Suspense fiction.
Classification: LCC PS3604.R3553 O59 2016b | DDC 813/.6—dc23
LC record available at http://lccn.loc.gov/2016014676

For Joe,
who believed when I couldn't

The heart will break, but broken live on.
—Lord Byron

PART I

before

Chapter One
July 2013—Three Months

On the day her life began to unravel, Jill Lassiter smeared sunscreen on her three-year-old daughter's soft skin and drove her, as promised, to the park.

It was a hot afternoon, and she held Sophia's hand as they crossed the road, leaning a little so her daughter's small arm wouldn't have to stretch too far.

While they walked Sophia chattered about the swings, about her plastic ring with the pink "jewel," about a small terrier being walked. The older woman holding the leash smiled at Sophia's cry of delight, but Jill's mind was elsewhere and she didn't really hear what her daughter said, pretending to listen with small sounds of interest.

Afterward, she'd feel guilty about this. What kind of mother didn't pay attention to her own child? Except she'd been thinking about two bar mitzvahs and a wedding she had to shoot, and attempting to mentally coordinate schedules so she and her business partner, Tania, could juggle them all.

"Let go, let go!" Sophia tugged to get free, and Jill released her hand, raising her camera as she watched her daughter run across the grass and struggle onto a swing. She was small for her age, but intent on doing everything herself. Jill offered a push and Sophia gravely accepted one, but didn't want her mother's help after that.

Jill stood to the side and snapped photos, watching her daughter's baby-fine blonde hair lifting as she swung forward and back. She had no premonition, no sense of imminent disaster.

There were few people at the playground on such a hot day. Even in the shade it was warm. Sweat darkened the hair near Sophia's temples, beaded slightly on her upper lip. Her cheeks were pink, but she didn't look as if she were getting sunburned. Jill could feel the damp against her own neck and lifted her dark hair for a moment to catch a breeze. She thought they would stay just a little longer.

When Sophia ran toward the slide, she didn't think to stop her. It was a safe, modern playground, with padding under everything, so that a child would have to work to skin a knee or scrape an elbow. She started to follow, but the crying of another child distracted her. Jill saw a mother struggling to support a howling infant in one arm while helping a little boy onto a swing with the other. The boy caught Jill's attention. She stared at him, caught by the familiar ache in her chest because he had dark hair and looked about the right age.

The baby's wailing and the other mother's

obvious distress snapped her out of it. "Here, let me help." She walked back to them, quickly giving the little boy the boost he needed.

"Oh, thank you," the mother said above the cries of the infant. "She's so hungry. Would you mind handing me that bag?" She nodded toward a large tote on the ground near her as she settled down on a park bench to nurse.

Jill set the bag down before hurrying after her own child. Helping the other mother had taken less than a minute. Two minutes at most. When she couldn't spot Sophia's blonde head bobbing above the brightly colored plastic she wasn't alarmed. Not yet.

She rushed toward the slide, using her free hand to shade her eyes. The slide wasn't like the old-fashioned ones, the single metal structures that burned the backs of your legs in the summer and had metal steps that were slippery when it rained. This was all plastic—a slide and a fort with tunnels and a climbing wall, and she thought Sophia was somewhere in that obstacle course. Only she wasn't.

Jill kept looking for that small blonde head, raising her voice when she called her name: "Sophia?" She expected to hear her daughter's high-pitched voice, to see her pop up, a question visible in her pale blue eyes. Except she didn't.

In that gap between Jill's first call and the frantic search that followed, there was a moment of such awful stillness that the only sound she heard was the startled catch of her own breath.

Other adults joined in her hunt, the woman with the two children, a man out jogging, an elderly couple walking, their voices joining hers until she could hear Sophia's name echoing through the park. She called David at work, babbling when he got on the line so that he had to say, "Slow down, slow down, I don't understand."

She didn't know who called the police, but they came before her husband, arriving in a screaming squad car. There were two of them, one short, one tall, both male, one white, one black, but beyond that she couldn't focus. She looked past them, constantly scanning the same territory over and over again. Swings, slide, wide empty field, the woods surrounding it all. Sophia had been standing right there and now she was gone.

"Does she have a history of wandering off?"

"Is she friendly with strangers?"

"Could a family member have taken her?"

She answered their questions, nervously checking her watch as they followed the route that Jill had taken through the playground.

"Did you pass anybody on your way here?"

"Who else was at the playground?"

They asked to see her camera and she handed it to them, showing them how to scroll back through the photos she'd taken. Her husband arrived, his car screeching to a halt behind the police cruiser.

David came across the field faster than she'd ever seen him run, tie flying, short blond hair in disarray, his face flushed. "Where is she? Have you found her?"

The police spread out to search. David retraced her route at a run before coming back to Jill with his hands on his head in disbelief.

A second police car arrived, then a third. Onlookers gathered on the fringes of the park. A female police officer placed a hand on Jill's arm, a touch that was supposed to be kind, but only unnerved her.

The police spoke quickly to one another and into radios, voices clipped and dispassionate, discussing doing a wider search of the wooded areas of the park and cordoning off all entrances and exits. Twenty minutes passed, then forty.

At the moment of despair, at the moment when fear overcame the guilt and Jill's body started to shake, Sophia suddenly appeared, standing in the shelter of some trees across the road from the park. She was more than fifty feet away, but Jill spotted her all the same, her small blonde head and white dress a beacon in all that green.

Jill pushed past the police officer and ran toward her daughter, calling to her with hiccupping cries. Her legs were leaden; she couldn't move fast enough. She was too scared not to scare her child, too, grabbing her with such intensity that her daughter started to cry.

"Oh, Sophia, Sophia." Her name was all Jill could utter, holding her tightly until David arrived breathless behind her, wanting to hold her, too. She passed the girl to him, but kept her hands on the little body, checking her back, her legs, for injuries.

The police tried to question the toddler. "Did you walk all the way over here by yourself?" Sophia shook her head and would only say no to every inquiry. She yawned, looking down, before mumbling, "I find a doggie."

The police looked relieved. "Is that what happened?" the female cop asked. "Did you follow a doggie?" She was smiling, the atmosphere suddenly relaxed. The news went around the small crowd that had gathered to search and they slowly dispersed, parents releasing their children back to the playground, couples walking away hand-in-hand.

"Do you think she might have followed someone walking their dog?" an older cop asked.

David nodded. "She's crazy about them, keeps begging us to get one."

Jill carried Sophia as they walked back with the police toward the parked cars. An older officer laughingly suggested that they keep their little girl on a leash, and David shook everyone's hands and thanked them repeatedly for their quick response. Jill tried to smile, but she was teary with relief. Some of the officers patted

Sophia on the head before taking off in their squad cars.

David opened the doors to Jill's car to let out the heat. "Don't wander off like that, Sophia," Jill said between kisses to her daughter's round cheeks. "You scared Mommy."

"My ring gots lost," Sophia mumbled, scratching an upper arm. Jill glanced at her chubby little hands and saw that the plastic ring with the pink gemstone was indeed missing.

"Don't worry," she said soothingly, "we'll find another one."

Sophia scratched her arm again. Jill pulled Sophia's hand so she could lift the cap sleeve of her sundress to see.

"She's got a mark here, David, she didn't have this before!" On the smooth skin of Sophia's inner arm was a tiny red pinprick with a slight swelling of the skin around it. "Jesus, someone's injected her!"

"What the hell—" Her husband grabbed his daughter's arm to look.

"They've drugged her! Sophia, did someone give you a shot?" She checked her daughter's blue eyes, but she couldn't tell if the pupils were dilated. Sophia stared at her mother, one thumb climbing to her mouth.

"It looks like a bug bite," David said, peering at the mark.

"That is *not* a bug bite."

15

At Jill's insistence, they drove to the nearest hospital. Jill held Sophia in the back of David's car, firing questions while he drove that Sophia wouldn't or couldn't answer. "How did you get in the woods? Did someone touch you? Did someone give you a shot?"

Sophia only kept up a mumbled singsong: "I find the doggie, I find the doggie."

An emergency room physician with dark circles under her eyes examined her arm. "It's hard to say. It looks like a small puncture mark, but it could be a bug bite." She gave Sophia a complete checkup and said they should give her a tetanus shot, just in case. The little girl howled when she saw the needle.

Jill held onto Sophia, wincing as the doctor inserted the needle into the soft fold of the girl's other arm and her daughter cried out.

"What about blood tests?" Jill asked as the nurse put an Elmo Band-Aid on Sophia.

The doctor looked up from the chart. "Tests? For what?"

"If someone injected her, you could check for drugs in her system, right?"

"I really don't think that's likely, Mrs. Lassiter."

"But you said yourself you can't tell. If she's been given a drug, we need to know."

David said, "Jill, do you really want to subject her to another needle?"

"No needle!" Sophia started wailing again.

"What if she's been drugged?" Jill said to David. She turned to the doctor. "Shouldn't you check for that or give her some preemptive treatment just in case?"

The doctor sighed. "I really don't think that's the case, Mrs. Lassiter, but we can run a tox screen."

Sophia howled and Jill opened her arms, but it was David she clung to this time. He seemed as upset as his daughter, holding her so tightly that Sophia had to tell him to stop squeezing her.

She had forgotten the pain of both shots by the end of the hour they had to wait while the hospital lab ran tests. She sat on the floor in front of a table strewn with old magazines and played with David's cell phone, amusing herself with a voice memo app. Jill sat next to her, a hand resting on one small shoulder until Sophia nudged it off. At fifteen minutes past the hour the doctor finally appeared looking at paperwork from the lab. "Negative for everything," she said, addressing Jill with a slightly patronizing smile. "There are no drugs in her system."

David drove them back to retrieve Jill's car. She sat next to Sophia, unable to be apart, running her hand repeatedly over her silky hair. "I shouldn't have looked away, she moves so fast these days."

"She needs to learn to stay with you," David said. He drove fast; she could see his hands gripping the steering wheel, read the tension in his shoulders.

"It's over," she said, trying to calm down, trying to calm him. "She's safe."

That night she dreamed of someone lurking in the woods waiting for her daughter, and of Sophia waving good-bye before being swallowed by the trees. Jill woke in a cold sweat and got out of bed in the darkness, padding silently across the hall to check on Sophia, surprised when she heard voices coming from her room.

In the muted glow of the night-light, she saw the outline of David sitting on the edge of Sophia's bed, the big-girl bed she'd lobbied for, not the least because she liked to climb out. She looked so tiny in it; the bed seemed huge around her. Jill stepped in the doorway and her husband looked up, startled.

"What's going on?"

"She had a nightmare."

Sophia whimpered and reached out to her mother. Jill took David's place and held her, rocking her daughter back and forth.

When the little girl slept she crept back to her own room, sliding back into bed next to David. He reached out his arms to hold her. "You know how much I love you, right?" he said. "Love you and Sophia?"

"Of course."

"You know I'd never let anyone hurt you?"

"What is it?" she said, searching his face in the darkness. "Are you afraid because of what happened today?"

He shook his head again, unwilling or unable to answer, but his arms tightened around her.

It was just residual anxiety. They'd faced every parent's worst nightmare and gotten a reprieve. It was only natural that they'd feel some leftover stress. Everything would be okay. Their daughter was here and whole, and what had happened to her was just an isolated incident. Nothing this bad would ever happen again; they had nothing to fear.

Jill was wrong.

Chapter Two
August 2013—Two Months

The real-estate agent had a nervous laugh and smelled of the peppermints she sucked to hide the fact that she smoked. They didn't. The smell of burnt tobacco lay beneath the peppermint odor, both of them nauseating, and emanated out of Patsy Duckworth's Land Rover whenever she opened the driver's door.

"Ready to see the next one?" she said with a big grin, as resolutely chipper after two hours as she'd been first thing that morning. She was a tiny woman who compensated with ridiculously high heels. It was amazing she hadn't broken her neck at one of the other houses. Bea Walsh nodded, unable to return the smile. They'd already seen five rental properties and none of them had been right. She'd known within two minutes at each house that it wouldn't work—they were too close to neighbors or didn't have finished basements—but she'd had to play along anyway, traipsing through rooms that didn't matter and pretending to appreciate features that weren't important.

"Are you looking for yourself?" Patsy had asked when Bea first came to the realty office, taking a not very discreet look at her left hand.

"Or are you sharing the rental with someone else?"

The gold of Bea's simple wedding band was burnished from years of wear. "It will be me and my husband."

"Any children?"

She'd looked away from the woman's prying eyes. "Just a small dog."

"Pittsburgh will be quite a change from Florida."

Bea just smiled.

A nervous laugh. "I guess you'll miss the sun."

If she closed her eyes, Bea could see the waves of heat shimmering above the asphalt of the hospital parking lot and feel the sweat dampening the armpits of her scrubs. "No."

They drove to the houses separately, Bea in her modest sedan trailing behind the woman's SUV through the wooded, hilly roads that lined Fox Chapel. "I think you'll like the location of the next one," Patsy said. "It's on a dead-end street; very private."

They were of a similar age, but while Patsy obviously struggled to hold onto her fading youth, paying lots of attention to hair, skin, and nails, Bea had ceased to care. Sixty-two years old last week and she knew she looked older, the stress of the past year deepening the once faint lines on her forehead and at the corners of her eyes. Her hair had more salt than pepper and she'd stopped tending to it, cutting it unfashionably short and no longer bothering to color it. The creases on either side of her nose were prominent and she blanched at seeing her face as she adjusted the rearview mirror, the physical changes shocking her, as did catching glimpses of her daughter's younger, prettier face hiding in her own.

She glanced at the address the agent had given her in case they got separated: 115 Fernwood Road. Bea entered it into her car's GPS and on the screen an arrow moved north, taking them northwest, along a stretch of wooded road and past the palatial estates of some of the wealthiest people in the country to much more modest homes. They'd been driving for seven minutes before the GPS signaled that they'd finally reached the turnoff.

A shield-shaped sign dangling from a wooden post announced FERNWOOD. The road itself was in bad shape, the asphalt skimmed away in parts so that the car bounced and rattled no matter how slowly Bea drove. It was uphill, a long stretch with one driveway peeling off to the right, and then another long stretch before a second driveway peeled off to the left. Still climbing, another thirty yards, and there it was, a narrow road barely visible through pine trees on the right. A black tin mailbox marked the end of the drive, with the number 115 adhered to it in peel-and-stick numbers. The five hung at a weird angle.

The driveway was paved with pea gravel, which sounded like buckshot spraying the under-carriage of the car. Bea couldn't hear anything over the noise and she couldn't look around, having to slow down and focus to keep on the narrow strip of road, which was only one car wide and meandered between the slender trunks of pines and maples growing so close on either side that feathery branches brushed the windows and tapped on the car roof.

Another two minutes and then the narrow drive suddenly opened up and there was the house, gray stone with a silvery slate roof, tucked against the hillside like fungi in a sea of green.

"It's really like an inverted two-story," Patsy said, indicating the attached garage at ground level. "The owner is willing to rent, but she'd really love to sell. She had a buyer last year, but it fell through. She's very motivated. Very." She waited for a response from Bea, but when none was forthcoming she laughed, raising a hand to her hair as if to smooth back an errant strand, but the artificial red helmet had been shellacked to her head with enough hairspray to ensure it didn't shift despite the late summer breeze.

The real-estate agent led the way, clicking up a flight of stone steps that climbed the hillside to the front door. Long grass crept up along the sides of the stone walls, and overgrown rhododendron bushes threatened what little light penetrated the wavy, dusty glass of its ancient windows. Bea could tell it had been vacant for a long time.

"This house was an estate caretaker's home years and years ago," Patsy said as she fiddled with the lockbox attached to the heavy wooden door. She took out the key and used it in the door lock, leading the way inside. "The estate still exists, apparently it's some sort of public trust now, but this house and two acres of land surrounding it were willed to the caretaker years ago. You'd be renting it from his granddaughter."

The house smelled musty and there was a faint odor of mothballs. Their footsteps echoed on hardwood floors darkened with age as they walked slowly through sparsely furnished rooms. There was an ancient green velvet sofa in the living room with two matching armchairs, the upholstery worn away in shiny spots and the legs of the chairs gouged with deep nicks.

"It comes furnished," Patsy said. "Isn't that wonderful?" Was she being ironic? Bea made a noncommittal noise and shifted her purse to her other shoulder. The day was overcast and the thick shelter of trees kept out what little natural light was left, making the house gloomy.

Lights flickered in a few rooms when she flipped on switches. Wallpaper covered some rooms, bubbling and peeling away in corners, while others were painted in faded, insipid shades of yellow or blue. Bea didn't care about those details. Looking out a front bedroom window, she caught a glimpse of roofline poking through the thick foliage. "That's the house we passed on the way up," Patsy said, "an elderly widower, but he's only here half the year—a snowbird."

Bea smiled slightly. It was the first truly private place she'd seen. "You said there's a basement?"

"Oh, yes, the lower level." Patsy led the way back down the hall to a door in the kitchen, which opened onto a steep flight of wooden steps. The light disappeared as they descended; it was like entering a tomb. At the bottom of the steps Patsy fumbled along the wall and an old fluorescent light flickered on above them, emitting a low hum. The ceiling was low; it felt claustrophobic. Patsy turned left, heading down a hallway lined on either side with rusting metal storage shelves, dust-coated mason jars lurking in the shadows. The hall ended in a T. Large round support pillars had been mounted in the concrete floor to the right and the left. Patsy stepped forward past a door standing ajar. "Here's the second bath." She flicked a switch and Bea saw a baby-blue sink and toilet from the seventies and a flimsy shower enclosure with a grimy glass door. Relentlessly upbeat, Patsy said, "A little cleanup, and this could be really nice."

To the left of the bathroom another door opened onto a utility area with an older-model washer and dryer separated by a laundry tub. To the right, the hallway receded into darkness. In the dim fluorescent light, Bea could just see the frame of a door partially hidden by the support pillar. "What's that?"

"That's the fourth bedroom." Patsy clicked her way across the concrete floor and tried the handle. The door creaked open. Dim light revealed a completely empty room. "Of course, technically this can't be considered a bedroom because there are no real windows." Patsy pointed at the one window, set high on the wall, but below grade, which looked onto a leaf- and debris-covered aluminum well.

"You could always freshen the paint," she added, tapping a dingy white wall. "That would brighten it up a lot."

Bea circled the space, examining the door that enclosed the bedroom. It was heavy and fit securely in the doorframe, not like those cheap hollow-core doors.

Patsy led them back up the hall and out another door into a musty-smelling garage. She pushed a button on the wall and a light came on as the garage door whirred slowly up and back against the ceiling. "This is obviously an update," she said as daylight rushed into the gloom. "It'll be great to have it in the winter."

The last thing they looked at was the backyard. Patsy led the way back up the stairs and out the kitchen door to the flagstone patio that ran the length of the house. Beyond it the hill had been graded and fenced, tendrils of ivy and overgrown grasses twining themselves between and around the wooden slats, separating a small strip of lawn from the woods that rose immediately behind it.

As they stood there, Bea heard the noise of a car bumping down the road, but she couldn't see it. "There's one other house way up at the top of the hill," Patsy said. "I'm sure you'd never see them." She swept an arm wide. "Isn't this a nature lover's oasis?"

Bea surveyed the loose and cracked flagstones, the overgrown shrubbery, and piles of last year's fallen leaves molding in corners at the base of each sagging fencepost.

"Well, take some time and think about the houses we've seen," Patsy Duckworth said, jangling her keys. "Or if you want to bring your husband back to look at any of them—"

"No," Bea said. "I'll take this one." She looked around the gloomy yard and smiled. "It's perfect."

Chapter Three

Journal—February 2009

Do you remember the first time we met? I believe that I can relive every detail, but memory is notoriously faulty and our first encounter was over three months ago.

So here is my undoubtedly flawed account: Rain. A cold, steady drizzle from a dingy sky. Umbrellas dripping on the lobby's marble floor. Two elevators pinging up and down twenty-eight floors. Hordes of half-asleep people waiting their turn. I am wide-awake; it is only my first month at the firm. Before stepping in the open car, I shake out my umbrella. It's black of course, everything in somber colors because I must compensate for my sex. Everyone trundles on, packed in close like a herd of peculiar sheep.

And that's the moment I met you. Or heard you. It was your voice first. A clear, low tenor, the first words you spoke to me: *"Hold the elevator!"* Not just to me, of course. Your voice—commanding, some might say imperious—does not move the other professionals who don't want to be delayed. The woman behind me shifts impatiently. I hear your footsteps—soon I will know that distinct, brisk walk—and I stick my soaking wet umbrella in the door just as it starts to close.

"Why did you?"

You asked me this recently, but not about our first meeting. We'd just made love in that awful, stale room, our clothes in a tangle on the thin red carpet, bodies and sheets equally sweaty, and suddenly it was that moment afterward when all feeling returns, life rushing back bleating its demands, and my body no longer held your interest. You twisted your wedding ring back on and wanted to know why I'd agreed to meet you. In that moment you wanted me to be responsible, to be the actor, to have pulled you toward what now seemed like purely, grossly animal behavior.

But back to that first meeting. Back to that moment in the elevator. Why did I hold the door? I can't see your face, not yet, but I like your voice. When the doors bounce back there is a collective groan from the other occupants of the car. Then you appear, slipping around the corner, dashing on board like it's the last train of the day. *"Thanks,"* you say, shaking your wet, blonde head like a dog, and then you look directly at me and your perfect, crooked lips part in a smile.

Chapter Four

September 2013—One Month

In the dim light of early morning, the high-pitched voice woke Jill before the blare of the alarm. "Mommy? Is it morning now?" A stage whisper. Jill cracked open an eye. Sophia stood in the doorway, a ghostly figure in a thin cotton nightgown. She'd been up once already, appearing at three a.m., tapping Jill's face and demanding to sleep with her. Jill glanced blearily at the clock; they'd made it almost to six thirty.

"Yes, it's morning now." She opened her arms and Sophia tiptoed to her, dragging Blinky, her well-loved stuffed dog, by one paw. Jill turned off the alarm before it blared and reached out a hand across the wide expanse of their king-size bed to touch David's bare shoulder. "Wakey wakey." He muttered something in response that got lost in his pillow, spread across his half of the bed like a large jungle cat, lying facedown with his arms curled above him. He wasn't a morning person.

Jill wrapped her daughter in a hug that pulled her onto the bed. This was real, here and now, not the recurring, anxiety-filled dream she'd woken from—an endless journey down a narrow, dimly lit hall, heart pounding, a familiar feeling of dread as she approached a closed door at the end. She always woke before opening the door; this time Sophia had woken her before she reached it.

Jill cuddled with her, breathing in the sweet, slightly milky little-girl aroma that was uniquely her daughter's. In the four months since she'd graduated from the crib, they'd been dealing with Sophia leaving her bed and coming into their room and their bed almost every night. This annoyed David, who'd advocated for the move to the big-girl bed, but not so she could keep them awake with her wiggling. He'd let her stay and snuggle for a few minutes before hauling her, tearfully protesting, back to her own room. While Jill agreed with him that Sophia needed to learn to sleep in her own bed, a part of her cherished the feel of that warm little body snuggled against hers. She held her close, feeling the anxiety slip away, just a little. "Who's the one and only ever Sophia?"

Sophia giggled. "I am!"

"You are!" Jill peppered her cheeks with kisses and then gave her a loud smooch on her tummy. It was a familiar ritual, a line from Sophia's favorite children's book, *On the Night You Were Born*, and mother laughed along with daughter.

"No kisses for me?" David smiled sleepily at them. Sophia clambered out of her mother's arms and onto her father's back, thumping him with little fists.

"Daddy, get up!"

David groaned, reaching behind him to fend her off, which made Jill laugh. She leaned over to give him a quick kiss on the lips and pulled Sophia into her arms. "I'll get breakfast started."

Downstairs, Jill switched on the coffee machine and poured her daughter a bowl of cereal, watching her eat it at the kitchen island, little knees tucked under her on the seat of the bar-height stool. Sophia had Blinky beside her and carried on an animated conversation with him while eating. She offered spoonfuls of soggy Cheerios to her toy, dribbling milk across the granite counter.

Jill let the chatter wash over her, yawning and staring blindly out the window above the sink while she reviewed the day ahead. Five appointments including an early photo shoot at an elementary school, but before that she had to get Sophia dressed and ready for David to drop off at preschool, then get ready herself before making the twenty-five minute drive into the city to the studio. She poured a mug of coffee and yawned again as she double-checked her calendar on her laptop. It was a wonder she remembered anything; sleep deprivation was becoming a permanent state. She felt on edge and David was already stressed, working long hours in the struggle to make partner at Adams Kendrick. If they could only get Sophia to sleep through the night in her own bed. And if only Jill could stop having that recurring dream. It woke her almost as often as Sophia.

"Have you seen my red tie?" David called down the stairs, snapping Jill out of her fugue. She sighed and rolled her eyes.

"Which one?" Yelling to be heard. David only owned at least eight red ties and they were always hanging in the same place in the closet.

"Mommy, no shouting," Sophia admonished, lifting her spoon from her Cheerios and waving it around.

David called, "The one with the little yellow shields."

"It should be on your tie rack," Jill called back, and then to Sophia, "Careful, baby, don't spill the milk."

"I'm not a baby."

"I know," Jill said. "You're a big girl."

There was a pause and then David's voice came again: "I checked, I can't find it. Did it go to the dry cleaner?"

"Hold on," Jill called. "I'll be right up." She wiped milk off the counter. "Are you done eating?"

Sophia tipped the cereal bowl to show her that it was empty.

"Good. Why don't you and Blinky go play in the family room while I help Daddy find his tie."

"Blinky doesn't want to play. Blinky wants more cereal."

"Maybe later," Jill said, taking the bowl from her and sticking it in the dishwasher. "Go play now. You can watch *Sesame Street*." She watched Sophia's little eyebrows dip down as a range of emotions played across the small face. She could see the word "no" forming like a storm cloud, but in the end the promise of TV outweighed the need to assert her independence.

"You can come, too, Blinky." She clutched her dog and wiggled onto her stomach to slide off the stool. Jill watched, ready to catch her if she fell, biting her lip to keep from offering unwanted assistance. She followed her into the family room and made sure Sophia was safely on the sofa with the TV switched on before she hurried upstairs.

David stood in front of the large mirror in the master bath buttoning a starched white dress shirt.

"Are you sure you checked the rack?" Jill headed into their walk-in closet.

"Of course." David came in behind her and reached for a pair of charcoal-gray trousers.

His suits were always conservative, the ties only slightly less so. She flicked through the rainbow of silk, rapidly eliminating most of the red ones.

"Here it is." She found the tie with the golden shields and held it out to him.

He had the grace to look sheepish. "Where was it?"

"Underneath the blue with red stripes and next to the yellow with blue flecks."

"I checked it twice!"

She refrained from saying "I told you so," watching as he slung the tie around his neck and rapidly tied it, muttering when he realized it fell too short.

Jill said, "Here, let me."

He turned from the mirror and she undid the knot, pulled the tie free and started again, deftly re-knotting it.

"You're a woman of many talents." David wrapped an arm around her waist, pulling her to him.

She relaxed in his arms even as she protested, "We don't have time."

"There's always a few minutes," he murmured, turning her face up to kiss her. There was a distinct if dull crash from downstairs.

She jerked away. "What was that? I've got to check on Sophie."

David drew her back. "She probably knocked over a toy." He kissed her lips, moved to her neck.

"Or she's hurt herself." Jill broke free and went to the door. "Sophie? Sophia, are you okay?" She could hear the TV, but no little voice answered her calls. "I've got to check on her."

David sighed. "She's fine, Jill. If she wasn't you'd hear her crying." She couldn't help the flinch, just a slight, involuntary reaction, but he saw it all the same. A stricken look crossed his face. "I didn't mean—"

"I know." *Don't think about it, don't think about him, not this morning.* She couldn't meet David's eyes. "I have to check on Sophie."

The anxiety was always there, flowing like an underground river through all her interactions with their child. It frustrated David; she knew he didn't understand it. For him what had happened, happened—the past could not affect the present. David kept all his feelings carefully compartmentalized, those he deemed "pointless" registered and put away. Past tense. For Jill the grief was still active, crouching at the edges of her life, prone to surprise attacks that left her as emotionally raw as if it had all happened yesterday.

Almost worse, though, was the legacy of everything they'd been through: Fear. "You can't protect her from everything," David had said more than once, watching her struggle to keep Sophia from any harm.

She ran down the stairs and through the kitchen into the family room. Sophia sat snuggled up on the couch with Blinky, staring mesmerized at the TV. "What was that noise, honey?"

Sophia shifted her gaze reluctantly from the TV to her mother's face, eyes glassy, looking like some underage drug addict.

"What was that noise?" Jill repeated, looking around the room. "It sounded like something fell over." The room looked as it usually did, floor covered in a chaotic jumble of Sophia's toys. Nothing seemed obviously out of place. It could have been one of her wooden blocks falling off something. Jill automatically stooped down to pick them up and toss them back in their bin. "Hey, you know you're supposed to pick up the toys when you're done playing." They were scattered all over the carpet.

Sophia moved her stuffed dog's head close to her ear, pretending to listen. "Blinky says someone was at the window."

"What? Where?" Jill immediately stood up and peered through the glass, but there was too little light to see more than outlines and shadows. She turned back, but now with that prickly sensation of being watched. "Are you pretending, Sophie? Or was someone really there?"

"Blinky saw her."

"Her?" A quick look back out the window, but peering through the twilight produced nothing but patio and the lawn behind it. Definitely Sophia's imagination, but Jill suddenly felt uncomfortable leaving her downstairs alone. "Let's go get ready for school."

"No! More Elmo!" Sophia shifted deeper into the couch.

Jill pulled her up, ignoring her protests, and sent her scrambling upstairs dragging Blinky.

She paused in the hall and then walked over to

the French doors that were between the kitchen and the family room. She switched on the outside light and peered outside before cautiously opening the door. The stonework patio and then the empty lawn, silvered with dew, stretched out before her. There was nobody out there. She started to close the door and saw that one of the tall planters flanking it had been knocked on its side, cracking the terra-cotta and spilling dirt and purple mums over the stone.

"What on earth?" Jill knelt and carefully righted it, scooping up dirt and flowers, patting it all back in some sort of order. She stood back up, looking around. What had knocked it over? Or who? There was no wind blowing. Could Sophia really have seen someone outside? No, it must have been the next-door neighbors' golden retriever again. The stupid dog was always loose, though his owners claimed they'd installed an invisible fence. Another argument against getting a dog. Usually he wreaked even more havoc, tearing through the flower beds, but those didn't look disturbed.

Puzzled, she walked back inside. David stood in the kitchen texting with one hand while he attempted to pour coffee into a silver travel mug with the other. He startled when she took the coffeepot out of his hand, shoving the phone into his front pocket. "I thought you'd gone upstairs—where's Sophia?"

She screwed the lid on the mug. "She's getting dressed."

"Is she okay?"

"Fine."

"I knew it." He hefted his briefcase off the floor and onto a barstool. "You worry too much."

"She says she saw someone outside."

"Really?" He sorted through papers, clearly only half-listening. "Would you mind dropping off Sophia this morning? Andrew's called an early meeting."

"This early?" Andrew Graham was David's mentor at Adams Kendrick, but he was married with kids, too. He didn't usually schedule quite this early. Was this the future if David made partner?

His phone started ringing, an insistent buzzing sound. He pulled it out and glanced at the number, but instead of answering slid the phone back in his pocket.

"Aren't you going to answer?"

He shook his head. "It's just Andrew again."

"Don't you want to know why he's calling?"

"Look, can you drop Sophia off or not?" David snapped.

"Okay, sure." Jill held up her hands. "Don't bite my head off." The phone stopped and there was silence for a long minute.

"Sorry." He sighed, running a hand through his hair. "I'm just stressed about this case." His phone started buzzing once more.

"I guess you're not the only one." She kept her voice cool.

David yanked the iPhone out of his pocket and switched it off. The buzzing abruptly stopped. He gave her a kiss and a rueful smile. "Forgive me, Jilly?" He was the only one who called her that; she softened a little, straightening his hair with her hand. He smiled, caught her hand and kissed it. "Thanks for doing the drop-off."

"I'll have to hurry—I've got an early shoot." She glanced toward the family room. "That stupid dog next door knocked the planter over and Sophia must have seen his owner coming to retrieve him. I didn't hear any barking, though, did you?"

"Barking? No." David shouldered into his coat.

"I'm really tempted to call over there and complain—that dog is a menace; do you think I should?"

"If you think it would do any good." He wasn't really listening, already lost to work as he grabbed his briefcase and headed for the garage. She picked up the coffee he'd forgotten, following after him as he slid behind the wheel of the beloved black BMW that he'd purchased after driving Andrew's virtually identical model.

"Thanks," he said as she handed him the mug, leaning out for a distracted kiss before backing down the driveway. Jill walked to the end of the garage and watched as he quick-reversed onto the cul-de-sac, tires squealing. He waved once before speeding away.

Their street was eerily still. Jill saw no sign of movement in the windows of the other large houses. No sign of the roaming golden retriever either. It was so quiet she could hear the hum of a bumblebee hovering over a rosebush near the end of the driveway.

This neighborhood of large new builds should have been priced out of their league, but the housing bubble had changed things. Someone else's foreclosure had seemed like a lucky break for them at the time, but perhaps it was only bad karma. They'd fled the city for a fresh start, had lived out here for almost three years, but for Jill it still didn't feel like home.

There were still several empty lots for sale on their street, weeds long since grown over the dirt because no one could afford to build anymore. The other houses built during the market frenzy all had the same overproduced feeling as theirs— cathedral-ceilinged entryways, enormous granite kitchens with wide islands, master bedroom suites with walk-in closets and jetted tubs—as if competing with your neighbors had been the whole point. Not that they knew any of their neighbors, not really. Expensive cars came and went daily, but she caught only occasional glimpses of the people inside. She knew the names of only a few. There was evidence of children, but she'd never seen any actually playing on the expensive swing sets sitting in the corners of the immaculate lots. Could one of these neighbors have been in her backyard? She shivered, feeling a chill despite the warm weather, and hurried back inside.

Upstairs Sophia sat on the floor of her bedroom doing a puzzle and wearing nothing but a pair of orange shorts. "C'mon, you," Jill said with a sigh. "You've got to finish getting dressed."

"No!"

Jill ignored her, pulling two dresses Sophia loved from the closet. "Do you want the pink one or the green one?" The advice from all the various parenting articles Jill had read said that you defused battles by offering a child choices. The experts had obviously never met a child like Sophia.

"No!" She stamped one little foot. "No dress, no dress, no dress!"

Jill winced at the piercing shriek. "You need to pick something, then, because we need to get to school."

"No school!"

"Yes, school, and Mommy's driving this morning, so we need to get going." Jill pushed Sophia gently but firmly in the direction of her closet. "Choose or I'm going to."

Ten minutes and as many tantrums later and

Sophia was dressed, albeit in a long-sleeved purple shirt that clashed with the orange shorts, and with her bare feet clad in snow boots. Never mind that it was September and already seventy-five degrees outside. Jill just stuffed a T-shirt and sandals into a bag in case Sophia changed her mind once her preschool class went outside.

As Jill wrestled Sophia into her car seat in the Toyota, it occurred to her that she'd once thought of people who let their children dress like this as bad parents. Now *she* was that bad mother. Parenting sometimes felt like a constant exercise in humility.

As they drove past the next-door neighbor's house, Jill noticed newspapers piled up on the driveway. Probably off vacationing somewhere. They were the sort of couple who had perpetual tans and spoke of their latest cruise the way others discussed what they were having for lunch.

She was racing along the winding suburban roads toward the preschool when it suddenly hit Jill: If the neighbors were gone then they couldn't have been in her yard and neither could their golden retriever. They always boarded the dog when they were away. For just a minute, before the endless minutiae of her daily life swept it out of her mind, Jill felt that same prickly sensation at the back of her neck. Then what—or who—had knocked over their planter? And who had Sophia seen at the window?

Chapter Five
September 2013—One Month

Finding a way into the house had been easy. Mabry Maids Cleaning Service traveled around Pittsburgh in cheery royal-blue vans emblazoned with a logo of a perky female in a short-skirted maid's uniform bending prettily at the waist with a feather duster outstretched in one hand. The sexism didn't seem to bother any of the women who piled out of the vans in front of 102 Wakefield Drive and other houses throughout Fox Chapel, nor did the fact that they bore little resemblance to their company's icon. They wore baggy pants and sneakers and royal-blue polo shirts with the company logo, some obviously well worn, the bright color faded from over-washing. The young ones tied their hair in too-tight ponytails and wore latex gloves to protect ten-dollar manicures. The older ones were thin and sinewy looking, or overweight with elastic-waist jeans stretched tight across ample bottoms, and some of them paused to take a smoke out-side, careful to pocket the butts so they didn't mar clients' pristine lawns.

Three women to a van, but sometimes that number climbed to four if the house was especially large. They took two to three hours inside each property, sometimes a little longer. Bea had staked out the neighborhood and created a careful record of days and times. The Mabry Maids visited 102 Wakefield Drive and two of its neighbors on Tuesday mornings usually by eight a.m. They were usually done at 102 by ten thirty a.m. and off the street before three p.m., moving from Wakefield to another street and then another before they were done for the day and heading back to a parking lot behind an old brick warehouse in the Strip District, where Mabry Maids maintained an office.

A short bald man with skin the color and texture of day-old porridge sat at the front desk watching TV on a small color set with a large cable box attached to it. He'd reluctantly turned down a court show and scowled up at Bea through dirty Coke-bottle glasses when she asked for an application. The place had smelled like male BO and microwave popcorn.

"We ain't hiring nobody new right now," he said, wiping his hands across the front of a dirty blue coverall before pulling an application form out of a scarred metal filing cabinet behind his desk. "You can fill this out, but don't expect no calls unless something happens to one of my girls."

At the end of each shift, once the Mabry Maids van had returned to the warehouse lot, the cleaning women split up, each heading off in different directions across the cracked asphalt. One woman got into a rusting Volkswagen bug and drove it to a small day-care center with dingy plastic toys fading in the fenced dirt patch that passed for a yard. She was out. The second woman seemed more promising, smoking menthols alone at a bus stop, but just as Bea approached, a Chevy truck roared up with a heavily bearded man in a flannel shirt behind the wheel and the woman tossed her cigarette, climbing into the cab with a big smile. That left number three, who turned out to be Donna, thirty-year-old childless divorcée and budding alcoholic. Bea learned all this at Vann's, a Lawrenceville fixture that was little more than a dark, nicotine-soaked shotgun row house with a bar running down one side of the twelve-foot space and small tables and chairs down the other.

Donna ordered a beer, followed by two more, every night except Thursdays and Fridays, when she celebrated the impending weekend with a string of White Russians. She believed because she didn't mix her alcohol she was not a heavy drinker. How many people like that had Bea seen over her years of nursing? Men and women suffering from ruined livers and pancreatitis? Donna was young enough not to exhibit the "tells"—veiny nose and slight hand tremors—but they were definitely in her future.

Bea had provided a free-of-charge wake-up call.

The previous Friday evening, Bea followed her into Vann's and took a seat at the end of the bar, well away from Donna's small table. It was just after five p.m., but the bar was steadily filling up, men and women pressing against one another as they ordered drinks, the men in tight-fitting T-shirts and jeans, the women wearing skimpy skirts or skinny jeans in a rainbow of colors. Donna had changed into a dress, a tight black jersey number that clashed with her skin tone, but set off the bleached blonde hair that she'd freed from a ponytail to back-comb and spray into something resembling a lion's mane.

An Indian summer. It was still so hot outside that the short walk from overly air-conditioned cars into the barely air-conditioned bar left patrons mopping at brows and plucking at necklines. Bea's hands were clammy against her glass. She'd made sure to arrive at the place ahead of Donna, securing a stool at the end of the bar. From this vantage point she could watch her in the smoked-glass mirror that ran the length of the room.

The bartender, a beefy young woman with a tattoo of orange flames jutting from the cleavage of her tank top, barely glanced at Bea when she placed her order. Vann's wasn't a place where everybody knew your name. Bea sipped her drink and studied the mirror.

When Donna began her second White Russian,

Bea slid her hand into her purse and pulled out the small syringe carrying a high dose of Rohypnol, hiding it in her palm and quickly depressing the plunger into her own White Russian. The lights were low enough that no one noticed. No one had noticed her taking it from the hospital either. One middle-aged nurse in scrubs was the same as another. She watched the mirror, waiting until Donna stood up and made her way through the crowded room toward the even skinnier passage-way that led to the restrooms in the back. The floor felt sticky under Bea's feet, but she moved rapidly through the noisy crowd after her, drink held high to protect it. The music faded as she pushed into the ladies' room. Donna was in a stall, but she always placed her drink on the little ledge above the sink. Bea switched drinks and headed into the second stall with drink in hand, almost colliding with Donna, who'd emerged tugging her dress down around fleshy thighs.

Bea waited in the restroom for two minutes, then made her way back out to the bar. Her seat had been taken so she stood and watched in the mirror as Donna sipped her drink. It was a hot night and she was always thirsty—it didn't take long for her to finish. Bea stayed until she saw the woman swaying from the drug's effects, waiting until Donna fell over, commanding everybody's attention in a way she'd never managed when she was conscious. Bea slipped unnoticed out of the noisy, hot bar onto the humid, quiet street; she sat in the parking lot until she heard the wail of approaching sirens.

The following Tuesday morning as the Mabry Maids climbed into their van, Bea approached wearing the blue uniform shirt and the same black wig she'd worn to apply for the job. "I'm Linda, Donna's replacement—she's in the hospital," she said to Rose, the woman in charge, who looked nothing like the flower and greeted her with a curt nod. Mr. Magoo at the office had conveniently waived the background check when he came up shorthanded. It had been enough that Bea had scribbled in the name of a Florida cleaning company on her fake résumé, listing Frank's cell phone number in case Mabry Maids called for a reference.

The younger woman in their trio, Liz, slipped on headphones once they were on the road, and Rose drove in silence, calloused hands knotted on the wheel. Bea slouched in the backseat and looked out the window, resisting the urge to fiddle with her wig. It looked like real hair, but it was best not to call attention to it. Her chest tightened when Rose pulled off Route 28 onto Fox Chapel Road. As they turned onto Wakefield Drive, Bea sat up, heart rate increasing like a moth fluttering.

The Lassiter house was so large, so luxurious. She'd driven past many times, each time struck again by its size. It was a neighborhood of massive homes, newer construction, and Bea knew that all of them would have the same soaring entranceways and vast kitchens that Frank laughed about. He'd done construction on homes like these during the good years. Sometimes he had described them to her at night, when they were sitting out on the screened-in porch off the back of their two-bedroom ranch in Tampa. "What do they want all that space for in the hallway? So everybody can sit there staring up at the ceiling?" He'd talk about how nobody who owned these homes did any housework. They'd hire cleaning crews and lawn crews and painters and plumbers and any service person they could think of to avoid doing any honest labor.

The family car was backing out of the Lassiter driveway as the van pulled up to the house. Bea averted her eyes as the Toyota sped past. Not that Jill would recognize her; only the child had seen Bea's face. Still, she had to be more careful. If she hadn't knocked over the planter that morning, trying to get a better look through the French doors, she wouldn't have been forced to dive for the cover of the bushes along the side of the house. It was lucky that the neighbors on that side were away or someone else might have spotted her.

It felt strange walking up to the house in broad daylight. Bea had to resist the urge to look over her shoulder and see if anyone was watching. Rose took a ring of keys from her pocket and used one to open the front door. Bea caught only a glimpse before the keys went back in Rose's pocket. She wasn't sure how, but she had to get the key to make a copy. No security system beeped as they trooped past the door; it appeared the Lassiters didn't have one. There was one problem solved. Before Rose could assign her a task, Bea immediately volunteered to clean upstairs.

The preschool drop-off had become one of Jill's responsibilities. "Just for a few weeks," David said, while he got through this difficult case. Jill couldn't say no, especially since the only other option was asking David's mother. "I know she'd be happy for the one-on-one time with Sophia," David had suggested, pulling out his phone.

"No, that's okay, I'll do it."

"You're busy, too, and she loves to help out. Why not ask her?"

The last thing Jill wanted to have to deal with in the morning was her mother-in-law. "She doesn't know how to use the car seat."

"I'm sure we could teach her."

"She doesn't want to learn; she thinks they're unnecessary. Don't you remember the last time she took Sophia out? She didn't even have the straps tightened."

"It's not that long a trip to preschool."

"She could still have an accident," Jill said, pretending she didn't see David shaking his head in frustration. "I can take Sophie; it's no problem."

And it wouldn't have been a problem, they were out the door more or less on time, except Jill had made it a mile down the road toward preschool when Sophia cried, "I forgot Blinky!"

Jill glanced at the dashboard clock. "Sorry, honey, but we don't have time to go back."

Sophia kicked and thrashed in the car seat, convulsing like someone receiving electroshock therapy. "Blinky! I need Blinky!" Fat tears rolled down cheeks turning pink with rage. She was quite capable of keeping this up all the way to preschool. Jill's temples throbbed.

"All right, all right. Settle down! We'll get him!" She squealed to a stop before making an awkward, and undoubtedly illegal, U-turn in the middle of the road. Cars in both lanes slammed on their brakes and hit their horns, adding to the cacophony. Jill waved a lame apology, racing back down the road toward home, certain she was being a terrible parent, but equally certain that she couldn't just drop off a sobbing Sophia at preschool.

Alone on the second floor, Bea donned latex gloves and ran a noisy upright back and forth over the plush, cream-colored carpeting. The child's bedroom was close to the stairs, with a bathroom between it and the master bedroom. Bea ran the vacuum into the room and quickly swept the floor while she surveyed the pale pink walls and white furniture. All of it high-end, of course. Switching off the machine, she ran a gloved hand over the child's bed, pressing a pillow to her face for a long moment, breathing in the child's scent. She flitted a dustcloth over shelves filled with toys, most of them neatly tucked into white wicker baskets lined with pink gingham. The young fairy princess walking down a country lane in the wall mural seemed to watch Bea as she plucked several blonde hairs from the soft bristles of a silver-backed brush sitting on the dresser.

Jill peeled back onto Wakefield Drive and pulled the car into the driveway, slamming it in park. Hitting the garage door opener, she exited the car leaving the engine running. Ducking under the slowly rising garage door, she ran back through the kitchen, startling one of the cleaners.

"Did you forget something, Mrs. Lassiter?"

Jill nodded, yanking out each kitchen chair before checking the family room. "Gray stuffed dog—have you seen him?"

"Sorry, no."

She ran up the stairs to the second floor, dashing

into Sophia's freshly cleaned room, checking the shelves and the floor and dropping down to search underneath the bed. No Blinky, but the cleaners hadn't vacuumed under there—she'd have to say something, but not today.

Where was the stuffed dog? She should put a homing device on the damn thing. Jill raced out of Sophia's room and down the hall.

The master bedroom was vast, hotel-like. Bea made the king-size bed quickly—she certainly knew how to do hospital corners—smoothing the deep blue duvet and arranging all the pillows. A pair of men's trousers had missed the laundry hamper in the walk-in closet and she retrieved them, taking time to check the pockets for anything useful. She wondered where David Lassiter put his things and checked the drawers in the closet until she identified his and hers. Business cards and receipts, a few odd coins. Jill Lassiter had a jewelry drawer, expensive pieces laid out like cold cuts in a deli case, ready for anyone to covet and steal. For a moment Bea considered taking a gold bangle, but something like that would surely be missed; she didn't need the police after her.

Leaving the vacuum running, she examined the attached master bath. A silk robe hung from a hook on the back of the door. Bea sniffed it, detecting Jill's perfume, and searched the pockets.

She took a few short strands of fair hair left in a comb on David's sink. She stepped into the massive shower stall, with its stone tiles and dual shower heads, carefully scraping up the dark hairs coiled around the drain.

"Excuse me?" The voice behind her shot Bea's heart rate into overdrive.

Jill had to shout to be heard over the vacuum. The cleaning woman hunched over in the master shower jerked upright. Jill said, "Sorry to interrupt you, but I'm looking for my daughter's stuffed dog. Old and gray, obviously well loved. Have you seen it?"

The older woman nodded, stepping out of the shower. "It was on the bed," she said in a gruff voice, eyes flicking to Jill's before looking away. One of her eyelids drooped, which she was obviously self-conscious about. Jill tried not to stare at that or at her weirdly asymmetrical black bob. As the older woman brushed past, Jill caught a glimpse of gray hair poking out one side and realized it was a wig. The woman switched off the vacuum as she crossed to the far side of the room. There, on an armchair, sat Blinky. The woman picked the toy up with a latex-gloved hand and held it out to Jill, who tried not to think about the germ transfer.

"Thank you! You're a godsend!" Jill took Blinky and bolted out of the room, racing back downstairs in a panic. In her annoyance and hurry she'd left Sophia alone in an unlocked, running car. She dashed through the kitchen and out the garage. The car was still there, still running, but the car seat—was it really empty?

"Sophia!" She ducked in the open driver's door, lunging toward the backseat. "Sophia!"

"Mommy?"

The little voice surprised her. Jill reared up, banging her head against the car's roof. Through painful fireworks she spotted her daughter crouched on the floor in the rear.

"Oh thank God!" Jill reached for her and Sophia stood up. "What are you doing out of your car seat? You scared me!"

"I want my doggie."

"I know, here he is, but you're not supposed to unstrap from your seat, are you?" Jill stretched out like a contortionist to haul her daughter back into the seat and fasten the straps. Sophia clutched her stuffed dog with a sigh that made Jill smile, tear tracks visible on her daughter's soft little cheeks.

For the second time that morning, Jill backed out of her driveway and headed for Tetterby Preschool. She glanced in the rearview mirror, watching Sophia burying her face in Blinky's gray "fur." She should really wash the dog; who knew what that cleaning woman had touched with those gloves?

• • •

"Linda?" Rose bellowed from downstairs. "Linda? Are you up there?" Rose's voice got louder. Bea could hear footsteps clomping up the stairs. She ran to pick up the vacuum wand and cast one last look over the room.

"There you are!" Rose stood in the doorway, looking exasperated. "Why didn't you answer me?"

"I didn't hear you over the vacuum."

"You should get your ears checked," the woman snapped. She looked around the master bedroom and gave it a grudging nod of approval. "This will do. C'mon, you can clean the kitchen floor."

While she mopped the tiles, Bea did a quick search of the kitchen, hitting pay dirt with a spare set of keys buried deep in a drawer. These went straight into her pocket. While the floor dried she did a rapid walk-through of the first floor, taking photos with a small digital camera that she'd hidden in a fanny pack worn under her uniform polo.

Just past the formal living room was a closed door, which turned out to be a study that looked like something out of a film set. Floor-to-ceiling bookcases in deep mahogany, lined with law texts and other works, and a few carefully chosen knickknacks—a crystal paperweight, a plaque from a law association citing David Lassiter as associate of the year, silver frames with pictures of the law school graduate and his wife and child.

An iMac sat on the desk. Password protected, of course, but Bea had read an article suggesting that people weren't clever enough with their passwords. She tried all the Lassiter names, then several combinations of initials and birthdates. The fifth try worked. Delighted, she searched the browser history and scrolled through David Lassiter's email account. The door banged opened and Bea quickly put the computer to sleep, pretending to dust around it.

"What are you doing?" Rose stood in the doorway, gloved hands on wide hips. "I'm the one who cleans this room."

"I didn't know." Bea lifted the cloth from the desk, clenching it in her hand. "Where should I clean next?" She locked eyes with the other woman, making her gaze wide and unblinking.

Rose looked away first. "Nowhere. We're done here—we got to get on to the next house."

Bea walked ahead of Rose, feeling the other woman's suspicion like a heat rash. What if she reported her to Mr. Magoo back at the office? Not that it would make any difference. By the time it mattered, "Linda" would be long gone.

Chapter Six

September 2013—One Month

For David the preschool drop-off took no more than five minutes—pull up out front, hand over Sophia to the one of the smiley teachers with a quick hug and kiss, and pull out into the queue exiting the parking lot. For Jill it didn't work that way. She couldn't just drop Sophia at the door with the crush of kids; she needed to walk her all the way into her classroom. A process the teachers discouraged because they felt it was disruptive. Even Sophia didn't like it. "Let go, Mommy!" she said, yanking her hand from Jill's as soon as they stepped in the door, running ahead of her down the hall to the classroom, still clutching Blinky. Jill followed after her; she knew it was silly, but she had to see Sophia safely into the room before she felt comfortable leaving.

Several female employees stopped Jill on her way out, wanting to know what had happened to David. "He's not sick, is he?" an aide asked, big eyes round with concern.

"Nope, just busy with work," Jill said.

"Oh, that's good." The young woman smiled. "He's such a devoted dad."

And wasn't Jill an equally devoted mom? She

was torn between annoyance and amusement as she hurried toward the main door; David, as always, had managed to charm all of them.

"Mrs. Lassiter? Can we talk?"

Jill turned to see the director of Tetterby Preschool, sixtysomething Mrs. Belmar, bearing down on her. Jill kept one hand on the door, holding out the other to forestall her. "I'm sorry, but I really don't have time this morning—"

"Just a quick chat," the other woman interrupted, beckoning with her hand even as she pivoted, leading the way back down the hall.

Once Jill followed her inside the office, Mrs. Belmar closed the door behind her, muting the sounds of a teacher leading a class in a chirpy, high-pitched good morning song.

"I'm so glad I caught you." Mrs. Belmar took her seat behind a wooden desk with a few carefully arranged silver-framed family photos and a large African violet in a white glazed pot. "Do you think Sophia enjoys being at Tetterby?" She peered at Jill through thick-framed glasses, short white hair floating around her wide, square face like a cumulus cloud—the only soft thing about her.

"Yes, very much so." Jill tried to meet the woman's gaze, but her eyes kept straying to the clock ticking away on the wall behind her. She had an early portrait shoot with a new client and her baby.

"That surprises me given what I've been hearing from her teachers." With large hands, the nails blunt cut and unpolished, Mrs. Belmar fiddled with a string of pearls resting on her chest. "They say Sophia's been having some trouble."

"Well, she was a little shy at first, but I think she's getting over that."

"Shy?" Mrs. Belmar gave a short, mirthless snort. "Oh yes, I think she's quite overcome that."

Jill tensed, finally focusing on the director rather than the rapidly evaporating window of opportunity to make it to the studio on time. "I don't know what you mean."

"What I mean, Mrs. Lassiter, is that Sophia neither listens to her teachers nor her classmates."

Jill sighed. "I'm sorry. We know she's strong-willed, but we're hoping it's just a phase."

Mrs. Belmar nodded, a tight smile on her face. "We certainly hope so too, Mrs. Lassiter. We'd hate to lose her."

"What are you saying? Are you asking her to leave?"

The older woman leaned forward, clasping her hands together on her desk. "What I'm saying, Mrs. Lassiter, is that Tetterby maintains a long waiting list, and if a child hasn't adjusted to the preschool experience within two months then it's probably an issue of maturity. Perhaps you should keep her home and try again next year?"

"No!" Jill practically shouted it. What would

61

she do if her daughter were home all day? She'd have to hire a nanny, which they really couldn't afford, or take Sophia to the studio. Jill would never get anything done. She cleared her throat, continuing more softly, "Please. I know school has been a big adjustment for Sophia, but please give her a little more time. I'll talk with her; we'll work on her listening skills."

Mrs. Belmar pursed her lips for a moment, then sighed. "All right, Mrs. Lassiter. We'll give it a few more weeks. But if things have not improved by then I'm afraid Sophia will have to leave."

She walked Jill back up the hallway to the exit, slowing as they passed the three-year-olds' room. All the children were sitting in a circle listening to the teacher read a story except for Sophia, who was standing alone at the wooden play kitchen with a sulky expression on her face, restlessly turning knobs on the play oven. Mrs. Belmar didn't say anything, but she didn't need to. Jill's anxiety turned up another notch, a slow burn suffusing her body as if she were cooking in the toy oven.

"I hope Mr. Lassiter is okay," Mrs. Belmar added as she said good-bye. "It's so nice that he brings Sophia in the morning."

As she sped out of the parking lot, Jill wondered why men were so often lauded for doing the most basic parenting. Jill was the one who got Sophia ready for school and picked her up every day, who provided the class with snacks when their turn rolled around each month, and who helped out at class parties and on field trips. David never did any of these things; very few fathers did.

Of course, in this case it might not be all fathers being appreciated, but just David, who'd won over the preschool staff with his effortless, boyish charm. She'd seen it happen time and again—older waitresses fawning over him at restaurants, saleswomen and -men gravitating toward him in stores. Even the teenage girls who worked the counter at their local coffee shop rushed to chat with him, always managing to remember his order, but never hers. Worse, all of his charm seemed unconscious. He reacted with a "who, me?" expression if Jill pointed it out.

What would he say about Sophia's problems at school? Would he think she was being overly anxious about this, too? She wished he had done the drop-off this morning so Mrs. Belmar could have spoken to him directly. Of course, she probably would have chosen to talk to Jill anyway; a child's problems were always assumed to be the mother's responsibility, not the father's.

Jill sped as fast as she dared on the back roads, but traffic ground to a halt, as usual, on Route 28. Stop and start, and then an accident on the bridge, and everyone trundled into one lane crawling past an ambulance and police cars. The river was a sluggish ribbon of dull pewter under a gray sky. She called Tania but it went straight to voice mail. "Hey, it's me. I'm running very late and we've got a client at nine—could you keep her entertained until I get there?" She hung up and called the studio, asking the same of their young receptionist, Kyle.

She took back streets off Washington Boulevard, but still pulled up over ten minutes late at the studio, a narrow storefront in Point Breeze. A large silver Volvo hogged two parking spaces out front. Jill had to drive a block farther down before she found a spot. She grabbed her bag and raced back up the street, just as the rain, which had been threatening all morning, suddenly fell. She held her purse over her head, running faster.

Looking through the front window, she could see Kyle talking to someone on the phone. He hung up as Jill pushed open the door, bell jangling.

"Is Tania here?"

He shook his head. "Nope."

"Great, just great," Jill muttered, brushing water off her clothes. Kyle stared at her blankly. He didn't seem to understand sarcasm. Early twenty-something, he was messy and not particularly self-directed. Still, he accepted minimum wage, which was all she could afford to pay, and more or less remembered to do the little required of him.

"I gave her tea," he said in a low voice, nodding toward the low-slung sofa and chairs across from the front counter that served as a waiting area, where Jill's first client of the day sat flipping through magazines on the coffee table while trying to entertain a fussy baby sitting in a carrier next to her. She was a small, plump, fortyish white woman with thin, mouse-brown hair, and she had a small, plump white baby with thin, mouse-brown hair. They wore matching oversize bright orange sweaters embroidered with pumpkins. The baby gnawed on a chubby hand, face and eyes red from a recent bout of tears.

"She's teething," the woman said in an accusatory tone when Jill apologized for being late. "If I'd gotten the appointment I wanted a month ago, like I tried, then we wouldn't have this problem."

"We'll just have to do our best to distract her," Jill said, trying a bright smile that the other woman didn't return. Jill led them down a hall to the back of the building and the actual studio, which she'd created by knocking the walls down between several small rooms to create one large space with a white backdrop, various props, large lights, and multiple cameras. They were offering a special on fall portraits right now—she'd hauled in some hay bales and pumpkins. A degree in art, but this was how she spent most of her time, the dream of being the next Sally Mann or Annie Leibovitz taking a backseat to the need to pay for rent and equipment. Family portraits and weddings supported the studio; the other photography, the art photography and the volunteer photography that were her passions, had to come second.

Over the course of an interminable hour, she took more than a hundred photos of the little girl. Baby alone, baby with pumpkins as props, and baby with mother. In a few shots the child actually smiled. A grumpy Madonna and Child commemorating a pagan holiday.

The woman seemed slightly less annoyed at the end of the photo shoot than she had been at the beginning. "I guess at least one of these will work," she conceded when Jill let her see the digital proofs. "Her father will probably like it." The baby squawked, sounding just as enthused, and Jill managed a faint smile. The woman would fuss over the price. As soon as she left she'd be on her cell phone complaining that she should have taken her child to a portrait studio at the mall.

She hustled the woman and child back out to the front of the studio, just as Tania walked out of the door of the production and developing room, followed by a huge, muscular white man with a tangled mass of dirty auburn hair and matching beard. Dressed head to toe in black and wearing mirrored sunglasses, he hoisted a backpack, also in black, onto his shoulder. With her blue-streaked blond hair and sparkly nose stud, wearing a flowing, post-millennial hippie skirt, Tania looked like a latter-day flower child, and combined aromas of patchouli and pot drifted after her. The client looked askance, clutching her child's baby carrier close as she passed them in the lobby, hustling out the door to the Volvo, as if one of them planned to snatch her child. Kyle stared unabashedly, mouth hanging slightly open. Jill realized she'd crossed her arms, so she let them fall to her sides, trying not to look like the mother who'd waited up all night for her rebellious teen daughter. What the client didn't know was that underneath her hippie-dippie exterior and beyond her terrible taste in men, Tania was a great photographer. And while Jill could find another photographer, Tania was also a longtime friend.

Not that the bonds of friendship didn't have their limits. "You must be Tania's boyfriend," she said, trying to be civil and struggling to remember the name of this latest romantic partner.

"Oh, yeah," Tania said, sweeping an arm toward the guy, who stood in the center of the lobby, arms crossed over his massive chest. "This is Leo."

The man's beard dipped, which might have been a nod. "Nice to meet you, Leo." Jill extended her hand, and he stared at it for a second before giving it a limp shake. He had a small but vicious-looking skull and crossbones tattooed on the side of his neck. "Leo dropped me off," Tania said. Standing on tiptoe to give him a lingering kiss, she murmured, "See you later" in a voice best left in the bedroom.

To avoid watching the good-bye, Jill focused on collecting the mail, which Kyle had left scattered on the front counter as usual. She sorted through it, stiffening slightly when she saw her mother's familiar scrawl on an envelope. The letter had been opened, though since it had "Jillian Lassiter Photography" on the envelope maybe Kyle had thought it was business correspondence. Not completely off base since it was undoubtedly a request for money. She shoved it into her pocket, unread, looking up when she heard the door close. Jill watched Leo sauntering off toward an old car before she followed Tania back down the hall to the production room. "Nice of you to show up."

"Don't be a bitch. I sent you a text, didn't you get it?"

"No." Jill double-checked her cell phone before holding it out for her friend and partner's scrutiny.

"Really? I wonder what happened."

"Let me guess—you were still in bed and a little distracted?"

"Do I detect a note of jealousy?" Tania said with a laugh. She grabbed Jill's arm and pulled her into what they sometimes still referred to as the darkroom, though now it was mostly filled with computer equipment to edit and print photos. "Isn't he hot?"

"Does this one have a job?" Tania's last boyfriend had been a professional moocher.

"Jesus, Jill!"

"Does he?"

"Yes, he has a job. God, you're like an old woman sometimes."

"Doing what?"

"I don't know—computers and shit like that." She waved airily as if the details didn't matter. "He's good with his hands."

"Oh, I saw that," Jill said.

Tania sneered. "What's the matter? Too little action in snooze-urbia?"

Jill rolled her eyes. From the day they'd become friends, fifteen years ago when both were freshman art majors at Carnegie Mellon, Tania had never missed an opportunity to comment negatively on suburban living, which she'd never actually experienced firsthand. She and Jill had bonded not only over a shared passion for photography, but also over being Pittsburgh transplants who'd been raised in larger cities by unstable mothers.

For all her criticisms of "Stepford living," Tania wanted the stability of this studio just as much as Jill, and it wouldn't exist at all if it hadn't been subsidized by suburban David's bourgeois job.

"Please tell me you haven't moved in with this guy," she said as Tania sat down at one of the desktops to download shots she'd taken at a recent wedding.

"Not yet." Tania looked uncomfortable. "But we're talking about it." She moved an average of once every year and a half, always convinced that a new apartment or, better yet, a new man's apartment, would bring her good luck. Jill was pleasantly surprised that it hadn't already happened with her latest lover.

"I think it's great you're waiting, taking your time."

Tania shot her a look, then sighed. "Actually, he still lives with his mother."

"He has a mother?" Jill blurted, adding hastily at Tania's offended look, "Sorry, it's just, he seems so, well, so *independent*."

"Everyone has a mother, Jill. He's very attached to his."

"And that isn't a good thing?"

"It's a little Norman Bates for me—his mother's a nut." Tania circled a finger near her ear. "I've got one of those already. I don't need a matched set."

Jill laughed, but couldn't stop the slight wince, glad that Tania didn't see. Did she still talk to her mother? The letter from Jill's own mother seemed to throb in her pocket. She wouldn't answer it, she'd stopped answering them some time ago, but she couldn't bring herself to throw them away.

"Anyway, he's getting his own place soon," Tania said, pulling Jill's attention back. "I think he could be long-term. He just gets me, you know? And he's into kids, too. You know how much I love kids."

"You're great with Sophia," Jill said, trying to hide what she really felt at the thought of flighty Tania becoming a mother. At least she wasn't lying; Tania *was* fantastic with Sophia, but that was very different from having a child to care for 24/7.

She and Tania reviewed the photos of the wedding, which they'd shot a week ago. A pretty young bride and her baby-faced groom, both of them looking so happy it was almost painful. There was so much promise in wedding photos. She wished she could freeze the moment, keep the couple just as happy as they were in the photos. But life would dim that light in their eyes. How long would it be before they figured out there was no happily ever after?

Where had that come from? Jill wasn't unhappy, not really. She turned away, shaking off the blues. "Let's get them in here to review the proofs." She gathered up prints from a session a few days before, black-and-whites of a man and woman holding an incredibly small infant in a hospital room, his eyes closed in every shot, his features perfect.

"Do you want me to mail those?" Tania offered, looking over her shoulder.

"No thanks, I'm going to drop them off next week." She never mailed these photos; she always delivered them personally. There were multiple prints and after a moment Jill discarded one in which the mother had started crying. Her grief was too raw, too painful—they wouldn't like that one. Jill blinked back sudden tears of her own, quickly gathering the photos together. She'd done so many sessions like this one, but they still moved her.

She searched the top desk drawer for the hidden place at the back where they kept the key to the large supply cabinet in the corner of the room, but it wasn't there. "Did you take the key?"

"It's probably in the door," Tania said, absorbed in sorting through the wedding proofs.

Jill turned to look at the cabinet, at the key sitting there. She swallowed hard, feeling more annoyance with Tania—always running late and now she couldn't even be bothered to hide the key? With a back door that opened on to an unlit alleyway, the studio was vulnerable to thieves. They'd had a break-in the first month after opening. Jill had installed a security camera outside, but when the camera got stolen it wasn't cost-effective to replace it. Instead she set up motion-sensor security lights, which were hit or miss, and installed a deadbolt on the back door.

She knew that wasn't enough, so she locked up everything of value inside. "Please remember to put the key away, okay? We don't want our stuff stolen."

"I'm not the one who left it out," Tania said, voice huffy. "Why do you always blame me for things?"

Because you're irresponsible, Jill thought. "I wish Kyle would put things back where they go."

"Kyle?" Tania gave her a puzzled look. "He doesn't touch this room, remember? You told him to focus only on the front desk and scheduling."

Jill fingered the key still sitting in the lock. Had she forgotten to put it back last night? She was usually so careful. "Were you in here yesterday afternoon?"

Tania looked up. "I wasn't here at all yesterday. I had the Nicholson party to shoot. You were the only one here, remember?" She gave Jill a smug look, implicit in her tone the fact that Jill couldn't own up to her own mistakes.

"I must have forgotten to put it away," Jill said, more to thwart Tania's sense of satisfaction than because she really believed it. Had she been so distracted that she didn't remember? Weird. Still puzzling, Jill opened the door and cried out as a tripod tumbled forward, slamming into her. It slid off her and she caught it before it hit the floor. "What the hell?"

Tania grabbed it from her. "Are you okay?"

Jill rubbed her shoulder and collarbone. "Yeah, just a little bruised." The cabinet was in disarray —boxes of photos shuffled through, cameras and other equipment obviously moved, which was how that top-heavy tripod, which was usually tucked against the back of one of the vertical shelves, had fallen out. "Someone ransacked this."

"Well it wasn't me," Tania said quickly. "It must have been Kyle."

"You just said this room is limited to you and me—so why would he even come in here?"

He hadn't. Once summoned, Kyle stood in the office doorway and swore up and down that he hadn't been in the back of the building "in, like, over a month, maybe more."

"Maybe we had a break-in!" he suggested, suddenly animated. "Do you want me to call the cops?"

"And tell them what?" Tania scoffed. "That our cabinet was messed up? Is anything even missing?"

Jill scanned the shelves again. "I'm not sure; I don't think so." All the equipment seemed to be there, but she couldn't swear to it.

"Then let's just forget about it." Tania waved two pieces of paper at Kyle. "I need you to send this invoice—the address is in the system—and I need you to call *these* clients and tell them their proofs are ready."

Jill followed him out to the front of the studio. "How long were Tania and Leo here before I finished with the client?" she asked in a low voice.

Kyle looked uncomfortable. "I don't know, maybe twenty, twenty-five minutes?"

Plenty of time to have gone through the production and equipment room in search of easy money. Fortunately, they kept that in the register at the front of the studio and at night she put that day's money away in a locked cashbox, which she stored at the back of a locked desk drawer until she could deposit it in the bank at the end of the week. On impulse Jill went to check the drawer, but it looked undisturbed, and so did the box, the money still there, along with a few checks written by clients.

She walked back down the hall to the production room. Tania had a Nikon slung around her neck like a piece of funky jewelry and was busy shoving another camera and some memory cards into her woven bag. "I've got to get to that shoot for the yoga school in Regent Square. Don't want to get any bad karma." She brought her hands together in a prayerful pose, laughing, and Jill mustered a small smile. She locked the cabinet, making sure it was secure before taking the key back to hide it in the top drawer of the desk.

The drawer was also in disarray. Jill stood there, staring at it. She hadn't noticed when she went to grab the key. She pulled opened the rest of the drawers, one after the other, and every one was just like the first.

"What is it?" Tania paused in the doorway.

"The desk has been ransacked, too." Jill said. "Was Leo in here alone?"

Tania's smile faded. "Of course not." She crossed to the desk and reached past Jill to check the drawers herself. "So some things have been moved—"

"Not some things, *everything*."

"Maybe, but maybe you or I moved them. We had a busy week last week, remember?"

"Not that busy."

"Nothing's missing, right? So no harm done."

"Listen, I don't think we should allow strangers into the office."

"If you mean Leo, he isn't a stranger and anyway he didn't go through the drawers."

"So what was he doing back here?"

Tania's gaze met hers, then skittered away. Her cheeks flushed. "He wanted a private good-bye."

"You were having *sex?* You had sex with your boyfriend in this room?"

"Keep your voice down!"

"Isn't any place off-limits to you? What if someone had walked in?"

"I'm not an idiot—we locked the door."

"He shouldn't have been back here at all. Don't bring anyone back here again."

"It was just for a few minutes—"

Jill held up her hand. "Just don't. Okay?"

"Fine." Tania spat the word.

They stared at each other for a long minute. Tania broke the gaze, turning toward the door. She gave a little laugh, but it had an edge. "Jesus, Jill, you're becoming paranoid."

Chapter Seven

Journal—April 2009

You must have seen me coming a mile away. I thought I was so sophisticated, with my law school degree and two new suits. I didn't under-stand how young I really was or how naive.

"You're so tense," you said to me that first time. *"Let me help you relax."* We were alone in the firm's law library and I'd taken off my jacket. I froze as your hands came to knead my shoulders, but I didn't move away.

I can't claim to be innocent in this; I know that. Months later you threw that at me. You said, *"You could have said no at any time."* But you were the senior member of the firm, you were the lawyer I was working for on that case, I was still in my probationary period. There are so many reasons I couldn't say no, the least of which was feeling flattered that you were attracted to me.

When you let your hand slip into the open neck-line of my blouse, I remember flinching and you laughed a little, said "whoops," and pulled back. Then you leaned in again, sniffing the air. *"God, you smell sweet. Is that your shampoo?"* And you lowered your head to my hair and I stayed still this time, embarrassed and unsure of how to respond. Your head dipped farther down and I could feel your breath hot against my neck. *"Or is it perfume?"* Then you pressed a kiss, just a little one, on my neck right below my ear.

I have wondered sometimes what might have happened if I'd reported what you did to the head of the firm. Would he have fired you, do you think? No one wants to get pinned with a sexual harassment suit, but wouldn't the senior partners be more likely to think they could contain it by sending you to sensitivity training? Whistle-blowers and complainers rarely make it far in any business. I was naive, but not stupid. The best course of action would be to forget it ever happened and stay quiet.

Only you couldn't forget.

Chapter Eight
October 2013—Two Weeks

Cosmo balanced on his hind legs on the passenger seat, front paws resting against the window of her old Ford Taurus while Bea slowly circled the cul-de-sac pretending to look for a house number. He enjoyed riding in the car, little ears perched at soft right angles, a quizzical look on his furry face. He was a rescue dog; Bea had driven to four different shelters to find him. There were plenty of other, bigger dogs available, lots of lonely-looking pit bulls, but she hadn't needed a dog for protection, she needed one that wouldn't frighten people. Something soft, small, and friendly; no barkers or biters or nervous dogs that peed on the rug.

There were no cars parked on the driveway of the Lassiter house; by Bea's calculations nobody should be home. She left their block and wove slowly through the rest of the neighborhood until she reached another cul-de-sac roughly parallel to the first, the two streets separated by hilly woodland. There were more lots for sale on this street, leaning realty signs and an overgrowth of dry, yellow weeds indicative of the recession. One house had its frame up, but construction had apparently stopped some time ago, given the frayed plastic sheeting wrapped around warping two-by-fours.

She parked out front, attaching Cosmo's leash to his collar and checking that her dark blonde wig was in place before exiting the car. If anyone asked, Bea was a would-be buyer of a new house, just taking a look at what this street had to offer. She zipped up her jacket and took one of the spec sheets from the plastic tube attached to the realty sign, pretending to study it. "Four bedrooms, three-and-a-half baths; unparalleled luxury only twenty minutes from Downtown Pittsburgh. Pick your own finishes!" Cosmo lifted a small hind leg and peed against the wooden signpost.

She urged him to explore the property, picking her way carefully over the lumpy ground until they were behind the half-built house and out of sight of the neighbors. From there it was approximately fifty feet across a barren field that would eventually be some family's backyard, and into the woods. Luckily, Cosmo didn't balk. He loved the woods, loved exploring anything new, the cheerful little mutt, and he pulled eagerly against his collar, straining the leash in her hand as he explored the cold ground with his nose.

Bea moved more slowly at first, blinking against the change in light. She kept her free hand outstretched to ward off low-hanging branches and tried to find a clear path through the dense foliage.

She didn't mind the dark, she'd never been afraid of it, unlike her daughter, who hadn't been able to sleep without a night-light and had woken Bea often with nightmares or fears of something lurking in the shadows.

Bea had been so tired on those nights, wanting sleep so desperately and worried that these night terrors would last, but in retrospect that time had been easy. She paused to catch her breath, thinking of how much harder things had gotten later on, how difficult it was to see your child suffering and not be able to make it all better with a hug. If she'd known it then, when her daughter was small, she'd have held on tight and never let go.

The hillside dropped steeply and she had to support her descent by grabbing the thin trunks of saplings. She disturbed small creatures as she plunged downward, a tiny vole scurrying out from some leaves and squirrels chittering complaints nearby. It was fairly quiet otherwise. Between her own labored breaths she could hear the far-off drone of an airplane. At the bottom of the ravine she paused along the edge of the shallow creek bed that ran its length and looked up the other side, trying to figure out where to go. It was too steep to see anything but more hillside, so she waded quickly across before trudging up the opposite hill, jerking the leash as Cosmo paused to lap at the dirty water.

Freezing water squelched from her sneakers with every step, and despite the cold she felt sweat trickling uncomfortably between her breasts and at the base of her spine. Her hands were damp and she had to pause several times to rewrap the leash and urge Cosmo up the hill. He wasn't so eager now, lolling behind her, his tongue hanging out of his mouth. She had water for him in the car, but it hadn't occurred to her to bring it. He moved slower and slower the closer they got to the top until finally she scooped him up in her arms. He snuggled against her shoulder like a furry baby, licking her cheek frantically, as if she were a melting ice cream cone, with a tongue that felt like wet sandpaper.

"No! Stop it." She pushed his little muzzle away until he got the hint, and she kept climbing. They were within sight of the top and she moved faster, stirred on by adrenaline to crest the hill.

They were still in the woods but on flat land again, and she could see the backs of the massive houses on Wakefield Drive. Things would look very different at night, of course, but she had to take the route at least once in the daylight to get the lay of the land. While she stood there, trying to figure out which house was theirs, she heard a faint clicking sound and a door opened onto the raised stone patio of the house to her left. A familiar towheaded little girl rushed out, followed more slowly by a dark-haired woman. Bea stopped, clamping a hand over Cosmo's muzzle to stop him from barking. They weren't supposed to be home; they must have pulled in right after she'd left their street.

The little girl was talking, Bea could hear a faint, high-pitched singsong, but she was too far away to make out what she was saying. Bea moved slowly left, making sure to stay behind several yards of trees, hoping that this and the afternoon sunlight would be enough to stop them from spotting her.

The mother looked nothing like the child—dark where the child was light, thin even bundled up in a jacket, with bony angles and high cheekbones, where the child was dimpled and rounded. Jill Lassiter's dark hair was loose today, worn down around her shoulders in a shiny wave. She took a seat at one of the chairs in a patio set and opened a folder that held something; photos, Bea realized, when the woman held them up to the light. Jill smiled at Sophia's pleas to come and play and said she'd be with her in a minute. And then the child ran down the stone steps and across the lawn straight toward Bea.

She froze, panic shooting through her, while Cosmo writhed in her arms. It was chilly out, but the child didn't seem to notice. She came closer, running on fast little legs, close enough that Bea could see the white furry lining in her pink wool coat. Close enough that she could hear her humming. Sophia seemed to stare directly at her and Bea, mesmerized, stared right back and then, just as suddenly, she realized that the child wasn't heading toward her but a playhouse at the back of the yard.

Bea had been so busy looking at the child that she hadn't noticed the little white house and she sagged in relief against the trunk of an oak tree. She could hear Sophia carrying on a one-sided conversation in the playhouse. "You want some tea? No, you're too little, bunny, but you can have a cookie." Things clattered and Bea moved left again, trying to see into the playhouse window, but the angle wasn't right. She could only make out shadows and hear the clear little voice directing her toys.

Over at the table the mother examined another photo before turning it facedown, rubbing her hands together to warm them, but clearly absorbed. If Bea stepped out of the woods she probably wouldn't even notice. The playhouse stood only a few feet away. She could see the child, could smell her. Bea inched forward.

The door of the playhouse slammed open and the child stepped out carrying an armload of stuffed animals. "Time to go for our walk," she said, mimicking an adult's voice.

At that moment an excited Cosmo pulled his muzzle free and barked twice, tail wagging. The little girl halted, head turning toward the noise, then dropped her toys and took off for the lines of trees yelling, "Doggie!"

Jill stood up from the table. "No, Sophia! Come back!"

Bea ducked behind a wide tree trunk, Cosmo thrashing in her arms. The little girl plunged into the woods; Bea could hear her small feet crunching through old leaves and pine needles. "Doggie! Doggie, where are you?" Her voice high-pitched and excited.

Jill Lassiter pelted after her, coming across the lawn faster than the child had before her. "Sophia! Come back here right now!" Angry and afraid.

Bea moved equally fast, slipping back through the trees the way she'd come, down the hill so hurriedly that she slipped and slammed her left hip hard against the ground. She scrambled up and behind another tree trunk, peering around in time to see Jill slipping sideways down the hillside, arm outstretched to catch her daughter before she toppled down the steep embankment.

"Sophia, wait!" Her voice shrill. The child slipped against loose acorns, they scattered ahead of her down the hillside, a light, rushing sound, and then Jill had Sophia in her grip, the child squirming just like the dog.

"Doggie! I want doggie!"

"There's no dog out here," the woman said, squinting as she tried to peer down into the depths of the woods. She hoisted the child onto her hip, gently scolding as she began a slow climb back toward the house. "You know you're not supposed to be in the woods alone; it's dangerous."

Bea waited, heart pounding, until they'd crested the hill before moving in the opposite direction. Cosmo scratched at her arms, struggling to get down, but she didn't dare release him until she'd gotten across the creek and halfway up the other side.

When Bea made it back to her own little house in the woods, Cosmo jumped against her legs, whining and barking to go out. "You were just outside," she complained, wishing Frank was around to take him out, but he could never be counted on to do anything domestic. Despite her exhaustion, Bea quickly let Cosmo out the kitchen door, and he lifted his leg next to the sagging fence. She had to force him back inside, and after she'd fed him and he'd lapped up a full bowl of water, he raced back and forth in the living room, trying to engage her in playing even after she'd sunk onto the old couch.

"Settle down," she told the little dog. "I'm too tired for this." When Cosmo jumped on her lap, she plopped him back on the floor, but gave up after they'd repeated this three times. "Damn dog," she muttered. "Just sit down there, then." She shoved him to the end of the couch and turned onto her side. Cosmo made a throaty, whining sound, but finally settled, his small body warm against her feet. She switched on the old TV and watched the local news, a roundup of everything awful that had happened in one day. She hated them all, these reporters with their smiley, overly made-up faces, feigning concern when you could see the lust for tragedy in their eyes, hear the sharklike glee as they recited it all: Murders and house fires, rapes and robberies. A veritable buffet of bad news; sidle up and gorge on someone else's sorrow. Bea sank deeper into the couch, fatigue overtaking anger. Her eyes closed.

She was in the passenger seat of a car watching the speedometer climb. They were going too fast, the car racing down the road and still the speedometer climbed—seventy, eighty, eighty-five—the needle trembling. The car shook. She told her daughter to slow down, but the girl just smiled. She was driving in the wrong lane, but she didn't seem to notice. Bea could see that they were going to crash. An approaching car came closer and closer.

Bea woke up screaming. For a moment she didn't know where she was, and then Cosmo licked her face and Bea pushed him away, sitting up on the couch, breathing hard, her throat sore. It had gotten dark—the only light in the room the glow from the old TV. She rubbed a hand over her face and looked at her watch. It was after seven—she'd slept for over two hours.

"I'm getting old," she said out loud, voice scratchy. The dog tilted his head to one side, looking at her quizzically before jumping against Bea's legs and whining until she stood and walked to the back door again. She let him out into the yard and stood there staring up at the night sky, pulled back into memory, a cold autumn night like this one, but long ago, her daughter pointing out the constellations to her mother, *"There's Ursa Major, Ursa Minor, and there's Orion. . . ."* Bea tried to remember the feel of those small shoulders under her arm, the smell of silky hair as she'd stooped to kiss the top of her head. She'd never fully appreciated that moment and all the hundreds of other small moments in her daughter's life.

"You can't undo it, Bea." Frank had come home without her hearing him. He stood beside her on the patio, a solid presence impossible to ignore.

For a moment she thought her husband was talking about the past, but then she saw that he'd dropped a Polaroid of the child that she'd taken that day at the park. "Give that to me; what are you doing with it?" She snatched it from the ground before he could retrieve it and pushed past him back into the house. He followed her inside, hovering as she hung up the set of keys she'd had copied. She hadn't used them today, but she would soon enough.

"It's never going to work," he said, not for the first time. "You need to let it go."

He'd always been negative; she felt the acid burn of long simmering anger. "Mind your own business, Frank!" She refused to look at him. If she didn't look at him, with any luck he'd get the message and disappear.

Chapter Nine

October 2013—Two Weeks

Jill had just finished taking engagement photographs for a couple at Frick Park when David called. It was late afternoon and she balanced her cell phone between ear and shoulder as she loaded camera cases, tripods, and other equipment into the trunk of her car. He sounded rushed as he always did at work. "Are we all set for tonight?"

"Tonight?" Jill pulled out the album she had to deliver and slammed the trunk shut. "What's happening tonight?"

"The firm dinner, remember? Andrew is going to be there and most of the other partners."

"Aargh, no, I completely forgot!" Jill slid behind the wheel and placed the album on the passenger seat. "Let's just skip it, okay?"

"I can't do that." David sounded aghast. "C'mon, I have to go and all the other spouses will be coming—what would they think if you didn't show?"

"I doubt anyone would notice. Besides, I haven't even lined up a sitter—how on earth will we find someone this late?"

"Call my mother." He said it so quickly that she

wondered if he'd planned it all along. "She'd be happy to watch Sophia."

"I don't want to do that, David."

"Why?"

"You know why. She feeds Sophia junk and she won't follow her schedule—"

"So what? She's a three-year-old for God's sake. How terrible is it for her schedule to be disrupted one evening?"

"—and she finds a million and one ways to criticize my parenting."

"C'mon, she's not that bad."

"Really? So she didn't tell me last month that I was to blame for Sophia's ear infection because I didn't make her wear a hat?"

"You're too sensitive, Jill. Just ignore what she says, that's what I do."

"Easy for you to say, you're not the one she criticizes."

"She loves Sophia."

"No one's doubting that."

"Then call her."

Jill groaned and David said, "Fine, don't call her. But I need you tonight so we've got to find a sitter."

Jill glanced at her watch. "I won't even have time to get ready at this point. I'm on my way to a client's now to drop off some photos—"

"Can't you drop them off tomorrow?"

"I promised them today."

"Then have someone else do it."

"It's too late, I've already left the studio."

"So just call and cancel. They'll understand."

"I can't do that, not with these people."

"This is for one of *those* families, isn't it?" David groaned when Jill didn't say anything. "It's like you keep tearing at a scab," he said. "Why do that to yourself?"

"Because I know how they feel," Jill said, struggling to explain to him for the umpteenth time what she could barely explain to herself. "I need to do it. It helps them. It helps to have someone who understands. It helps me."

There was silence on the other end of the phone, but she could hear his frustration. In a way David was right—every photo shoot she did for charity reminded her—but what he didn't understand, what she couldn't talk to him about, was that she didn't need to be reminded. Ethan was always there, a constant presence, not like picking at a scab at all, really, because the wound had never healed.

After a moment David sighed and said, "I don't want to argue, it's your choice. But please, at least call my mother and ask, okay? I'd do it myself, but I can't break away, especially now."

"Especially now" had been going on for months. If the latest case reached a successful conclusion then he would certainly be promoted before the end of the year. This was according to Andrew, who as a partner himself couldn't explicitly say anything, but had been encouraging David to think positively about his future with Adams Kendrick. "Come on," David said, his tone softening. "How often do we get to go out in the middle of the week? It could be fun."

"Of course I'll watch Sophia!" To the average listener, Elaine Lassiter's voice sounded nothing more than warm, gracious—the perfect mother-in-law and grandmother. Friendly and outgoing, a charmer just like her son, and once, long ago, she'd charmed Jill, too. "Do you want me to pick her up from day care?"

"No thanks, I can get her from preschool." Jill emphasized the last word, her grip tightening on the steering wheel.

"I'm sure she'd love to go home early—it must be so hard on her to sit in day care all day."

"She only does the extended option three days a week."

"Well, I don't know how you career girls do it." Elaine's voice was light, her laugh a melody. "I'm sure it must be hard leaving your child every day."

"Sorry, Elaine, hitting traffic—I'll see you at six. Thanks!" Jill pushed the off button with force, pretending it was Elaine's face. "Annoying witch!" That woman always made her feel bad no matter how many times Jill tried to tell herself not to listen, that what her mother-in-law said didn't matter.

She must have done something in a past life to have not one, but two difficult mothers. The letter from her own mother had gone into a box at home unread, but it was undoubtedly just like every other letter she sent; they arrived at regular intervals: "Dear Jill, life has been hectic with the move, but this new job looks exciting. Things are a little tight right now, with the economy the way it is and moving expenses, but soon I'll be making enough to finally buy that dream home we always talked about. After so many years, I can say that I've finally found my bliss. . . ."

Things had always been tight; her mother always chasing rainbows in search of her "bliss." Jill couldn't recall a time in her childhood when they'd ever completely settled down. No sooner did they move to one place than her mother was announcing that she knew, just knew, that the life she really wanted was in another city or state. She blew through careers and relationships like tissue paper, working as an artist, a secretary, and eventually in health care, leaving lovers behind without any visible sign of discomfort. Jill's father had been a musician or a science teacher or maybe the door-to-door salesman who'd once given her mother a ride from Indiana to Pennsylvania. It was only when Jill reached adulthood that she'd

95

stopped to ponder that her mother's only real attachment was to her.

A bright spot amid all the dim memories: a neighbor who felt sorry for her, giving Jill a Polaroid camera as a good-bye gift. She'd suggested that Jill use it to document the move and she could still remember aiming out the window of the unair-conditioned cab of a U-Haul snapping scenes during a long drive South. She'd fallen in love with photography, and her passion, unlike her mother's, had been lasting.

She'd fled that chaotic life for college, staying on in Pittsburgh after graduation ostensibly because of a job she'd landed at a local ad agency. That was the story she told if asked, but it was only partially true. The whole truth was that Jill had been desperate to find roots.

Enter David, a law school student when they met, whose own background practically shouted stability and normalcy. Elaine and Bill Lassiter had been married forever and lived in the same split-level in the suburbs that they'd moved into as newlyweds. What had seemed so appealing at first—the homemade meals, the family camaraderie —soon revealed its dark side.

Everything about Jill was alien to her mother-in-law. She'd been a stay-at-home mother and still clung to her children, calling multiple times a week with advice or to ask when they were going to visit. Elaine was obsessed with David's professional success, but thought Jill choosing to keep working outside the home after having a child was wrong. She called constantly to check up on Sophia. A possessive grandmother, she pressured Jill about trusting her only grandchild's care to "strangers," but she was also critical of Jill's parenting and often referred to Sophia as her baby, which made Jill bristle.

She tried not to care. She told herself that Elaine was just a lonely old woman who'd formed no life outside of her kids, but it was hard to remember when she was face-to-face with the woman. Elaine made snippy remarks to Jill, little verbal potshots about her looks, her parenting, her career, and all delivered with a smile. If called on it, a rare occurrence, Elaine would get all wide-eyed and say, "Why I was just teasing! Jill knows I didn't mean anything, right?" Her only redeeming quality was that she truly, genuinely, loved and doted on Sophia.

Jill decompressed as she drove, trying to relax her shoulders and breathe deep, working to forget Elaine and concentrate on winding through a maze of city backstreets to Morningside, a working-class neighborhood with boxy brick homes and small, neat lawns where pumpkins and Halloween ghouls competed for space with plaster Madonna shrines. She pulled into an empty spot and backtracked down the sidewalk to a tiny brick house with white metal awnings over stoop and windows.

Jill hurried up the front steps and rang the doorbell. The wind had picked up, lifting a strand of blue ribbon tied to the lamppost. Probably the remnant of baby balloons hastily cut down; she could picture some well-meaning family member tying them there, then hurrying to take them down. The curtains were drawn in the windows, but Jill expected someone to be home. It was barely two weeks since she'd seen the Dilbys at the hospital.

At last she heard footsteps approaching. Cathy Dilby opened the door slowly, as if it took tremendous physical effort. She'd aged in the short time since Jill had last seen her, or perhaps it was just that she'd put on makeup and combed her hair for the photos, and now her skin looked washed out and her hair hung in lank brown strands. She blinked at the bright light, giving Jill a confused once-over.

"I've brought your photos, Mrs. Dilby," she said, holding out the album.

"Oh, yes." Recognition in the eyes, an attempt at a smile. "Please . . . come in." She shifted slowly back to let her enter, tugging the sides of a pilling cardigan closer to her body. Up close, Jill saw that her eyes were bloodshot and she clutched a wad of crumpled tissues.

Jill stopped short in the hallway, confronted by boxes of various sizes and colors, all of them holding baby supplies—a stroller, a bouncy chair, blankets, a baby bathtub, and dozens of tiny outfits. "We're giving back the things we got at the shower," Cathy Dilby explained in a lifeless voice. "Some people said we should hold on to them, but I can't have them in the house—not now."

There were footsteps on the stairs, and Tom Dilby stepped into the hall hauling another box—the crib. "That's the last of it," he said to his wife before he noticed Jill.

"She's brought the photos," Cathy said. Tom came immediately to his wife's side and shook Jill's hand. His face was also strained, dark circles under red-rimmed eyes, but he seemed to be holding it together for his wife's sake.

"Thanks for coming—let's take a look." He gently eased the album from Cathy's limp hand and ushered her over to the sofa in their cramped living room. Jill followed, perching across from them on an armchair while Tom set the album on the coffee table and slowly turned the pages. Cathy teared up immediately, but she smiled, too, touching her son's image. No one would ever guess that the child was dead.

When Jill first learned about bereavement photography, and Now I Lay Me Down to Sleep, the charity that provides free photography sessions for families of stillborn or terminally ill newborns, she'd felt compelled to volunteer. Some people thought it was morbid, but she knew how precious it was to have photos to remember your child no matter how brief his or her life. She had her own precious album tucked away at home that she still looked at. David didn't want photo reminders, so couldn't understand why this was a kind service for grieving families. It was also something Jill was uniquely qualified to do, but he was right—it was so hard to take these photos, so hard not to think constantly of Ethan.

"They're beautiful," Tom Dilby said, voice gruff. He glanced at Jill, then away, swiping roughly at his eyes with the back of a hand.

"He looks so peaceful, doesn't he?" Cathy Dilby sounded slightly more animated.

"Yes, definitely."

Jill sat with them for another few minutes while they talked about their son, waiting for a lull before excusing herself.

Tom Dilby walked her to the door. "I wasn't sure how I felt about this, but Cathy wanted to do it. Now I'm glad. Once all this is gone"—he swept a hand out to indicate the pile of baby supplies— "what else will we have left to show that he really existed?" His voice broke on the last word and she felt a lump in her own throat. He coughed, embarrassed, stepping past her to open the front door. He shook her hand with both of his. "If we can ever return the favor, just let me know. Anything at all."

Jill had to take a moment to compose herself once she was alone in the car. As she drove away, she looked back at the Dilbys' small brick house with that sad little scrap of blue ribbon dangling from the lamppost. If she came back a year from now would they still be together? Sometimes she wondered if she and David would have pulled through if it hadn't been for Sophia. Relationships, like life itself, could be so fragile.

A glance at the clock pulled her out of her musing. She raced toward the preschool, keeping one eye out for cops and another on the dashboard clock. Fox Chapel's roads were twisting and narrow, with almost no shoulder, and some sections heavily wooded. A shower of leaves blew across the asphalt, a rainbow of red and orange.

She pulled into the preschool lot just as another parent was leaving. Sophia stood in the doorway, a forlorn figure clutching the teacher's hand. Jill ran up the steps. "So sorry I'm late."

"No problem. We had a good day, didn't we, Sophia?" The teacher's smile seemed forced and she glanced at her watch. "We're working on listening, aren't we, Sophia?"

Jill's heart squeezed at the tired look on her child's face. She and David had talked to Sophia after Mrs. Belmar's warning and things had been improving, but at what cost? Maybe the director was right and Sophia was just too young to be there. She took Jill's hand, clutching Blinky and several crayon drawings, all of them of dogs. She showed them to Jill as she was buckled into the car seat. Dog in a park, someone walking a dog, a dog chasing what looked like a ball but what Sophia informed her was a "fizbee."

"These are great," Jill said. "I love the blue color you used for this dog."

"That's just peetend," Sophia said. "Dogs is not blue."

"You're right, dogs are not blue. What color are dogs?"

Sophia perked up a little, chattering happily about her current favorite subject as Jill slipped behind the wheel. As she raced out of the almost empty parking lot, headlights flashed on and another car pulled out behind her. Jill turned out of the lot and the other car followed. It was dark and the wind had picked up. Leaves flew around the car as Jill raced down the hill. Pause at the stop sign, turn signal clicking. Traffic suddenly opened up and she shot left, surprised when the other car followed her. Jill drove as fast as she could, foot flashing between accelerator and brakes, taking turns so tightly that the tires squealed, but her eyes kept straying to the rearview mirror. The car remained close behind her the whole way home, making every turn that she did.

Oblivious, Sophia chattered on about school, talking about the "mean teacher," but Jill couldn't focus, her attention on the other car. When she turned onto Wakefield Drive, Jill slowed down, waiting to see if the other car would turn in, too, but it zipped past.

So it hadn't been following them. Jill laughed a little.

"What's funny?" Sophia asked from the back-seat.

"Mommy's imagination," Jill said.

She couldn't quite shake the unease and she waited until the garage door was fully closed before getting out of the car. She hustled Sophia into the house and up the stairs. "You better pick out some toys and games; Nana's going to want to play with you."

With Sophia occupied, Jill quickly changed, throwing on a formfitting blue dress that David especially liked. She smiled at her reflection in the mirror, imagining his reaction.

The doorbell chimed and Jill grabbed her pumps, carrying them as she raced down the stairs to let her mother-in-law inside. The front door was unlocked. Taken aback, Jill paused, wondering how that had happened. She and David came in and out of the house through the garage; the front door should have been locked.

The doorbell chimed again, then a third time. Elaine Lassiter was trying to peer through the sheer-curtained windows that flanked the door. Jill yanked it open.

"Where were you?" Her mother-in-law stepped

103

inside hauling two bags loaded down with what looked like a refrigerator's worth of food. "I thought something happened to you or, God forbid, Sophia."

Jill ignored the insult, leaning in to air-kiss the older woman's cheek. "You didn't have to bring dinner."

"Oh, it's no trouble." Elaine led the way to the kitchen, making herself right at home like she always did, plopping her bags on the island and unpacking. "I knew you didn't have time to cook, not with getting back so late from your busy job, and I didn't want poor Sophia to suffer—"

"Speaking of Sophia, I better go say good-bye." Jill ran back up the stairs and down the hall to her daughter's bedroom. Sophia stood balanced precariously on the sill of the window that looked out onto the backyard, her hands and face pressed against the glass.

"Get down from there!" Jill grabbed her around the waist and lifted her away.

"Lemme go!" Sophia protested, squirming in her mother's arms. "Me watching a doggie!"

Jill set her down, but held on to her, crouching so they were face-to-face. "That's dangerous, Sophie. You could fall through the glass."

Sophia plucked at her mother's grip with tiny fingers, shrieking, "Let go!"

"Is everything okay up there?" Elaine's voice

came from the direction of the stairs. Jill released Sophia to stop the noise.

"Everything's fine," she called. Sophia gave her mother a baleful look and scrambled back on top of a toy bin that she'd overturned near the window. So that was how she'd gotten up there. Jill's concern overrode a brief feeling of pride in her daughter's ingenuity.

"No," she said, lifting Sophia off the plastic bin, righting it and moving it away from the window. "You do not climb onto the window ledge; it's not safe."

"I want the doggie," Sophia cried. "Let me see the doggie."

"What doggie?" Jill asked. She picked Sophia up and held her at the window. Had another neighborhood dog gotten loose? The sun was setting and Jill peered through the gloom, but there was no dog in sight. "Where was the doggie, Sophie?"

"In the trees." Sophia pointed a chubby index finger toward the woods at the back of the property. "The doggie lives in the trees."

It had to be her imagination; Jill firmly believed that. Or tried to. She felt the same unease she had earlier. When they went downstairs, she made sure to check the locks on all the doors.

Chapter Ten

Journal—June 2009

You cornered me one evening in the parking garage. *"I haven't stopped thinking about you,"* you said. Corny, right? Classic romance-movie stuff, but name me a woman who doesn't like to be admired or told she's beautiful. It helped that I was tired and disheveled after hours of searching case law, and feeling pretty low at the thought of going home alone to my cookie-cutter townhouse.

Of course, you are not responsible for my vulnerability. That is entirely on me. But you are responsible for stalking and seducing a col-league. In court you'd call my words inflammatory, but I think they're accurate.

You offered to buy me dinner and that seemed innocent. You offered to drive us to the restaurant in your car because parking was tight. You knew that after dinner, after we'd shared a bottle of wine, after we'd talked about law and life and you'd pulled personal details from me and flattered me by listening intently to everything I had to say, after all that you were intending to fuck me in your car.

I have thought a lot about that night since and I must say it was artfully done. You pretended that you'd made a wrong turn down that isolated side street and it seemed perfectly natural when you pulled over under a bridge overpass to consult a map, claiming your GPS was broken. Leaning over me to fetch a map from the glove compartment, you banged the door hard against my knee and insisted you had to *"kiss it better."* You pressed your lips lightly against my knee and then you pushed my skirt up and kissed above it and then you kept going. I tried to push my skirt down, but you held my hands out of the way. And then you fixed me with those eyes of yours and pushed the skirt right up until you'd exposed my stockings and lace underwear. I remember the sense of shock, of shaking, of wanting and not wanting.

After that it's all a bit of a blur. I'd had a lot of wine, it was late, you were smiling as you eased my stockings down, easily holding my hands out of the way, saying, *"Ssh, it's okay, you're okay,"* when I protested. There was nothing rough, not that first time. You kissed my thighs and when I flinched you kissed my face and you kept saying things like, *"Does that feel good?"* like it was all being done for me instead of to me. It occurs to me now that I should have guessed by how swiftly and easily you managed it that this wasn't the first time you'd had sex with someone in your car.

Here's where your mastery really comes into play: I met you again. This is what I'm most ashamed of. Fool me once, etc. . . . Why did I, a top student in law school, a high achieving woman, allow you to get anywhere near me again? How did I let you mind-fuck me into believing that this was a love relationship?

Chapter Eleven
October 2013—One Week

Adams Kendrick was a large and growing law practice, a corporate merger between two competitive firms and about to add offices internationally. Someone at the firm had chosen an overpriced new restaurant called Sprout, or Seed, or Spore, or some such name that in its very simplicity managed to be pretentious. Anointed one of Pittsburgh's best new eateries, it was haute cuisine meets farm kitsch with pitchforks as door handles and miniature trowels as serving spoons. The food was elegantly presented, yet absurd: Pork-belly pâté shaped like a pig on a bed of radish shavings, preemie lamb chops encased in quivering slices of mint jelly. It was also, oddly, a series of increasingly smaller courses. Jill tried to make the single, albeit jumbo, scallop in this latest course last longer than two bites.

David would laugh about the food later, but right now he was too engaged in conversation to notice. Corporate people were never really off work, and the pressure was palpable. Lawyers, on the whole, intimidated Jill with their quick wit and expensive suits. They were too gabby, too eager to impress. The women were as bad as the men, all toothy smiles and shoe-polish-shine hair. They made her uncomfortable, tongue-tied, and she ended up retreating to corners at firm events. David got annoyed by this, pressing her to make more of an effort. "You're a beautiful, intelligent woman—I want to show you off," he'd say, presenting her to colleagues like a hothouse flower, which only made her more nervous.

Yet hadn't she chosen this life? Hadn't she been attracted to David in part because he pursued a law degree? The pragmatist in her, the girl who wanted to eat well and not have to worry about the electricity being cut off, that girl had passed over the MFA candidate, and the passionate Broadway wannabe, and the bearded philosophy major for the boy who had a plan in place for a secure financial future. "How bourgeois," Tania had commented years ago when Jill told her that David was in law school. So how could Jill blame him when he turned out to be competitive and driven and, well, relentlessly lawyerly? She had made her choice and now she had to live with the side effects.

She took a healthy sip of wine. The only thing she did appreciate about these events was their commitment to booze. No alcohol-free celebrations for Adams Kendrick, and tonight's dinner was no exception. They'd had the cocktail hour where she'd enjoyed her first glass of wine and now, finally, they'd moved on to dinner. At least this evening's event was smaller than many others; it appeared to be a trial run for David and a few other associates. She knew some of these people, recognized others. An older partner, a silver-haired man whose name she'd immediately forgotten, smiled across the table at her. "And what do you do, Mrs. Lassiter?"

"I'm a photographer."

"How interesting!" He smiled. "I'm sure that's fun."

"It can be." She took another sip of wine. She'd discovered long ago that her work was unclassifiable for the people in David's world, a fantasy job, something they assumed could be done with little to no effort or training.

"I've always wanted to take up photography," Mr. Silver Hair said as if on cue. "Maybe when I retire."

She smiled. "What a coincidence—I'm thinking of taking up law when *I* retire."

The man blinked, smile faltering. He reached for his own glass of wine and took a big swallow.

"This is nice, isn't it?" Paige Graham, Andrew's wife, said from her end of the table, winking at Jill as she deftly turned the conversation. "It's so refreshing to get an evening out with the grown-ups."

Mr. Silver Hair smiled again, visibly relaxing. This was familiar territory. "How are the children?"

"Oh, they're just fine. Growing like weeds—

James is going to be taller than me soon, isn't that hard to believe?"

Paige was a petite woman, fragile looking next to Andrew, who was as tall as she was short, but her stature and bone structure were deceiving. She could eat more than her husband and sickeningly never put on a pound, but she was always so friendly and bubbly that Jill couldn't help liking her.

"How old is he now?" Jill asked to keep the conversation going.

"Seven. He's in second grade this year. It just goes by so fast."

Andrew turned toward his wife. "What goes by so fast? Dinner?"

"No, silly." She smacked his arm playfully. "Childhood." She and Andrew laughed together.

In every way they were a golden couple, the sort of people who inspired Ralph Lauren commercials. You couldn't live in Pittsburgh and not know about the Graham family. The name was associated with so many buildings and philanthropies; there was even a museum in New York named after them. Children were taught about Thomas Graham, Andrew's industrialist great-great-grandfather who'd made a fortune in steel and whose son and grandson had managed the company after him. Andrew's father, the senator, split his time between Washington and a fifteen-acre guarded enclave in Fox Chapel.

Andrew had gone to Princeton, like his father and grandfather before him, and then on to Duke for law school, where he'd met Paige, a Southern magnolia from a Georgia family with ties almost as prestigious as his own. Their wedding had been featured in *Vanity Fair* and *Town & Country*.

Jill had been nervous when she first met Andrew, self-conscious and despising herself for being so. She'd never been a fangirl, never pined after celebrities or waited overnight to get tickets for her favorite band. Yet there she was hanging around the offspring of a famous family, stuttering and blushing and have trouble looking him in the eye. It had taken months before she'd felt even semirelaxed.

Mr. Silver Hair looked at Jill. "Do have children, too, Mrs. Lassiter?"

"A daughter. She's three."

"Such a sweet age," Paige said with a sigh. Jill thought of Sophia's tantrum that evening over staying home with Nana instead of coming with them. "Hmm," she said. She tried to catch David's eye to share the private joke, but he was absorbed in another conversation.

"Children are a blessing," the older man intoned, taking another big swig of red wine. Broken capillaries laced his nose. Just how much had he had to drink?

"How many do you have?" Jill asked, less out of interest than to be polite.

"Two. The heir and the spare." He guffawed.

"Are they lawyers as well?"

"No, no, they didn't want to follow in my footsteps. Shoes too big to fill, I suppose." He chuckled again, took another large sip. "Our daughter's a medical examiner outside of Chicago. She's couldn't escape the law altogether —she gets called to testify in criminal cases."

"Oooh, that must be an interesting job," Paige said. "Can you share any stories?"

"She had a tough case recently." He lowered his voice. "A young man found dead—"

David suddenly stood up from the table, and when Jill looked over at him he pointed at his phone, mouthing, "be right back." She smiled and turned her attention back to the conversation, where Mr. Silver Hair was still holding forth. "—all evidence of foul play. They claimed to know nothing about it, but of course they were the first suspects."

"Of course," Paige said. "The parents are always who you suspect when a child dies."

Jill flinched, shifting in her seat to try to hide it. Andrew noticed. She saw him touch his wife's hand, saw the look that passed between them. Paige spoke fast, stumbling to explain, "Oh, I didn't mean, that isn't who—not you, Jill. I didn't mean you."

Jill had to force a smile. "Sure, I know."

"Of course you're right." Mr. Silver Hair looked

from Paige to Jill and back, trying to hold on to the conversation. "They *do* always suspect the parents."

"Excuse me." Jill pushed back from the table, looking away from the distressed expression on Paige's face, weaving through the crowded restaurant to the restrooms where she had to take a second to scrutinize the icons on the doors— hen or rooster—before pushing through the correct one and locking herself in a stall. She stood there trembling, waiting for the rush of emotions to pass.

It was silly to be this upset. Just a stupid comment. The conversation had nothing to do with her, nothing to do with what happened. "What people say has no power over me," she mumbled, trying to channel something a therapist had once told her. She squeezed her eyes shut, trying not to cry. It didn't help. She was back in the nightmare, walking down a hallway, sunlight falling across the carpet, dust motes hanging in the air. A faint scent of woodsmoke from a neighbor's fireplace. The distant sound of a crow cawing. The soft footfalls of her feet in carpet. Closer. Closer.

Jill forced her eyes open, pressing her hands so hard against the stall door that the tips of her fingers turned white. She didn't want to relive this. She wouldn't. She had barely talked about that day with Paige; she'd hardly talked about it at all, even with her closest friends, but somehow they knew. Everyone knew what had happened to the Lassiters. A cautionary tale, a hushed "there but for the grace of God" story. Was God really so stingy with grace?

Tears spilled over and Jill swiped at them, blinking hard. She'd never been one to cry in public. A stoic child in response to her mother's histrionics. She listened to make sure the restroom was empty before opening the stall door. A teen girl came in while Jill stood at the sink. Jill kept her head down, washing her hands while the girl primped, adjusting her push-up bra, and applying a fresh layer of sticky lip gloss. Had Jill ever been that happy and carefree? Once the girl had gone, she wet a paper towel and pressed it against the back of her neck for a moment, practicing the girl's relaxed smile in the mirror. It looked fake.

She lingered in the alcove outside the restrooms, in no hurry to get back to the table. If she called to check on Sophia then she'd have to talk to Elaine, and she had to summon the stamina for that. The cell connection in the restaurant was spotty. She ducked into the lobby area, trying to get a dial tone.

Through the front glass she could see a woman talking to someone on the sidewalk with her arms waving, obviously agitated. The long hair, blonde and shiny under the restaurant lights, was what caught Jill's eye. She dialed her home number, listening while it rang and rang while her hand strayed to her own hair. The woman wore a long fur coat—could that possibly be real? Jill watched as the woman took a step forward on impossibly high heels.

"Hello?" Her mother-in-law finally picked up the phone.

"Hi, Elaine, I'm just calling to check on Sophia."

"Who is this?" Elaine sounded crabby, and Jill felt her own temper rise.

"It's Jill." She raised her voice to be heard. Who else would it be? The man taking reservations raised an eyebrow. Jill turned her back on him. "How's Sophia? Is she asleep yet?"

"She's fine," Elaine said. "We're watching *Snow White* together."

Jill glanced at her watch. "Her bedtime's eight o'clock—it's almost nine."

"I know, Jill, I can tell time, you know."

The woman outside raised her hand as if to slap someone, and a man's hand shot out and grabbed her wrist. He stepped into view and Jill, shocked, let her phone drop to her side. It was David.

"Hello? Jill? Are you still there? Hello?" Elaine's bleating came from far away. Jill raised the phone back to her ear. "Sorry, I've got to go." She hung up on Elaine's complaint. David and the woman exchanged a few more words and

117

then he turned and sprinted back into the restaurant. Without knowing why she did it, Jill ducked back into the alcove so he wouldn't see her. She waited until he'd passed, face set in a grimace, before hurrying out to the front entrance, hoping to see the woman. The street was empty in either direction; she'd disappeared.

"There you are," Andrew announced in his typical life-of-the-party fashion when she got back to their table several minutes later. "David was about ready to send out the cavalry."

Paige laughed, but it was a little nervous and Jill could tell that she'd been the subject of the conversation in her absence. David smiled as if nothing was the matter, pulling back her chair, searching her eyes as he murmured, "Everything okay?"

"Yes. You?"

"Yes, of course." He smiled, squeezed her hand. Who was that woman? And what had she and David been arguing about? Jill couldn't ask him now; it would have to wait. She tried to put it out of her mind, but she kept seeing the woman's hand raised to slap him.

The conversation had moved off the subject of children and back into the safer territory of law. "Of course, this was the real purpose of tonight's dinner," Paige said with a sigh. "Andrew wants to discuss the caseload with David. If it wasn't for these events, I swear I'd never see him."

"Hey, I always show up for a free meal," Andrew said and he and David both laughed. Jill smiled weakly. She listened as Andrew, David, and Mr. Silver Hair talked for a while about their case, a lawsuit against one of the largest construction companies in Pennsylvania, getting into such a detailed discussion of the particulars of building contracts that Jill found her attention wandering.

"Drew says David's on the fast track to partner," Paige said in a conspiratorial whisper, leaning closer, blonde bob swinging over high cheekbones. She smiled knowingly. "And he's not the only partner who feels that way."

"That's great." Jill tried to share her enthusiasm, but all she could think of were the longer and longer hours that David had been working in pursuit of making partner. He was tired all the time, the shadows under his eyes becoming permanent, frown lines more prominent. His shoulders were often stooped from hours spent writing or poring over case law. They had little time to socialize, and what time they did have always seemed to be eaten up by work-related events.

As if she could read her thoughts, Paige suddenly said, "Are you coming to the Halloween party next week?"

"Um, maybe, that is, we're going to try." Put on the spot, Jill couldn't think of a creative out fast enough. She'd delayed RSVPing to the invitation for the party hoping that some excuse would present itself. Every other person Jill knew relied on e-vites or just posted an invitation on Facebook. Not Paige. Her invitations were old-fashioned and sent by regular mail, always sent early and always preceded by personal pressure so she could lock every holiday down. "You've got to come, we've got so many surprises planned for this year. It's going to be so much fun!" Paige clapped, catching Andrew's attention. He leaned over, wrapping an arm around her.

"What has Jill got to do, darling?"

"Come to our Halloween party."

"Of course she's coming, you all are, aren't you?" Andrew smiled at Jill, then David, clearly expecting him to agree.

"Of course," David said. Andrew's smile broadened. Jill kicked her husband under the table, and he shot her a look that said clearly, *What did you expect me to say?*

The ride home was quiet, tension-filled. Jill stared out the window and watched the still, dark water far below her as they drove over the Fortieth Street Bridge, leaving the lights of the city behind. She felt restless, hungry for something more, though she'd had enough food and a little too much wine. Why couldn't he just socialize with them alone? She always came away feeling annoyed as well as inadequate.

"Sorry about tonight," David said. For a moment she thought she must have spoken out loud, but then he added, "The food was okay, but that place is so pretentious, don't you think?"

"Yeah." She kept her head toward the window, looking out at the night sky.

"Larry thinks it's great, but I bet he's the only one." He laughed, downshifting to turn off the highway.

"Why did you say yes to the Halloween party?" She turned to look at him.

David turned his attention from the road to her for a second, obviously caught off guard. "Don't you want to go?"

"I wanted time to consider it. I don't think you need to jump every time Andrew asks."

His face tightened. "I don't."

"You do. If he asks, you always say yes."

"Christ, Jill, not this again." David sighed.

"Not what again? What's that supposed to mean?"

"This is my *job*. I *have* to socialize with them. Why is that so hard for you to understand?"

"You *want* to socialize with Andrew. There is nothing in the job description that says you *have* to spend that much time with him."

They were at a red light. David turned to her, jaw tight. "First of all, Andrew is my friend—our friend. And yes, I want to hang out with him. Why wouldn't I? He's a well-respected lawyer—"

"From a rich and famous family."

"That has nothing to do with it."

Jill just laughed. "Oh, c'mon, you're saying you don't think it's cool that he's a Graham?"

The light turned green. David floored the accelerator, tires screeching as he made a left turn. "Look, don't go to the Halloween party. No one is forcing you."

"That's not my point."

"Then what is your point? Because in case you don't realize it, this job is what gives us the comfortable life and the big home—"

"I didn't ask for a house that size, you wanted it—"

"—and the studio. Like it or not, this job lets you pursue your job!"

It felt like a slap, the words ringing in her ears. He never threw that in her face, never. Jill turned away, too angry to speak, but not before seeing regret cross his face. "I'm sorry," he said. His hand covered one of hers, squeezing. "I shouldn't have said that, Jilly."

She pulled her hand away. "Who were you talking to outside?"

"What?"

"The blonde woman. I saw you talking to her outside the restaurant. Who is she?" She turned to see his face.

David stared at her, then looked back at the road. "Are you spying on me or something?"

"No, I was making a phone call. Just answer the question."

"Is this jealousy? Do you want me to ask about every guy you photograph?"

"I'm not jealous, I'm just asking who you were talking to—the woman with the fur and the heels."

David downshifted, turning right onto another dark road. "She's just a lawyer from another firm—Leslie Monroe. She's upset about a case."

"All that arm waving was about a case?"

"What is this? Are you some expert in nonverbal communication now?"

"You don't have to get defensive."

"How do you think I'm going to react? It's like you're accusing me of something."

"I'm not accusing you of anything—should I be?"

"Of course not. She's just an annoying woman—"

"She tried to *hit* you. That's a lot more than annoying."

"What are you trying to say, Jill? She's a crazy lawyer. You don't believe me? Here, take my phone." He jerked it from his suit jacket and thrust it at her. "Call her up! Ask her why she's so batshit. Go on—take it!"

"I don't want to call her." She tried to push his hand away, but he held it out, the car veering slightly at he looked away from the road.

"C'mon, you don't trust me—take it!"

"Watch out!"

The BMW had swerved into the other lane. An oncoming SUV slammed on its horn as David dropped his phone and yanked the car back into their lane. Silence for a long moment as he concentrated on driving, both of them breathing heavily. "I'm sorry," he said after a long minute. "She's a miserable woman and I'm taking it out on you. Let's forget it. I'm sorry you didn't have a good time tonight."

"I didn't say that."

"No, you didn't, but I know this evening isn't your thing."

Now it was her turn to sigh at how defeated he sounded. "I didn't mean it like that."

"It'll get easier once I'm partner," he said. "I won't have to impress anybody anymore."

"I know." Except she didn't. Andrew's hours were just as demanding as David's and he was a partner, so she didn't hold out hope that things were going to suddenly change for the better. David had been promising for years that things would be easier—easier once he'd graduated from law school, once he found a good firm, once he passed the first year. There was always some new challenge that sucked up all his available time. Sometimes she thought that he used work the way some people used alcohol, as a way of anesthetizing himself from life's harsher realities.

She thought of Ethan then, as if what had happened were a touchstone against which everything else in their life could be measured. Tears spilled over before she had time to swallow them down.

"Jill?"

"It's okay, I'm okay." She swiped at her eyes; she wouldn't talk about it, she wouldn't say his name out loud, because if she did the tears would never end. The car suddenly veered right, skidding slightly on gravel, as David pulled into one of the small parking lots for the hiking trails that rose in the wooded hills around them. It was empty at this time of night.

"Hey, c'mon, don't cry." He shut off the car and reached for her.

Jill tried to fend him off. "I'm fine. We have to get home."

"No, you're not fine." He smoothed the tears gently from her face with his thumbs. She'd always loved his hands; they were massive next to hers. "It's okay. We've got time." He kissed her gently and she returned it. She kissed him the second time, desperate to think of something other than loss, other than work and parenting and the daily stress of a life that often felt as if it had gotten away from her. He kissed her back, wrapping a hand around her head and pulling them together with an urgency that matched hers. His other hand slipped between her legs and then they were both moving, shedding clothes and shifting seats, and he lifted her on top of him, entering her in an act that was as much about desperation as love.

Chapter Twelve
October 2013—One Day

Sophia was going as a fairy princess to Paige and Andrew's Halloween party in a sparkly pink costume she'd chosen herself. "No, me do it!" she yelled as Jill came to help her zip up the tulle and satin that Sophia was struggling with since she wouldn't relinquish the light-up wand clutched in one little fist.

"Fine, you do it." Jill threw up her hands and walked out of the room.

"Are we ready to go yet?" David popped his head out of his study as she came downstairs. "We're already late." He'd gotten himself ready and seemed to assume that meant that everything else would just get done without his help.

"No, David, 'we' are not ready. Maybe you'd like to help out and get your daughter dressed?"

Her husband groaned and headed upstairs, taking them two at a time. She could hear him working his charm on Sophia: "My goodness, are you a fairy princess?"

Shaking her head at the sound of Sophia's giggles, Jill headed into the kitchen to pack up the brownies that she'd made as their contribution, absurd since the party was undoubtedly catered, but she wasn't comfortable arriving empty-handed. But then she was rarely comfortable when they socialized at the Grahams'.

Both Andrew and Paige were friendly and out-going, and so down-to-earth that Jill felt like a witch for not embracing their company. Certainly David thought she exhibited working-class snobbery toward them. He was practically the president of the Andrew Graham fan club. "He's a great guy," he'd said before introducing her. "You'd never believe how much money he has."

Except Jill was always acutely aware of how much they had, and it wasn't only their material wealth. Andrew and Paige had three children—James, Andrew Junior, and Matthew. Paige had easy pregnancies, yet looked like a woman who'd never given birth. She thought it was cute that her sons' initials spelled JAM. Their annual Christmas photo card, which resembled an ad for Brooks Brothers Kids, always had JAM emblazoned somewhere on it. One year the photo featured the three boys surrounding an enormous stoneware crock of grape jam, with pieces of bread slathered with jam held just below their smiling mouths.

The Grahams lived in a mansion rumored to have been a wedding gift from Andrew's father. It was less than ten miles from Jill and David, but several significant zeros away, a three-story brick Georgian with an enormous front swath of emerald lawn and a slobbering Saint Bernard. It was half past five by the time the Lassiters arrived, but the party was already in full swing, as evidenced by the cars parked in a long line along the road. The Grahams' dog came bounding down the stone walk to greet them, as always making a beeline for Jill, seeming to intuit which person cared the least for big dogs.

"No, get down!" She tried to block him, but he leapt up anyway, landing big dirty paws smack against her chest.

"Hey, stop trying to cop a feel, fur ball," David said, laughing as he helped her push the beast away, which wasn't easy with Sophia in his arms. Jill brushed at her blouse as Sophia leaned out of her father's arms, trying to get to the dog.

"Stop that, Bruno! Heel!" Paige called from the doorway. She came clicking down the walk in high heels, clapping her hands at the dog. He ran to her, tail wagging excitedly. "I'm sorry about that," she said as she reached them. "Isn't this weather just terrible? And it was so nice yesterday. That's Pittsburgh for you." She threw out her arms to hug Sophia, exclaiming, "Who is this beautiful princess?"

"It's me!" Sophia giggled, as David handed her over. Paige and Sophia had a mutual admiration society, which made it a bit easier for Jill to accept that next to Paige she'd always look frumpy. Sophia said things like, "Paige wears pink lipstick," and "Paige is so pretty," which felt like indictments of Jill's fashion sense. They were like a before-and-after style show: Jill in jeans and a black blouse and flats, her hair tied back in a loose knot, while Paige wore a clinging black jersey dress that showed off her flawless figure, paired with high-heeled leather boots that screamed sex and high fashion in equal measure.

"C'mon in and enjoy yourselves," she said, handing Sophia back to David and traipsing ahead of them up the stone walk, her slight hips canting with every step.

The house was packed with people. Adams Kendrick didn't host many functions that included family members so most people took advantage of this one, especially those with kids. David swung Sophia down to the floor, but she shrank back against him as a gang of boys dressed as Power Rangers came racing through the house shooting at one another with Nerf guns. "Outside, boys!" Paige called, striving to be heard over the din. "Monster Mash" played loudly in the background. "Drinks at the bar and the serious food is in the dining room," Paige said. She bent down to talk to Sophia. "Do you want something to eat, honey, or do you want to see the surprise out back?"

"Surprise!"

What Andrew and Paige referred to as "out back" was approximately six landscaped acres. It had been transformed into a Halloween paradise, complete with waitstaff dressed in showy costumes, miniature jack-o'-lanterns hanging from the trees, and an enormous hay maze. "Wow, that's big!" Jill exclaimed and a woman standing nearby smiled.

"Andrew said it took over two thousand bales to create."

"Amazing." Leave it to Andrew and Paige to top themselves. They hadn't stopped at the maze: Pony rides were being offered off to the left and to the right was a bouncy castle. Gas torches and dozens of other jack-o'-lanterns lit the night and the crescent moon added to the festive air. Despite the cold and the fact that it had already rained heavily once, turning the grass slick and muddy, there were parents with children lined up. Jill expected Sophia to choose the pony ride, but she dropped Jill's hand and headed straight for the maze.

Jill understood why when she spotted the young woman dressed as a fairy princess handing out cotton candy at the entrance. "Are you a princess, too?" the woman said as she delivered a pink fluffy cloud on a paper cone to Sophia's waiting hand.

Sophia nodded, unexpectedly shy. The cotton candy was bigger than her head. She darted under the arched entry following a young couple and Jill hurried after her. "Wait up, Sophie!" she called as her daughter rounded the first corner. Straw had been sprinkled along the path to try to sop up the

131

mud, but Jill slipped in it as she hurried. The bales were too high to see across, and arranged in narrow channels that were at most three people wide.

Jill followed Sophia at another intersection to the left; the young couple disappeared to the right. They were suddenly alone. Sophia trotted ahead, wand in one hand, cotton candy in the other. They turned another corner and passed a clown juggling. His wide painted face with its huge grinning mouth and red triangles drawn around the eyes was creepy, but Sophia just laughed with delight as he pulled on and off his red nose, juggling it along with a handful of small balls. He winked at Jill. Two more turns, left, then right, then straight on for about six feet. Jill thought she heard a distant rumble of thunder. They kept turning corners, sometimes backtracking when they hit a dead end. Jill lost count of how many turns she took, lost all sense of direction. The heavy, earthy smell of hay was overpowering. She felt sweaty despite the cold; it was claustrophobic. At one point she heard people laughing and realized that they were just on the other side of the bales. She had to resist the sudden urge to push the hay over to get to them. "I want a pony ride," Sophia announced.

"Okay," Jill said, "but first we've got to find our way out."

Now she led the way, with Sophia falling behind.

The remainder of the cotton candy dropped to the ground, immediately coated in straw and mud. "Just leave it," Jill said as Sophia whined, trying to pluck off the straw. A few drops of rain fell, then a few more. The clouds were heavy and gray, hanging low in the night sky, ominously portending a downpour.

Sophia let it drop and took her mother's hand. They continued at an even slower pace. Jill felt the prickly walls moving closer, the smell of wet hay and dirt overpowering. She could hear voices in the distance, but they were alone in there and would never find the way out.

She swallowed, clutched Sophia's hand more firmly, and dragged them around another corner. A man in black walked ahead of them. Jill felt immediate relief; they might be lost, but at least they were no longer alone. She hurried after him, slowing as he paused at the end of that passage, standing there with his back to them, deciding which way to turn. "Maybe he knows the way out," Jill said to Sophia. Just as they reached him, he turned around.

The cry tore from Jill's throat. A monster stared back at her, a contorted skeleton's grimacing face, with fangs for teeth, and dark sockets where the eyes should be. Then the man reached up a hand to peel off his face. A mask, just a mask, but Sophia was screaming. She jerked free of her mother, pelting back the way they'd come. Jill ran after her. "Sophie, stop! Wait! It's just pretend." She caught her daughter in her arms and held her tight as the three-year-old struggled, still yelling. "Sophie! Stop it!" Jill shook her a little and the child burst into tears. Jill picked her up and rocked her for a moment, waiting for her own heart rate to return to normal.

The man holding the mask called, "Sorry, it's just me!" It was Andrew. He grinned sheepishly as Jill came back toward him carrying Sophia, who clung to her, sniffling. "Sorry about that; I guess it's more effective than I thought." He reached out to Sophia, but she shrank from him, turning her head away. "I'm sorry, sweetheart. You know Uncle Andrew wouldn't hurt you."

More drops of rain. Jill shifted Sophia in her arms. "Can you show us how to get out of here?" He led the way quickly through the rest of the maze, talking the whole time about how much work he'd had to go through to get the maze built, while Jill barely listened. The few drops of rain became a sprinkle, and if that rumbling was any indication, they were at most minutes from a major downpour.

They emerged from the maze just as the storm clouds opened and Jill, along with everyone else, made a run for the house. "Pony!" Sophia protested, wriggling in her mother's arms. "I want to ride the pony!"

"Here, let me take her," Andrew offered, lifting

Sophia from Jill's arms. "You don't want your princess dress to get ruined do you?" he said to Sophia.

They hurried up the wide stone steps onto the veranda and through the French doors behind a group of laughing adults and children. Andrew put Sophia down at her mother's feet. "There you go, sweetie—nice and dry."

"So where do you keep this gun collection I keep hearing about?" a balding man Jill vaguely recognized said to Andrew. Paige was passing by with a tray full of Halloween-themed cupcakes and grimaced.

"Just make sure none of the kids are around," she said to her husband. Then she rolled her eyes at Jill. "Boys and their toys."

Jill hoped that this was one passion that David wouldn't share with Andrew. He'd gone target shooting with him a few times, but so far he'd expressed no desire to own a gun of his own.

"I want to ride the pony," Sophia whined, pulling on Jill's shirt. "I want the pony!" She tried to go back out the door, but Jill pulled her away.

"Not now," she said, bending down to look Sophia in the face. "It's a thunderstorm right now, we can't ride the pony in the storm, it's not safe."

Sophia dropped to the floor, kicking and screaming, her face flushed like a ripe apple. "Pony! Pony! I want the pony!"

"Stop it!" Jill snapped. She was conscious of

other parents staring at them, at her. She knelt and hauled Sophia up, holding her firmly. "We're not going to ride the pony at all if you don't stop screaming."

This only made Sophia's wails louder. She kicked and flailed and managed to hit her mother in the nose. Jill reeled in pain, clutching at her face and letting go of Sophia in the process. The little girl immediately darted past another group coming in the door and ran back out into the storm.

"Damn it all!" Jill jumped up, one hand still holding her nose, and pushed past the crowd to go after her. She found Sophia running across the wet lawn toward the pony, which was tethered to a post, head down, enduring the rain while his minder huddled under an umbrella nearby. Lightning arced across the sky. "Get back here!" Jill yelled, but the thunder drowned her out. Fear quickened her pace. She lunged for Sophia, but just as she touched her small shoulder Jill slipped on the sopping grass and fell to the ground, pulling her daughter down with her. Sophia promptly started crying again and Jill struggled to her feet, pulling Sophia up, too. "This isn't safe," she said over her daughter's cries, hauling her back toward the house just as another bolt of lightning crackled overhead, illuminating a crowd of partygoers standing at the floor-to-ceiling windows watching them.

• • •

"It's no big deal," David said later, after she'd endured the stares and whispers of other guests and after they'd been fussed over by Paige, who offered Jill a change of clothes, only to rescind that offer seconds later, since they probably "wouldn't fit." Several hired helpers brought them towels, which were quickly smeared with muddy streaks. A lifetime later, though it was probably only twenty minutes, they were finally, blessedly, heading home.

"Easy for you to say—you weren't there." No, while Jill had been dealing with their child, David had been talking Glock and Smith & Wesson with Andrew. "I can't believe Paige lets him keep guns in the house."

"They're locked in a safe and he keeps his study locked, too."

Jill glanced back at Sophia fast asleep in her car seat wearing just her little undershirt and panties. Her face and hair were sticky with cotton candy, the mud-soaked princess costume on the floor at her feet, and her beloved wand still clutched in one small fist. She looked angelic. Jill sighed. "I'm sure I'll laugh about this someday."

"Yeah," David said, sounding relieved. He chuckled. "It is pretty funny—"

"I said someday, David. Not tonight."

"Sure, okay." He drove with one hand, reaching out to stroke her hair with the other. "Ooh, what

137

is that?" He lifted his hand away, trying to peer at his palm and the road at the same time.

"Probably mud."

He sniffed, nose wrinkling. "Actually, I think it might be pony—" He stopped abruptly and reached for a tissue from a box in the center console, wiping it off. The BMW swerved a little.

"Are you saying I have pony shit in my hair?" Horrified, Jill grabbed tissues and swiped at her head.

"No, probably just mud." David stared scrupulously ahead.

"Oh my God! It is shit!"

"It's no big—"

"David, if you tell me it's no big deal again, I swear I'm going to smear pony crap all over you!"

"Okay, okay—calm down." He slowed to turn on to their street. The front lights glowed from several neighbors' houses. A flash of lightning and Jill pictured again the faces of all those people crowded at the window watching her struggling with Sophia.

David pulled into the garage and shut off the motor. "You go ahead and take a shower—I'll give Sophia a bath."

"Thanks." Jill tried not to touch anything as she got out of the car. "Be careful, she's probably covered in it, too."

David unlocked the back door and reached in to the car seat. "We're not afraid of a little equine excrement, are we, Sophia?"

Jill trudged into the house, still feeling upset and embarrassed. What must those people think of her and her daughter? That Sophia was a spoiled brat? That Jill was a terrible parent? She'd certainly given them lots to talk about.

The upstairs hall was dark, which was the only reason she noticed light pouring from under the door of the spare bedroom. Strange. They were almost never in that room; it was set up as a guest room, but they mostly used it for storage. Jill opened the door and looked around. One side of the double closet stood open. Jill looked inside. Extra bedding sat gathering dust on the shelves, and some of her dresses and the tux that David wore approximately once a year hung in garment bags from the rod. They kept nothing else in there, so why was this even open? Had the cleaners been in there? A few metal hangers pinged as she slid the door closed. She looked around the rest of the room. An old clock ticked quietly on the dresser. The duvet on the bed seemed a little rumpled, as if someone had sat on it. She must have brushed against it, Jill thought, pulling it straight and smoothing the cloth with her hands. One more look around, before she switched off the light and pulled the door closed again. Odd.

She continued down the hall to the master bathroom, shedding her filthy clothes on the tile floor, and sighing with relief as she stepped under the warm spray of the shower. She took her time, shampooing her hair twice, wishing it were that easy to wash away the entire evening. She didn't think she'd ever be able to look some of those people in the eye again.

Finally pony free, clean, and more relaxed, Jill slipped on her robe and hurried down the hall to the main bath, where she found David kneeling by the side of the tub, washing Sophia.

"Hi Mommy!" Sophia grinned up at her, fully recovered.

"Hey, feeling any better?" David smiled at her. He lifted Sophia from the tub, wrapping her in a towel. She looked like a little cherub, all peachy pink from her bath, hair sticking out in all directions. He looked handsome, kneeling there with his shirt-sleeves rolled up, his hair falling forward into his eyes. Jill leaned down and kissed him. He pulled her to him with wet hands and kissed her again, lingering.

The buzzing of his cell phone interrupted. David let go to slip the phone from his pocket, but he shoved it back when he saw the number. "I'll call them back."

"Go ahead," Jill said. "I can finish with this little madam."

"I'm not madam," their three-year-old chirped, "I'm—"

"Sophia," Jill and David finished with her. They all laughed.

"You sure?" David said, but he was already on his feet with the phone in his hand.

"I'll put her to bed; you go."

He thanked her with another, faster, kiss as she took the towel from him. "Here you, lift up, sweetie." Jill dried under Sophia's arms and around her neck where the hair continued to drip. She pressed her head in the towel, rubbing gently while Sophia giggled, and finished with combing her hair. "There. You're all set. Go get your pj's on." She shooed her playfully out the door and Sophia ran giggling down the hall to her room.

Pajamas were rejected in favor of a nightgown, which Sophia wriggled into with only a little help. "Okay, time for bed," Jill said, pulling back the covers. She wasn't surprised when Sophia bypassed her and ran to the bookshelf instead, hauling a familiar book back to Jill and thrusting it into her hands. "Story, Mommy!"

"What's the magic word?" Jill prompted, putting the book aside for a moment to get Sophia into bed and tuck her under the covers.

"Please!" Sophia snuggled against Jill, who sat on the edge of the bed and opened the picture book that was her daughter's favorite. "On the night you were born," Jill began, no longer having to look at the words, but turning the pages so Sophia could enjoy the pictures. When she got to

Sophia's favorite part, the little girl chanted the lines along with Jill, "until everyone heard it and everyone knew, of the one and only ever you!"

By the time the story was finished, Sophia's eyelids were drooping, but she reached for a hug as Jill bent to kiss her good-night, mumbling, "You're my one and only ever mommy."

"And you're my one and only ever Sophia." Jill held her tight. "Sweet dreams." She checked that the night-light was on before switching off the room light and pulling the door almost closed behind her.

As she stood outside Sophia's room, waiting a minute to make sure that she settled into sleep, Jill heard a door close downstairs. David must be in his study. Had he finished the call? Jill walked to the head of the stairs and listened for the familiar sounds of David locking up for the night, but she heard nothing. Maybe he was still on the phone.

She padded barefoot downstairs and crossed the cold slate entry tiles to get to his study. There were no voices. She tapped quietly before opening the door. The lights were off. If her husband had been in there, he'd left. "David?" she called, closing the door behind her. There was no answer. She wrapped her robe more tightly around her as she walked toward the kitchen and the back of the house.

The kitchen was dark. She reached for the lights,

switching on the patio ones as well, and cried out as something moved outside the French doors, jumping when she spotted an inquisitive raccoon. "Shoo!" She rapped the glass and he scurried off into the darkness. Jill stood there for a second, puzzled. Maybe it was the raccoon she'd heard, though she could swear it had been a door closing. It had been a click. Definitely a click.

Jill pulled a bottle of Pinot Grigio from the fridge and poured a glass. Something creaked like footsteps at the front of the house and Jill dropped the glass. It shattered on the tile floor, spraying wine and shards everywhere. "Oh shit!" She knelt to pick up the biggest pieces of glass, crying out when a large shard sliced two of her fingers. Coin-size drops of blood spotted the tile floor, then the sink basin as she ran the cuts under water. Just small, thin cuts, but they bled so much. She bound them with a paper towel before cleaning up the mess with a broom and dustpan and then going over it again with a dish towel to mop up the blood.

When it was finally clean she headed back upstairs with two more glasses and the open wine bottle, bare feet moving soundlessly over the carpet.

David stood in the walk-in closet with his back to her, talking on his cell phone. "No. Absolutely not." He rubbed his forehead, pinching the bridge of his nose. "Because it can't happen again." She set the wine bottle and glasses on the bureau and David whipped around, face ashen. He said, "I've got to go," and pushed the off button. "Christ, Jill, how long have you been standing there?"

"I just got here." Jill poured a glass of wine and held it out. "Sorry. I didn't mean to startle you. Who on earth was that?"

"Nobody important." David slipped the phone in his pocket and took the wine glass. "Thanks. Did Sophia get to sleep okay? I didn't want to open her door and risk waking her."

Jill nodded. "She's out—it was a long day." She poured her own glass of wine and took a sip. "It didn't sound like nobody."

"Who?" David took a sip and put his glass down on the dresser. He focused on unbuttoning his shirt.

"The person you were talking to—it sounded important."

"Trust me—it was nothing interesting. Just work." He saw the makeshift bandage on her hand and grabbed her wrist. "What happened?"

"Nothing, I broke a wine glass."

"How did you do that?"

"Scaring myself." She told him about the strange click and then hearing what she'd thought sounded like footsteps.

"You probably just heard me or Sophia. Sound travels."

But Jill remembered something else. "Did you go in the guest room today?"

David slipped off his shirt and balled it, tossing it in the hamper. "No. Why?"

"The light was on in there."

He took another sip of wine. "So? One of us must have left it on from the last time we went in there."

"I'm never in there."

David shrugged. "Maybe I went in to get something."

"What? There's nothing of yours stored in there except your tux."

"Okay, so maybe the cleaners left it on."

"They don't clean that room most of the time. It doesn't need to be cleaned. And the closet door was open, too."

David set down his glass and rested his hands on her shoulders, massaging lightly. "Hon, c'mon. You had a rough day and you're letting your imagination run wild." His hands moved from shoulders to neck. He brushed her wet hair out of the way and bent down to kiss the tender skin at the nape. "You need to unwind."

Jill leaned into his touch, wanting to believe him.

Chapter Thirteen

Journal—August 2009

You left early again and I'm splayed on the bed, your seed spilling out of me. At the end you never want to linger. You believe in the quick finish. It has taken me some time to cut through the flattery and charm that brought me literally to my knees. That's where you like me to be when I suck your cock. Is that too vulgar for you? I picture you wincing, though this is precisely the sort of language you prefer when you tangle your hand in my hair and use it to control my head.

When we are together, you tell me that we have an incredible connection that you just don't have with your wife. Not that you've ever called her that or called her anything at all. "Home" is the euphemism. "I don't have this at home," you say. "You're the only soul mate I've got."

I know, I know. Stupid, right? I am the classic dummy when it comes to male behavior. Your secretary tried to tell me once, did you know that? She approached me in the ladies' room, the one that the male partners like to crow about whenever gender discrimination issues come up because they added three more stalls and think that makes them supersensitive to women's issues. We stood at adjoining sinks. "Do you mind if I tell you something?" She had a smile on her heavily powdered face, and it didn't occur to me that it would be anything less than friendly. I gave her an expectant smile in return, standing there with the water running. "You're not the first easy lay in this firm and you won't be the last, so stop thinking that you can fuck your way to partner."

My face flamed; I felt offended, misjudged. I didn't realize the real message behind her warning, not for some time.

I think about leaving every day, but I'm too inexperienced to attract the attention of another decent firm. Every interviewer asks why I'm leaving my present firm, but I can't tell them the truth, can I? I'm stuck, which means I'm stuck with you because as much as I long to end it, the truth is that I've fallen in love with you. It's an illness, this sort of obsession. I know you're bad for my health, but like a smoker reaching for "just one more" from that pack of cigarettes, or the dieter who justifies eating that slice of chocolate birthday cake, I keep acquiescing.

You've never said you'll leave your wife, but I fantasize about it all the same. We don't talk about her, but she looms large between us when you're fucking me, D. Sometimes I think I can even see her, a ghostly apparition hovering in a corner of the room during every encounter—watching, judging.

I have seen her for real, you know. Once we actually rode the elevator up together. I recognized her from the photos you have on your desk, the pictures of a life that you should be having with me. She's a beautiful woman, and I felt a surge of jealousy that she got to be with you, sleep with you, wake up next to you every morning.

Chapter Fourteen
November 1, 2013—The Day

Jill woke suddenly, startled by something. She sat up in bed, heart racing, while David lay snoring softly beside her. A glance at the clock showed it was 6:27 a.m. Her alarm would go off in three minutes anyway. She'd had the nightmare again, another endless journey down a shadowed hallway, the feeling of dread gaining in intensity the closer she got to the door at the end. Except she'd woken sooner this time and she didn't know why. She had the sense it was something external, a noise of some sort, but she couldn't hear anything beyond David's heavy breathing and the low hum of the furnace kicking on.

She slipped out of their king-size bed and padded into the large master bathroom, the tile floor a sudden chill under her feet. The first day of November and there had already been flurries. Soon the remaining leaves would fall and winter would arrive with the promise of lots of snow. She hated the cold, but she did love photographing the clean, unbroken sweep of a snow-covered hillside or the starkness of black tree trunks against a perfect expanse of white. And Sophia loved the snow—making snow angels and snowmen, throwing snowballs. Jill smiled remembering Sophia's grin as she'd clomped through mounds of snow in the pink sparkly boots she'd worn last winter.

Thinking of Sophia made her realize that they'd gotten through the night without her crawling into bed with them.

David was still lying in bed when Jill came out of the bathroom. She leaned down to kiss him. "Good morning."

" 'ello," he mumbled into his pillow.

"Notice anything?"

He stared up at her, bleary-eyed. "Um, you're more awake than I am?"

"Sophia slept in her own bed."

"Great." He yawned and rolled up to a sitting position with a groan. "Then why don't I feel any more awake?"

She smiled and slipped into the silk robe hanging from a hook on the back of the bathroom door. "You can have the shower first; I'll get Sophia up and start the coffee."

It was dark in the hallway. She pulled the robe tightly around her, trying to rub warmth into her arms, and padded down the long hall to her daughter's room. The master bedroom was at one end of the second-floor hallway, separated from three others by a laundry room and the large main bath. Sophia's door was a tiny bit ajar, the way they left it every night, because Jill wanted to be able to hear her daughter if she needed them.

Jill listened at the door for a second, then slowly pushed it open. In the dim light coming through the gauzy curtains she could see the bed piled high with the blankets that Sophia loved to snuggle under. "Good morning, sleepyhead," she called in a soft singsong, walking quietly across the carpet to the bed. She put her hand on the top blankets, expecting to feel the warmth and firmness of her daughter's small body, but her hand sank into softness instead.

"Sophia?" Jill pushed down on the blankets, then pulled them off. Her daughter wasn't there. Surprised, Jill switched on the light, looking around the room. "Where are you, sweetie?"

She took a quick peek under the bed, hoping to find Sophia stifling giggles underneath, but no such luck. Jill sighed and headed out of the room and down the stairs to the first floor. Twice, lately, they'd had a variation on the sleepless theme with Sophia going downstairs to make her own breakfast, in both cases before five a.m. The first time had involved cereal scattered across the counter and floor and a half gallon of spilled milk. The second time, it was grape jelly smeared on every available surface. Worse than the mess, however, was the fear that Sophia would try to use the stove or toaster on her own. The first time, Jill told her that she could help make breakfast like a big girl, but she had to wait until the morning and had to have Mommy or Daddy's help. The second time, David spoke to Sophia very sternly and put her in time-out for three long minutes, during which she sobbed loudly and heartrendingly. Jill thought they'd gotten through to her, but apparently not.

She rounded the corner into the kitchen with a scold on her lips, only to stop short. All lights were off and the kitchen was dark. "Sophia?" No sound, except the steady drip of the kitchen faucet that they kept meaning to fix. No food out on the granite island, no dishes because she'd left the wine glasses and bottle upstairs. All the chairs were pushed in at the kitchen table. No one had been there.

The rest of the first floor was in shadows. Jill crossed out of the kitchen and into the empty family room beyond, tripping over one of Sophia's stuffed animals lying on the floor. She put it up on a shelf, surprised that Sophia wasn't curled up on the sectional in front of the TV. She moved on through the dining room, her footsteps quick enough to make the crystal glasses tremble in the china cabinet, and into the living room. There was no sign of Sophia anywhere.

Jill felt uneasy. She ran back upstairs taking the steps two at a time. "Sophia? Sophie, where are you?" She went back into her daughter's room. "If you're hiding it's time to come out now." She opened the closet door and swept her hands between the clothes on the lower rack, separating them. No Sophia. She checked under the bed again and then strode out of her room and through the next door into the empty guest bedroom. No Sophia.

Real fear came first as a tiny prickling feeling. She checked the bath, then Sophia's bedroom again, before running back toward her own, the sound of the shower in the master bath getting louder. "Sophia? Are you in here?" She dropped to her knees and looked under the bed before checking the walk-in closet. The shower stopped and in the quiet she could hear herself panting. David came out of the bathroom toweling his hair.

"What's wrong?"

"Sophia's not in her room."

He stopped drying and stood there with the towel in his hands. "She's probably downstairs making breakfast again."

Jill shook her head. "She's not. That's the first place I looked."

"Well, where else could she be?"

They stared at each other for a second, then Jill ran to the window while David said, "Could she have gone outside?"

Jill scanned the backyard. "Did you lock the French doors last night?"

"I don't know, I think so."

"You think so?" She couldn't see her anywhere.

"Oh my God, do you think she could have left the yard?" She turned and saw David pulling on jeans and hurried past him to do the same.

"No," he said, yanking a T-shirt over his head. "At least I don't think so."

Jill ran from the room and heard David racing down the hall behind her. Back down the stairs and through the kitchen to the family room and the French doors. She stepped onto the back patio, the cold air like a slap against her face. She scanned the dark yard rapidly, searching for her daughter. It was still so dark out; would she really have gone outside on her own? "Sophia!" Her cry scattered a group of crows resting in an oak tree, and they rose shrieking into the air. David came out with the flashlight they kept under the kitchen sink, the beam bouncing erratically off bushes and the wooden play-house.

Jill ran toward it and David followed. Sophia loved the little white house accented with pink shutters and door and real window boxes, a birthday gift from David's parents. "Sophia?" David called this time, his voice louder than Jill's. A light came on in an upstairs window of a neighbor's house. The playhouse was empty; the toy table set with cups and saucers, and one of two small wooden chairs lay on its side.

Jill thought it looked untouched. "She hasn't been in here."

154

David swung the flashlight up and over the rest of the yard. Nothing.

"Do you think she would have left the yard?"

"No," she said at once, then hesitated. "I don't know. I don't think so."

Beyond the lawn the yard sloped down into woods. "It's so dark," David said. "Would she really wander this far in the dark?"

They'd talked about getting a fence, but had deemed it an unnecessary expense. It wasn't as if they had a dog, though Sophia kept asking for one. Jill suddenly wished that they'd gotten the dog; if they'd gotten the dog they would have gotten the fence and Sophia would be here.

"Sophia! Sophie, where are you?" Jill's voice seemed to echo in the silence. There was no answering cry. "We've got to check the woods."

Jill hurried after David down the dark hillside, flashlight bouncing off tree trunks and low-hanging branches and once the ghostly wide eyes of some animal almost as frightened as they were.

She tripped over a tree root and fell heavily to the ground, her hands sinking through a dense carpet of pine needles and molding leaves before slamming into rock-hard soil, the smell of decay souring the air around her. She clambered to her feet, glancing back at the house as the sun crept up, a frightening ribbon of blood orange spreading on the horizon. For just a moment, in a trick of light, the dark windows at the back of the house made it look like a large, leering face.

Reaching the ravine within seconds of David, she clambered over the rocks that formed the bottom, following him down the creek toward the culvert that ran under the road over fifty feet away. Icy water soaked through her shoes, but Jill barely felt it. She screamed Sophia's name until her throat was raw, but when they reached the entrance to the culvert she tried again, her voice echoing off the concrete walls. A raccoon exploring a small pile of debris in the corner bared his teeth at them for a moment before running out the opposite end. It was deserted, but David ran its length anyway, bent over, running the flashlight all around.

"Where is she?" Jill's voice cracked; she was sweating despite the cold.

David stopped at the end of the culvert for a moment, hands on his knees and head bent, catching his breath. When he turned back seconds later the look on his face frightened her.

"Call the police."

PART II

after

Chapter Fifteen

Day One

By the time detectives arrived, Jill had recounted multiple times the story of how she had discovered Sophia missing. Originally to the young, acne-scarred patrolman who arrived first, and then again and again to the older, more senior officers who came after him.

Jill's jeans had dark stains on the knees and her hands were scraped and dirty. Inside she felt empty, scraped and hollowed out, like the jack-o'-lantern sitting on her own front porch. She didn't think she could replay this nightmare one more time, but that was exactly what the detectives expected her to do.

"We've already told the other officers," David said with exasperation when the male detective asked Jill to repeat the story again.

"Yes, I understand, but I haven't heard it from you." Detective Ottilo moved ever so slightly, turning his attention fully to Jill.

They were in the living room, Jill and David seated together on the sofa like teenagers being grilled by parents before their first date. They'd been asked to sit down in there so that they didn't interfere with the police work going on in the house around them. Beyond them, in the front hall, police officers moved in and out hauling various cases and bags. Fear warred with a feeling of violation.

"So you checked outside," Detective Ottilo prompted in a quiet voice. Jill wondered how he could be so calm. He was late forties or early fifties, tall and skeletally thin with short-cropped gray hair, sharp cheekbones, and pale and penetrating gray eyes. He wore brushed steel reading glasses taken from the pocket of his charcoal gray suit. Even his tie was a dull pattern of black and silver. He looked as muted as he spoke. His partner, Detective Finley, couldn't have been a greater physical contrast. She was a short, curvaceous woman in her thirties with fiery red hair and the sort of milky skin that burned like paper in the sun. She wore a clingy emerald green wrap dress and long, brown high-heeled boots, and her blue eyes darted around the room, taking in everything before settling back on Jill and David. If Ottilo looked like an accountant who ran marathons, then Jill thought Finley resembled an Irish version of the Barefoot Contessa. Neither of them matched her mental image of a detective, and why were they both sitting there wasting valuable time?

"When we couldn't find her in the woods, I called the police and then we both searched the house a second time, like the 911 operator told us to," she repeated, struggling not to speak in a rapid monotone just because she'd told the story one too many times. It didn't begin to convey the horror of it; it couldn't convey the fear.

"What happened to your hand, Mrs. Lassiter?"

"My hand?" Jill glanced at the Band-Aids she'd taped around two fingers. "Nothing, I broke a glass and cut myself picking it up."

"Last night?"

Jill nodded and Ottilo made another mark in his small notebook. He'd been making occasional scribbles all along, his eyes rarely leaving her face. She avoided his gaze, watching the traffic in the hall with her arms wrapped tightly around her midsection. Gradually aware of pain in her arms, she glanced down to find her nails digging into the skin. She was surprised she could feel anything. Fear had given way to panic and that, in turn, had given way to a certain numbness. Maybe this was shock? Apparently, she wasn't the only one who thought so, as Ottilo flagged down a young uniformed officer with instructions to "get Mrs. Lassiter a glass of juice or ginger ale or water if you can't find anything sugary." Bizarre to be a guest in her own home.

Detective Ottilo looked back at Jill. "So the front door was locked this morning?"

Jill nodded. "Definitely. I remember locking it last night. We don't use the front door all that often; we usually come in through the garage."

"And both that door and the garage door were closed?"

"Yes."

"So you went out the French doors, between the kitchen and the family room, which were unlocked?"

David had been talking to his office on his cell phone, but he hung up in time to catch the question. "We've told you all this already! We went out the French doors and they probably weren't locked. This is a safe neighborhood—we don't always remember to lock those doors."

"Sophia could have unlocked them," Jill said. "I don't know if we locked them last night, I can't remember." She pushed a hand against her forehead, willing herself to see it—her hand reaching for the door, turning the knob. "I don't think it was locked this morning."

"What time did both of you go outside?"

"I don't know," David said. "Sometime after six thirty?" He looked at Jill for confirmation.

"Six thirty-five? Six forty?" Ottilo turned his gaze back on her.

"I don't know." Jill struggled to think clearly. "I can't remember. I wasn't thinking about the time, I was thinking about finding my daughter!"

A cluster of officers in the hall turned as her voice rose. Tears pricked in her eyes and she struggled to hold them back, feeling the detective's stare like heat against her skin. The young officer came back with a glass and offered it to her. She took a sip and choked on the cloying sweetness of the artificially flavored orange drink that they kept in stock only for David's mother. The officer was speaking in a low voice to Ottilo. That's all they were doing—talk, talk, talk.

So much time had passed. If Sophia had wandered off, she could be miles away by now. And if someone had taken her . . .

Anxiety forced Jill up from the couch. "I can't just sit here talking." She paced to the living room window, pushing back the curtains. "I'd rather be out looking. Are they checking people's yards? Sophia likes animals—she might have gone to look at someone's dog."

"Has she wandered off before?"

"She's not supposed to leave the yard, but she went into the woods a couple of weeks ago," Jill said. "That's why we checked there first."

"And the park a few months ago," David added. "She wandered off there."

Jill whirled around; she couldn't believe she'd forgotten. "She didn't wander off, someone tried to abduct her!" She quickly described what had happened, trying to include all the details. "She had a puncture mark here." Jill pointed to the spot on her own arm. "It looked like she'd been given a shot or—"

David interrupted. "You're the only one who saw that, Jill."

Detective Ottilo stopped writing and looked up. "There was a needle mark on your daughter's arm?" He leaned forward in his seat, pen poised for their reply.

"Yes," Jill said just as David said, "No."

He said to Ottilo, "Our daughter was gone for about thirty, maybe forty minutes, probably roaming around in the woods. There was a small mark on her arm and Jill was understandably upset. It looked like a bug bite to me, but we took her to the ER just to make sure. They didn't find anything."

"Did the police file a report?" Ottilo asked.

"I don't know," Jill said. "They left before I found the puncture—"

David interrupted. "Look, we're wasting valuable time here. That had nothing to do with today, except to explain that our daughter wanders off. You should be out looking for her, not sitting here discussing things that happened months ago."

"Of course it has something to do with today— it could be the same guy," Jill snapped.

"What guy? We never saw anybody and you know as well as I do that Sophia is always taking off."

"So your daughter routinely wanders off?" Ottilo asked, looking from Jill to David and back again.

"No," Jill said just as David said, "Yes." Then

he repeated, "Why aren't you out looking for her?"

"We have officers looking for your daughter as we speak, Mr. Lassiter." It was Detective Finley who spoke this time. She perched in an armchair across from them, next to her partner in a matching chair, tapping a pen against her knee. "The state police have issued an Amber Alert for Sophia. Do you have a recent photo we can give to the news media?"

"I'll get you one." Jill headed for the stairs, anxious to do something.

Detective Finley fell into step behind her and Jill wondered why she needed an escort until they got to the top of the stairs and she saw police officers milling about the second floor, one of them coming out of Sophia's bedroom, another on his hands and knees dusting for fingerprints on the door, and still another checking the linen closet. It shocked her into stopping.

"This is just routine," the detective said. "We have to follow procedures, Mrs. Lassiter." Voice calm, she touched Jill's arm, a gentle pressure to steer her toward the bedroom. Jill swallowed hard and looked away; it felt so invasive, and it only got worse when she entered the master bedroom and saw a police officer coming out of the attached bath.

"My daughter was not in here this morning," she said, trying to control her indignation.

"Sorry, ma'am." The officer glanced at the detective before exiting.

Jill's bedroom was as she'd left it earlier that morning, bedclothes in a tangled heap, David's towel tossed on the floor, her robe a silk puddle next to it. It felt like a lifetime ago, not just a few hours. Detective Finley picked up a five-by-seven photo of Sophia from a display on the dresser. "Is this recent?"

"Yes, I took it this summer." Jill stared at Sophia's smiling face over the other woman's shoulder. There were over a dozen photos on the dresser and most of them featured Sophia. Sophia alone, Sophia with friends, Sophia with Jill or David.

"Is she an only child?" Detective Finley was looking at the other photos and Jill saw her gaze rest for a moment on a small photo of an infant in a baby-blue onesie.

A split-second hesitation before Jill said, "Yes." She looked away from that photo and reached for a headshot of Sophia giving a shy smile to the camera. "Here, this is another recent one." The detective took it, but Jill saw her glance stray back to that small, single photo.

As she walked back into the living room Detective Ottilo said to David, "We need to know who's been in the house besides the three of you in the last twenty-four hours."

"No one. We were at a party yesterday, but we came home early."

Ottilo nodded. "Okay. Anyone in the last few days?"

Jill shook her head, impatient. "No, the cleaning crew comes earlier in the week. We already told the first officer."

"We're going to need contact information for your cleaning crew." Ottilo paused scribbling to ask, "Do you have family here?"

"My parents," David said. "They live in Fox Chapel. I have a sister, Diane. She lives in Philadelphia."

"What about you, Mrs. Lassiter?"

She shook her head. "No, I don't have any family nearby." When he continued to stare at her, she added, "There's just my mother. She lives—" She struggled to remember the latest postmark. "—somewhere down South. We're estranged."

"Could any family members have taken Sophia?" Finley asked. "It could be for any reason at all—dispute over parenting styles, wanting to see their grandchild . . ."

"No," David said bluntly. "My parents wouldn't take our child, that's ridiculous."

"We will need to talk to them anyway. It's all routine, Mr. and Mrs. Lassiter."

"It isn't routine for us," David snapped.

Jill's felt suddenly weak-kneed. Why hadn't she thought of it immediately? "Sophia's adopted."

Chapter Sixteen

Journal—October 2009

I told you today. I'd carried the news around with me for over a week, waiting for the right moment. I think some part of me knew that there was never going to be a right moment, not with you.

I expected surprise, but not the shock that followed, or the anger. "This is the twenty-first century," you said, gaping at me like I'd announced terminal cancer. "You're telling me you didn't use birth control?"

"I thought I'd taken it—"

"You thought?" You had that awful voice you get sometimes in court, the one that says whatever the witness has testified to is completely and unquestionably idiotic.

"You didn't wear a condom," I said, but you weren't listening. You already had your phone out, scrolling through search screens.

We were sitting in your car. I didn't plan it that way, but it's appropriate, don't you think, since that's where it all started? You'd pulled into the motel parking lot and I didn't want to share this with you in that cheap, awful little room with the pasteboard furniture and the TV bolted to the wall.

"We need to get you to a clinic as quickly as possible," you said. "I'll arrange it all, you don't have to worry about cost."

I said, "A clinic?" My turn to sound shocked, and you smiled, patting my arm.

"Don't worry, not one of those awful ones with protestors out front. There's a private one I know about."

I didn't really think about that comment until just now. How do you know about this private clinic? How many times have you had this same conversation?

"I'm not going to get an abortion."

The look of even greater surprise on your face would have been comical if I hadn't pictured this conversation going in a completely different direction.

You switched into your whiskey-smooth voice, the one that makes me feel like believing any-thing you say. "This desire of yours, to selflessly have this baby to help another couple, that's really great of you." You were stroking my hair and I pulled back.

"No, no, I'm going to keep it."

You flinched. You actually flinched. And then you said that that was the stupidest thing you'd ever heard. "Are you out of your mind? This will ruin both of our careers!"

You told me how I'd never keep up with the work, you told me that there was no way on my salary that I'd be able to afford more than the worst day care for my child. My child. Not ours. You told me that if I proceeded with this stupid plan that you wouldn't be able to help me, that I'd end up without a job. "You couldn't stay at the firm, don't you see that?"

I started to cry and you sighed. "Look, I'm not trying to hurt you, but this is how it is." I cried harder and you wrapped an arm around my shoulders, pulling me close against your expen-sive suit, something you usually don't do until you're undressed because you care so much about your clothes. "Don't cry," you said. "It's going to be okay." The only thing to hope for is that you'll change your mind before the time comes to give our baby up.

Chapter Seventeen

Day One

Bea's shoulders ached from hauling the bag, her arms twitching with fatigue. She had to concentrate to keep the wheel straight as she drove. Be careful, keep within the speed limit. The last thing she wanted was to attract the attention of police at just after five in the morning. There were no streetlights in this damn suburb; she could barely see the road.

The duffel bag sat on the floor of the backseat on the passenger side; she'd been afraid to leave it in the trunk. She'd pulled out of the copse and onto the road as quietly as possible, but there was no way she could avoid using the headlights. It was cloudy and had been bitterly cold in the woods; the night was so complete that she could barely see a hand in front of her face. The yellow headlights glowed like flares in the darkness.

A small sound from the backseat. Bea glanced in the rearview mirror, cursing when she saw the bag moving. She still had close to ten minutes of driving before they reached the house. Bea increased her speed, watching the arrow move along the little map on the GPS mounted to her dashboard. Calculated arrival at destination: six minutes, twenty seconds.

As she came around a bend near the turnoff for Fernwood Road, flashing lights suddenly appeared. Bea slammed on the brake as she saw a police cruiser blocking the road. Behind it, in the glare of headlights, she could see several large trucks and a cluster of men in yellow hard hats. The whine of an arc saw; sparks shot up in the air.

It was too late for Bea to turn around; a police officer waving a flashlight strode toward her car.

"Go back, turn around," she willed under her breath, but he kept coming. She tilted the rearview mirror to see the bag in the backseat. The zipper was partially open. Bea reached back to zip it fully closed, but the metal slipped in her fingers, then stuck. "Damn it!"

The cop approached the driver's-side door, squinting against the glare of her headlights, and made a circular motion with his hand, instructing her to put down her window.

She lowered it a crack. "Yes, officer?"

The flashlight blinded her for a moment as he ran it over her face before lowering it. "Ma'am, this road is temporarily blocked for the next few nights for road work. Where are you heading?"

"Fernwood Road."

He nodded, his face bisected by shadows. Young and overly muscular, biceps straining his uniform jacket. "We can let you through in a minute, just sit tight." He ran the flashlight lazily over the interior of the car and Bea fought to keep her face relaxed and hands on the wheel. Her gaze flicked to the rearview mirror and back up to the cop's inquiring eyes. The bag was twitching; could he see it?

"You're out late," the cop said and she knew he was fishing.

"Yep." She tried to smile, pulled her lips back from her teeth, imagined that her pale face must be gleaming when everything else was so black. Black! She'd forgotten that she wore all black—the pageboy wig, the hoodie, the pants, even her socks and shoes. Damn, it looked odd. Had he noticed?

"You work a late shift?"

Like it was any of his business. A bead of sweat trickled down the side of Bea's face despite the cold. She looked up at what she could see of the young man's face. "Yep."

If he asked where she worked, she wouldn't know what to say. "Will it be much longer?" She spoke quickly to distract him.

"Shouldn't be; let me check." He turned toward the construction just as the sound of the arc welding stopped. In the sudden quiet an audible moan. The cop turned back. "What was that?"

"I didn't hear anything." Her voice sounded high and false; did he notice? The cop's flashlight shot back to her face and she thought he must see the sweat soaking her temples, pooling in the hollow at her collarbone. It was only thirty degrees, but she felt soaked in sweat. Her chest hurt, the familiar pain of angina radiating from the center out. She wanted to massage it, but her hands stayed glued to the steering wheel.

The officer hitched up his belt with the flashlight still in his hand, its beam bouncing erratically over the car. A startling glimpse of something white in the rearview mirror. A tiny hand.

"Wait a minute." The man's voice rose as the beam of light stilled on the backseat. "What's that?"

Chapter Eighteen

Day One

Detective Ottilo's calm slipped; he looked genuinely surprised. "Adopted? So her birth mother might have taken her?"

"No," David said. "There's no way. It was a closed adoption."

"Maybe she found us," Jill said. "Haven't you always wondered if she might?"

"No," he said, flatly. "Never."

But Ottilo ignored him, asking, "Has she ever tried to contact you?"

Jill shook her head, sinking farther into the couch. "But maybe somehow she got our address—"

"That's ridiculous," David said sharply. "It would be illegal. It was a closed adoption— closed as in we knew almost nothing about the birth mother—we didn't even know her name— and she knew the same about us."

Detective Finley said, "Still, it's possible. We need the agency's name and number."

"We didn't use an agency," David said. "It was a private adoption."

"Then you used a lawyer?" Ottilo said, adding, "Was it someone from your firm?"

"No, a colleague set us up with an adoption attorney. John Antkowiak."

"We'll need his phone number and all of the information you have from the adoption."

David grimaced, but stood up. "It's in the study." Detective Ottilo followed him after exchanging a quick look with Detective Finley. Before Jill could interpret it, a young police officer rushed to Ottilo's side, speaking rapidly, but too low to overhear.

"What? What is it?" Jill asked, but they ignored her, the uniformed officer heading back down the hall toward the kitchen with Ottilo striding after him.

Finley called, "Mike?"

Ottilo glanced back at her, face grim. "We've got something out back."

Jill ran after the detectives, down the hall. A cluster of police officers and a few crime-scene technicians crowded the kitchen and the back door. Detective Ottilo pushed through them with the officer who'd fetched him, but when Jill tried to follow, Detective Finley stopped her with an outstretched arm. "Let's wait here a minute."

"Is it Sophia?" Jill stood on tiptoe trying to see over the crowd. "Have they found Sophia?"

"What's going on?" David rushed into the room. "Have they found her?"

"Sophia isn't out there." Detective Finley didn't budge.

"Then who is?" David demanded. He sounded angry, but Jill could hear the fear underneath it. "This is ridiculous—you can't stop us from moving around our own house." He started to push past the detective, who was several inches shorter and at least fifty pounds lighter, and the woman's hand shot out and circled David's wrist. She had his arm up and behind his back before Jill could react. He cried out in either surprise or pain, and Jill cried, "Let him go!"

A male police officer stepped in from the other room and two other officers turned from the back door. Commotion came from outside, the crowd dispersing, and Detective Ottilo turned back to them.

"It's all right," he said and Finley abruptly released David.

"What the hell is going on!" he said. His shirt had come untucked; he was red in the face.

Jill's searched Ottilo's face. "What is it? What did you find?"

"There are traces of blood on the patio," Ottilo said.

Jill couldn't move, she was frozen in place. "Oh my God."

"Blood? What the hell—is it Sophia's? I want to see it." David made another move forward and this time it was Ottilo who caught him, holding the other man firmly by both arms.

"You cannot go out there, Mr. Lassiter. We need

to preserve the evidence; the fewer the people the better chance we have." He let him go and turned to Jill. "You said you cut your hand yesterday?"

"Yes, I bled on the kitchen floor, maybe some of it got tracked outside."

"But you didn't go outside when you cut it?"

Jill shook her head. A momentary hope that it was just her blood, not Sophia's, evaporated. "How much blood was on the patio? It's Sophia's blood, right? Oh my God." She didn't realize she was shaking until Detective Finley put a steadying hand on her arm.

"Don't jump ahead, Mrs. Lassiter," she said. "We don't know anything yet."

Detective Ottilo moved one arm around David's shoulders and both of them were escorted out of the kitchen. Jill couldn't stop trembling. How could she and David have missed seeing the blood outside?

There was a sudden commotion at the front door, and Elaine Lassiter pushed past an officer trying to restrain her.

"She insisted on coming inside," a young patrolman said to Detective Ottilo.

"Of course I insisted! I'm the grandmother!" Elaine turned her back on the man as if he were an annoying waiter. She scanned the room, spotting Jill first, but going straight to her son. "David!"

"Hi, Mom." He went to her open arms, and after she'd held him, Elaine reached out an arm to Jill, who got pulled into the older woman's small but iron-tight embrace. As always, a pungent aroma of Shalimar wafted in with her. Jill pulled back first, raising her eyebrows at David to demand why he'd called his mother. He avoided her gaze.

"We could barely get on the street," Elaine said with wonder and indignation. "There are police cars a mile deep outside. Your father dropped me off; he's going to have to park clear down at the end of the road."

Detective Finley moved to a front window with her cell phone, apparently directing some cops outside to deal with through traffic. Elaine looked her up and down before turning her attention to Detective Ottilo. "What's happening? Have you searched the neighborhood?"

"Everything possible is being done, Mrs. . . . . ?"

"Lassiter. Elaine Lassiter. I'm David's mother. Do you have any suspects?"

"I'm really not at liberty to discuss the case with you, Mrs. Lassiter."

"I just want to be sure that everything is being considered. Have you located the birth mother?"

Jill recoiled and David said, "Mom!"

Elaine said to Ottilo, "They don't like to talk about it, but really—isn't the birth mother the first person you should look at?"

"We've already talked about this," David said. "Not that it matters. We got Sophia when she was a day old. It's almost as if Jill gave birth to her."

"But she didn't," Elaine said in her usual blunt manner, looking straight at Jill. "And the birth mother could be anybody." She turned back to the detectives. "You hear these things all the time, women taking back their children after they give them up. That's why I argued against adopting—"

"Stop it, Mom!" David cut her off, red in the face. Jill got up from the couch and crossed to the window, holding her arms protectively across her chest.

"Well, I'm just trying to help." Elaine managed to sound both indignant and wounded at the same time. Her voice grated on Jill. In the silence that followed, the ticking of the mantel clock seemed suddenly louder, an indictment of her as a mother, the biological clock that had ticked away inside her but hadn't been enough to produce a healthy, living child.

Ottilo's cell phone rang and he carried it with him into the hallway, talking so quietly that even when she strained Jill couldn't hear what was being said.

"Mr. and Mrs. Lassiter, we'd like to take your fingerprints," Detective Finley said. Jill turned from the window, wondering why they needed to do it again, but Finley was talking to her in-laws. Bill Lassiter had slipped into the house without his wife's fanfare. Tall and slightly stoop-shouldered, he stood there in his usual quiet manner letting his wife take the lead.

"We're not suspects, are we?" Elaine said.

"It's routine—we need to identify all the prints found in the house."

Elaine and Bill followed Finley into the dining room. It was at that same table, over a dinner orchestrated for that very purpose, that Jill and David had announced to his parents that they were adopting. Elaine had given them plenty of reasons why they shouldn't do it—it was too soon after what happened, the child wouldn't be their own flesh and blood, who knew what bad genes the child could carry—while Bill sat nodding his head in apparent agreement, a concerned look on his face. It was at such moments that Jill saw clearly why Bill was an accountant, not a litigator, and why David was such an effective one. He'd inherited his mother's quick wit and verbal repartee, and he'd answered every argument thrown at them.

From the dining room, Jill heard Bill say, "David and Jill know that we would never do anything to hurt Sophia."

On that point, at least, they were in total agreement. Despite their reservations about adoption, once Sophia was actually born David's parents came on board as doting grandparents, eager to spend as much time with her as possible and showering her with attention and gifts. Jill thought that they'd forgotten about the adoption, given that Elaine was prone to making comments like

"She looks so much like David," or "Isn't that exactly what Diane did at that age?"

Apparently they'd never forgotten. It had festered below the surface, perhaps a secret fear for Elaine that she'd lose her granddaughter. That Jill shared the same fear should have been a bond between them, but it couldn't be, not after what had happened. Jill turned back to the window, pressing her hands against her temples as if she could push away bad memories. She stared out at the cul-de-sac crammed with vehicles; alien to see it this crowded. A news van had joined the patrol cars, reporters sniffing around like stray dogs.

David said, "What the hell are they doing?" She turned away from the window as he flung himself back down on the couch, gesturing at all the strangers passing through their house. "I see lots of police, but what are they actually doing to bring her home? Have all of the neighbors been questioned yet?"

The officer standing at the front door shifted, staring at him before looking away, and Jill could tell that he and the other cops were judging David—the arrogance of this high-priced attorney expecting that they could just snap their fingers and make everything okay. It didn't help that he sounded peevish, the voice of a man expecting things to work for him as if the universe had decreed him exempt from all pain and suffering.

Ottilo came back into the room. "There's been a development." His eyes were alight.

David leapt up. "What is it? Have you found her?"

Clenching her hands, Jill recited a silent prayer: Let it be Sophia, please let them have found her, please let it be.

"A neighbor reported seeing a strange car parked near the entrance to your street last night—"

"Was Sophia in the car?" Jill interrupted.

"We're waiting for confirmation, Mrs. Lassiter. The only other thing I can tell you is that a car matching that description was stopped by police sometime early this morning. There was a child in *that* car."

"It's her," Jill said. "It's got to be Sophia."

"It could be her, Mrs. Lassiter. *Could* be. We don't know anything yet—they're checking on it as we speak."

The home phone's shrill ring made everyone jump. David said, "I'll go," and headed into the dining room. Every time it rang they had to take it in there, waiting for an okay from the technician working on recording the calls. In case the kidnapper called. Kidnapper. The very word sounded ludicrous, like something out of a nineteenth-century novel. Jill watched as the technician gave the go-ahead and David picked up the phone. "Hello? Oh, hi. No, nothing yet." He shook his head at the technician who switched off the recording, stifling a yawn as David told whoever was calling that he'd call back on his cell phone. He strode down the hall to his study and Jill returned to the window, but not before noticing that Detective Ottilo had followed after David, his expression inscrutable. She looked outside again. A second news truck had pulled up alongside the first. They would have to talk to the media at some point—they needed help to find Sophia—but the very thought made her shudder.

"People don't just vanish; this doesn't make any sense," Elaine Lassiter said for the third time, repeating it to anyone who would listen. She paced from the dining room to the living room and back, while Jill tried to ignore her, until her father-in-law finally took his wife by the hand and led her to an available armchair.

David came back into the living room looking slightly more animated. "That was Andrew," he said, coming to stand next to Jill at the window. "He's on his way."

"Why did you call him?"

"I texted him earlier about the adoption attorney; the number I have for him is out of service. He said he'd track him down. Andrew's the one who suggested Antkowiak, remember?"

Ever since adopting Sophia, Jill had dreaded the day that she'd be confronted by her child's blood mother. She and David had decided on a closed adoption hoping if not to avoid then at least to delay a meeting with birth parents. In the era of social media, it seemed impossible to hide from anyone. Just the month before, Jill had read an article about birth parents connecting with their biological children through Facebook. She'd always assumed the day would come, but some-time in the future, not now. And she'd always assumed that the primary emotion when that day arrived would be anxiety, not hope.

"I want the birth mother to have taken her, isn't that strange?" she said to David. "What if she's the one who was driving the car they stopped."

"I don't care who it is—I just want them to find Sophia." David's cell phone pinged. He frowned as he read the text.

"Is that Andrew?" Jill tried to look at his phone, but David turned it off and slipped it back in his pocket before she could see. "Was that him?"

"No, just someone else from work."

She was about to ask why they were calling since he'd contacted the office hours ago to say he wouldn't be coming in, but another cell phone's distinct ringing distracted her. She heard the detective growl "Ottilo," and she started toward him, but Detective Finley stepped in front of her, holding a legal pad and a pen. "I'd like you to make a list of everybody who's been in this house in the last month and anybody who's been in contact with Sophia in the same time frame."

Jill wanted to know what was being said on that

phone call, but she took the pad of paper. At least it was something tangible to do. She took a seat as the female detective handed paper and pen to David, repeating the same instructions. Apparently they were going to compare lists.

Elaine Lassiter came to stand near David, reading his list over his shoulder. "Has anyone checked the cleaning people?" she said to the room at large. "The company says they do background checks, but those aren't reliable. Just look at that case out West—"

"Why don't you make some coffee, Mom," David said. Elaine looked as if she couldn't decide whether to feel annoyed at being interrupted or flattered that they needed her help. Watching her, Jill was reminded of Sophia's shifting moods, and she felt a terrible ache, a yearning for her daughter so strong that she felt nauseous. She forced her concentration back to the names she'd scribbled down, trying to believe that this list would do any good. She wrote Tania's name, then hesitated. Should she add Leo? Tania's boyfriend hadn't met Sophia as far as Jill knew, but there had been an afternoon weeks ago when she'd had to ask Tania to watch Sophia when Jill had an unexpected scheduling conflict. She'd dropped Sophia off at Tania's apartment; who was to say that Leo hadn't been there with her or that he'd hadn't come over after Jill left? She thought of him having sex in the office with Tania, thought of how everything in the office seemed to have been rifled through. Had he been searching for drug money? Would he take a child if he thought he could get money for her?

She mentioned it to the female detective when she handed her the list. Finley immediately circled his name. "Do you have a last name or a phone number?"

Jill shook her head. "But Tania will know. I can call her—"

"No." The detective held up a hand. "We'll take care of that, Mrs. Lassiter." She took David's list as well and walked off with them. Jill returned to her vigil at the window. A woman wearing red slacks and a black, puffy down coat was leaning back against one of the news trucks smoking a cigarette. A man sat in the door of the cab, camera equipment between his feet. As Jill watched, the woman laughed at something he said and then glanced at her watch. Time was dragging for them, they looked bored, while for Jill time was hurtling along like a train switched to the wrong track, unable to avoid the disaster looming ahead.

"You've only lived in this house a few years, is that right?"

Startled, Jill turned to see Detective Finley behind her. The woman was stealthy; Jill hadn't heard her coming. "Yes, we moved right after—" she caught herself. "I mean, before Sophia was born."

Jill wondered how the detective knew how long they'd been in the suburbs, then caught a glimpse of her mother-in-law chatting with a police officer in the other room. Elaine Lassiter didn't understand boundaries and thought that any news was hers to tell.

"So you don't know many of the neighbors?"

"No. Are you sure that they checked all of their houses and yards?"

Finley nodded. "No sign of your daughter, but we've got officers canvassing other streets, farther out." She looked out the window, then said casually, "Before moving out here you lived in the city?"

Jill nodded. She didn't want to make idle chitchat. "How often will they repeat the Amber Alert?"

"It will keep up at regular intervals until we call it off," Finley said. "What made you leave the city?"

David answered for her. "The same thing that makes lots of people move—starting a family, lower housing costs, better schools."

Finley turned back toward him. "Privacy?"

"That was one factor," David said. "We were also tired of apartment living."

"It seemed like a safe place to raise a child," Jill added. She hadn't directed it at him, but David looked distressed and she remembered how much he'd pushed for the move, extolling the virtues of the suburbs.

Ottilo came back into the living room and David immediately said, "Was that call about the car that was stopped?"

"It was a single eyewitness report—" he began, but Jill interrupted him.

"But they stopped a car, you said there was a child in it." She dug her nails into her palms. It had to be Sophia in that car, please let it be Sophia.

Ottilo looked at Finley, then sighed, taking off his reading glasses and rubbing his eyes. "I'm sorry. There are always false leads in cases like this. The child in the car wasn't your daughter."

The breath Jill hadn't realized she was holding came out in a whoosh like a door closing. She stood there, disappointment acid in her mouth. David staggered back to the sofa, rocking slightly, his head in his hands.

Fifteen minutes later, the young police officer at the door announced Andrew's arrival, saying "It's Senator Graham's son" in an awed tone that drew a reproving look from Detective Ottilo.

Andrew had obviously come straight from the office, this was clearly an interruption in his day, but he acted like a man with all the time in the world, brushing a few drops of rain off his wool topcoat before he took it off and draped it over a chairback. His charcoal suit was immaculate, the sheen in his peacock-blue tie catching the light. "I got here as soon as I could," he said to both Jill and David.

David stood up slowly, as if his body hurt, and went to shake his hand. "Thanks for coming, I really appreciate it. What did you find out?"

Jill couldn't make herself move. She didn't realize that she'd crossed her arms protectively over her chest until Andrew crossed the room to embrace her.

"How are you holding up?" he said in a low voice, his expression grave. Gratitude for his kindness overwhelmed Jill; she choked back a sudden wave of tears as hope rose inside her like a swimmer coming up from deep water. She had to clear her throat before she could ask, "Have you found—"

"The birth mother?" Elaine Lassiter talked right over her. "She's the one who's got Sophia, right?" Jill's mother-in-law stood in front of Andrew barking up at him like a small dog. "I knew it was the birth mother, I knew it. It happens all the time with adoptions. The minute I heard Sophia was gone I said to Bill, 'I'll bet it's the birth mother.' Where is she?"

Andrew looked nonplussed. "She's dead."

Chapter Nineteen
Day One

"It's nothing," Bea said to the cop, panicked, but his light moved away and instead of the car door being yanked open, the officer abruptly walked off, and Bea realized he'd been talking to the road crew, not her.

Seconds later, he waved Bea through and she drove past as quickly as she dared, terrified that the cop would follow. The car bounced and rattled up cratered Fernwood Road, so loud she feared it would wake neighbors she'd never seen. It was even noisier when she turned onto the pea-gravel driveway at 115. Bea slowed to a crawl, inching the car between the trees that seemed to squeeze it on either side. She jumped when a branch scraped the roof like a ghostly claw. It was a relief when the headlights finally shone on the house.

"Home sweet home," Bea muttered and hit the garage opener.

The door rose with a quiet whir and she pulled the car inside. She didn't move until the door was completely closed; then she rushed the bag into the house. It wasn't moving anymore. She set it on the concrete floor and pulled down the zipper and the child's head emerged, downy hair first, like a chick peeking out of its shell.

The toddler's skin felt damp, but that was a common side effect of the drug. Bea brushed fine strands of blonde hair back from the flushed cheeks and leaned down to listen, reaching into the bag to find a wrist and take the child's pulse. Blue eyes shot open, startling her.

"Oh!" Bea cleared her throat. "Hello." She looked down at Avery, and the little girl looked up at her. There was silence for a long moment as they appraised each other. Then the child opened her mouth and wailed.

"Ssh, it's okay. You're okay." Bea kept up a soothing mantra as she slipped on a fresh pair of gloves and spread a sheet on the floor. She lifted the child from the bag onto the sheet and quickly stripped her, setting aside the nightgown and tiny panties. The child was still too dopey to do more than cry in protest, her head listing to one side, then the other, when Bea cut her hair, cropping it short all the way around, careful to catch the fine blonde strands in a plastic bag.

She clutched the stuffed dog that she'd been holding when Bea took her, floundering dopily as Bea forced her into a new pair of pajamas. At last they were on and Bea hoisted the child into her arms, groaning at the weight, as she carried her upstairs. She put her down on the old velvet sofa and covered her with a blanket. The child's eyes fluttered open and closed. It would take time for the effects of the drug to wear off.

Bea dropped down on the couch next to her, completely exhausted. Adrenaline forced her up again fifteen minutes later, pushing her back downstairs where she slipped on another pair of latex gloves, carrying the duffel bag into the utility room and setting it on top of the washer. Unzipping the side slot, she took out the used syringe and dumped it in a small trash bag to dispose of later in some city bin. A second syringe went back into her medical kit. Benzodiazepines were effective tranquilizers. It had been easy enough to put on her nursing scrubs and slip unnoticed into area hospitals. Harder had been getting the various drugs, which were always locked up. Or supposed to be. People were careless and she took advantage of that, being sure never to take too much from any one place to avoid provoking an investigation. The trickiest part was mixing the drugs and monitoring the dosage. Bea wasn't sure how much Avery weighed, but she'd made a conservative guess and clearly it hadn't been quite enough. She would have to use more next time.

The duffel bag went into the trash and she stripped off all her clothes and divided them into two other trash bags. It was a pity to get rid of perfectly good clothes, but simply not worth the risk to save them. She changed into clean clothes she'd left in the laundry room for that purpose and picked up a small, brand-new white pillow, pulling it free of its plastic wrapper which declared it to be extra firm, and placing it on the washer. She stretched the child's nightgown around it and went to fetch the knife. She practiced for a moment, just as she had every day for weeks, before thrusting the knife hard through the nightgown and into the pillow, feeling the blade quiver as it cut through cloth and sank into the polyester fluff. She jerked it out and repeated the thrust, slightly lower this time, then again and still once more. The blade was coated with bits of white fiber when she was finished, the nightgown shredded down the front.

She hustled back upstairs to the kitchen, where she collected the glass test tubes she had taken from the freezer and placed in the fridge to thaw overnight. She took one of the vials from the plastic rack holding them and held it up to the light, swinging it gently side to side. The dark red liquid moved with it and she smiled.

She'd done thousands of blood draws over the years, so that day in the park had been quick. The child had struggled, of course, but chloroform on a cloth worked fast and Bea had been able to retrieve three vials and get the child lucid again in pretty short order. A quick peek at the child, who hadn't stirred, and then back to the basement, where she examined the child's nightgown again before pouring the blood across the knife holes, soaking the front of the little cloth. It poured easily, just as if it were fresh and hadn't been frozen for three months.

The old clock radio she'd found in the basement showed almost seven a.m. Time was ticking away. Had they discovered the child missing? Had the police been called? She placed some of the hairs she'd collected in different places on the nightgown, some of them on the cloth, some with the blood. It was good to give the police plenty of DNA to work with. She wondered if the story was on the news yet. The very idea excited her and she couldn't wait any longer, turning on the radio with the sound turned down very low. She didn't want Avery to hear it.

Chirpy announcers were talking about the prospect of snow so soon after Halloween, about local trick-or-treating, about whether the Penguins would do well in that weekend's game. "C'mon," Bea muttered. She leaned against the washer, careful not to touch the nightgown. The blood was tacky to touch now, drying in patterns. An ad for incontinence played, then one for Viagra, then one for some nasal allergy spray. Sweet Jesus, was everyone in this country drug dependent?

"And now, some breaking news." The announcement alerted Bea. She stood upright. "State police have issued an Amber Alert for missing Fox Chapel toddler Sophia Lassiter. I repeat, an

195

Amber Alert has been issued for three-year-old Sophia Lassiter of Fox Chapel, reported missing from her home sometime this morning. Sophia Lassiter is white, with short blonde hair and blue eyes, approximately thirty-three inches tall and weighs approximately thirty pounds. Anyone who sees a child matching Sophia Lassiter's description is asked to contact the police."

"Mommy!" The child's cry was piercing; Bea jumped, banging into the washer. She ran up the stairs as the child wailed, "I want my mommy!"

The little girl struggled up to a sitting position as Bea reached her. "It's okay," she said, reaching out to help the child get her balance. "You're okay."

The child shrank from her touch. "Mommy!" she wailed again.

"Sssh," Bea crooned. "It's okay. Are you hungry?" She pointed over her shoulder at the peanut butter and jelly sandwich on the dining room table that she'd prepared before she left. Her daughter had loved pb&j; it was her favorite. Didn't all kids like it? She'd stocked up on bread and peanut butter and on mac and cheese and apple juice. "I know you must be hungry, Avery. Come and eat some food for me." It felt odd but good to finally say the name out loud. Her daughter's favorite name for all her dolls when she'd been little; convenient that it worked equally well for boys and girls.

"My name's not Avery," the little girl said.

196

"That's your real name."

"My name is Sophia."

Bea shook her head. "That was just a pretend name. Your real name is Avery. It's a pretty name. Try it. Say Avery for me."

"Sophia!" A shout.

Bea rubbed a sweaty palm against her pants leg, glad that the house was remote. No one was likely to hear them; they were alone in the woods.

As if she could understand, Avery screamed louder. "Sophia! Sophia! Sophia!" The last cry ended on a wail and she began to weep again, eyes creasing into tiny slits and face turning red. Bea walked to the table, peeled back the plastic wrap from her own sandwich, and took a bite. What she really wanted to do was sleep. Her head kept throbbing in equal time with her chest, but it wasn't safe to give the child another sedative, not so soon after the last one.

"Doesn't your dog want some food?" she said loud enough to be heard over the little girl's wails.

The crying stopped and Avery, who'd been clutching her stuffed dog tightly in her arms, suddenly lifted one of its floppy ears and whispered into it. Then she looked at Bea and nodded.

"Does he like peanut butter and jelly?"

"Just jelly, no peanut butter," Avery said, but with a glower.

"I'll make him a jelly sandwich," Bea said,

getting up from the table and walking into the kitchen. She glanced over her shoulder and saw Avery wiggle off the couch and move slowly to the dining room. Bea didn't say a word as the child climbed up onto a chair and picked up the sandwich.

With the crying ended, another noise became noticeable. *Scratch, scratch, scratch* against the kitchen door. Bea had left Cosmo in the back-yard last night. There was food and water for him outside, but he still wanted to come in. He knew that someone else was in the house; the question was how would he react? How would Avery? Cosmo was a friendly little dog, and Bea wasn't worried as much about him as she was about the child.

Cosmo barked, just a single sound to attract attention, but it was loud enough that Avery heard. She swiveled around on her chair to stare wide-eyed at Bea. "Do you has a dog?"

Bea nodded. "Do you want to meet him?"

"Yes! Yes!" Avery scrambled off her chair, still holding on to her stuffed dog. Bea opened the back door and Cosmo shot into the kitchen, little nose down and up sniffing wildly. He stopped in front of Avery and barked once, small tail wagging like crazy.

"Hello, doggie! Hello!" She bent to pet his head and then his side. "What's his name?"

"Cosmo."

"Hello, Cosmo! Good doggie!" All of a sudden she paused and looked at the dog more closely and then up at Bea. "I sees him at the park and at my house."

The hairs rose on Bea's body. It hadn't occurred to her that the child would remember the dog. She said to distract her, "Do you want to eat your sandwich with Cosmo?"

It was important that the child ate. Hungry children were cranky children, and Bea didn't want any more tantrums. The little girl ate with Cosmo at her feet, offering bites of the jelly-only sandwich to her stuffed dog. Bea refilled the small mug of milk and sat across from Avery. "What's *your* dog's name?" she asked.

Avery gave her another mulish look. After a moment she mumbled, "Blinky." Her chair wobbled and Bea reached out to catch it, only to feel a sudden numbness in her left arm.

She clutched it, walking into the kitchen in search of the nitroglycerin tablets. She paused with the pill bottle in her hand. When had she taken the last one? Was it three hours ago or four? She needed to keep better track; she swallowed one anyway, looking out the kitchen window at the woods rising behind the house. Gray light, the sun rising somewhere behind the clouds. Wind blew roughly through the trees, trunks groaning like boats tossed in a stormy sea. Leaves poured onto the cracked patio. Soon the trees would be completely bare. Would anybody up the hill be able to see them? Bea tried peering through the foliage, but it was still too dense.

"I see you went ahead and took her."

She whipped around. Frank stood in a dark corner of the kitchen, arms crossed. She put a hand to her chest. "Stop sneaking up on me!"

"You're a stubborn woman, Bea."

"She belongs with us. Can't you see that?"

Even with his face half in shadow, making his expression hard to read, she could feel his disapproval.

"I only took what was mine to take," she added, looking away from that hard face and walking back to the child. She waited until Avery was done eating to say, "I have a surprise for you." The little girl simply stared at her with that same sullen expression. "It's downstairs." Bea pointed toward the hall and the door to the basement steps. Avery swiveled in her chair to stare at the door, and then looked up at Bea for a long moment in a very adult, almost suspicious way. It made Bea uncomfortable. "Don't just sit there," she said. "Go downstairs and see what it is."

The child hesitated, then slid off the chair and walked slowly through the kitchen and into the shadowed hallway, Bea following behind her. Avery reached a hand toward the doorknob and stopped. "What is it?"

"I can't tell you, it's a surprise," Bea said,

hovering behind her. "Go on, head downstairs."

Bea hit the light switch at the top of the stairs, a single bare bulb illuminating the shadowed stairs and a bit of the concrete floor at the bottom. The little girl shook her head, took a step back. "No."

"You won't get the surprise if you don't go down." Bea tried to hide her impatience with a light tone.

"No!" The child took another step back, bumping into Bea's legs.

"Just hold on to the handrail." Bea pushed the child forward, her hand on one small shoulder. "C'mon, you can do it."

"No! No, no, no!" Avery pulled out of Bea's grip and took off running down the gloomy hallway.

"Get back here!" Bea chased after her.

The little girl rounded the corner, but then she tripped and fell. "Gotcha." Bea hauled her up and dragged her back down the hall.

"I wanna go home!" Avery wailed.

"Let's see what's down here first," Bea said, grasping the child's small hand and forcing it on to the handrail. She half-walked, half-carried Avery down the wooden steps into the basement, reaching for another switch at the bottom. Two long fluorescent bars flickered on, humming. Bea led her down the hall to the door partially hidden by the steel support pillar.

"It's behind that door," Bea said. "Go on, open it."

"No, no, no!" Avery's shrieks increased in volume.

"Here, I'll help you." Bea walked the child over and forced Avery's hand to cup and turn the knob. She pushed the door open for her, shoving the child into the room.

Bea watched, waiting for the explosion of happiness. She'd painted the walls a cheerful pink and found a wooden bed at a garage sale. It looked a lot like the one in the child's old room. Cheaper probably, but still a good match. She'd found a toy shelf at a Goodwill and filled it with toys that she bought and some that had been her daughter's. She'd bought a striped rug at Target to cover the cold concrete floor and even remembered to get a night-light. It was a nice room, but when she looked down to see Avery's reaction, the girl's face was slack; she wasn't smiling at all. She seemed indifferent.

"Whose room is this?" she said.

Of course! Bea had forgotten how kids think. "It's yours. This is all for you." She spread her arms wide. When Avery didn't move she gave her a little push in the back to get her over the threshold.

"This is not my doll," Avery said, fingering a little baby doll that Bea had bought.

"Yes it is. She's yours. All of this is yours. Here's a tea set. You can have tea parties."

"Mine's purple." Avery ran one little finger over

the new, pink teapot. She didn't sound enthusiastic. Bea felt a little annoyed. Didn't the child appreciate anything?

"Don't you have something to say? What's the magic word?"

The girl's lower lip slipped out. She pulled her stuffed dog into her arms and shook her head.

This child had been spoiled, that was plain to see. Bea shook her own head. "Thank you. The magic word is thank you."

The child still didn't say it. Bea sighed. She didn't have the energy to deal with this now; they'd have plenty of time. "You and Blinky have fun with your new toys," she said.

Avery stared after her as Bea walked backward toward the door. She felt uncomfortable with how the child kept looking at her. It wasn't polite to stare like that.

She left Cosmo in the room with Avery and closed the door. She slid shut the bolt lock she'd installed and, predictably, the child started to wail. The door shook slightly and Bea knew that Avery had banged on it. But there was hardly any noise coming out—the door and the walls were solid.

Chapter Twenty
Days One, Two, and Three

Before Jill could ask to see the death certificate, Elaine Lassiter snatched it from Andrew's hands. "Are you sure you've got the right person?" she demanded, scanning the document with a stunned expression. "Maybe this is the wrong woman?"

"I'm sure, Mrs. Lassiter." Andrew sounded unusually somber. He took the certificate back from Elaine and offered it to David, who glanced at it, his expression unreadable.

"Could we concentrate now on who *has* taken our child?" he said, passing it to the detectives. "Why aren't there any leads?"

Jill recoiled at his disdainful tone. David was looking at Detective Ottilo, but she had been the one who thought Sophia's disappearance was tied to her adoption. Strange to think that if she'd found out just two days ago that Sophia's birth mother was dead, she would have felt relieved.

"It'll be okay," Andrew murmured. "They'll find Sophia."

He stayed on until well into the evening, until Jill urged him to go. "Paige will be putting the boys to bed—you need to be there to say goodnight." Just saying the words felt surreal—Andrew's sons waiting safely at home in their beds. All over the country children were going to sleep in their own beds, but her child's bed was empty. Andrew hugged her again and clapped David on the shoulder, promising to return the next day.

She and David went upstairs sometime after eleven when her in-laws finally went home and the police had cleared out, leaving behind crime-scene tape, used coffee cups, and crumpled take-out bags. Two different police vehicles remained parked out front, one from Fox Chapel, the other from neighboring O'Hara, with officers whose jobs seemed to be both to keep watch and to keep the media at bay. Two news vans had parked along the street, clearly camping out. Jill moved through her nightly routine on autopilot, pausing only when she changed out of her jeans and started to cry as she stared at the dirt-caked knees from that morning's frantic search. She gulped sobs back, brushing the wetness from her cheeks, refusing to break down. Nothing good would come of her tears; if she started to cry she might never stop.

But the tears came again later, after she slipped into bed next to David, fear pressing down on her like the weight of too many covers. David was awake, too; she could tell by his breathing, but neither of them spoke. She thought of what it had been like after Ethan, those first days when she'd felt his absence like a constant ache, and now that wound had torn wide open and she longed to stroke Sophia's soft cheeks, kiss the small spot at the nape of her neck, feel a dimpled little hand slip into hers. Tears spilled over, hot and silent, running down Jill's cheeks and dampening her pillow. Exhaustion eventually carried her into sleep, where she dreamed of Sophia calling to her from far out at sea, where she bobbed in an inflatable ring that the waves kept pulling farther and farther from shore. Jill struggled to get to her, swimming through waves that rose higher and higher around her. She woke up with her throat hoarse from crying Sophia's name.

The police showed up at 6:30 a.m., more news trucks following them into the cul-de-sac. Sophia's disappearance had been on every evening broad-cast. Now reporters were jockeying for position at the front of a growing crowd.

Jill looked out at the cars, but couldn't spot Andrew's among all the traffic. She hoped he'd be there in time for the press conference. She dreaded going out there. Jill had always been more com-fortable behind the camera than in front of it. She peeked through the living room curtains at the swarm of news media that had been alerted that she and David would be giving a statement and swallowed hard, nervously smoothing her hair with her fingers.

"Remember, it's important that you mention your daughter by name," Detective Ottilo said. He'd been giving instructions to her and David for the last ten minutes. "An abductor might think of your child as an object of their fantasies instead of as a real person—by naming her you help destroy that illusion."

Fantasies. Jill thought she might vomit. How many times had she watched parents of missing children give teary appeals on TV? Had any of them ever done any good? She rubbed her eyes, exhausted.

"Hey! Where do you think you're going with those?"

Jill turned from the window to see David confronting an officer heading out the door carrying both of their laptops along with the desktop from David's study. "You can't take my laptop," she said, hurrying toward them. "I need it for work."

"It's routine, Mr. and Mrs. Lassiter." Detective Ottilo stepped between them and the officer. "We have to examine everything."

"There's nothing on those that will help you find Sophia," Jill said.

"You'll get them back ASAP," Detective Ottilo said in his infuriatingly calm voice. "Don't focus on that right now; you need to think about your media appeal."

David threw up his hands and stalked away, grim-faced. Jill crossed her arms to hide the trembling. They were powerless to stop the police, powerless to control anything that was happening. More than thirty hours had passed since they'd last seen Sophia and a bunch of strangers crowded on their lawn wanted a piece of them, a close-up of emotional parents to lead every newscast. "I don't think I can do this."

"Yes you can, Mrs. Lassiter," Ottilo said. "This is important. You'll do anything you can to get your daughter back, right?"

"Of course," she said, stung. She picked up the photo of Sophia that they'd been instructed to hold and stared at her daughter's sweet little smile, steeling herself. Ten minutes later, Jill and David headed out the door followed by multiple police officers, who formed a phalanx around them.

Cold air stung Jill's face, strands of hair pulling free from her loose bun to whip at her cheeks. She realized belatedly that she should have done something about her appearance. She must look terrible.

"Jesus," David muttered, and she didn't know if he meant the cold or the growing crowd at the end of the driveway. The reporters spotted them, turning en masse and rushing forward. "Mrs.

Lassiter! Mr. Lassiter, who took your daughter?" Microphones thrust in their faces; someone bumped against Jill, knocking her off balance. David caught her by the arm before she fell.

"Mr. and Mrs. Lassiter, what happened to your child?"

Jill tried to keep her voice clear and steady as Detective Finley had instructed. "Yesterday morning we discovered our three-year-old daughter, Sophia Lassiter, missing from our home. She is our only child and we miss her terribly." Her voice trembled and David picked up where she'd left off.

"Sophia is a loving, trusting little girl. Her mother and I need her back with us; we cannot go on without her."

Jill held up the photo, trying to keep her hands steady. "Please look carefully at this picture of Sophia and call 911 if you've seen her." She could hear the whir of cameras as they zoomed in on the photo. "I'm speaking now to the person who's taken Sophia. I'm begging you to please return our daughter."

David wiped roughly at his eyes, obviously crying, but she stood dry-eyed beside him. It had always been this way; she'd always shut down emotionally in public. Detective Ottilo stepped in front of them. "Allegheny County police, local officers, K-9 units, and trained search-and-rescue personnel will join volunteers from the community to conduct a broader search of the area beginning at ten tomorrow morning. That's all for now. Please step back."

"Do the police have any suspects?" someone in the crowd called.

"The investigation is just beginning." Ottilo sounded completely calm, as if this was something he dealt with all the time.

"Do you have any eyewitnesses? Has anyone seen Sophia?"

Ottilo said, "That's all we're at liberty to discuss right now." He signaled to Finley and she motioned to Jill and David to head back inside. Jill had David behind her, one hand on her lower back, as they headed up the walkway, leaving Ottilo to deal with the clamoring. She heard the last shouted question as Finley ushered them back in the front door. "Do the police consider Mr. and Mrs. Lassiter suspects in the disappearance of their child?"

Jill stopped short to hear his response. "We're exploring all possibilities," Ottilo said. "Everyone who has had contact with the child is considered a person of interest."

David nudged Jill, raising his eyebrows. This is what Andrew had brought up yesterday, whispering to them in corners when the detectives were otherwise occupied. "Be careful not to say too much," he'd warned. "Remember—they go with what seems easiest and obvious. The lowest

210

common denominator is the two of you." David nodded knowingly and Jill hadn't been surprised. It made perfect sense, but it was different hearing the police actually admit that they were suspects.

"Let's get out of the cold." Detective Finley stood holding the door open for them, her face neutral. She waited for Jill and David to follow her, like school kids called in from recess, before closing their own door behind them. Jill slumped on the living room sofa, cold and trembling all over. She reached for a glass of water and gulped it down. Finley said, "That went well, good job." It sounded so obviously pacifying that Jill snorted.

David moved to the window with his arms crossed over his chest. "Let's hope it works."

"I need to get more copies of that made." Finley held out her hand for the photo of Sophia that Jill hadn't realized she was still clutching.

Ottilo came back inside talking on his cell phone; Jill heard something about "search dogs" as he headed down the hall toward the kitchen. When she went to use the bathroom she felt as if she should be asking the police for permission.

She lingered in the powder room, splashing icy water on her face before running water over her wrists, trying to shock away the numbness. She had a surreal déjà-vu feeling and knew that she'd felt the same before, after Ethan. It was as if the woman she was inside, Jill's real self, retreated until all that was left was this shell, this body, that was useless to do anything on its own. She stared into the mirror at the shell, noting distractedly the vacant expression in her sunken eyes, the sallowness of her cheeks, the limp hair. Disintegration took such little time.

When she came out of the bathroom, Tania was there, setting up her laptop at the dining room table, taking little notice of the police technicians who looked variously mystified or offended by this fast-talking woman with gypsylike clothes emanating a mixture of patchouli and lentils. "I got the website set up," she said when she spotted Jill. "Come take a look."

She'd suggested it last night, calling to tell Jill about all the missing-children websites, talking about them as if they were trendy and seemingly surprised that Jill had never seen one. She'd offered to set it up and Jill was surprised that she'd actually followed through with it. "I added the most recent shots I had of Sophia, but we can always add more," Tania said, clicking rapidly through a couple of pages. Across the top of the home page it said BRING SOPHIA HOME, in a bright, bold font. "You should think about offering a reward," she informed Jill and David. "People pay more attention when money is involved."

She seemed to know so much about this kind of thing—why? Jill thought again of the studio being ransacked and how Tania had been so blasé about it. Suspicion must have looked like hesitation on Jill's face because Tania said, "I know it's crass, but some people won't do the right thing unless they're compensated, you know?"

"No," Jill said. "I don't know anyone anymore."

The morning's search had been mentioned on every nightly news broadcast, but Bea was still surprised to see a young police officer preventing cars from turning onto the street and directing them to park along the side of Fox Chapel Road instead.

Her chest constricted when he looked directly at her, but it wasn't the same cop from that night. She'd taken the precaution of swapping the license plate on her sedan with one she'd stolen off a similar car in the vast wasteland of a Walmart parking lot. There were thousands of four-door sedans like this one, hundreds of thousands, probably; nondescript cars that no one would look at twice. The GPS had the route she'd taken from the house two nights before, but it had seemed bad luck, maybe even dangerous, to follow the same path. She'd gone a different way; it was easy enough to let the GPS reroute.

The bored expression on the patrolman's face didn't alter as he waved his hand, indicating that she should follow the car that had just passed, and she pulled onto the shoulder ahead behind a dark blue minivan. She checked the dashboard clock. Seven fifteen. She had two, maybe three hours to make it back before the child woke up. A plump man and even plumper woman got out of the minivan, followed by an equally roly-poly teenage boy. They passed Bea as she got out of the sedan, and she had to squeeze against the car so they could get by. "Here for the search?" the woman said to her with a somber expression, but avid, hunting eyes.

Bea said, "I just want to be of help."

"Us, too." The woman nodded at her husband and son. "Terrible what this world is coming to if you've got to worry about your children in your own home."

She was the sort of person who relished the drama of other people's tragedies, desperate to feel important, interested in attracting their own fifteen minutes of fame by claiming to be "best friends" with a victim they'd met once in passing.

She hated people like this woman and her passive husband and son, but she nodded at the woman's babble as if she agreed, falling into step with them because there was safety in numbers. They turned onto the street, and she smiled when she saw just how many people were there. It was even colder today than the day before and she'd chosen her clothes with care, wearing a short, puffy jacket in dull blue with a gummy waistband. The color repelled attention and the extra padding and waistband concealed what she carried. She couldn't resist checking, running her hand lightly against the small bundle resting against her ribs. She had to keep reminding herself not to reach in and touch it.

"I'd just die if I was the mother," a young woman said, but she had that same strange excited look in her eyes that Bea recognized. People like that were there for the show, the media spectacle, all the while hiding behind the belief that they were really helping.

The crowd was so big that it was hard to see through all the people. Bea moved away from the fat family, pushing through the horde so she wouldn't be standing on the fringes. It was easy to spot people on the margins and she could see several news trucks and camera crews panning the crowd. If she buried herself within it, no one would notice her. She'd worn a different wig today and pulled a dull oatmeal-colored knit cap over it for extra camouflage. Her head itched, but she didn't dare scratch it. Fortunately it was sunny enough that her sunglasses didn't seem out of place.

An elderly couple stood on one side of her; they looked like they were out for a day of bird-watching, both of them in hiking boots and heavy winter jackets, the man with binoculars slung around his neck. On the other side of Bea stood a skinny teenage girl with shiny, straightened hair and a fur-trimmed white coat and boots that screamed ski bunny, and next to her stood an older, heavier, wrinkled version of the girl. "I just can't believe something like this happened out here," the girl whispered to the woman. "It's, like, so safe out here and they seem so, like, normal."

"You can never tell," the woman said, adding in an even lower voice. "It usually turns out to be the parents."

The number of people who arrived to search surprised and moved Jill. Despite the cold, despite the short notice, a small cluster of volunteers had grown to a large crowd filling the cul-de-sac and lining most of the street. The media was still out in force, too, and there were cops galore. She wondered if every police officer in the county was there. The search dogs hadn't arrived and Ottilo was upset about it. He'd had his cell phone glued to his ear for the last twenty minutes, but he waved at the special officer in charge of the search, mouthing, "Just go ahead."

They were standing at the end of the drive-way, Jill huddled in her coat, David next to her, trying not to notice the cameras recording their every move, listening to the special officer issuing instructions to the crowd with the help of a megaphone.

"We'll move in groups of eight to ten. If you spot something, stop, and blow the whistle that you've been provided. An officer will come and assist you. If you find something, don't touch it; wait for a trained officer or investigator to retrieve it. Obviously, we're all looking for Sophia, but we're also looking for any evidence that can lead us to the person or persons who might have taken her." He dropped the megaphone and offered it to David.

"Thank you all for coming this morning," David said, his voice wavering. "Jill and I are humbled by the community support. Let's bring Sophia home."

Bill and Elaine Lassiter stood with the crowd and Tania not too far from them. No sign of Leo with her. Jill wondered if the police had already talked to him. She saw other faces in the crowd that she recognized—a woman from the gym, the children's librarian who knew Sophia from story hour, the old man from the dry cleaner's. The neighbors were there, too; she recognized the couple with the rampaging golden retriever and the older woman who lived alone in the house closest to theirs. There were many more people that she'd never seen before and some of them stared at her and David with frank curiosity.

At the first short blast of the whistle, Jill started across the lawn with David and the others in their group, walking about two feet apart, moving toward the back of the house while other groups fanned across both sides of the cul-de-sac.

"We found a five-year-old child last year over three miles away from his own house, stuck in a shed in someone's backyard," Ottilo had told her. "It's seems improbable, but even little kids can go incredible distances."

"What month was it?" Jill had been busy collecting Sophia's pillow and a shirt that she'd worn two days ago because the dogs would need to sniff them to pick up her scent. They weighed nothing—so light, so insubstantial.

"What month?" Ottilo looked confused.

"Did the boy wander off when it was warm? It would be okay if it was warm out, but it's so cold. How long could she last—" Jill stopped, swallowing hard, her hands tightening on Sophia's things.

"Let's not look ahead, Mrs. Lassiter," the detective said firmly. "You need to stay focused on bringing Sophia home. We can't worry about what-ifs."

But what-ifs were all that pounded away in her brain. She veered between wild, magical thinking —that some kind elderly couple had taken in Sophia—to the darkest thought—that Sophia was dead. Dead. Even thinking the word made Jill shake. She focused hard on the ground, murmuring "I'll find you," over and over again like a prayer as she walked along, searching for any sign of Sophia's presence—tiny footprints, a scrap of clothing, the toy dog that she'd loved to a uniform grayness.

Andrew had shown up to search, along with some of David's other colleagues, and Paige Graham had come, too, with their children in tow, all of them wearing matching hiking outfits that looked like they'd been taken straight from the pages of L.L.Bean or some more exclusive outdoors catalog company. Paige had come by earlier to drop off several loaves of beautifully wrapped, homemade pumpkin bread. "I know it's not much, but I wanted to do something for you," she'd said, catching Jill off guard with a big hug. The woman was a more glamorous version of Martha Stewart. As soon as she thought this, Jill felt guilty; her judgment would bring bad karma.

Jill had always thought of herself as mildly superstitious, but Sophia's disappearance had loosed something inside and she couldn't stop playing mind games. If she didn't look up for ten minutes, then Sophia would be all right. If she didn't watch the clock, they would find her. If she only believed that Sophia was fine, then she would be fine.

She'd always been skeptical about unbridled optimism, dismissive of people who insisted that you could keep bad things at bay if you only entertained positive thoughts, but now she embraced it with a true believer's zeal, striving with every step to know that it was all okay and that Sophia would be found; any minute now she would wander out of the woods just like she had that day at the park.

Bea smiled involuntarily before averting her gaze, stepping around the bird-watchers and moving even deeper into the crowd. She listened to the police officer giving instructions, but her eyes were on the couple. Jill looked terrible— pale skin, eyes red-rimmed, hair that looked like it hadn't been combed. Satisfaction lit like a little coal inside Bea, warming her. David looked just as bad, his face puffy as if he hadn't slept, and his voice shook as he thanked them for helping to bring back his daughter. Bea made a scathing noise and turned it into a cough as a woman shot her a surprised look.

Police divided up the crowd and Bea moved into a far group that she hoped would lead to the culvert. She caught a glimpse of the Lassiters moving at the front of another group and she wondered at the police allowing them to participate, feeling a momentary panic that what she'd planned all along wasn't going to happen. But then she remembered how many times this had happened before—family members would make tearful pleas on television and lead the searches for their missing spouses or children, and later would come their inevitable arrest. It was just a matter of time; Bea pressed again to feel what she held in her jacket.

Jill focused on the grass, trying not to notice how it crunched underfoot, hardened from a frost, which had silvered the trunks of trees and etched the remaining leaves. She looked to her right and saw David searching the same way, his eyes locked to the ground, his face tense.

Please let me find her, she prayed. Please God, whoever, wherever you are, please bring her home. She'd never been a particularly religious person; she hadn't been raised in any church, though her mother had been fascinated with saints and their followers. She'd dragged Jill to numerous Catholic churches, where they lit candles and stood below the passive, plaster representations of people whose devotion mostly seemed to have caused them to die in horrific ways. Jill had enjoyed the smell of incense, though, and the flicker of votives, and she could remember wondering what it was like to believe as passionately as the silent old women kneeling alone in hard wooden pews clutching their prayer beads.

If Jill had been devout, if she'd been a believer, might God have protected her and her children? Did it only work that way? Did the Almighty really require constant reverence and attention to return even a little of the same?

Jill followed other searchers across the lawn and into the woods. The pace slowed in the thick carpet of leaves. It was so cold. Jill's breath hung in faint clouds in front of her as she moved slowly down the hill. Could it really only have been the day before yesterday when she and David ran down this hillside on their own frenzied search? The hill sloped sharply, at a steeper pitch, and Jill had to catch the thin trunks of sapling maples and oaks to keep from falling. It got darker and colder the farther down they went and her mood dropped along with it, as if they were descending from earth to the underworld.

She caught a glimpse of blue, but when she frantically brushed aside the leaves, it was just the cracked shell of a robin's egg caught in the center of a small brown nest that must have fallen from a tree long ago in the spring. She thought of Sophia spotting one like it last year, the way her blue eyes could look startling like that robin's-egg blue, the color so bright and pure in that same way, and how they seemed to sparkle when her daughter was excited, running across the yard to show her, *"Look, Mommy! It's a teeny, tiny birdie!"*

The cracked egg seemed like a bad omen. As she stood staring down at it, two sharp blasts of a whistle pierced the woods.

Chapter Twenty-one
Day Three

The dogs arrived as Bea's group started across the yard. She heard excited barking and turned back to see a man wrestling to restrain three large German shepherds pulling against their leashes. A police officer held something up to the dogs' faces, and the way they sniffed at it frightened Bea.

She had to hurry. Those dogs were coming; it was a matter of minutes. At least she'd planned her position well: her group landed on top of the concrete culvert and she watched the people in front of her split off, some of them moving one way around it and others going over it. She stayed to the left, reaching the little creek at the base of the hill just outside the entrance to the concrete tunnel, where she paused, pretending to adjust her boots. Searchers passed, one woman asking if she needed help, but Bea shook her head. She heard a dog barking, glanced back up the hill and caught a glimpse through the trees of sweating coats and salivating muzzles. They were coming. Quick look left—the man searching the half-frozen creek had turned away. The woman creeping through the tunnel had her back to Bea. It was now or never.

She unzipped her coat and unzipped the plastic bag, slipping its contents into the muddy water at the edge of the concrete. A layer of ice had formed on one corner and she used the tip of a stray branch to shove the garment under it, before shifting some leaves toward it with her foot.

"What is it? Do you see something?" The man to her left had turned around.

"I don't know, there's something caught under the concrete, but I can't see very well down here," she said and the man—large and ruddy-faced—ran to her side.

The dogs were close now, straining at their leashes, pulling ahead of their handler, who was practically sliding down the hillside. Bea hurried up the opposite hill, glancing back to watch as the searcher squatted for a moment to peer at the ice shelf just before the dogs plunged through the creek to his side. Then the man bolted upright and reached for his whistle.

The sharp blasts stopped Jill short. The whole row of searchers halted for a moment, before continuing on, but Jill couldn't move. "What if it's Sophia?" she called to David. "What if they've found her?"

David's eyes locked with hers, his face ashen. He came to embrace her, moving one hand to the base of her neck and pulling their heads together for a moment. "It's going to be okay." But it sounded like he was trying to convince himself.

Ottilo came running down the hill with another officer just behind him. "C'mon," David said, hurrying after him and Jill stumbled forward, trying to look past the leaves falling silently from the trees, through the shafts of sunlight dappling the cold, hard ground. She could see nothing, nothing at all except more trees and fresh leaves falling on molding ones, hundreds of new leaves covering the old ones. What if Sophia had fallen out there and been buried by them?

When they reached the shallow creek at the bottom Jill saw that it was frozen in sections, a thin layer of ice covering the water running over a bed of brown and gray rocks and pebbles, darker brown silt underneath it all. She looked to her right and saw the search dogs near the culvert and a police officer stringing crime-scene tape around the trees next to it. Ottilo and a couple of officers huddled near the entrance to the concrete pipe. She wanted to go to them, wanted to see what they'd found, but she was afraid. She kept imagining the blood on the patio, the blood that they'd missed. What else had she and David missed when they ran through there? She heard a faint whistling sound and realized it was her own keening.

The detective turned and there was something in his face, a grimness, which scared Jill even more. She reached for David's hand. He called to

Ottilo, "What is it? What have you found?" But the detective turned away, climbing back up the hillside without answering.

Bea scrambled up the opposite hillside, hearing the dogs clamoring behind her. Could they smell Avery on her? She'd paused along with everybody else at the whistle blasts, peering back through the woods as if she, too, wondered what had been discovered, but then the dogs pulled their handlers on and Bea no longer cared about anything but getting out.

She checked her watch. Only thirty minutes left before Avery would wake up. Bea was tired from climbing, but there were other people older than she was out there, diligently pressing forward into the backyards of the houses at the top of the hill. One of them would probably step in the dried remains of Cosmo's shit, left behind the half-constructed house that she'd used as her excuse the first time she ventured into these woods.

She kept walking, pretending to search the path in front of her, all the while hearing the dogs behind her and knowing that at any minute they'd be on her, barking. She wanted to run, but people would definitely notice that and it would take even longer to get back to her car.

As she continued up the hill the dogs came running straight at her. Bea froze, holding her breath, waiting for them to leap on her. She could see the whites around their eyes, the foam-coated mouths hanging open, teeth sharp. One of them paused, sniffing her, nuzzling in to her coat and Bea fought down her panic, leaning back and struggling not to run.

"Get off her!" The handler was a short white man with cheeks red and raw like slabs of uncooked meat. He jerked on the leash, glancing at Bea for a split second. "Sorry about that." The dogs bolted away, springing past her up the hill through the leaves while the man huffed along behind them. Then they were gone and she was standing there, shaking. Her feet hurt and her chest felt odd. Not like a heart attack, at least she didn't think so, but palpitating all the same, and despite the cold she felt clammy. She scrabbled through her coat pockets, searching for her tablets, but she'd forgotten to carry them with her, she'd left the bottle in the car. Other volunteers spread out, searching this next street and the wooded hillside beyond, but Bea turned back.

Some other searchers were backtracking down the hill they'd just climbed, and she joined them, moving in a line back through the woods and up and out the way they'd come, marching slowly across the frozen grass in the Lassiters' backyard under a hard sun. Bea needed to be done, needed to sit down somewhere and take some slow, deep breaths. Out from the shelter of the trees, a cold wind whipped at her face; the sun blinded her. She stumbled and someone cried, "Watch out!" Then a man grabbed her arm and before she could shake him loose, her other arm was also taken.

"Okay," the first man said, "we've got you."

For one terrifying second, Bea thought she'd been discovered, but then the other man said, "You're going to be okay."

"I'm fine," she protested, trying to pull loose, but they held fast, leading her to one of the metal chairs sitting next to a folding table that someone had set up to hold supplies and information for volunteers. The cold press of metal against her backside didn't help Bea. She struggled to rise, but the men's hands held her down.

"Here, have some water." A female voice and then hands pressing a bottle into hers. Bea dutifully gulped it down, afraid they'd try to pour it into her if she didn't. It helped; her heart rate slowed just a fraction. She looked up to thank the woman and when she saw her the grip on the water bottle gave way. Jill Lassiter caught the bottle before it hit the ground and offered it back to her. "Here you go. You should probably drink some more."

"Thanks." Bea ducked to hide her face, pretending she needed to catch her breath.

"How do you feel?" the man on her left asked. "Any pain?"

Yes. Her chest was pounding again and Bea could feel sweat pouring down her neck and back.

She shook her head, hoping her distress didn't show.

"She looks pale," the second man said. "She should be seen by the paramedics."

"Let them help you," Jill Lassiter said and offered a hand to help Bea up from the chair. Bea put her hand in the other woman's, trying not to look at her.

"Thank you so much for coming out to search," the woman said, squeezing Bea's hand, giving her a sad smile. "We really appreciate it."

Bea mumbled something, but it didn't matter, the men were hustling her away and down the driveway, where other volunteers milled around alongside police officers. People stared with frank curiosity and Bea saw a cameraman, relegated with the rest of the media to the center of the cul-de-sac, turn in her direction.

"I'm really okay," she insisted. "Please stop dragging me."

The men were young, both of them in their twenties or early thirties, and the suggestion that they'd do anything of the kind to an older woman obviously offended their sense of themselves because they stopped at once. One of them, a guy prematurely balding, thrust his beaky face into hers and tried to follow the movement of her eyes. "You're probably dehydrated," he said. "You need to get all of that water in you, and then you'll feel better." He moved his hand to the bottle and she quickly raised it and took another gulp, anxious to prove that she didn't need any further assistance.

She caught a glimpse of the roly-poly family heading at a slow pace out of the cul-de-sac and seized the opportunity. "Thanks, but there are my friends." She pointed at the family disappearing down the road, raising her hand as if one of them had signaled to her. "I've got to go."

She walked away without looking back, moving as quickly as she could, which wasn't very fast at all, not with her chest hurting this way. She drank more of the water, some of it splashing onto her chin, and it actually helped, but what she really needed were those tablets, those damn nitroglycerin tablets that she'd forgotten to slip in her pocket. She wondered if the men who'd helped her were watching and wished that the roly-poly family would slow their waddle. They were like a family of overgrown ducks, bottom heavy each one of them, and surely she could catch up.

Mama duck suddenly paused, bending over to tie her shoe, and Bea called, "Hello there," not having to work hard to sound friendly. The mother looked around in the midst of checking her other stretched-out tennis shoe, and almost lost her balance.

"Careful!" This time it was Bea catching someone. "You don't want to fall." The woman's arm was plump and pliable. It reminded Bea of a loaf of soft-baked bread. She felt a genuine surge of affection for these people and remembered an old toy. "Weebles wobble but they don't fall down," she murmured, too low for the family to hear.

At last, in the privacy of her car, she found the little vial of pills and swallowed one. The young police officer barely glanced at the car as she drove past, and once she was out of sight she floored the accelerator. It had all taken too long; Avery would be waking up by now.

They were doing roadwork again just before the turnoff. She sat behind a row of cars, waiting five full minutes before the laconic-looking young woman holding the pole with the STOP sign turned it to SLOW. Bea ignored that sign, speeding into the left turn, the car screeching as she pulled onto Fernwood Road. She sped up the hill, banging over potholes, screaming past an old man walking along the side of the road. She slowed down, then, but it was too late. He'd taken notice. She could see him in the rearview mirror, an elderly man bundled up against the cold, holding tight to a walking stick as he stared after her car.

Maybe he saw her turn off at 115, but then she disappeared beneath the trees, winding up the narrow, pebbled road as fast as she could. Finally she reached the house. The garage door was partially open again. It had a tendency to stick and she'd forgotten to make sure it closed all the way. She pulled in now before it fully rose. She could hear banging and wailing as soon as she opened the door to the house. Cosmo came running down the stairs, barking furiously in time with the noise, a furry percussion instrument jumping against her leg. Bea limped down the hall as fast as she could, reaching out| to one of the basement's steel support columns for balance. The child's cries got louder the closer Bea got to the door. She'd thought it was soundproof; had anyone heard it outside?

"Down!" She shooed Cosmo away, fumbling to slide back the bolt on the door. Avery scrambled, bawling, wild-eyed and mouth open, to the far corner of the bed, and pressed her back against the wall. "All right," Bea called above the noise, "It's all right, I'm here."

She reached for the child, trying to soothe her, but the little girl only wailed louder, kicking out, her small foot making contact with Bea's chin. She cried out in pain, stumbling back, clutching her face for a moment while she waited for her vision to clear. Her ears rang from the noise. Between the child and the dog the neighbors were probably calling the police.

"That's enough—there's no reason for crying like that." Bea grabbed the child's legs and yanked her flat on the bed. "Stop it!" she shouted, straddling Avery. "Stop it right now!" She used the weight of her body to hold down the child's legs and captured Avery's hands in one of hers, holding them above the girl's head. The child was hysterical; she had to silence her. Bea held her free hand over the child's mouth. She could feel the little girl's teeth against her palm for a split second before Avery bit her. "Aaugh!" Bea snatched her hand away, shaking it, as the child's cries burst forth again.

Panic mounting, Bea snatched a pillow from the bed and pressed it against the child's face. "You have to stop," she begged, pushing more firmly as Avery tried to dislodge her by jerking her head right and left. "Be quiet," she begged, pressing the pillow more firmly against the child's face. "Just be quiet."

Chapter Twenty-two
Day Eight

No one would tell Jill and David what had been found in the volunteer search, but afterward, the atmosphere changed. The FBI field agents who'd joined the investigation and helped coordinate the search had left. The recording set up in the dining room was virtually abandoned. By the morning of the eighth day a lone officer sat at the table drinking a cup of coffee and reading the paper. Finley muttered into her cell phone in the living room and the young, acne-scarred officer watching the front door wouldn't meet Jill's eyes. Ottilo stood talking to a crime-scene tech in the kitchen, but stopped, abruptly, when she and David walked in the room.

"What's going on?" David asked as the tech brushed past them. Jill felt Ottilo's scrutiny as she poured mugs of coffee for both her and David, but when he spoke it was in that perfectly reasonable voice that she'd learned to distrust. "We'd like you both to come down to headquarters today and take a polygraph." He waved his hand in a casual gesture as if he were swatting away a fly. "It's standard in cases like this, just a formality."

David said, "We need to talk to our lawyer first; I want him present."

"Lawyer?" Ottilo repeated the word as if it were profanity, eyebrows rising along with his voice, but Jill didn't believe his surprise. "I'm not sure why you want an attorney with you, Mr. Lassiter, but I have to tell you that any delays could impede our investigation."

"We're not delaying anything," David said. He pulled out his cell phone to call Andrew.

Ottilo glanced at his watch. "Suit yourselves, but tell him to meet you there. We've got this scheduled for eleven."

"The police station is only ten minutes away," Jill said.

"Not the Fox Chapel station," the detective clarified. "Allegheny County Police headquarters. We've got a polygraph expert there."

He insisted on giving them a ride and David finally acquiesced. It was early morning, gray and drizzling. Surprisingly, only two news trucks sat parked outside the house and no reporters could be seen. "Probably afraid of melting their makeup," David muttered, and Jill managed a small laugh. Anything to push away the feeling that what was already a nightmare situation had suddenly gotten much, much worse.

Initial interviews had been done at the Fox Chapel police station, the left side of an attractive redbrick building with a neatly manicured lawn and lovely trees out front. First Jill, then David had given official statements while sitting at an

235

oval table with the detectives and another officer present. Andrew had been there, too, but more as a supportive presence. Even when they'd been asked to sign their statements it had seemed more of a formality than anything else. This change in location signaled that this was not a formality, no matter what Ottilo claimed.

The Allegheny County police had their head-quarters in Point Breeze, in an old industrial park not far from Jill's studio. She'd passed by the area plenty of times without paying any attention. The limited media presence back at home had lulled her into complacency. She wasn't prepared for the crowd of reporters rushing toward the unmarked car as they pulled into the lot next to the building. The crowd jockeyed for their attention, one man even banging on the trunk of the car. Jill jumped at the noise, flinching from the crowd. "How did they know we'd be here?" she whispered to David.

He looked grim. "It's a tactic—the police probably alerted them."

Suddenly Andrew was there, striding down the sidewalk like he'd come straight from court, his arms outstretched to block them from reporters, long dress coat open over a double-breasted suit, polished wing tips hammering the pavement, cold wind ruffling his pale hair. "The Lassiters will not be answering any questions!" he said loudly. Jill had never been so happy to see him.

As if they'd only just noticed the media's presence, police officers emerged from the building and began shouting at the reporters. "Back up! Get back!" Andrew and Detective Ottilo ushered Jill and David into the station ahead of them, stopping only once they were inside with the doors firmly closed behind them. Andrew clapped David on the shoulder and took Jill's hands in his. "Okay? Hanging in there? This is terrible, but you're going to get through it."

Jill tried to smile, but couldn't. The lobby reminded her of the DMV or another government agency, except for the framed photos of uniformed police officers and a large Allegheny County Police Department seal. Beyond the lobby it was like any other boring office complex, with cubicles and metal desks, and industrial carpeting under-foot. Ottilo led them down a hallway and Jill caught a glimpse of Sophia's picture mounted on a whiteboard alongside shots of the Lassiter home. It was disconcerting to see an enlarged shot of Sophia's room; she recognized the pink bedding. Ottilo led them past that room, ushering them through another door.

They were in a large room with a window against the back wall and rows of filing cabinets lining another. At a square table in the center, a small man with tightly cropped red hair stood with his back to them setting up a computer monitor with wires connecting it to a metal box, which was attached in turn to something that looked like a blood pressure cuff.

"This is Detective Boyle, our polygraph expert," Ottilo said, and the man turned and blinked at them, nodding his head in greeting with a tight smile. He had a slightly upturned nose and freckles and wore a green tie.

"It will take approximately forty-five minutes to administer the test," Boyle said in a surprisingly deep voice. "I'll take you one at a time. You'll be asked a series of questions and this—" He tapped the computer monitor. "—will record the truth of your answers. Your responses will register via this equipment. . . ."

He went on and on, pointing to each item on the table with small, freckled hands. Watching him made Jill think "leprechaun," and she was afraid that she'd say it out loud, as if she had selective Tourette's, and she could feel hysterical laughter bubbling up inside her. God, what was wrong with her? There was nothing funny about this. She pressed her lips together and looked away.

Andrew interrupted the technical spiel. "My clients are cooperating only because they have nothing to hide, but they'd prefer not to waste any more time than is already being wasted here."

The little detective looked offended, but he only said, "Who wants to go first?"

Jill glanced at David before Andrew answered for them, "I'd say David."

"Okay, Mrs. Lassiter. If you'll come with me, we'll have you wait in another room."

Andrew caught her arm before she left the room and whispered, "Don't say anything to anybody. Do you understand? Don't get fooled into having any kind of conversation."

Jill followed Ottilo down the hall to a windowless room, empty except for a rectangular table and three straight-backed chairs. "It shouldn't be too long," the detective said as he left, closing the door behind him.

She took a seat at the table and imagined what David was doing in the other room. A large, round clock ticked away high on the wall and she stared at it, trying to calculate how long Sophia had been gone. She pulled out her cell phone to call Tania, but there was no coverage in the room and she slipped it back in her purse. Her fingers tapped against the scarred tabletop. She was reminded of all the different waiting rooms where she'd sat anxiously awaiting news—the bland peach walls of the waiting room at the fertility clinic, the cold blue chill of the emergency room, and the nautical-themed reception area at the adoption lawyer's office. But there had been other people in those rooms, magazines to read or some piece of wall art to stare at—blurry beachscapes were popular—while listening to soft music playing in the background.

The police made no attempt to soften anything.

Harsh fluorescent lighting, nothing to distract her from the endless ticking of the clock. There was a camera mounted in one of the corners. She stared at it, suddenly conscious of her appearance, the clothes that she'd picked without really seeing them—jeans and a sweater and boots that were scuffed. She pulled her feet under her and smoothed a hand over her hair.

The clocked ticked on. Jill thought she might go mad. She circled the table multiple times, counted how many footsteps it took to cross the room. She wondered if this was what it was like to be in solitary confinement, this horrible dragging out of every second, the agony of being alone with only her own anxiety for company.

The door suddenly opened and Detective Finley stepped in holding two steaming insulated cups. "Thought you might like some coffee," she said, offering one to Jill. She took a seat at the table. "You take it with cream, right? If not, this one's black."

"This is fine," Jill said. "Thanks."

"How you holding up?" Finley eyed her over her own cup. She took a seat and sat back in her chair as if she had all the time in the world.

"Okay."

"You must be exhausted," the detective said.

"Yeah." Jill wrapped her hands around the cup and tried to inhale its warmth. Exhaustion didn't really describe it, it was more like moving through a fog, or as if everything and everyone was going on about their lives and she was trapped, like an animal in a zoo exhibit, growing passive the longer she was captive.

"It shouldn't be too long now; then you can go home and get some rest."

Did this woman really think that she could sleep? Jill noticed that the detective had a thin gold band on her ring finger. Finley saw her staring and smiled. "Just got married last year."

"Congratulations."

"We want to start a family soon. Do you want more children?"

"Maybe," she said. That insensitive, invasive question asked by so many people. The first few years of marriage it had been the joke of every older couple they encountered. *"When are you kids going to have kids?"* Always the casual assumption that Jill could just produce a child anytime she wanted to, that all it took was having unprotected sex and, presto, out would pop a baby in nine months.

Finley took another sip of coffee, eyeing Jill over the cup. "Children take up a lot of time. It's hard to juggle having a child and a career, isn't it?"

She said it so casually, but Jill remembered Andrew's admonition and drew back internally, feeling her body tense. "At times."

"It must be stressful."

Was she hoping for some sort of confession? Jill stared back at her, at that pretty, fresh face, and thought of what Detective Finley would look like as she aged, the lines that time and stress would chisel into that pale skin, the creases that childbirth or the lack thereof would etch into her forehead and at the corners of her eyes. Laugh lines were also tear lines.

She stayed silent, pretending to be absorbed in her coffee, but afraid if she took a sip, the cup would tremble and spill. "No more stressful than anything else in life." That was a neutral thing to say; nothing could be made of that.

"I've heard that children are harder, though. Hard on you, hard on your marriage. It's easy to understand how accidents happen, how well-meaning people hurt their children. Especially when they don't share the same blood."

Jill saw the alertness behind the open demeanor, saw what was being done there, and even though she understood it was Finley's job to dig for information, she felt a sudden hatred so deep that she wanted to punch the other woman.

She leaned across the table and Finley immediately mimicked her pose, eyes widening. Jill felt her hands twitching, and had to keep them on the coffee cup to stop from grabbing the other woman. "I love my daughter just as much as if I'd given birth to her," she said slowly, looking directly in Finley's eyes and emphasizing the present tense. "I didn't hurt her; I wouldn't."

Before Finley could respond the door behind her suddenly opened. Ottilo stood outside with David behind him. "Your turn, Mrs. Lassiter."

The leprechaun attached the wires to Jill's body quickly and impersonally, touching her only when he had to and explaining the procedure for a second time before taking her through a series of questions. It reminded Jill of taking tests in school and how nervous she'd always been about being accused of cheating, worried that if she so much as glanced at someone else's paper she'd be disqualified.

Andrew stood to the side, leaning against the wall with his arms crossed. He'd taken off his coat and draped it over a chair, and he'd given her a reassuring smile when she came in the room. She was grateful to have him there.

A series of bland questions lulled her. She relaxed a little. The leprechaun stared impassively at the computer screen, his voice even with every question. "Did you cut your fingers on broken glass?"

"Yes."

"Did you hurt your daughter?"

"No." Jill startled and Andrew shifted. The leprechaun didn't change expression, just kept asking questions.

"Did you kill your daughter?"

"No!"

Finally it ended. Jill felt damp through her armpits and along her hairline. She looked at the leprechaun. "How did it go?"

"Everything worked just fine," he said, unhooking her from the equipment without really looking at her.

"When will we know the results?" she asked, feeling again as if this were some doctor's appointment, but Andrew had his hand under her arm, helping her to rise, and spoke before the leprechaun got a chance.

"Let's go, Jill, we're done here." He led her out of the room and she saw David coming down the hall with Ottilo. He looked washed out, the skin under his eyes dark and puffy, but he gave her a little smile and squeezed her hand.

"You okay?" He kept his voice low.

She nodded. "You?"

He nodded, holding on to her as they waited at the front of the station for Andrew, who'd offered them a lift home. He pulled up in front of the station, honking his horn to clear a path. Jill and David ran the gauntlet of reporters.

They had to get home soon. They were appearing on an upcoming segment on the *Today* show, the camera crew coming to their home for the shoot. Andrew had set it up; he'd said that they needed to get the national media "on your side."

"You make it sound like politics," Jill had

protested, "as if we've got to win some sort of popularity contest for the election."

"Oh, it's worse than politics," Andrew replied. "You can't afford to lose."

Jill left the front seat of the car for David and climbed in the back, resting her head against the leather seat and closing her eyes, letting their conversation wash over her. Her stomach hurt, nausea rising like a storm. Andrew and David discussed polygraph testing, their inadmissibility in court, while she agonized over whether she'd passed. She could sense that she hadn't done well, she just knew it, and what would that mean? She pictured Detective Finley's face leaning across that table, thought of her prying questions. Jill hadn't lied on the test, but she'd lied to her. Parenting *was* more stressful than the rest of life, much more stressful. She remembered the first few days at home with Sophia and how she'd jerk awake to that distinctive, high-pitched wailing, feeling like it pierced her skin. She remembered heating bottles of formula as fast as she could and of cradling Sophia in her arms and offering her the bottle and being amazed at those little hands reaching up to cup it even before she could really grab hold. And she remembered those eyes, Sophia's dark blue baby eyes staring at her as she drank, an intent, unblinking stare that had left Jill trembling with the sudden realization that for this tiny human being she was the center of the universe.

"Did you kill your daughter?" No, never. Unthinkable. Except she knew what it was like to be so tired that you couldn't see straight, that you wanted to do anything to stop that endless crying, that you wanted nothing more than to catch a few more minutes of sleep. She knew what it was like to grit your teeth until they hurt with the effort not to lash out at a stubborn toddler. She knew the secret that most parents never uttered—that you didn't fully understand child abuse until you'd had children of your own and when you heard stories about other parents harming their children you felt almost shaky with relief that it hadn't been you.

Andrew and David had moved on to discuss a case they were dealing with at the firm, and she marveled at David's ability to compartmentalize. He'd always been good at switching between work and home. Much better than she'd ever been. If she'd had a fight with David or a difficult morning with Sophia, she carried the stress with her into the studio and sometimes she'd have to sequester herself in the darkroom for thirty minutes or more, doing some repetitive task until she could drive the sickening feeling of disagreement from her mind.

How would she ever drive this from her mind? People were resilient, she knew that firsthand, but surely there was a limit, a moment beyond which nobody could fully recover? *"Did you kill your daughter?"*

The bile rose quickly, like a rogue wave, and she sat upright, slapping the seat in front of her. "Stop the car."

"Jill? What's wrong?" David's head turned to look at her, but Andrew had already figured it out, jerking the car over to the side of the road and shuddering to a stop along the pebbles and grass. She struggled to open the door, the cold air rushing in at her face, and stumbled out, falling to her knees and heaving into the dry, sparse grass.

Her stomach felt as if it was trying to turn itself inside out. She felt David's hand on her shoulder, a solid, hot weight, but she couldn't stop, the same horrible retching sound over and over, but there was nothing but bile and a thin, dark drizzle of coffee.

"I don't think she's eaten," David said to Andrew. "Do you have any water?"

"Let me check."

She was aware of dirt underneath her hands, of gravel digging into her knees. Hair came loose from her ponytail and whipped about her eyes, which were already tearing.

Andrew and David spoke above her, their words lost because she was heaving again, though there was nothing left to expel. David lifted his hand from her shoulder for a moment, stood, but then he came back, squatting next to her. "Here, drink this." He handed her a bottle and she took a quick swallow, immediately gagging on the sugary taste.

"Sorry, but all I had was an energy drink." Andrew hovered behind her. The sudden trill of a phone made everyone jump and Andrew said, "I've got to take this—hold on." It didn't matter where they went; Andrew's phone always had connectivity.

"Any better?" David asked, rubbing his hand soothingly up and down her back. She nodded shakily, getting to her feet. David helped her stand and they heard Andrew's voice rising.

"When? Where did they find—" He'd turned from them, walking toward the hood of the car. Jill ducked into the backseat and fished tissue from her purse to wipe her mouth.

"Better?" David said, but he wasn't looking at her, but at Andrew, who paced back and forth several feet ahead on the road.

Jill, wrung out and weak, discovered that fear had not been expelled with the contents of her stomach. The drawn look on Andrew's face made her aware that it was still there, like a heavy layer of silt left at the bottom of a parched riverbed.

"What?" she said. "What is it?"

He snapped his phone shut, looking away for a moment, before finally meeting their gaze.

"They've found a body."

Chapter Twenty-three
Day Eight

"It isn't confirmed," Andrew said. "They don't know if it's Sophia." He had to raise his voice to be heard above Jill's cry. It came from somewhere deep inside her, a guttural, inhuman noise. "We have to go to the morgue," Andrew continued, his face pale. "They need you to, well, to identify her."

Jill stared blankly out the car window, waiting for a traffic light to change. They were moving so slowly. It wasn't confirmed, they didn't know that it was Sophia. Images of her daughter cycled through her mind—Sophia rolling over, learning to walk, her first tooth, her first solid food, the first time Jill had held her in her arms. All of these images played, a photomontage Möbius strip. She couldn't be dead; wouldn't Jill feel it inside if her daughter had left her? She remembered what it had been like with Ethan, how she'd known something was wrong, how she'd had that feeling.

The morgue was in the Allegheny County Medical Examiner's Office, a long, two-story building on Penn Avenue with a few wooden picnic tables out front. Was that to make it seem cheery? They just added to Jill's surreal feeling. A patrolman waved Andrew into a fenced lot across the street, just as a police car, lights flashing, pulled up behind them. Detective Ottilo leapt

out and came toward them. Jill stepped out of Andrew's car, amazed that she could walk—she felt completely disconnected from her body, everything was numb.

Ottilo fell into step with the three of them, grim-faced. "It hasn't been confirmed," he said. "We don't know if this is Sophia."

Jill swallowed hard, managed to ask, "Why don't they know if it's her?"

The detective hesitated, rubbing a hand over his face. "The bod—the child was found in the river," he said at last. "It's hard to identify after a certain amount of . . . decomposition."

"My God!" Jill sagged, swaying like a puppet whose strings have been dropped. David caught her and together with Andrew, they supported her through the sliding doors and into the morgue. Quiet inside, the quiet of the dead, but strangely peaceful, too, like a church or temple. Across a tiled floor, a guard sat at a wooden desk. He paged the medical examiner and indicated some padded benches. Jill took a seat and then David began to hyperventilate and sank down next to her, dropping his head between his legs for a few minutes, struggling to breathe normally.

The medical examiner looked like an aging hipster, with a carefully knotted bow tie peeking out at the top of his lab coat, carefully groomed beard, and square, black rimmed reading glasses. He talked quietly with Ottilo off to the side for a moment before coming over to them. "Does your daughter have any birthmarks or moles?" he asked in a solemn voice. "Or any other identifying marks?"

"She has a birthmark on the back of her knee, a tiny café-au-lait spot," Jill said. "And she has a few red splotches at the base of her hairline." She raised her own hand to her neck to show where. "Little red marks—they call it stork bite."

"Anything else? What about her teeth?"

"Teeth?" David asked. His face was a queer yellowish color, and Jill reached for his hand.

"Does she have all her baby teeth?"

"Oh, yes," Jill said. "She hasn't lost any teeth yet, she's too little—" Her voice broke on the last word and she raised her hand to her mouth.

"She has a little cowlick," David said. "It's a lot like mine, right here." He pointed to his hairline, along the part, where the short blond hairs turned into a whorl pattern.

Sophia did have one like that, in almost the same place. Jill hadn't really thought of it before, beyond being grateful that they'd shared this in common because it helped David bond with his adopted daughter.

"Can I do the identification?" Andrew asked.

The medical examiner shook his head, looking

regretful. He took his glasses off and rubbed them against his lab coat. "It must be a family member."

"I'll do it." David staggered to his feet. He said to Andrew, "Stay with Jill, okay?"

Andrew immediately moved next to her on the bench, but Jill waved him away, getting to her feet. "No. I have to see her."

"I don't recommend it," the medical examiner said in his quiet voice. "She was in the water for many hours." He reminded her of a priest, speaking slowly and reverentially.

Ottilo said, "We don't need both of you, Mrs. Lassiter—you don't have to do this to yourself."

"I'm her mother; I have to see her." She knew that she would never believe the answer if she didn't see with her own eyes.

The medical examiner looked at her intently for a moment and then nodded his head. "It's this way."

Andrew came with them, trailing along behind as they followed the medical examiner down a long, painfully white corridor. The farther they got from the lobby the more it resembled a hospital rather than a church. There was a strong citrus smell, cleaning fluid or air freshener, probably supposed to mask the earthier smells of blood, death, and decay, but they were there underneath, fecund and frightening.

The hall ended in double swinging doors marked AUTHORIZED PERSONNEL ONLY. The medical examiner pushed through and they followed, Ottilo, David, Jill, then Andrew. No one spoke, the only sound the occasional squeak and rhythmic click of shoes crossing tile floor. They were in a large, open, chilly room. On the left were rows of what looked like stainless steel refrigerator freezers. To the right a pockmarked woman wearing a lab coat sat reading a magazine at a small table. She stood up and at a nod from the medical examiner walked over to one of the drawers. Jill's heart raced; the fluorescent lights above her seemed too bright. She clutched David's hand.

The drawer slid open like a filing cabinet and there, covered by a sheet, was an impossibly small body. Tears flooded Jill's eyes. The morgue assistant stood at the side watching them and waiting, her jaw moving as if she were chewing gum.

"Ready?" The medical examiner's voice seemed to come from far away. Jill felt as if everything was blocked out except that single, slight bundle on the tray. How would she survive this? How would she go on if this small body were Sophia's?

David squeezed her hand and nodded at the morgue assistant. She peeled the sheet back slowly and Jill dug her nails into her other hand. Chalklike skin, so white, naked, fragile, all blue veins and odd marks and the pale hair slicked back from a tiny face that looked as if it had been smeared a little, the features blurred as if it were made of wax that had melted slightly. Jill leaned forward, staring hard at the little girl, but it was hard to make sense of this child that was no longer a child. She could hear her own panting. She said, "Turn her over. Can you turn her over?" Her voice higher than normal, not her voice, someone else's. The morgue assistant carefully moved the body—so insubstantial, so easily shifted—and Jill and David searched the back, the hairline and that little, pale cavity behind the knee.

All at once Jill sank to the floor, her legs giving way completely, tears pouring in a rush down her face, like standing under a shower. "It's not her," she cried, smiling up at David and the medical examiner through her tears. "It's not her, it's not Sophia."

Chapter Twenty-four

Journal—June 2010

No one raised an eyebrow at the hospital, but I was conscious of being the only woman giving birth alone. You said you couldn't get away, but it's clear that you aren't one of those men who find pregnancy a turn-on. The last time you saw me I was seven months and huge and the look that flashed across your face was horror.

Everyone has seen some depiction of the birth experience and knows what is supposed to happen: The doctor declares, "It's a girl!" and the wriggling, impossibly tiny, remarkably monkey-like little form is put on the mother's chest for her to hold. This didn't happen. Someone cut the cord and immediately took our baby away.

I'd pleaded with you to reconsider keeping the child. "No one needs to know. I won't tell anyone that you're the father."

"It would come out. Someone would notice eventually."

I had to ask a nurse weighing our child whether it was a boy or a girl. She answered me with her face turned away. I begged to hold her. The young nurse looked at the doctor. She looked uncomfortable. She said, "I don't know if that's a good idea under the circumstances." She meant the woman from the adoption agency standing quietly by the door with a car seat.

You found the agency and arranged everything. That was after you found me a job at a crappy little firm in another county. "Lay low for a while," you said. "Just until after the birth."

I've lived like a virtual hermit, seeing none of my old friends, commuting back and forth every day up until I went into labor, turning down the offers of my new coworkers to grab a drink after work. I didn't even tell my family, per your advice. "Why get them excited about a grandchild they aren't going to be allowed to see?"

"Please," I pleaded with the nurse. "Please let me hold her. Just for a moment."

They relented. They placed her in my arms, our little girl, and I touched her soft, silky head and counted each one of her impossibly small fingers and toes. I wanted so much to say it had all been a terrible mistake and I was taking her home, but I was exhausted and I couldn't hold on when they came to take her out of my arms. I cried, tears sliding from my eyes and into my hair, and the doctor and nurses bustled around me pretending not to notice.

I couldn't hold on to her so I'm holding on to what you promised me the last time I saw you—that I should be able to come back to the firm next year. Along with that, I'll also be coming back to you.

Chapter Twenty-five

Day Fourteen

The little girl who would not answer to Avery huddled on the couch staring at the TV screen, mouth hanging slightly open.

"You could have killed her the other day," Frank said, hovering over Bea as she started preparing dinner. "You almost smothered her."

"She's fine." They could have macaroni and cheese—what child didn't like that? Her daughter used to love it and she'd loved TV too, staring at that dumb, glowing box that Bea had wanted to get rid of, but Frank insisted on keeping. She couldn't get rid of this TV either; she needed to watch the news and it helped to have something besides Cosmo guaranteed to keep Avery entertained. She was watching a cartoon now, what looked like a kitchen sponge with arms and legs talking to a starfish wearing bathing trunks. Bea didn't understand it.

She walked back out to the living room, waving her hand in front of the screen, trying to break the little girl's fixed concentration. "Avery. Avery, listen to me. Avery!"

The snap made the child shift in her seat and Cosmo looked up from his bored vigil at her feet, but instead of looking over the little girl just hugged her toy dog more closely. Bea could tell from the set of her jaw that she was being purposely ignored.

"Fine then, you'll get what I want to make," Bea said.

She filled a pot of water at the sink. Frank said, "She's afraid of you."

Bea brushed her hand to move him away from the stove. "She's not afraid, she's just stubborn." She set the water to boil.

When the mac and cheese was ready, she fixed a bowl and called to the girl again. "C'mon, Avery, dinner's ready."

In response, the child bolted out of the living room and down the hall. Bea frowned as she heard the basement door slam. This child was spoiled, probably the result of living with those awful people. She'd watched the press conference replayed a dozen times; the woman was an ice queen and her husband was an attention-seeking liar. Did anyone buy his crying act? Well, they wouldn't for long.

She poured a glass of wine and took a large sip, relaxing a little as the warmth spread through her. The pasta was gummy, disgusting really, but the wine made it palatable. She left Avery's dish of mac and cheese on the counter and carried her own bowl into the living room, switching through the channels on the TV until she found the local news. There was new footage of the Lassiters pushing through a throng of reporters to get into a police station. They played that clip twice before replaying footage of the search. There was a single crowd shot, but Bea felt reassured when she couldn't spot herself in the mass of volunteers. She sat down on the couch, mesmerized by the coverage. The reporters seemed to like Jill Lassiter's face—they zoomed in on it often enough—and much was made of where they lived.

"Who could have taken Sophia Lassiter from this upscale home in what had been considered a safe neighborhood? Police are not releasing the results of the search eleven days ago, but Channel 11 has learned that police recovered something related to the case and that item has been sent to a crime lab for analysis." Bea recognized the reporter, a young bleached blonde with glossy red lips and an unwholesome gleam in her heavily mascaraed eyes. She probably looked at this as an opportunity to advance her career.

"Jill and David Lassiter agreed to polygraph tests, but police aren't releasing the results." More footage of the couple with a familiar-looking well-dressed man, dodging reporters outside of the Fox Chapel police station. Jill Lassiter flung up a hand to block a reporter's mike.

"Mommy!"

Bea dropped the bowl of mac and cheese and

spun around. Avery stood in the doorway staring at the TV with big eyes. Bea had been so caught up that she hadn't heard her come back upstairs. "Mommy!" The child ran toward the TV with outstretched hands, and Cosmo, who'd made short work of the spilled mac and cheese, ran toward her, barking. Bea quickly reached for the remote to shut it off. When the picture vanished, Avery cried out as if she'd been stabbed.

"I want Mommy! Where's Mommy!" She touched the TV screen, looked behind it and then tried to take the remote out of Bea's hand, stretching her little arm until it was almost out of its socket, straining and jumping, her fingers waving fruitlessly in the air. "Give me my mommy!" The dog, confused, jumped against the girl's legs, then Bea's, yipping in time with the child's cries. The noise was too much for Bea.

"Stop it!" she yelled over the din. "Stop it right now!" She had to get away, carrying the remote with her into the kitchen, but the child followed, still sobbing, and the dog followed after the child. Bea's heart thudded in her chest, and she yanked open an upper cupboard door and shoved the remote deep inside, slamming it shut. The child's wailing only increased. She followed Bea back to the living room, pulling at her, trying to climb her. Bea detached one hand, then the other, only to have the first return and suction on again.

She panicked at the thought of someone overhearing and swung the child up, hauling her out of the kitchen and into the hall, fighting to carry her down the stairs. She put her down hard on the basement floor. "Scream all you want now! Nobody will hear you!" Her own voice sounded ragged and harsh and she looked at her trembling arms; they were covered with red marks.

"Mommy! Mommy! I wanna go home!" The child's screaming hadn't abated, though it was ragged, too, and hysterical. Bea hauled the child over to the laundry tub and turned on a faucet. Cupping a handful of icy water, she turned and splashed the child full in the face.

The little girl yelped, a different cry, and stopped in shock, her mouth open, eyes rolling back in her head. Bea paused, her own hands shaking and dripping. For a moment the only noise was both of them breathing hard and the water rushing into the sink behind them. Then the little girl started to cry again, but quietly, and she dropped to the floor, folding like a paper doll.

"You've hurt her again." Frank stood there surveying them, hands on his hips.

Bea turned off the water, splashing some on her face first. Her heart still beat obscenely fast and she clutched the sides of the metal tub and gulped the air like an asthmatic. "Mind your own business."

"You're supposed to be a healer," he said. "Remember? Do no harm."

"Don't lecture me on medical ethics, Frank!"

"Who's Frank?" The child's voice surprised Bea. She turned to see Avery looking from her to the empty basement. "Who are you talking to?"

Frank had gone. In the sudden silence Bea could hear a distant buzzing sound, short and sharp. It stopped, then started up again. The doorbell.

Panicked, Bea fumbled on the shelf where she stored the needles, hurriedly pulling one free of the pack and filling the syringe before turning to the child, but she was gone.

"Avery?" Bea hissed. She ran out of the utility area, heading for the basement stairs. Avery scrambled up them, one hand reaching toward the door. "Get back here!" Bea lunged for her, catching her by the ankle just as the child turned the doorknob. The child cried out, but Bea dragged her down, wrapping a hand over her mouth before sinking the needle into the child's arm. She twisted in Bea's grasp for a moment, eyes wild, before falling limp. Bea hauled her dead weight into the basement room and bolted the door. The doorbell buzzed again. She rushed up from the basement, only to stop short at the top of the stairs.

Pressed up close to the kitchen door, hands cupped to his face as he peered through the glass, stood a police officer.

Chapter Twenty-six

Day Fourteen

Bea quickly stepped out of the basement, closing the door behind her. She marched to the kitchen door, watching the patrolman startle as he saw her. She cracked open the door. "What is it? What do you want?"

He was young and lanky with dark hair cropped too short for his round face. "Police, ma'am. Are you okay?" His words came out as puffs in the frigid air.

"Of course. Why wouldn't I be?"

"We had a report of screaming coming from this residence, ma'am. Do you live here alone?" She saw his gaze linger for a moment on her lazy eye, but then he looked past her at the kitchen, glancing one way, then the other.

"No, my husband lives here, too."

"Is he home?"

"My husband?"

"Yes, ma'am."

"No, he isn't here right now."

"Is there anyone else in the house with you?"

Bea shook her head. "No. Well, except my dog." She forced a smile, trying to look friendly. "What is this about, officer?"

"One of your neighbors reported screaming."

"From this house?"

"Yes, ma'am."

"Well I don't know what they thought they heard, but no one's been screaming here, officer. We're too old for that much excitement." She chuckled.

He flushed, a rusty red color flooding his spottily shaved cheeks, and shifted his feet, hitching up his uniform belt. "Why didn't you answer the front door?"

"I didn't hear it. I was in the basement doing laundry."

He peered at her and Bea met his gaze and held it, holding the smile. He broke first, looking to his left before turning back to her. "You're sure you're okay?"

"Positive. I don't know what the neighbors thought they heard. Maybe they heard me yelling at my dog?"

He hesitated. "You mind if I come in to take a look?"

Her hand tightened on the doorknob. "Of course not," she said. "Come on in."

He stepped past her into the kitchen, looking around. She circled her hand around the hypodermic in her pocket. The cop saw the macaroni and cheese and before he could comment on the second bowl she said, "We keep it in stock for our grandchild, but my husband and I have gotten a taste for it." She saw him glance at the wine bottle, but he didn't comment.

He stepped into the living room, looking around. "Where is your husband?"

"It's poker night. He's out with friends." Frank had never played poker in his life.

The officer nodded, then walked down the hall, poking his head inside her bedroom door, his face impassive. He turned the knob on the second door and she tensed, hand tightening on the needle. "Which neighbor called the police?" she asked, trying to pull his attention toward her even as he pushed open the door. She realized with relief that the heavy drapes across the room's rear windows cast the room in shadows, obscuring the furnishings.

"I don't know," he said, barely glancing at the room before moving back toward the kitchen. It had to be the old man she'd seen the other day. The cop reached his hand toward the door to the basement and she said, "Careful—my dog's down there. He's not friendly." As if on cue, Cosmo barked from behind the door and the man moved his hands to hitch up the heavy belt again. His radio squawked and he picked it up. "Negative on the domestic. Homeowner's unaware of any screaming and I don't see a problem. Heading out."

She walked him to the front door. "I appreciate

the police checking up, but some of the neighbors, well, some of the old ones don't have enough to do—I wouldn't trust what they say."

He smiled a little. "And what do you do, Mrs.—"

"I was a nurse," she said. "I'm retired."

She stood at the door and waited, watching him walk down the front steps that wound down the hill to the gravel driveway, where a patrol car sat with the bar of lights on top spinning. She waited until he'd gotten in the car, raising her hand in good-bye, smile fixed on her face. Just like any other neighbor, any solid citizen. Police weren't viewed with suspicion by the people in this tax bracket. She waited, shivering, until the car disappeared down the wooded driveway, and then the smile dropped and she fled inside the house and bolted the door, sliding the old chain in place for good measure. She walked down the hall to the second bedroom, flicking on the lights. The photos she'd taped to the wall stared back at her, single shots, group shots, and the formal portraits that she'd stolen from the studio. What would the officer have made of those if he'd seen them?

"Busy, busy little Bea," Frank hissed, hovering in the doorway. "Don't you need to check on the child?"

"Shut up!" She pushed past him, but he followed her down the hallway.

"What if you've killed her this time? What then?"

"Leave me alone! I don't want you here!" She screwed her eyes shut, hands clenched in fists, and when she'd opened them he'd gone.

The child was lying motionless on the floor where Bea had left her, limbs akimbo, face pale and beaded with sweat. "Avery, c'mon, it's okay now, you can wake up." Bea knelt beside her, grabbing one tiny wrist to check for a pulse. She couldn't find it and for a horrible moment she thought Frank was right and she'd killed her. What then? What would she do? Sweat broke out on her own face. Her hands felt slippery on the child's waxy skin. She circled the wrist again, pressing, uncomfortably aware of her own pulse jumping harder than it should be. Nothing, nothing. She dropped the little hand and moved to the child's throat and there she caught it, a faint but steady thumping. "C'mon, little girl. Wake up now." She hauled the child up and over to the bed and then sank down next to her, waiting for her own heart rate to return to normal.

Chapter Twenty-seven
Day Twenty-Two

Humming. Sophia humming a little song. Jill followed the sound through an empty playground, across a dry field. She saw her daughter stepping out of the woods, just like that day in the park, only this time Sophia was barefoot and in her nightgown. As Jill ran to her, Sophia turned and disappeared back into a sea of green. Jill followed, calling her name. And then it was a hallway and she was walking toward a door at the end of it, and she could hear humming coming from behind the door. She could feel her heart thudding in her chest as she turned the knob.

Jill woke before she opened the door, her face wet with tears. She reached a hand toward David, but he wasn't there. She sat up, still feeling tired, reminded of the utter exhaustion that she'd felt when Sophia was a newborn and Jill's days had been an endless cycle of feeding and changing diapers and only being able to sleep during those precious few hours that her baby slept.

"David?" It came out as a croak. She swung her legs over the side of the bed and thought of Sophia poking her head around their bedroom door. The need to hold her daughter was so great it made Jill's bones ache.

She staggered to the door and pushed it open, hearing faint voices coming from downstairs. What was it? Were the police back again?

When she came downstairs, tying her robe around her, she realized it was only the TV. David sat in the family room with his back to her, glued to the set. The local news station was playing clips from their *Today* show appearance again. And Andrew had thought doing a national news show was a good idea.

"You need to get in front of the story," he'd insisted. "You've made the national news any-way —an attractive couple with a missing child? The media laps it up." Jill hadn't wanted to do it, but Andrew had agreed to the interview before telling them, and to cancel had seemed worse. Not any-more. Worse was how stiff she looked on camera. She'd been front and center during the interview, flanked by David and Andrew, but something about being better groomed than at the press conference had made it worse; she'd looked even more emotionally detached.

She stared transfixed, hating it but unable to stop watching. "What are they saying?"

David looked up at her. "Nothing important." He reached for the remote, but she got to it first.

"Don't, I want to hear." She turned up the volume. They'd cut from the *Today* show clip to a solemn-faced blonde announcer. "—every parent's worst nightmare, but the question on everyone's mind this morning is: Are Jill and David Lassiter telling the truth about their daughter's disappearance? Our reporter, Sean Dunlop, brings us the story."

Another cut to a young man with dark eyes and sleek hair who'd adopted the same serious mien. "Folks in Pittsburgh this morning are asking what happened to little Sophia Lassiter, only three years old"—one of the photos of Sophia flashed on the screen—"who vanished from her wealthy suburban home in the early hours of a peaceful November morning. As we enter day twenty-two with no sign of Sophia, attention is increasingly focused on her parents, Jill and David Lassiter, and people are starting to ask if they know more than they've been saying."

They went to a taped clip then, the reporter interviewing a woman who Jill recognized, another preschool parent, someone she'd seen every day, at every drop-off and pick-up, but had never met by name. "You hate to think it, but the parents are usually involved in cases like these," the woman said. "Her mother is a cold woman— you can tell on the TV, the camera doesn't lie."

Jill swore. "I knew it was a bad idea! I've seen that woman daily, smiled at her, chatted with her, and now all of a sudden she thinks I'm cold? Just because I can't cry on command?"

"That's why I didn't want you to listen to this." David reached for the remote, but Jill held it out of range.

"No, I want to hear it." The camera cut to another person, a man this time.

"You can't help but be suspicious of them," the guy said with a knowing smirk. "I mean, c'mon? What is the likelihood of someone breaking into your house and taking your child? Especially in that neighborhood."

They went back to the reporter and as the camera panned wide, Jill realized with a start that they'd taped the segment right in front of the house. The reporter said, "Police have yet to name Jill and David Lassiter as suspects in the disappearance of their daughter, Sophia, but say that everyone is a person of interest."

"God, turn it off." David stood to wrest the remote from her hand and this time Jill didn't fight him. He sighed as she blinked back tears. "C'mon, you can't listen to that crap."

"But it's true. I do look cold. *I* think I look guilty. Why can't I cry when it would actually do some good?"

"It doesn't matter, none of it matters." David pulled her into an embrace and she clung to him for a minute, gulping. She could feel the tension in his arms, see the same tension in his eyes. He said it didn't matter, but he didn't mean it. He knew better.

The phone rang, startlingly loud. Jill pulled away to answer it, swiping at her eyes and clearing her throat. "Hello?"

"What the hell were you thinking?" Tania said. For a second, her mind still on the news, Jill thought she was talking about the *Today* show, but without waiting for an answer Tania bulleted on, "I've just spent three fucking hours at a police station and Leo is still there."

"It's routine—they have to talk to people we know." Jill felt as if she were channeling Detective Ottilo.

"They said you gave them my name. My name and Leo's. That you said we had something to do with Sophia's disappearance."

"I didn't say that, I swear." Jill saw David looking at her, eyebrows raised.

"Then what did you say?" Tania demanded. "My landlady saw me leaving in the back of a police car, Jill. Do you really think I did something to your kid?"

"No." And as soon as she said it the dark kernel of suspicion Jill had felt evaporated, like a shallow pool of murky water exposed to the sun. Of course it wasn't her friend and business partner, of course not. "I don't think you did anything."

Tania wasn't appeased. "But you think Leo did?

She hesitated and the other woman leapt on it. "You *do* think he did, don't you? Why? Because he isn't some button-downed nine-to-five conformist he must be a kidnapper? A pedophile?"

"What do you really know about him?" Jill countered. "Other than that he's like every other one of your boyfriends—all of them rebels without a cause, either current or former addicts, with shady pasts and a penchant for sex. I don't know what he's done, Tania, but then neither do you because knowing him would mean you'd have to let go of the romance and face the very real possibility that underneath the cool sunglasses and tattoos the guy you're sleeping with might not just play the bad boy, he might really be one."

Silence when she'd finished. She'd stunned Tania; she'd stunned herself. It was the most honest she'd ever been with her, and after a long minute, Tania returned the favor. "It's been so easy for you, hasn't it?" Her voice was cold, harsh. "So easy to judge when you're married to a perfect man and living the perfect little life in your perfect rich world. Only it's not so perfect now, is it?"

"Tania, please—"

"I told the police what you said, about wishing you could just take a break from parenting? I told them about that conversation and about the time you said you wished kids came with a volume knob, so you could just turn it off when she had a tantrum."

Jill felt hot, then cold. "That was just talk. I love Sophia, you know I love her."

"The police asked me and I answered—"

"They already suspect us, Tania!"

"It's just routine. Isn't that what you said, Jill?"

Before Jill could reply, she heard a dial tone. The phone rang again almost immediately and she answered, "Tania—"

"Nope, sorry, it's Andrew. I've been trying to reach David, but I keep getting voice mail. They want you both back down at police headquarters."

Chapter Twenty-eight
Day Twenty-Two

Cameras clicked and flashed, blinding Jill as she ran with David and Andrew past the gauntlet of reporters gathered along North Lexington Street outside county police headquarters. She struggled not to duck her head because Andrew said that made them look like suspects. Act like you normally would, he said. But there was nothing normal about having dozens of people in your face shouting, "Mrs. Lassiter, where's Sophia?" "Did you kill Sophia?" "Do you have any idea who took your daughter?"

Detective Ottilo greeted them in the lobby, offering them coffee, which Jill was glad to accept. It gave her something to do with her hands. He led them down a hallway, pausing outside a room similar to the one Jill had sat in alone only two weeks before. "We'll be conducting separate interviews today, so if you'll just have a seat in here, Mrs. Lassiter—"

Andrew cut him off. "Absolutely not. That was not agreed upon."

"It's standard procedure—"

"If you had advised me that you intended to formally interview my clients, I would have arranged for another attorney to be present."

"No problem," Ottilo said with a hard smile. "We'll interview the Lassiters one at a time so you can be present for both."

Andrew glanced at his watch. "Unfortunately, I have to be in court later today; you'll have to reschedule." He ushered Jill and David back up the hallway.

"I could charge you with obstruction," Ottilo said, hustling after them.

Andrew snorted. "I'd like to see that hold up."

Ottilo stopped them in the lobby. "Fine," he snapped, his usual composure gone. "We'll do *today's* interview together."

Andrew and David exchanged a quick smile as they followed the detective back down the hall. Jill wasn't optimistic that the upper hand would last. Ottilo ushered them into a larger room and shut the door hard behind them. Not quite a slam, but he was clearly upset. The detective grabbed a chair standing against the wall and hauled it to the far side of the table so there were three seats instead of two. "Sit down." He pulled up his own seat across from them and slapped a folder onto the table, glancing toward the camera mounted in the opposite ceiling corner and angled to give it a full view. He cleared his throat, "Okay, for the record I'm Detective Michael Ottilo interviewing Jill and David Lassiter in the presence of their attorney, Andrew Graham."

David took a sip of coffee, acting nonchalant, but Jill thought his hand trembled. She took off the plastic lid and blew on hers though she didn't know why she bothered. What difference did it make if she burned her tongue? She couldn't taste anything anyway.

"You have to eat," David had said last night, "you're going to get sick." She'd eaten an apple to appease him, cutting it into thin slices, eating them slowly one by one, realizing when she was halfway through that she couldn't taste the fruit, could barely even smell it. Lately it was as if all her senses were lost, as if the only things she could taste and feel were fear and longing.

Ottilo opened the folder and perused two documents before sliding them across the table to Andrew. He pulled on his reading glasses and picked up the papers, David edging closer to take a look. Jill kept her eyes on the detective.

"Those are the results of the polygraphs," Ottilo said, sitting back, rocking on the legs of his chair. There was silence for a long minute while Jill and David read the reports that Andrew passed to them. There was a lot of technical jargon. Ratios, probabilities—what did it all mean?

"As you can see, the results for both of you are inconclusive," Ottilo said.

"This is why you brought us down here?" David tossed the paper back at the detective. "These don't say anything and certainly nothing that I didn't already know. When are you going to stop wasting time on us and find the person who took our child?"

Andrew put a hand on his arm. "Let me," he said in a low voice, then to Ottilo, "I agree with my client, detective. There is nothing here."

Ottilo sat up, the legs of the chair landing with a thud on the carpet. "Inconclusive does not mean you passed."

"What does it mean?" Jill asked.

"It means there are no clear results," David said.

"No," Ottilo said. "It means that you aren't being completely truthful."

"But it didn't say we were lying, right?" Jill said.

"It means that the tests are bunk and he knows it," David said. "They're almost meaningless, which is why they can't be used in court."

"That's partially true, Mr. Lassiter." Ottilo smiled, a thin, tight smile. "A prosecutor could not use these results in a courtroom, but it doesn't mean that they're worthless. Police use them to steer us either toward or away from suspects."

"I've been waiting for this," David said, and he sounded both angry and, underneath the anger, afraid. Andrew put a hand on his arm and David sat back in his chair, arms crossed against his chest.

Jill said, "Where are you going with this?"

"Let's look at the facts to date." Ottilo spread one of his bony hands and ticked the items off on his long, skeletal fingers. "First, your daughter disappeared from your house. Second, by your own admission there was no sign of forced entry or abduction. Third, there was blood found both in your kitchen and on your patio. Fourth, there have been no ransom demands and no one else has seen your child since the night before when she threw a major tantrum at a Halloween party. Fifth, the polygraphs indicate a certain amount of deceit. What does all of that say to you, Mr. and Mrs. Lassiter?"

"Don't answer that," Andrew said to David and Jill. He pushed the papers back across the table and sneered at Ottilo. "Is this why you brought them down here? There is nothing substantive here."

Ottilo smiled, but he had a nasty gleam in his eyes. "There's more, Mr. Graham." At that moment the door opened and Detective Finley stepped in carrying a paper bag. It looked like a normal grocery bag except on one side it had evidence printed in large black letters followed by a check box that someone had filled out. She saw LASSITER and #10 before Finley handed the bag to Ottilo and leaned against the wall behind him with her arms crossed. The lights in the room seemed glaring. Jill leaned forward in her chair, all her muscles tightening. "What's in that?"

Ottilo didn't answer. He pulled a pair of latex gloves from his pocket and pulled them on; it seemed excruciatingly slow. He opened the bag and reached inside, all the while watching their faces. She was reminded of a crazy magician who had performed at a birthday party Sophia had been invited to last year—the dramatic pauses, the constant gauging of the audience's reaction. Ottilo lifted out something pink that had reddish-brown splotches. He unfolded it on the table.

"What is that?" David demanded.

"It's Sophia's nightgown," Jill managed to say, feeling strangled. She reached across the table to touch it, but Ottilo pulled it out of her reach.

"We found this near the culvert in the woods behind your house, Mrs. Lassiter," he said.

"Oh no, please no," Jill shrank in her chair, staring horrified at the small item of clothing. She thought of putting it on Sophia, of pulling it over her head and helping her button the two tiny pearl buttons. They were still there, smeared in that reddish brown along with the rest of the gown.

"The lab is still testing the blood," Ottilo said. "Preliminary tests show that it's A positive. There's more than a ninety percent likelihood that the blood is Sophia's. The only question is how it got there."

"How on earth would we know that?" David's face had paled. "Jesus Christ."

Ottilo ignored him, watching Jill, who couldn't stop staring at the tiny garment. "You've lost another child, right, Mr. and Mrs. Lassiter?"

It was a like a blow. Jill's gaze jumped to the detective's. She had to clear her throat before answering. "Yes."

Ottilo held up the folder like a poker hand, surveying its contents for a moment before closing it and placing it back on the table. "Three years ago, shortly before you adopted Sophia?"

He probably had the date in front of him. Jill couldn't steady her voice. "Yes."

David said, "This is unbelievable—what does our son's death have to do with this investigation?"

"Yes, I fail to see the relevance," Andrew started, but Ottilo held up a hand to stop him even as he consulted the folder again.

"Your son was nine months old when he died?"

"Ethan," Jill whispered.

"Excuse me?"

"His name was Ethan." She wrapped her arms around her stomach and focused on the tabletop, afraid that she might throw up.

"Ethan. Right. And how did Ethan die?"

Andrew said, "Now look here," but David spoke over him. "SIDS. The doctors said it was SIDS."

"Sudden Infant Death Syndrome." Ottilo said each word slowly, and he was still staring at Jill, his cold gray eyes boring into her. "And you were the one who found him?"

Before Jill could answer, David spoke for her, "What the hell is this? Why are you asking about our son?"

Ottilo's eyes didn't leave Jill's face as said rapidly, "He cried a lot, right? Do you remember telling the police that your son 'cried more than seemed normal'?"

"I don't remember—it was over three years ago." Jill blinked rapidly, trying to hold back tears. She didn't want to cry in front of them. It wasn't true. She did remember. She remembered all of it, everything that had happened that day framed in excruciating detail in her memory. She tried not to think about it, but already she could hear her footsteps climbing the apartment stairs to the second floor, see the dust motes hanging in the sunlight spilling from the skylight across the narrow hallway, obscuring the closed door that sat in shadow at the end of it. She could still remember that she'd felt grateful—oh, dear God —because he'd taken a longer nap, because she had been in need of a rest and he was still sleeping. Grateful until she'd climbed the stairs to check on him, until she'd walked down that endless narrow hallway and knew that something was wrong.

"Sophia was a crier, too, right?" Ottilo said. "She was pretty strong-willed, isn't that right?"

"Do you have a point, Detective?" Andrew sounded angry. "I consider this harassment."

Jill closed her eyes and ducked her head, pressing her hands hard against her temples, but she couldn't stop the past from surging forward. Like floodwaters breaking over a wall, her memory of that day engulfed her, pulling her under and into that hallway again looking at that door. The same hall and the same door that she visited over and over again in her dreams as if dreaming about it could somehow change the outcome.

The voices fell away and she was standing there again in the silence. The terrible silence. It shouldn't have been so quiet. Her footsteps stopped outside the door, listening, even as she put her hand on the cool metal knob and turned it. She opened the door, the feeling of dread like going off a high dive at the pool as a child, the absolute knee-knocking fear and aloneness of that moment, followed by a stomach-dropping free fall into nothingness when she saw the still, small body of her son lying facedown in his crib.

A loud thud against the table jolted her back. Detective Ottilo had thrown a book in the enter. "What is that?" David said even as Jill reached for it, knowing it instantly by the green marbled cover. "It's mine," she cried as Ottilo pulled it out of reach. "Give it back!"

The detective ignored her, opening the book

and turning the pages instead. Photos of Ethan, all of the pages were Ethan, each image lovingly attached to the heavy paper pages with old-fashioned black paper corners. They were all the same setting, the same approximate pose, but taken over time, showing Ethan sleeping in his crib—one a week since they'd brought him home from the hospital. Thirty-nine photos, two per page, all of them in black-and-white.

She'd started it as an interesting experiment, to see how quickly an infant changed, but after two months it had turned into something more—an art project, her own untitled exhibition, a personal tribute to her son.

The detective stopped on the last page with its two photos. The first, at the top of the page, had been taken the week before Ethan died. He was on his side, his eyes closed, one little hand curled in a fist, the other resting against his side. The photo below it was of the empty crib. She'd taken it that first Friday, two days after his death, at the same time that she'd taken the others, going up to that room alone, overwhelmed by grief and needing to express it in some more personal way.

"What *is* this, Mrs. Lassiter?" Ottilo said, tapping the last page.

David was trying to see the photos. Ottilo turned the album to show it to him and Jill saw confusion and something else—repulsion?

"It was just a way to remember him, a way to frame those moments." She stumbled through an explanation of her art while the detective stared at her the way she'd once seen a cat staring at a bird. He waited for her to finish before he glanced at the other detective.

"We thought these were strikingly similar to some other photographs you've taken," Finley said, opening the folder she carried and slowly and deliberately laying out a series of photographs as if they were tarot cards while everyone at the table watched in silence.

Each one was a shot of a child apparently sleeping in his parents' arms. It was only if you looked closely that you could see that the children weren't alive.

"These are personal," Jill said, "they belong to the families who asked me to take them."

"These photos look an awful lot like the photos you took of your son," Ottilo said, aligning the album with the row of photos.

"They're supposed to look just like those photos, they're supposed to help the parents with grieving."

"What it looks like, Mrs. Lassiter, is that you have a preoccupation with death."

"That's absurd," Jill said, glancing at David, but there was something in his face—he was thinking about what the detective said.

Ottilo said, "When Ethan died, you were the one

who found him, Mrs. Lassiter, and when Sophia disappeared, you were the last one to see her. Don't you think that's odd, Mrs. Lassiter?"

"I didn't do anything to Ethan." Jill's voice shook, but with rage as much as fear. "He was my son, Detective. My son."

The detective's eyes bored into her. "And Sophia? Did you do something to Sophia? Tell me what happened and we can end this charade right now."

"What charade?" Andrew said.

"Mrs. Lassiter, did you hurt your daughter?"

Jill recoiled. "No!"

"This is ridiculous," David said. He rammed his chair back and stood up from the table. "We're not going to just sit here and let you accuse us."

"We're not done, Mr. Lassiter," Ottilo boomed. "Sit down!" He stood up, too, his own chair slamming into the wall behind him an indication of how much strength was actually in that whipcord frame.

Andrew was on his feet as well, and he placed a hand on David's shoulder. "Let's all just calm down." David shook him off, but he sat back down in his seat, arms crossed. Andrew took his seat and Ottilo sat down after him.

Jill took a shaky breath as Andrew said, "Have you found anything of substance besides the nightgown?"

"Yes," the detective said, "but not in the woods."

He held the folder up again, reading something slowly, before leaning sideways to show it to Finley, who whispered something in his ear. Ottilo put the folder down and sat forward. "Many people aren't aware that whatever they erase from their computers gets stored on the hard drive. We have computer experts who can pull up a user's search history even if it's been cleared and email messages even if they've been deleted."

"Fascinating." Andrew had adopted a bored tone. "Are we going anywhere with this?"

"Our experts found some interesting items in your search history, Mrs. Lassiter: You looked up area landfills—"

"No I didn't!"

"—and replacement knives from Henckels, coincidentally the same manufacturer as the set in your kitchen that's missing one."

"This is crazy!" Jill looked from Ottilo to the others in the room. "I didn't search for those things. I didn't!"

"You can't prove anything with that," David said angrily.

"I want to see the official report," Andrew said, but Ottilo ignored him, turning his attention to David.

"Do you know a Leslie Monroe, Mr. Lassiter?"

The name sounded familiar. Where had Jill heard it before? She looked at David, but he glanced at Andrew before looking back at the detectives.

"She's an acquaintance," he said after a few seconds.

"Just an acquaintance?" Detective Ottilo feigned surprise. "She's a lawyer with Goldberg, Winthrop, and Shaw, isn't she? Didn't your firm work with them on a big case several years ago?"

Jill stared from the detective to David and back. What was going on? What did this lawyer have to do with Sophia?

"It was a long time ago," David said. His face flushed and he avoided Jill's eyes.

"Didn't you meet Leslie Monroe last month for drinks?" Finley said.

"She called me," David said, but Andrew cut him off.

"Don't answer that!" he snapped. "This is not relevant to your investigation, Detective."

Finley barely glanced at him. "Mr. Lassiter, you were asked by the polygraph examiner if you'd had any extramarital relationships."

Jill shot David a look then looked back at Finley. "Extramarital? An affair?"

"Your answer to that question was no. The polygraph indicates that this was deceitful."

Jill remembered where she'd heard that name. The blonde woman in the fur coat reaching out to slap David outside that stupid restaurant what seemed a lifetime ago. *"She's just a lawyer from*

288

another firm." She felt sick remembering how David had gotten defensive. *"Are you spying on me?"*

"This has nothing to do with my daughter." But David's voice shook. He wouldn't look at Jill.

"Did you have an affair with Leslie Monroe, Mr. Lassiter?" Ottilo said.

Jill waited for him to deny it, to try to convince them that it was all a misunderstanding, that this was strictly a professional relationship. David stared down at the table for a long moment and then he looked up at Ottilo and Finley, his profile as handsome as ever, his hands coming up to rest flat on the table. She saw the red staining his cheeks and knew his answer before he even opened his mouth.

"Yes."

Chapter Twenty-nine
Day Twenty-Two

Avery seemed groggy and her skin was pale. Bea needed to get some vitamin D capsules for her. In the meantime she'd let her out to the yard to get some sunlight, however little there was on these shorter days, the end of the year when darkness descended. "Do you want to go in the yard and play with Cosmo?" she said and the child's eyes brightened. Bea bundled her into a boy's coat that she'd gotten at Goodwill.

Predictably, Avery fought her on it. "No coat!" she said, thrusting the brown jacket away.

"No outside without the coat," Bea countered and the little girl complied, though she did it with her lower lip sticking out in a pout.

"I like pink," she said, plucking at the brown sleeves with her tiny hands.

"We'll get you a pink one later." Bea stood back to look at her. With her cropped hair and male clothing no one would guess she was a girl. She wrestled a dark blue knit cap on the child's head and only then did she open the kitchen door and let the child and Cosmo head out into the fenced yard. Avery's pout vanished. She laughed, running around the yard throwing handfuls of leaves while Cosmo barked excitedly.

Bea stood in the doorway watching them. The air was fresh, if cold. She pulled her cardigan tighter around her, crossing her arms for warmth. The air smelled of rotting leaves and traces of woodsmoke from a faraway chimney. Another year passing. Her daughter always liked this time of year, enjoyed the run-up to the holidays. Thinking about her hurt, like brushing up against a bruise. She frowned, forcing her mind off the past. Focus on the present and the distressing lack of action on the part of the police. What was it going to take before they made an arrest? Did they have to have all the dots connected for them? She knew that DNA testing took time, but she'd thought that this case would be a priority, that they'd be able to rush it through.

It was too cold to have the door open for long. "Avery, time to come inside," she called. The little girl ignored her, or perhaps she didn't hear. She'd found a stick and was playing fetch with Cosmo, laughing happily when the little dog chased after every throw. "Avery!" Bea raised her voice and the child looked at her this time. "Come back inside now. Let's go, Cosmo, you too." Bea clapped her hands at the dog, but he took one step toward her before pausing and whining, looking from the three-year-old to Bea.

"No!" Avery said, stamping a sneakered foot. "Cosmo wants to play!"

Bea sighed. She'd forgotten how much energy it

took when children were little. And this child wore her out with the constant arguing. She started out the door to get them, but it was too damn cold to have this fight without a coat. She called, "I'll be right back," and headed to the front closet.

A crunching noise outside made her jump. She hurried to the window just as a blue SUV came up the gravel driveway. The car looked familiar. Bea tugged on her coat and ran down the basement stairs to the garage, pressing the button and ducking under it as it slowly lifted.

A woman came around the side of the SUV, an enormous handbag on the shoulder of her bright white coat, waving and calling "Hi there!" She dropped the cigarette from her other hand and ground it out with a preposterously high heel. Damn, it was the real-estate agent. Bea grimaced as Patsy Duckworth came traipsing toward her, a nasty smoke smell trailing after her.

Bea went down to meet her, moving as far from the house as she could. "Hello, Patsy." She tried not to cough on the lingering haze of smoke. "I was just on my way out."

"Sorry to drop by unannounced, but you are a hard woman to reach." Patsy gave her character-istic nervous laugh. "I've left you multiple messages; didn't you get them?"

"The machine hasn't been working," Bea lied.

"Oh dear, well, it's a good thing I came out here then, isn't it." She laughed again while Bea just stared, willing her to go away. "Bad news, I'm afraid," Patsy pressed on. "There's a buyer for the house—the one we had last year who fell through? He's back, offering more money, and Mrs. Stephens has decided to accept the offer."

It took Bea a second to process. "The rental agreement is through next year."

"Yes, I know, but there was that clause in the contract, remember?" The agent reached into her overstuffed mustard-yellow handbag and pulled out a pile of papers, flicking through the stapled pages with nicotine-stained fingers. "Here it is: 'Terms subject to expire if a buyer is found for the property' and that's what you signed—"

"How long?"

Patsy stared stupidly. "How long?"

"When do we have to be out?"

"Oh, of course." Patsy smiled. "By the end of the month. They want this transaction completed before the end of the year. Tax reasons; I'm sure you understand."

"That's not enough time."

Patsy's smile wavered, corners quivering for a moment. "I know it's come as a shock, but I'm sure we can find you and your husband another rental. Unless you're ready to buy?" The corners of her mouth upped another half-inch, Cheshire Cat grin firmly back in place. Did she know how moronic she looked? "Barring any major damage, you'll get your full security deposit back."

Bea laughed at that. "Any damages? The place is a dump."

Patsy's eyes lit up as if she found that funny, but then she said in a sweeter, high-pitched voice, "Hello there! Who are you?"

Bea whirled around, but she knew before she saw her that it was Avery. The child had come around the side of the house; Cosmo nowhere in sight. She glanced from Bea to the agent, head tilted shyly for a moment, before she announced, "I want to go home," and headed toward the SUV.

For one very long moment, both women just stood there watching the child crunch determinedly past them down the gravel driveway. Bea snapped out of it and thinking fast, hustled after her, saying in a singsong, "C'mon, Avery, let's get you into the car." She swept the child into her arms, but Patsy Duckworth was faster in those stupid shoes than Bea had anticipated.

"Is this your grandson?" She reached out a manicured hand to touch the child's cheek. "He's just adorable!"

"Yes," Bea said, moving with Avery toward the car. "We've got to get going—"

Patsy just chuckled. "How old is he? Three?" she said to Bea, and to the child, "What's your name, little guy?"

Avery ducked from her hand. "Soph—" As she spoke, Bea shifted her arm and pressed the child's head against her shoulder, muffling the answer. She said to Patsy, "He's shy."

The child yanked her head back. "Put me down!"

"It's okay, sweetie, I'm going to get you in the car, we need to get to the doctor." The child immediately wriggled in her arms, struggling to break free.

Patsy's hand drew back. "Oh, is he sick?" She opened her purse and Bea was sure she was searching for hand sanitizer.

"Woke up feeling bad," Bea said. "I told my daughter that I'd take him to the doctor."

"I didn't know you had a daughter." The agent wiped her hands on a tissue, smile firmly back in place. "Does she live around here?" Couldn't she take the hint that this wasn't a good time to talk?

"Baltimore," Bea said. "They're visiting." Avery scratched her arm and Bea cried out, loosening her hold. The child slipped to the ground and darted away, running past the SUV and down the drive.

"Avery!" Bea ran after her. "Come back here!"

The child lost her footing, slipping in the pea gravel. Bea was on her, dragging her up. "Let go! Let go!" the child screamed. "I want my mommy! I wanna go home!"

"His eyes do look a little glassy," Patsy mused, staring at the child, but keeping her hands far away. "He could be coming down with something; I'd better let you go."

"Yes," Bea agreed, trying to mimic Patsy's laugh. "Got to get this little boy in the car." She turned to head back into the garage with the child.

"I'm not a boy!" the child cried. "I'm Sophi—" Bea discreetly pressed her hand over the child's mouth.

"Mrs. Walsh? Just one more thing."

Caught off guard, Bea spun around. The damn real-estate agent had come up behind her without Bea hearing. Patsy Duckworth's eyes widened as she registered the hand covering Avery's mouth. Bea immediately shifted it, pretending she was stroking the child's face. "You'll feel better soon."

Avery struggled, reaching out to Patsy. "I wanna go home!"

"Is everything okay?" the agent said, smile faltering. "Sounds like this little boy really needs his mother."

"I'm not a boy!" The child cried, voice hoarse.

Patsy looked perplexed. Bea forced a laugh. "He likes to pretend he's someone else sometimes." She opened the rear car door and plopped the child onto the backseat, then closed the car door to cover the wails. She rolled her eyes at Patsy. "Kids; you know how it is." She tried to hide her panic behind a big fake smile of her own.

"Of course," the agent murmured, but her smile was definitely gone, replaced by a furrow between her eyes. "I just wanted to let you know that the buyer will be coming to see the house with a home inspector. He wants to get the property checked again before the papers are signed. I'll make sure it's late in the month, though, and I'll call before-hand, of course."

"Of course." Bea waited for her to leave. Avery's wails were barely suppressed by the car door. She'd climbed up on the seat, was banging her little hands against the window.

"Well, I'd better get going. If you're sure you don't need any help."

"I'm sure." Bea smiled again, one hand clenched on the door handle. "He's just high-strung."

Finally, Patsy headed back down the driveway to her car. Bea yanked open the car door and hissed, "Sit down right now!" Her voice must have scared the child; she scrambled to obey. Bea looked back down the drive. Patsy glanced back, looking doubtful, and Bea raised a hand, waving good-bye. She waited, watching the other woman climb back into her SUV and execute an awkward three-point turn before heading back down the drive. Bea waited until the other car had dis-appeared beneath the thick canopy of trees. She waited until she could no longer hear the spray of gravel or the roar of the motor.

Avery was curled up on the seat whimpering, face red and blotchy from her tears. "Stop crying," Bea snapped, reaching in to haul her back out. "You've got nothing to cry about."

"I wanna go home," the child dared to say again, but in a teary whisper this time.

"This is your home," Bea said matter-of-factly, carrying her back inside the house and almost tripping over Cosmo. Somehow the dog had gotten back in the house and was scratching at the door out to the garage, trying to get to them. The child must have put him back in the house. Bea put the child down, staring at her with narrowed eyes. "I think we're going to keep you inside from now on," she said, squatting to take off Avery's coat and hat. She took the child's hand and led her toward the bedroom.

"No!" Avery dug her heels in the floor. "No! I don't wanna go!"

"Too bad." Bea huffed as she lifted the child under her armpits to drag her the rest of the way. She pushed her through the door into the room. "Bad girls have to do a time-out in their room." She slammed the door and drew the bolt across it. The child's smothered cries could be heard through the door; small fists hammered against it.

Cosmo bared his teeth at Bea, growling. She clapped her hands at him and he cowered, retreating, tail between his legs, into a dark corner of the basement. "Good, you can take a time-out, too." She climbed back up the stairs and closed the basement door to drown out the child's cries. Her hands shook a little as she pulled the cork from the bottle of wine on the kitchen counter. The real-estate agent's visit had unsettled her. She poured a glass of cabernet and took a healthy swig.

"Isn't it a little early to be drinking?" Frank sat at the kitchen table, looking disapproving.

"Oh mind your own business," she muttered. They would have to leave here much sooner than she'd anticipated. She didn't know how they'd travel with the child; it would be too risky. "I guess your plan isn't going to work after all." Frank's voice was heavy with sarcasm.

"You're wrong." Bea carried her glass to the kitchen door and locked it. "You've always underestimated me." She took another swallow, savoring the sharp yet warm liquid before letting it slide down her throat. Bea stared blankly out the window in the top of the door without seeing the sunshine dappling the carpet of leaves outside. This was just like chess, which her daughter had learned at school and tried to teach her. Frank hadn't been interested, dismissing it as a game for nerds, but Bea had listened to the instructions if only for the sheer pleasure of hanging out with her teenage daughter. She could still see those slim fingers moving the carved pieces around the board, carefully explaining what each piece could and couldn't do. Bea drained her glass, trying to dull the ache that always came when thinking about her daughter.

Focus on the plan. The plan was like chess. She just had to consider the cause and effect of each possible move.

"Well then, how are you going to make it work?" Frank demanded, sounding slightly slurred, which was funny since Bea was the one drinking.

"Never you mind," she said. "There's always a contingency."

Chapter Thirty

Day Twenty-Two

Jill had broken her arm when she was young and the pain of having it set had been a high-pitched, blinding white pain, like the shrieking of a teakettle. It felt like that again as she listened to her husband recount the details of his relationship with another woman.

"It's been over for a long time," David said to Ottilo. "It has nothing to do with Sophia."

"How did you and Ms. Monroe meet?"

"I don't know—a company retreat, I think." David glanced at Jill, but she wouldn't look at him. She thought of those twice-a-year weekends, of David leaving on Fridays with an overnight bag and a quick kiss and arriving home exhausted but cheerful on Sundays. He used to complain about the retreats, say that he didn't understand why a law firm actually thought that putting a group of lawyers together in an enclosed space for an entire weekend was a good idea. They'd laughed about it. She wanted to vomit.

Andrew cleared his throat loudly. "Again, I object to this line of questioning. I fail to see how this has anything to do with Sophia's disappearance."

Ottilo ignored him. "Isn't it true that you told Leslie Monroe that you wanted out of your marriage?"

Andrew said, "Don't answer that."

"No. I want to." David leaned forward in his chair, wiping a hand over his face as if it would wash away the stress. "I might have said that, but that was years ago. We—Jill and I—were going through a bad patch in our marriage."

A bad patch. Was that like a bad batch? Jill thought of how easily David tossed things out when he cooked, how often he began again. *It didn't turn out; I'm starting fresh.* Is that how he thought of their marriage? Of her? This one didn't work, so I'll just find someone new?

"Wasn't the only thing holding you in your marriage your daughter?"

"No!"

"You didn't tell Leslie Monroe that Sophia was the only thing holding you back?"

"What? No! I never said that."

Ottilo consulted his notes. "Did you meet Leslie Monroe on September nineteenth?"

"She called me—"

"Yes or no, Mr. Lassiter?"

"Yes, but it wasn't—"

"Leslie Monroe says that at that meeting you told her that you couldn't leave because of Sophia."

David pressed his hands against his temples. "I

302

told her that things were different now—Sophia was just one of those differences—"

"Mr. Lassiter, Sophia was the only thing standing between you and a new life. If it wasn't for Sophia you'd be free to be with Ms. Monroe—"

"I don't want to be with Leslie!"

"If you could just get rid of Sophia—"

"No! I didn't hurt her!"

Andrew said, "This is outrageous speculation!"

They were all yelling, three male voices raised in accusation and justification. Only Jill and Detective Finley were silent. Jill could feel the other woman staring at her, but she wouldn't meet her gaze. Her skin felt hot, tight. When this happened to men it was called being cuckolded. Was there a similar word for women? She couldn't take anymore. She stood up, headed to the door. David called after her, "Jill, wait!"

She kept walking, out the door and down the hall, but stopped in the front lobby when she saw a crowd of reporters still clustered outside the station. The desk sergeant stared at her. "Can I help you?"

"Is there a back exit?"

He pointed down another hall, which led to stairs and an exit onto a parking lot. She stalked out into the cold, wanting to get away from the building, away from everything, and then she remembered that they'd come in Andrew's car and she had no way of getting home. She stopped walking and David was on her, trying to wrap her in his arms.

"Please, let me explain!"

"Get off me!" She fought him, knocking his hands away until he dropped them to his sides.

"It meant nothing to me, you have to believe me. She meant nothing!"

"Get away from me." Jill backed away, arms clutching her stomach. She turned and walked in the opposite direction, heading toward what she hoped was a way out around the other side of the building. She felt as if she were being torn apart, piece by piece. Soon there would be nothing left of her. But David wouldn't stop; he ran after her, walking backward in front of her, trying to see her face. She looked away from him, staring down at the pavement, studying the cracks in the asphalt and wondering what it would be like to disappear into them.

"It was nothing," David said. "I swear, it was just sex."

"What does that mean? What is *just* sex?" How could something that intimate be "just" any-thing? She was aghast at him and at her own naïveté. She wondered how many times he'd lied to her. How many times had he really slept with this woman? Where had he met up with her? A terrible thought crossed her mind. "Did you bring her to our house?"

"What? No, never, I wouldn't do that."

"Oh, so there are some lines you won't cross?"

Andrew had come out of the building and was standing a discreet distance away. Jill felt a moment's shame at seeing him standing there, witnessing this, but anger at David overcame any sense of discretion.

"Jill, please! I only met her a few times. We were going through a hard period, remember?"

She laughed bitterly. "How could I forget? We'd just buried our son, David. You were fucking her when our son was barely in the ground!"

"It was a terrible time—I was vulnerable, we were vulnerable."

"I didn't cheat on you!" She pushed past him and strode over to Andrew. "Can you please take me home now."

"Of course. Let's go."

David trailed them to the car, where Jill took the front seat rather than risk David trying to climb into the back with her. David took the seat behind her and she felt his breath on her neck. "I'm so sorry," he whispered, but then Andrew got in the driver's side and David sat back. They rode in silence broken only by Andrew as they approached the cul-de-sac.

"This news is going to be leaked, I don't see any way to avoid it, but you need to keep a united front, weather the storm."

"I agree," David said. "I think I should go to the office. It looks bad if I don't—"

Jill got out of the car while he was still talking, pushing through the crowd of reporters and past the open-mouthed patrolman. She saw another patrolman sitting on the sofa munching on a fast-food burger, the grease-stained wrapper splayed on the coffee table. "Eat that in the kitchen or get out of my house!"

The man mumbled an apology, but Jill ran past him and up the stairs to the second floor. She went into their master bedroom and did something she'd never done before—locked the door.

Within seconds she could hear David's foot-steps pounding up the stairs and coming down the hallway. She lay on her side on the bed, her back to the door with bent legs pulled to her chest, hands over her ears. But she could still hear him, his hand on the doorknob, trying to turn it. Knocking on the door. "Jill? Jill, let me in."

The noise seemed to echo in her ears. She remembered being at the seashore with Sophia and showing her how to hold a conch to her ear and listen to the noise of the sea. Where had he been then? Off fucking someone else?

"Don't do this, Jill. Please."

But she wasn't doing anything. He'd done it. He'd brought this poison into their lives. She thought of how casually he'd lied at the restaurant. He'd lied to her repeatedly. How often had he been with that woman during that time? Had he bedded her and then come home to Jill? Had he compared them, finding fault with Jill? She tried to remember what he'd said to her at the time, but couldn't.

"I've got to go to work," David said through the door. "We can talk when I get back." Silence. She made no move to fill it. "I'm sorry, Jill," he said in a lower voice and she knew he was pressed right up against the door. "I know you don't believe me, but I never meant to hurt you."

It was strange how intense emotional pain could become physical. Jill felt as if she had the flu. She thought of all the times that she and David had made love while they were trying to conceive. The thermometers and ovulation kits and record keeping they'd mastered to keep track of something that other people managed with seeming ease. She thought of the day they'd come home to their apartment with Ethan and she'd nursed him in this same bed, while David hovered around grinning from ear to ear. She thought of the worst days of all, the days after Ethan's death, when she'd barely left her bed, shuffling to the bathroom and back and willing herself to die.

The tears she'd held back finally spilled from her eyes in a hot wave, and there was relief in shedding them. She cried and cried, thinking of that tiny torn and stained nightgown and how the detective had referred to Sophia in the past tense. Jill had barely survived the loss of one child—how would she survive the loss of another? And how monstrously unfair that in addition to losing Sophia she had to lose the last remaining relationship she cherished, on the same day.

But hadn't she known her marriage was in trouble back then? Hadn't she sensed David pulling away at the time, but been too afraid to ask about it because she couldn't handle another loss, not after Ethan? And really, if she looked back, hadn't their marriage been under stress even before Ethan? Hadn't they been simply hanging on, burned out by infertility treatments and demanding jobs?

The darkest months after Ethan's death were a blur to her. Swallowed whole by grief, she was amazed she hadn't simply died from it. How could he even think about sex during that time? The selfish bastard—she'd thought they'd been in it together, working through their grief even if individually, adopting Sophia, moving on as parents and partners.

But it was all a lie. She wondered what it had been like, his first meeting with this woman. The other woman. It was something from a made-for-TV movie, not her life. She'd heard David say something once about other lawyers at the retreats, how they viewed it as a free pass from their marriage. Don't ask, don't tell. Had he been testing her with that information? Judging how gullible she was, how ready she was to believe that he'd done nothing when he was away on those weekends?

Her body felt so heavy and her eyes ached from crying. She closed them and fell into a deeper sleep than she had had in days. She dreamed she was trying to find Sophia, that she was searching through room after room of a house and then suddenly she opened the last door, but instead of Sophia what she found was David in bed with a faceless woman.

It shocked her awake. Jill sat up, blinking. The sun was starting to set; streaks of orange covered the bedspread and carpet. She stumbled out of bed and into the bathroom. The face in the mirror was puffy and salt-streaked, hair a tangled mess. She washed her face, ran a brush through her hair.

She listened at the door before opening it. There was no one in the hallway and she walked slowly down the stairs. It surprised her to find David in the kitchen.

"I thought you were going in to work?"

"I did." He'd pulled his tie loose and the sleeves of his crisp white dress shirt were rolled up. He was standing at the window, staring out at the backyard with a drink in his hand. "They asked me to leave."

"What?" Surprise overcame her resolve not to speak to him. "You're kidding."

"Apparently employing a child killer is bad for the firm."

"Did they actually say that?"

He gave a mirthless laugh. "Oh, of course not. They suggested that it would probably be a good idea to take a break, that I needed to concentrate on my family situation." He took a swig from his glass. "That's what they called it—a *situation*."

"I can't believe they actually asked you to leave."

"Oh, it was all very polite." He laughed, a harsh sound, and then his voice went deeper and she knew he was imitating one of the senior partners. "Of course you understand that this does not reflect on your performance, but we must think of the firm."

"But what about Andrew? I know he wouldn't support that."

He turned from the window to look at her. "The partners are having a meeting now; they'll let me know tomorrow. He's trying his best, but he's probably going to be outvoted. He told me as much."

"What did you say when they asked you to leave?"

"What could I say? No? It really wasn't presented as an option. I said I was sorry my situation had inconvenienced the firm and I left."

"Situation." She repeated the word, thinking how antiseptic it was, and how wildly inappropriate to describe the disappearance of their child.

The doorbell rang, startling them both. "Isn't the officer still outside?" Jill said.

"It could be Andrew," David said. He headed toward the front hall. "If it's another one of those reporters I'm not going to be held responsible for what I do."

She followed behind him and saw him swing the door open. A middle-aged woman with long, graying hair stood on the doorstep. She wore a purple tunic-like garment over black stretch pants with black boots and she had a silvery scarf looped around her neck, but it was her eyes that captured most of Jill's attention. They were a strange shade of blue, so pale that they appeared almost translucent. "Hello, are you Mr. Lassiter?"

"We're not giving interviews," David said, moving to close the door, but the woman stepped forward, sticking her foot inside.

She smiled. "I'm not a reporter." She peered around David and spotted Jill. "You must be Mrs. Lassiter. I'm Glynnis Moonday."

David said, "I'm not sure what you're selling, Ms. Mooday—"

"Moon-day," the woman corrected with the same smile.

"Moonday. But whatever it is, we're not interested."

"I'm not selling anything. I'm here to help you."

"Are you with the police?"

"No, but they've used my services before. I'm a psychic."

"Oh dear God," David said.

"I know about your little girl."

Jill knew she should send the woman away. Early on in the investigation, before they became the prime suspects, Ottilo had warned them about people like this. "Every nut in the country will try to contact you," he'd said. "Don't answer their calls. Just refuse to talk to them."

"You need to leave," David said, moving to close the door.

"I just want to help you find your daughter."

"We're being helped by the police, but thank you anyway." David pushed against the door, but the woman wouldn't move. She'd fixed her gaze on Jill.

"Do you want me to leave, Mrs. Lassiter?"

Jill knew she should say no, knew that there was no basis in fact, that it was just superstitious nonsense, but she couldn't do it. David had the door half-closed. "Wait!"

He stopped, shocked. The woman pushed her way back inside. "I'm here, Mrs. Lassiter," she said in a soothing voice. "I'm here to help."

David looked at Jill. "What are you doing?"

"Let's just hear what she has to say."

"Why? To give us false hope? This woman is a fake—there is no such thing as psychic ability."

"It's okay, Mr. Lassiter," Glynnis Moonday said,

but her strange eyes remained fixed on Jill. "I'm used to skeptics."

"Do you know something?" Jill asked. "Have you seen Sophia?"

The woman smiled. "Not physically, no."

"But mentally? In images?"

The woman nodded. "Yes. I've seen her."

"Where is she?" David demanded. "If you can see her then tell us where she is."

"Spirit doesn't work that way, Mr. Lassiter."

David snorted. "Of course not."

"What can you tell us?" Jill asked. She felt like she did as a kid when she'd wanted so desperately to believe that Santa Claus existed.

"Can I see her room?"

Jill hesitated, but the woman was already moving toward the stairs. David took Jill's arm. "This is crap," he hissed. "All she wants is money."

"If she doesn't know anything then we're no worse off than we were before," Jill said.

She hurried up the stairs after the woman and watched her wander down the hall until she stopped inside the doorway to Sophia's room. It was gloomy, but she didn't put on a light. Jill came into the room every single day, unable to stay away even though just being there was like pulling off a scab. She could see dust on the butterfly mobile that hung from the ceiling, turning silently. The room looked untidy, but not the way Sophia left it, with toys scattered around and her clothes left in piles. It was disheveled from searching. The sheets tossed back where she'd pulled them, the drawers open where the police had searched. The clothes in the closet separated where strange hands had pushed the hangers apart. Jill felt the gnawing ache in the pit of her stomach, but she stayed, watching Glynnis Moonday survey the room.

"Can I touch something of hers," she said in a quiet voice.

Jill looked around; everything was Sophia's. "Does it matter what it is? Do you want clothes?"

"Does she have a favorite toy?"

"It's gone—missing, I mean."

"Was it a stuffed animal?"

Jill clenched her hands. "Yes."

Glynnis Moonday moved forward and paused next to the bed. It looked so small, but it had been Sophia's big-girl bed. She'd been so excited to move out of the crib, but Jill wished she'd waited another year. Why hadn't she waited? From the minute that bed was in the room Sophia got up at night. Although she'd climbed out of her crib, too, and that was why they'd gotten the bed in the first place, because Jill was afraid she'd hurt herself falling over the high sides of the crib. But no matter how many times they'd spoken to her, Sophia would sneak out of bed. The danger had been there all along, but Jill hadn't recognized it.

The psychic reached down and put one hand on

the pillow. Her hands had prominent veins and her nails were long and painted a deep red that was chipping. Jill didn't want her to touch it, didn't want her there in Sophia's room, another stranger picking among her things, but she wanted it at the same time. The woman held her hand there for a moment, pressed into the pillow, her long, graying hair hanging around her face. Then she straightened up, moving her hand away and turned toward Jill. Her odd eyes rolled back in her head and Jill felt the hair on the back of her neck rise.

"I see trees. Lots of trees. And there's a dog."

"Blinky? Is it a stuffed animal?"

If the woman heard her she didn't acknowledge it. "I see water. Running water."

"Is she near the river?"

The woman looked down again suddenly and her eyes came back into focus. "I can't see it," she said.

Jill heard a snort behind her and turned to see David in the doorway. She ignored him. "What does that mean?"

"I'm sorry, I don't know," the woman said. "You need to put those images together with other evidence."

"Yes, very helpful," David said. "Trees and water. Wow, I hope we can find some of those."

Glynnis Moonday looked at him. "The reading wasn't as strong as it could be because his negative energy is blocking."

David made a derisive noise, but Jill ignored him. "Please," she said, touching the woman's arm. "Please, is she, that is, did you actually see her?" She couldn't bring herself to ask directly, but Glynnis Moonday did it for her.

"Is she alive? I feel her energy, Mrs. Lassiter," she said. "But it's very weak."

"What does that mean?"

"She's here, but I don't know for how much longer."

"Oh, no—is she hurt?"

"I can't tell, not without spending more time. If you want to engage my services—"

"No," David interrupted. "No more. Get out." He pushed past Jill and grabbed Glynnis Moonday's upper arm. "Get out of our house. Now."

"Let go of me," the psychic protested.

He pulled her into the hall. "Go."

"If you don't stop, I'll have you charged with assault."

"And I'll have you charged with fraud."

Jill ran after them. "Stop it, David. You could hurt her."

The woman shook herself free from his grip. "I'm leaving. Spirit doesn't stay where the energy field is so negative."

"Good riddance to you and Spirit," David said.

"Please!" Jill ran after her. "Is there anything

else? Anything at all?" She touched the woman's arm and Glynnis Moonday turned her strange eyes on her. "You lost another child," she said, staring deep into Jill's eyes. "You're afraid because you already lost one child and you don't want to lose another."

Jill let go of her, stunned, and the woman swept out the door. David slammed it behind her. "And you didn't have to swallow that bullshit."

"How do you know it's bullshit? Did you hear what she said about Ethan?"

"She could easily have found that out. Why are you sucked in by her voodoo? It's just false hope."

"It's better than no hope," Jill said. "What else do I have left?"

She walked away from the stricken look on his face, heading to the kitchen where she gathered empty coffee cups and a crumpled fast-food bag from the table and she threw them out, the small action spurring her to keep moving. She wiped the kitchen table and then the countertops. Someone had run the dishwasher, so she emptied it, losing herself in the mindless task. At some point she became aware of David standing in the doorway watching her, but she didn't acknowledge him.

Too soon there was nothing left to clean. She stood at the sink looking over the backyard, sponge clutched in one hand. David cleared his throat. The noise was loud in the quiet of the room.

"I didn't mean to hurt you."

It was so feeble. The words were so stupidly feeble. They ignited a spark within her. She turned so she could see his face. "What did you mean to do? Did you think that fucking another woman was somehow going to help us?

He winced at the obscenity and she felt glad. She wanted more than a wince, she wanted to wound him in the same way that he had her. "Did you hurt Sophia?"

He made a sound as if she'd punched him. "God, no, of course not. How can you say that? How can you even think that?"

"Did that bitch you sleep with hurt her?"

"Jill! My God!"

"You saw her nightgown. You saw the blood."

"I didn't do anything to her and neither did Leslie. I swear."

"How can I believe anything you say? You're obviously an accomplished liar."

"I wouldn't lie about that—"

"No, only about our marriage."

He turned to the side, one hand reaching for his stomach and she was pleased, desperately pleased to see him clutch himself as if he were in physical pain.

"You were alone with her," he said after a

minute, his voice so low that at first she thought she'd heard him wrong.

"Are you accusing me?" The anger had turned toxic; it was a real thing crackling in the air between them.

"You were alone with her that night—"

"Yeah, while you were on the phone with your whore!"

"And the next morning, I was asleep."

Jill felt blind rage consuming her. "You bastard! I can't believe you're even suggesting that."

"She's a handful, you're always saying that. You lose your temper with her—"

Jill laughed, a harsh, ugly sound. "How would you know? You're barely around. You don't know anything about my parenting."

"I'm around enough to see that you get frustrated by her behavior."

"And you don't? For God's sake, David, do you really think that getting frustrated with a strong-willed three-year-old means that I hurt her?" Jill couldn't stop shaking, she didn't know how much was emotion and how much sheer adrenaline. "What did I do, David? Did I stab her?"

"Stop it." David turned from her.

"No! I want you to tell me what exactly I did to our daughter. Did I smother her in her sleep?"

"I'm not going to listen to this." David walked out of the room, but Jill ran after him.

"If you're going to accuse me, I'd like to know what it is you think I've done."

He didn't answer, walking into the living room where he stopped in front of the windows. Through the sheers, Jill could see the outline of the large crowd hovering, always hovering there like some lost herd of sheep, at the edge of their property. "Why do you think it's me instead of that whore you've been sleeping with."

David finally turned to look her in the face. The expression in his eyes frightened her before he spoke. "Because you're the last person who saw her."

Chapter Thirty-one

Days Twenty-Two and Twenty-Three

"I'm going to stay at my parents' for a while." David walked into the family room with an overnight bag in his hand. Jill could see his reflection in the window. It was almost nine and far too dark to see anything, but she stared into the darkness anyway, nursing a second glass of wine.

"I've got my cell phone—you can reach me on it or at my parents' number." He stood there as if he expected her to try to stop him. Jill didn't turn around. Of course he'd go to his parents. They would welcome him with open arms. They'd find a way to blame Jill for his infidelity, just as they probably blamed her for Ethan's death, and for Sophia's disappearance.

After a minute David left the room, and a few minutes after that she heard the front door close. Her shoulders dropped a little and she took a swig of wine and settled on the couch, glad that he was gone. She couldn't have shared a bed with him tonight; she didn't know if she'd be able to again.

It was odd being all alone in the house; she couldn't recall when that last happened. She finished the wine and dragged herself up to bed, sure that between emotional and physical exhaustion she'd fall right to sleep, only she didn't. All alone in their king-size bed she couldn't stop thinking about the stories of betrayal she'd heard over the years and how she'd pitied women who claimed to be clueless to what their husbands were really doing. How could they have missed the signs? There were always signs. She'd judged these women, thought of them as either stupidly oblivious or willfully blind. So which was she? She found herself replaying all the things that should have made her suspicious and the times that she had been suspicious, but had allowed him to convince her not to be. How stupid she'd been not to realize, to think that somehow her marriage was exempt from the possibility.

Her own mother had tried to warn her off men early. "Liars and cheaters, most of them. I think it comes with the package. You've got to do for yourself in this world, because woe be unto the woman who thinks she can depend on a man."

She'd thought her mother was just negative because she'd been unlucky in love, but lying there alone in the darkness, it suddenly made sense to Jill. She wondered if David had ever been faithful, if he'd meant it when he said he loved her, if anything he'd ever told her was the truth. Every business trip he'd taken now underwent her mental scrutiny. Her desire to know everything about what had happened forced her out of bed, at one in the morning, to search through the closet, turning out his suit pockets to see if he'd left anything behind. She caught a glimpse of herself in the mirror—a wild-eyed and wild-haired woman wearing nothing but a long T-shirt and panties. She felt foolish and crawled back into bed, except again she couldn't sleep, but this time her thoughts were consumed by Sophia.

If she were dead, wouldn't Jill feel that? She'd felt it with Ethan, felt his absence before she'd found him in the crib, but maybe that was because he'd been biologically tied to her. Maybe it didn't work that way for adoptive mothers, but was mother's intuition about biology or love? She loved Sophia just as much as she had Ethan, even if that love had started in desperation and despair. She could feel Sophia's presence, just as surely as she'd felt Ethan's absence. That bloodstained nightgown didn't prove anything. She was sure her little girl was alive, but maybe that was because she needed to believe Sophia was out there, somewhere. She needed that now more than ever.

At some point Jill must have drifted off. When she woke up it was still dark and she reached automatically across the vast expanse of bed in search of David before her mind caught up with her body and she remembered. Felt the awful plummeting that had been with her every morning since Sophia's disappearance. She opened her eyes and glanced at the clock. Just after six. Her body clock kept its time even where she had no life left to schedule.

She showered and got dressed, moving on autopilot, but desperate to hold on to some routine. A voice inside screamed that this was going to be her life from now on, all alone with only her own thoughts for company. She struggled against it, heading downstairs to make breakfast just as if it were any other morning. Except it wasn't. She was alone and the fridge held only an old heel of bread, some limp celery, and a carton of milk so out of date it had curdled. She winced at the sour smell and tossed it all in the trash before eating handfuls of dry cereal straight from the container.

She would go to the grocery store. This was something to do, something that needed to be done. It was better than sitting at home and brooding. Better than going to the studio. She'd had to lay off Kyle last week—too many sittings had been cancelled and there were no new orders to fill. Tania had stopped coming to the studio of her own accord. Even the bereavement photog-raphy had ended; the organization had dropped Jill from its rolls.

She was aware of a new patrolman in the car at the end of the drive as she backed out. He raised the car radio to his mouth as she drove off, and she knew that he was calling to tell someone that she had left the house. Were they tailing her? She checked in the rearview mirror multiple times as she drove to her local store, but she couldn't tell.

The parking lot at the grocery store was filling up, unusual for so early in the morning, but then she checked the date on her phone and understood. Thanksgiving shopping; the last weekend before the holiday and people were trying to beat the rush. She'd had plans for the holiday once; it seemed like someone else's life, but that had been her less than a month ago. She pushed her cart slowly down the aisles, feeling strangely detached. As she tried to focus on choosing a head of lettuce she caught a woman staring and whispering to the man next to her. She left the lettuce and moved on to another aisle.

There was a line at the deli and as Jill waited her turn she caught more strange looks and saw people nudging one another and whispering. When they called her number, she raised her hand, but the deli man just stared at her for a long moment, accusation in his eyes.

"A half pound of turkey breast please," she said, staring right back at him, but her voice sounded high and abnormal. He finally turned to slice the turkey, but said something under his breath to one of the women behind the counter and she looked at Jill, too, with hatred in her eyes.

"Here." The man dangled the bag of turkey just out of reach and Jill had to lean forward to grab it. He got a nasty smile on his face, and she guessed he thought she'd killed her daughter even if he wouldn't come out and say it.

She threw the bag in her cart, anxious to go. She pushed on, grabbing milk and bread. She thought that they were almost out of Life cereal and Sophia really liked Life the best, and then Jill had to stop moving and clutch the cart because for a split second she'd forgotten, and the pain of Sophia's absence roared back.

"Mrs. Lassiter?"

A voice behind her made Jill jump, startling the woman who'd pushed a cart up against hers.

She looked familiar, but Jill couldn't place her. Young, short black hair, and wearing blue jeans and a T-shirt. The woman obviously saw her confusion and said, "I'm Liz Meyer, one of Sophia's preschool teachers."

"Oh, of course, I'm so sorry." Jill had lost her mind. How could she have failed to recognize this woman that she'd seen every day? "How are you?" She stretched out her hand to touch Liz's arm, but the other woman recoiled.

"What are you doing here?" she said, her sweet voice a hiss.

Jill's hand dropped. "The same thing you are." She pushed her cart away, but the other woman pursued her.

"You've got some nerve showing your face in public. You should be ashamed."

Other shoppers turned to stare. Jill stared

straight ahead, moving faster toward the checkout.

"What did you do to her?" Liz demanded, pushing her cart alongside Jill's. "I know you killed her just like you killed your son."

Jill abandoned her cart and any pretense of shopping. She hurried toward the exit, Liz in pursuit. "You can't run away!" the woman called. "We know what you did!"

Jill held back the tears until she was alone in the car. Her cell phone, switched to silent, vibrated in her pocket. It was David calling; she didn't answer. She didn't want to talk to him. At that moment, she wasn't sure she'd want to talk to him ever again. She squeezed her eyes shut, leaning back against the headrest. Then all at once she sat up. She knew who she did want to talk to.

Shadyside early Saturday morning was filled with joggers and thirtysomething women wheeling young children to coffee shops in expensive strollers. Jill turned off Walnut onto a parallel street, following the house numbers until she found 113.

She had to circle the block a few times to find parking, and it started to snow, a few tiny flakes, as she made her way back to the redbrick apartment building. She ducked under the faded black awning and scanned the names posted next to the buzzers, and there it was in small letters in the slot for Apt. 8B: MONROE.

It hadn't been hard to find the address—Google was an amazing thing. She was about to buzz when an old woman dragging a laundry cart struggled out the door. Jill held it open for her and slipped inside. There was no doorman and no one else waiting for the elevator. She rode up to the eighth floor and headed down a dimly lit, carpeted hallway. Faint smells slipped under the doors—fried onions, dryer sheets, wet dog. She pressed the small black buzzer at 8B, taking pleasure in holding it down. There was a peep-hole in the door. Jill turned sideways, so her face was obscured. After a moment she heard a chain being released and the door opened a crack.

"Yes?" Leslie Monroe peeked around the corner of the door, wearing nothing but a terrycloth robe. Her feet were bare, her blonde hair tousled.

"Late night, Leslie?" Jill asked and slammed the door open, pushing past the other woman into the apartment.

"Ow!" Leslie Monroe pressed a hand to her forehead where the door had hit her. "What the hell are you doing?"

"Where is she?" Jill poked her head in the first door, but it was just a powder room. She yanked open a door on her left and a pair of snow boots fell out.

"What do you want? You can't just come barging in here!" Leslie hurried after her, one hand clutching the robe at the neck.

"Sophia!" Jill called. She turned back to Leslie. "I know you took my daughter, where is she?" She stalked past the small kitchen and into an empty bedroom, dropping to her knees to check under the bed and pushing aside clothes in the closet before moving on.

"There's no one else here," Leslie protested, but Jill ignored her, ducking into the second bedroom across the hall. Clearly the master—the bed was unmade, covers thrown back as if Leslie Monroe had just gotten out of it. There was no one there, not in the small walk-in closet or the full bathroom.

Jill strode back out to the living room with the other woman right behind her, checking behind the drawn living room curtains and looking out at the small balcony.

"You're David's wife," Leslie Monroe said with sudden recognition. "I saw you on TV."

Jill turned to confront her, breathing hard. "What did you do with her?"

"Do? I haven't done anything. I don't have your daughter."

"Have you hurt her? Did you kill her?"

"No, no, of course not! Look, the police spoke to me—I haven't seen your daughter."

"Sophia!" Jill called again.

"Listen, just calm down." Leslie held out a placating hand. "I swear to you—I haven't even seen your daughter, much less hurt her."

Jill pressed a hand against her head. She'd been so sure that Sophia was there, that this woman had taken her. Leslie Monroe backed away from her toward the kitchen.

"I need some coffee—do you want a cup?" she said, bumping into the kitchen counter and edging around it to get into the kitchen without turning her back to Jill, who was suddenly aware of how crazy she must look. Unwashed hair scraped back into a ponytail, faded jeans, an oversize old sweater with one sleeve unraveling.

She dropped into a chair, and Leslie took this as assent and poured Jill a cup of coffee. "Do you take cream or sugar?"

Jill shook her head.

"Here we go." Leslie carried two mugs out of the kitchen and offered one to Jill.

Was that supposed to be a fair exchange, Jill wondered. Her husband for a cup of coffee? She took the cup, staring hard at the other woman, who flushed and looked away, sitting down in a chair that left some distance between them. She adjusted the tie on her robe again and ran a hand over her thick mane of blonde hair, smoothing it.

She was a voluptuous woman, late thirties, with ample breasts, big eyes, and full, pouty lips. It was easy to see why men found her attractive. "I'm sorry about your daughter," she said. "I heard about it on the news."

"The police said you have an alibi for the night of her disappearance," Jill said, staring her in the eye. She'd thought this would be hard, but anger had displaced any awkwardness.

"I was in Chicago," the other woman said, adding, "on business," as if Jill might have thought otherwise.

"How long have you been screwing my husband?" The words poured out of Jill's mouth before she had time to think about them.

Caught in the middle of taking a sip, Leslie Monroe spluttered and coffee spilled down her chin in a messy trickle. "We're not, that is, we're not anymore." Leslie Monroe was one of those people who blush completely and unattractively, a fiery color starting at her ears and throat and spreading across her entire face.

Jill waited, staring at the other woman, while Leslie Monroe's blue-green eyes darted away from her, seeking anywhere else to settle. "Did you have sex in my bed?"

The blush deepened. "No. Never. I wouldn't do that."

"So seducing another woman's husband is enough for you?" Jill found it exhilarating to be so direct.

The other woman frowned, and Jill suddenly saw the wrinkles around her eyes and mouth, and the harsh lines that age had carved on either side of her nose. Someone had forgotten her Botox.

"I didn't seduce anybody; David approached *me*."

"Did you know he was married?"

"So what if I did?" Leslie Monroe tossed her head a little, her hair falling forward to reveal darker roots. "That's his problem, not mine."

You bitch, Jill thought. Her hands gripped the coffee cup and she had to breathe for a minute to maintain her equilibrium. "When did it start?"

The other woman waved her hand in the air as if this was completely unimportant. "I don't know. Three years ago? Four? It doesn't matter; it's over."

"Where did you meet?"

"My place or hotels." Her lips curved slightly. "I've always enjoyed room service."

"If it's over why did you meet him for lunch last month?"

Leslie sighed and glanced at the clock. "A client referral. I'm a lawyer, too, but I'm sure the police told you that."

"Did you have sex last month?"

She laughed, startling Jill. "In the dining room at The Carlton? Credit me with a little more discretion."

"Why did the relationship end?"

"Why don't you ask him?"

"I'm asking you."

She sighed again. "It's over—move on, I'm sure he has."

"What does that mean?"

"It means I'm sure he's got some other woman now, so why don't you go question her."

"Did he tell you that?"

Leslie Monroe rolled her eyes. She took a sip of coffee before answering. "Look, once a cheater always a cheater. All men stray—fidelity is not part of their nature. I'm sure David has had affairs with other associates at his firm; he isn't the only one."

Jill's mind reeled. Multiple affairs? Could he really have cheated repeatedly without her finding out? What if another woman, angry with David or jealous of his married life, took Sophia? "Who are the other women?"

Leslie shook her head. "I don't know—he wouldn't talk to me about something like that, it's not polite."

Great to know that whores had standards. Jill gritted her teeth. "Someone took my daughter— if you're right and David had multiple affairs, then it could be one of those other women."

Leslie gave her a half smile. "Like I told the police, I don't know who else David was seeing, I just know that his firm had a lot of extra-curricular activity."

"I need names."

The other woman laughed. "I can't give you any. I don't work for Adams Kendrick, remember?"

"But you've worked with them—who are the other women?"

"Oh, God, I don't know." Leslie Monroe put her cup down on the glass coffee table next to an issue of *Cosmo* and sat back in her chair. "There was that skinny front desk girl—Karen somebody? I know she was with someone, but I don't think she's David's type. There was a young associate—Lisa? Lee? Something like that. She was a hot little number; I'm sure he noticed. David's always had an eye for pretty things, but I'm sure you know that."

She stood up, stretching a little like a cat. "I don't know what more you want from me. Details? David's good in bed, he likes to give and receive oral pretty equally. Is that what you want to know?"

Jill felt her own face getting hot and the other woman saw it and smiled, a nasty little smile with plump lips parting to reveal capped teeth.

"Doesn't he do that with you? Well, he does like to hear some response."

Jill's grip on her self-control suddenly loosened along with the hand gripping the mug. She threw the cup of coffee in the other woman's face and walked out.

Chapter Thirty-two

Day Twenty-Three

A tour bus returning from a casino had gone over the side of a mountain road in West Virginia, and the grisly accident scene was being featured on every station. Bea rapidly switched through the channels, frustrated to discover that the disappearance of Sophia Lassiter was no longer top news. Damn reporters! Hyenas, all of them, their limited attention spans drawn away by fresh kill.

She had to wait through five more stories before they finally did a piece on the missing child. "Tension is high in Pittsburgh on the twenty-third day since three-year-old Sophia Lassiter vanished from her parents' Fox Chapel home."

Tension. That was all? She'd practically gift-wrapped this case for the police; she didn't understand why they hadn't made an arrest. Bea switched the TV off in disgust. If she and Avery had to be out of this house before the end of the month then she had to do something else, make the final move.

The real-estate agent had called last night to tell her the date for the inspection. "You're welcome to be there, of course, but it will probably be easier if you and your husband could arrange to be out of the house that morning." Oh, she'd *arrange* to be out of the house. She'd *arrange* to be gone for good well before the inspection.

It was early afternoon, Avery's usual naptime. Bea paced from the living room to the second bedroom, trying to move quietly, before settling in front of a DVD to watch, for the umpteenth time, as her daughter ran around in that small yard they'd had when she was young, jumping through a sprinkler, face radiant in the way that only little kids could look. Before life disappointed them.

"We were happy then, weren't we?" Frank had slipped in to take the seat next to her. He laid his arm along the back of her chair, letting his hand lightly cup her shoulder, but it felt more like a restriction than a comfort. She shifted in her seat, trying to lose herself in the past, but she couldn't relax. She'd been unsettled since the visit from the real-estate agent. Patsy Duckworth had been a little too interested in Avery. What if she'd recognized her? If the police came to the house again they'd do a more thorough search—there was no easy way to explain the outside bolt on the bedroom in the basement. They had to move, but what would she do with the child if they went back to Florida? How could she go back to the hospital full-time when she had Avery to look after? Day care cost a fortune; there was no way she could afford that plus rent on a condo.

"I tried to tell you," Frank said, and for once he

didn't sound superior, just sad. She pressed a hand to her head, which was throbbing, while her daughter danced silently on the screen in the little ruffled blue bathing suit that Bea could remember buying for her years ago. Strange how the past was so clear now, memories rushing at her vivid and intense, while things that had happened more recently—the years alone with Frank, for instance—were fading into obscurity, a blur of sensation.

She'd tried so hard to make things right. She'd wanted to be a perfect mother, working hard to give her daughter the opportunities she'd never had, but somehow she'd alienated her only child in the process.

And what of the child asleep downstairs? When she'd found Avery, the only thing Bea could think of was how this was her chance. Her second chance. An apology of sorts and a redo button. But life didn't give you any redos, there was only the now. She had to move, that was a given. Except she couldn't go without seeing the Lassiters arrested. It wasn't fair. She'd done all this work, she'd come this far, and for what? To have them fall into that limbo of so many parents of missing children, held under suspicion, certainly, but never having to pay for their sins? It wasn't enough, not nearly enough.

Bea left Frank watching the video and went down to the basement. She tiptoed past the bedroom door, which she'd left open a crack, a concession to Cosmo, who liked to be free to come and go, but had taken to curling up against the child when she slept. The little dog lifted his head and looked at her quizzically, but didn't bark. Bea donned latex gloves before pulling a bag from the closet. She carried it upstairs and spread paper towels on the kitchen table before opening the bag. In it was a dish towel and wrapped inside was a knife with a long, sharp blade. It was an expensive item. German steel, very thin. The kind of knife that people with money bought at overpriced cooking stores. She'd found it in the draining rack in the Lassiters' kitchen.

She considered the knife while she waited for the blood to thaw, feeling the heft of it in her hand, before testing its feather-thin blade against an orange. It sliced through the rind cleanly, with only the faintest pressure. This was the last remaining item that she'd taken, this and the used dish towel. Both likely had usable fingerprints on them. If this didn't work, then nothing would.

She coated the blade with the child's blood, smearing it over the carbon steel before dabbing more onto the wood handle, pleased when she saw a fingerprint suddenly outlined. She wiped the blade down roughly with more paper towels; it looked like someone had done a fast cleanup. With most of the blood gone she fetched a

338

Ziploc bag of the child's hair and carefully adhered a few blonde strands to the blade, and then she rewrapped the knife in the original dish towel and put the bundle back in the plastic bag.

Where could she plant it? That was the big question. There was no way she could get back in the Lassiter house without getting caught. David's office? Too many people. She sat at the kitchen table resting her head in her hands, mentally running through all possible alternatives. This was her last big move, the final, decisive play that would bring closure. "Where can I put it?" she said out loud, calling on her daughter for help. Her angel would help her; she always had. Bea closed her eyes, picturing her daughter's smiling face, and just like that, she knew where to go.

Bea hummed as she changed into a church lady's polyester dress and the brown wig, before heading back downstairs and prepping a syringe. She tiptoed into the child's bedroom. Avery lay curled in a ball on the bed, fast asleep. Cosmo growled softly as Bea gently tugged one arm down and placed the syringe on the soft inner skin. The child suddenly rolled, some of the drug spilling from the needle onto the sheet. Bea cursed. How much had she lost? She held the hypodermic up in the dim light from the window, trying to see. It would have to be enough; the child was stirring. She quickly tugged the child's arm back down, bracing for the initial jerk as the needle slid inside. The child's blue eyes flew open and Avery stared at Bea for a moment, alarmed, before her eyes rolled back in her head. Bea released her arm gently and walked out without bothering to tiptoe, pulling the heavy door closed behind her. Cosmo could stay with the child; if she happened to wake, the dog would comfort her.

She was still humming as she backed out of the garage, the bag with the knife on the seat beside her.

The tears came again as Jill drove away from Leslie Monroe's, hot, angry tears that she brushed away with her hands, determined not to break down. She would not cry over that stupid bitch; she refused. Had Leslie been telling the truth about David? Had he really slept with other women as well? If David *had* cheated with other women then why hadn't the police mentioned it? Wouldn't they have uncovered that in their investigation?

Her phone buzzed as a text came in from him: *Stopping by home to get some boxes to clean out office; partners suggest an "indefinite leave of absence."* Code for being fired. So the firm wasn't immune to the court of public opinion; apparently Andrew's support only went so far. Jill wondered if the rest of the partners knew about David's infidelity and whether that had played any part in the decision. For a moment she felt angry on his behalf and sorry for him, too, but then another text came in: *Talk when I get there?* Trying to take advantage of the moment to win her sympathy. She ignored the text. She didn't want to see him—not like this, not now. She needed to talk to Andrew first; he would tell her the truth about David, she'd force it out of him. He didn't answer his cell phone, so she drove straight to his home.

There were no cars in the driveway at the Grahams'. Jill parked in front of the first bay in the three-car garage and marched to the front door. She rang the bell and heard the complicated chime. Silence. She heard the noise of an airplane, but couldn't see it through a hanging curtain of heavy clouds. It was so cold. She shivered and rang the bell a second time. Again the ridiculous peal of bells. Where were they? It was early Saturday morning, wasn't somebody home?

At last she saw a shadow coming through the glass, and then one of the Graham boys opened the door wide, barefoot and dressed in a soccer uniform, a piece of toast in his hand.

"Hi," Jill said. "Is your father home?"

He shook his head and took a bite of toast, crunching loudly. "Who is it, Jamie?" Paige came down the center staircase behind him. Even in a hurry she walked like the pageant queen she'd once been, descending the stairs as if she were arriving at a debutante ball.

She looked picture-perfect, too, even casually dressed in jeans and a sweater. "Jill?" She sounded wary, and instead of ushering Jill in she pulled her son back. She poked her head out the door, looking quickly right and left as if afraid that some neighbor might be watching.

"I need to see Andrew," Jill said.

"Oh, I am sorry, honey, but Drew's not here. He's gone into work. You know how lawyers are—even weekends are billable hours." She laughed, a light, twinkly sound that held more relief than humor, and started to close the door.

Jill put her hand against it. "When will he be back?"

"Not until late." Paige pushed against the door. "I'm sorry, Jill, but I've got to take the boys to soccer," she said, adding to her son, "Jamie, go get your cleats on." She gave Jill a tight smile before closing the door in her face.

Despite the cold, Jill felt hot with embarrassment as she walked back to her car. Anger warred with the shame; why should she care what Paige Graham thought of her? Had she really expected Miss Perfect to react differently than everyone else?

She backed out of their driveway, pulling over at the end of the street to try Andrew's cell again. Straight to voice mail. As she sat there trying to decide what to do, Paige drove screaming past in her Mercedes SUV. On impulse, Jill followed her over a familiar network of hilly, narrow roads to end up at the playing field where she'd gone so many times with Sophia. A game was just ending and the field and parking lot next to it were crowded with parents and children. Jill parked illegally on the shoulder, waiting until Paige had gotten her sons out of the car and onto the field before she ran across the hard grass to confront her.

"—can barely keep up with all their activities," Paige was complaining to another mother when Jill touched her arm. She swung around, and at any other time the dumbfounded expression on her face would have made Jill laugh.

"What are you doing here?" Paige said, taking a step back as if Jill had a virus.

"You know what happened at the police station, don't you?" There was something in Paige's gaze and the way it darted away. Jill persisted, "Did you know about David?"

Paige looked embarrassed. "For heaven's sake, Jill, this is not the time or the place—"

"I need to know."

They were attracting attention. Mothers had stopped watching their kids running around the field and turned their way. One woman held a Starbucks cup poised at her lips, looking from Jill to Paige and back again as if they were the better sporting event.

Paige was nothing if not keenly aware of

attention. "Not here," she said through a clenched smile, and stomped toward the parking lot. Jill followed. Paige didn't stop until they were on the far side of the lot, out of sight behind some cars, where she whirled around, arms crossed. "I can't believe you came here," she said, the veneer of Southern hospitality giving way like soft wood to reveal the rot underneath. "Nobody wants you here; they don't trust you around their children."

"I went to see Leslie Monroe," Jill said.

"Who?" Paige asked, but she'd stiffened at the name.

"I know you know who that is. What else did Andrew tell you? Leslie Monroe told me that David had multiple affairs. Is that true?"

A crow cawed like a woman's high-pitched scream. Paige looked in its direction, then back at Jill. "I think you should talk to David about that."

"He's moved out."

Paige frowned a little, her smooth forehead marred by a little V between her eyes. "When's he coming back?"

"I don't know. I don't know if I want him back," Jill said, and when she saw the slightest glimmer of pity in Paige's eyes she used it. "Please tell me—I need to know the truth."

"I don't want to be responsible for ruining a marriage," Paige said in a prim voice.

Jill gave a short, bitter laugh. "David's done that all by himself."

Paige sighed. "All right, I'll tell you, but then I want you to leave." She waited for Jill's nod of agreement. "Okay, this is what happened. Several years ago I went to meet Andrew at work. My sister took the kids unexpectedly, and I thought I'd surprise him, take him out to dinner, you know."

Get to the point, Jill thought, but only nodded, afraid to say anything to stop the other woman.

"It was late. All the secretaries were gone, of course, but no one else was around either. Just a few of the office lights were on. David's office was one of them, but the door was open and he wasn't in there. I continued down the hall to Drew's office, but he wasn't in there. I thought maybe he was working in the firm's library, so I kept going. I was a little nervous—it was so dark in the hallway. I saw some light coming from under the door to the library, so I tapped on the door and heard someone say, 'Come in.' I pushed open the door and that's when I saw her."

"Who?" Jill said, confused.

"One of the first-years. I recognized her. She was lying on one of the tables and she was completely, well, naked." Paige lowered her voice on the last word, leaning toward Jill. She whispered the rest: "Not a stitch of clothing, legs spread wide, a come-hither smile on her face, until she realized it was me. She screamed and bolted up, trying to cover herself and I screamed, too, and just turned tail and ran."

"But what does that have to do with David?"

"She was expecting *him,*" Paige said. "Apparently they met there regularly—it turned out that my husband wasn't even in the building, he was just covering for your husband because David had asked him to."

"Andrew knew David was having an affair with one of the associates?" Jill felt sick.

"No, not that it was an associate. He knew that David was meeting someone—he'd overheard him on the phone, apparently, and David had confided in him and asked him not to say anything."

Jill felt slimy just hearing the story, as if she'd been the one to fuck a colleague. "You said years. This was several years ago?"

Paige nodded, shivering from the brisk wind blowing through the lot.

"But why didn't Andrew tell me? Why didn't you?"

"Do you really think I would call a woman up and tell her such a sordid little story? To what end? I knew you two were already having problems, this was not too long after, well, you know."

"After Ethan's death."

Paige winced at his name. "Yes." Her gaze flitted away from Jill's, then back. "Andrew was

346

furious when he found out it was an associate. He said David could have lost his job and could have cost Andrew his job, too, for covering up for him. I know he talked to David and David agreed that he'd never see the woman again. Of course, the firm got rid of her, too."

A referee's shrill whistle made them both flinch and Paige's face hardened. "I've told you everything I know," she said. "I'm going to go watch my son's game and you're going to leave before someone calls the police." She stalked back toward the field without saying good-bye.

"What was her name?" Jill called after her.

Paige turned, but kept walking. "It doesn't matter, Jill, it was a long time ago and she left the firm soon after that."

Jill ran after her. "You said you recognized her—what was her name?"

Paige hesitated. "Lyn," she said finally. "Lyn Galpin."

Chapter Thirty-three

Journal—October 2011

I waited outside the office yesterday in the cold. By the time you finally appeared my body had started to go numb and I couldn't move for a moment, mesmerized by the sight of you laughing and talking, a hint of red silk tie visible at the top of your wool dress coat. You were talking to someone I vaguely remembered, another lawyer, but I didn't really register her face, not at first. I was too busy looking at you, D.

I saw the little double take you tried to hide when I stepped directly in your path. Your eyes, which had once raked over my body with desire, now looked right through me. You wore the blank look that one reserves for waiters or other service people—the maid who cleans your hotel room, the valet who fetches your car. It was then that I finally realized what should have been obvious all along. I was just one more of these people in your life. I was of no more consequence, and just as replaceable.

Even as I write this you are probably in bed with that new version of me. Does she look at you with that same mixture of yearning and desire to please? You described me once as the American version of a geisha, and I was stupid enough to take it as a compliment.

But I'm not nearly so complacent. The idea of a short-term arrangement existed in your mind, not mine. You'll laugh, but I believed that you truly loved me. You never told me that these declarations were limited to three-hour time slots on particular afternoons or weekends.

I didn't really realize until that day on the street. I didn't want to know. Ridiculous when you think about it—how deluded not to realize that your lack of phone calls and visits since the birth were because you lost interest, not because you were keeping our secret safe.

I dressed up, did you even notice? It took just over eleven long months to lose the extra pounds, but I did it. I chose a dress you always liked, the blue one that hugs my hips just so. It was so cold, but I left my coat open so you could see it.

If you'd smiled at me, acknowledged me in any way, I wouldn't have gone home and torn that dress off my body. I wouldn't have cried you out of my system, shoving that dress high on a closet shelf and knocking loose a folder I'd hidden away.

There's so much paperwork in any legal trans-action; pages fluttered to the floor like doves settling in to rest. The thing that jumped out at me was my signature over all the adoption agency's pages. My signature, not yours. Where your name should have been was a single typed word: Unknown.

And that's when I knew that the someone I was missing wasn't you.

Chapter Thirty-four
Day Twenty-Three

A lot had changed in the last few weeks. Bea circled the street, pretending to search for house numbers, but she needn't have bothered. The only vehicle on Wakefield Drive was a single patrol car parked outside the Lassiter house, and the middle-aged officer behind the wheel didn't look up from his newspaper. No more news vans and clamoring groups of reporters. The bus accident had lured all of them away, but they'd be back. She'd see to that.

Someone was home; the BMW sat in the driveway. As Bea circled back, the front door suddenly opened and David Lassiter stepped out carrying a couple of boxes and an overstuffed briefcase. She watched as he tossed both into the trunk of the car.

What did that mean? Had he moved out of the house? Bea drove to the end of the street and pulled to the side of the road, thinking. Seconds later, the BMW came tearing by, kicking up a cloud of leaves, and Bea held her cell phone to her ear and turned her head away as it passed. She waited a second and pulled out after it, careful to stay two car lengths behind. David Lassiter turned onto Route 28 heading toward downtown Pittsburgh, and she struggled not to lose him in multilane, fast-moving traffic. It was only twenty minutes later, when he took the North Shore exit, that she realized where he was heading.

The parking garage next to the office tower that housed Adams Kendrick was virtually empty on a Saturday, but David zipped past all the open spots, pulling into one when he'd reached the seventh floor, the level with a walkway across to the office building. Bea idled halfway up the floor below, then drove past his car, climbing up a level and pulling into a spot where she could look down at the floor where he'd parked. David Lassiter had his back to her, digging into the trunk of his car. She waited until he stepped through the walkway door, stuffed briefcase in one hand, box in another, before starting her car again. She pulled into a spot close to his and waited again, listening to the engine pop and ping. Nobody passed. She slipped on her gloves and dug the copy of the key out of her purse. As Bea walked to his car she heard footsteps, someone approaching, and she quickly turned back to her sedan. A young woman passed, high heels clicking on concrete, yawning as she approached a compact car ten feet away. Bea watched until she'd driven off, looking up and down the length of the garage before approaching David Lassiter's car again. She opened the driver's side and popped the latch to the trunk. Empty except for a cardboard box. Bea shifted it over and tugged at a corner of the floor mat, lifting it just enough to slip the knife underneath.

"Hey! What are you doing?"

Bea jerked upright, slamming her head against the raised lid. "Hey, you!" David Lassiter was coming toward her, frown on his face, carrying a full box in his arms. She slammed the lid shut and ran to her own car, fumbling for her keys.

"Stop!" He dropped the box, cardboard splitting as it hit the ground, books and papers exploding onto the dirty concrete. He ignored it, running at her as Bea lurched into the car and slammed the lock button. His fist punched the rear of the car and she jumped.

"Damn it!" She forced the key in the ignition, but he was at the driver's-side door, pulling on the handle.

"Stop! Who are you?" He had an iPhone out; he held it up to the window.

"Shit!" The motor turned over and Bea put the car in reverse, stepping on the gas. The car leapt back, dragging David Lassiter with it. He held onto the driver's door, banging on her window, as she jerked the gearshift into drive, but he still wouldn't let go, running alongside her as she increased her speed, heading down the ramp. He would have to let go; she would make him. She turned the corner hard and dislodged him. He stumbled back, just as another car came speeding up the ramp. It was too late for David Lassiter to react, too late for the other driver to brake. The front fender of the oncoming car hit him hard, sending him flying backward as if his body were weightless. Bea kept driving; behind her she heard brakes squeal and something land with a heavy thud.

David's cell phone went straight to voice mail. Jill struggled to sound calm: "Are you still at the house? We need to talk—I'll be there soon."

She wanted to catch him off guard with the information, she wanted to see his face when she said Lyn Galpin's name, but when she pulled into the garage his car was gone.

"He was here about forty minutes ago," the older patrolman said when she walked to the end of the driveway to ask him, looking up from the paper to glance at the watch digging into his pudgy, freckled arm. Jill thanked him, walked back to the house. The study door was uncharacteristically open, as was the glass lid on one of the antique barrister bookcases. It was as if David no longer cared about anything except getting in and out as quickly as possible. She shook with leftover adrenaline, slamming the lid to the bookcase down, pleased when she saw a hairline crack appear in the glass.

She punched the redial button on her phone. It

rang only once before she heard David's smooth voice. "David Lassiter isn't available right now. . . ."

She could barely control the tremor in her own. "I know about the other women, David. I know about Lyn Galpin, you bastard." Except she didn't know, not really. She knew nothing about this woman—did the police? She started to dial Detective Ottilo's number, stopped. They wouldn't care, not when they were convinced that she'd killed her own daughter. But this Lyn woman could have taken Sophia. Except she didn't want Sophia, she wanted David. What if she'd killed Sophia? It was unlikely, just as unlikely as Leslie Monroe. Jill tried to convince herself of that even as she began searching the study for something, anything, related to Lyn Galpin.

She had to find her, to know. No matter how illogical it was, this was the only thing Jill had—there were no other leads. She yanked open every desk drawer, sweeping things off the surface and dumping files out on the floor. There was nothing, no mention of other women, no secret stash of business cards or withered collection of cocktail napkins with inked phone numbers bleeding into the paper. No scribbled messages: *Call me.* There were no love letters, no receipts for jewelry that she'd never received or trips she hadn't known he'd taken. There was nothing, absolutely nothing, and yet she kept hearing Paige's whisper, *"She was expecting him. Not a stitch of clothing."*

She sat down in his leather chair and plugged in the desktop computer the police had returned. David obviously hadn't touched it since. She tried to open his email, but hit a block. She'd always thought he was careful because of work, but had it really been to hide another life? It took several more minutes, but eventually she found a neatly typed list of passwords tucked away in the far back of a bottom desk drawer. She searched his mail and other files, but there was no mention of a Lyn Galpin. She did find Leslie Monroe's initials on his online calendar, which only spurred her to keep searching.

She tore law books from the shelves and opened them, shaking their pages for anything hidden between, but one after the other came up empty. She let them fall to the floor until she was wading through mess. There was nothing, absolutely nothing. She sank back down in the desk chair and surveyed the chaos she'd created, defeated except for a bitter satisfaction at knowing just how much David would despise seeing his precious study torn apart.

The cursor on the screen blinked on and off. On a whim, she opened a search engine, typed in Lyn Galpin's name. It took a few seconds, the little icon spinning, before a series of articles appeared, one after another.

LYN GALPIN CHARGED WITH DUI MANSLAUGHTER
LOCAL ATTORNEY CHARGED IN DEATHS OF FOUR
NO TRIAL FOR GALPIN ANYTIME SOON

"What the hell?" Jill clicked on link after link, scanning articles. Could this really be the same Lyn Galpin who Paige had told her about? Yes, there it was, buried in one of the first articles, a mention that she'd started her career at Adams Kendrick. Only she hadn't stayed there; she'd left the firm for reasons unknown and ended up at a small firm in Butler County. Later had come this terrible accident. December, two years ago. Jill remembered it vaguely, there'd been lots of news coverage, but she'd been busy with work and the upcoming holidays. It had been only their second Christmas with Sophia, the first one where she was walking and really engaged with what was happening. Jill remembered the happiness of that year, but also the bittersweet feeling that came with every milestone. The joy in watching Sophia grow sometimes made her miss Ethan even more. How had David been around that time? Had he acted any differently? He had to have known about this; he had to remember this woman. Unless Leslie Monroe was right and Lyn Galpin had been just one in a string of women and none of them meant anything at all.

Jill fought another wave of nausea. How could she have missed the signs? She thought of the times she'd come upon David texting and how he'd hurriedly hide his phone and how there'd been so many days when he'd call last-minute to say he had to work late. Everything seemed suspect now. She googled images of Lyn Galpin and pictures flooded the screen—a sweet face, pretty in an ordinary sort of way. Her long blonde hair was her best feature. Is that what had attracted David? Leslie Monroe also had blonde hair. Was that the look he preferred? In which case, why had he married a brunette? She flicked through page after page, looking at static images and then footage of the accident caused by this second woman who'd had sex with her husband. Eye-witnesses and at least one member of the media had taped the accident—there were multiple variations on YouTube. A real winner, Lyn Galpin —obviously driving drunk, her car weaving in and out of traffic.

Many of the articles speculated about her alcoholism, and how that had played a part in her professional slide. They bordered on libel, as did the tabloid headlines: DRUNK DOPE RUINS CHRISTMAS and LONELY LAWYER'S SELFISH DECISION. The tragedy had been picked up by the national news—a good-looking woman accused of killing five people. Jill jumped as the doorbell pealed, then pealed again, and someone pounded loudly with the knocker. The patrolman stood huffing on the front step, doughy face creased with concern.

"Is it Sophia?" she demanded. "Have they found her?"

He shook his head. "It's your husband. There's been an accident."

Bea slowed just a fraction as she exited the parking garage, afraid of getting pulled over for speeding. Her adrenaline was still high, pushing her heart into overdrive. Stupid! Stupid! She banged the steering wheel, furious at herself for getting caught. He'd seen her and, worse, he'd probably taken her picture. But she was disguised. Bea touched her wig for reassurance. His phone had probably been crushed along with him anyway, so it didn't matter.

She headed back home through the crowded streets of the Strip District, filled with Saturday shoppers visiting wholesale fishmongers and old-school butchers and stocking up on imported pasta and cheese at Pennsylvania Macaroni. Beyond these streets, the crowds thinned, gave way to businesses deserted on the weekends. When she spotted what had to be one of the city's last remaining phone booths, she pulled over, struck by an idea. As she stepped out of the car, her heart rate suddenly surged and her legs turned to jelly beneath her. She plopped back down in the seat, coins dropping from her hand onto the dirty ground. Her pulse was more erratic than she thought. Despite the cold air rushing at her, she felt hot, her scalp prickling under the wig, her body sweaty. For a moment it was as if all she could hear was the thud of her own heart fighting to find a steady beat. She struggled to pull off the wig and then she leaned back in the seat, fumbling to reach the glove compartment and her pills. The tablets rattled as she struggled to get the cap off. There weren't too many left; she'd have to get more. She stuck one under her tongue and waited for it to dissolve, waiting for the subsequent steadying of her heart rate while breathing like a drug addict waiting for a fix. Police sirens increased in the distance.

A minute slid by, then two. Impatient, she leaned down to scoop up the coins, and white spots exploded in front of her eyes. She clutched the door handle until the worst of the dizziness passed and then staggered over to the phone booth. Just before dropping the coins in the slot, she stopped and went back to the car to put on gloves. She wiped down the coins and what she'd touched of the booth before making the call.

"Police tip line." A bored, metallic voice.

"I saw David Lassiter—"

"Who?"

"David Lassiter. The one with the missing little

girl. I saw him hiding something in his car in a garage—"

"Slow down, ma'am, I'm having trouble understanding you."

The Plexiglas walls were scratched and covered with graffiti. Bea's breath fogged the FUCK YOU FUCKER! scrawled in purple Sharpie. "David Lassiter hid something in the trunk of his car—I saw him in a parking garage near Sixth Street and Penn Avenue."

"Did you see the make of the car?"

"Yes, it's a BMW. I didn't get all of the license, but I think the first letters are J, B, and C."

"Okay, got it. We'll pass it along. Can I have your name?"

Bea hung up the phone and crossed back to her car. She'd parked in a tow-away zone in front of an empty storefront with large FOR SALE signs yellowing in the window. Had anyone seen her? Would they remember if they had? Not that it mattered. No one would remember an older woman in a brown wig and shapeless, gray wool coat. People were attracted to shiny, pretty things; they ignored the ugly.

A police car lurched around a corner onto the road, lights flashing. Bea looked straight ahead, hands gripping the wheel as the siren wailed, but it screamed past without the driver so much as glancing in her direction. She smiled as she pulled the car back onto the empty road and sped away.

Chapter Thirty-five

Day Twenty-Three

The older patrolman became a maniac behind the wheel of the patrol car, his siren parting traffic like Moses at the Red Sea. Jill jumped out when he screeched to a stop in front of the emergency-room doors at Mercy Hospital, running inside and into chaos. Police officers milled around a waiting room crowded with patients, among them a man with a blood-soaked towel wrapped around his hand, a woman trying to soothe a screaming child, and an elderly man holding a leaking bag of ice to his leg while arguing with an obese young woman trying to help him into a wheelchair. Jill pushed through the crowd to the front desk.

"My husband was just brought in by ambulance. Lassiter, David Lassiter."

The harried-looking nurse shuffled through papers. "He's in surgery right now; they just took him back."

"Surgery? For what?"

"Mrs. Lassiter." A police officer she didn't recognize materialized at her elbow. "Your husband was hit by a car."

"Where? How did it happen? Is he going to be okay?"

"All I can tell you is that he sustained some pretty serious injuries," he said.

The nurse interrupted. "You can go to the waiting room, Mrs. Lassiter. Go out that door, take a left to go into the main entrance, then take the green elevators to three and follow the signs."

The hospital was confusing. She took two wrong turns before finding the waiting room. It was at least quieter than the emergency room, if only slightly less congested. The people waiting looked anxious or resigned. Some people stared blankly at the television monitor playing a talk show where an anorexic female host promoted a new book on weight loss. Others flipped through old issues of *Ladies' Home Journal* and *Sports Illustrated*.

Jill couldn't sit. She paced the room, looking from the clock to the large closed doors stamped HOSPITAL PERSONNEL ONLY. The patrolman who'd brought her appeared, sinking into a seat nearby. Jill got a cup of coffee from the high-tech machine in the corner, but couldn't take more than a few sips.

Thirty minutes passed, then an hour. People passed in and out of the doors, but no one for her. Had David died and they weren't telling her? The thought made her sick—she had to swallow hard a few times—and that feeling, in turn, gave her pause. She was so angry with him, so full of rage. If he'd been in front of her earlier in the day *she* could have run him over. She didn't want to care about him, her rational mind told her most definitely not to care, that he'd betrayed her and their marriage, but she couldn't ignore the fear that washed over her at the thought of losing him. No matter what he'd done, she couldn't simply stop loving him.

Just before the two-hour mark a woman in scrubs came through the doors from the inner sanctum, searching the room. "Mrs. Lassiter?"

Jill stepped forward. "How is he? Is he okay?"

The woman gave her a grim smile. "Your husband was hit full-on by a car. The trauma caused a pneumothorax—a collapsed lung, which we've repaired; and a severely fractured left arm and leg. He's also suffered a concussion, several cracked ribs, and some lacerations. He's critical, but stable."

Jill staggered and the doctor grabbed her arm to steady her. "Can I see him?"

"He's in recovery," the doctor said. "You can see him once we've moved him into a room."

When they finally gave her the room number, Jill practically ran to the elevators. She was surprised when a few police officers, including the patrolman who'd driven her, got on with her. She was even more surprised to see Detective Ottilo on the fifth floor. He flashed one of his enigmatic smiles. "Hello, Mrs. Lassiter."

She brushed past him into David's room, ignoring the patrolman stationed at the door. The shades were drawn and a doctor and several nurses surrounded the bedside. When one of them moved she saw David lying still and white against the bleached hospital sheets. For a moment she flashed to Ethan lying in his crib. But there were oxygen tubes protruding from David's nose, an IV attached to a vein in his hand, and a heart-rate monitor registering with steady beeps. He wasn't dead; he hadn't left her. She dropped her purse and coat on a chair, and a nurse moved aside so Jill could stand next to the bed.

David's skin looked unbelievably pale, except for the places where it was scratched and bruised, Rorschach inkblots of dark purple around his temple, left eye, and chin. His shirt had been removed, his chest was bandaged, and his left arm was in a cast. His left leg was in a longer cast and there were steel pins protruding from it. "Oh, David," Jill whispered, eyes watering.

"I'm sorry, but I need to check his vitals," the nurse said, touching her arm gently. Jill brushed a soft kiss on the only uninjured spot she could find on David's forehead and stepped out of the way. The nurse picked up a plastic bag on the tray table next to the bed and handed it to her. "Here are his things; you should hold on to them so they don't disappear." Jill looked in the bag and saw David's keys, cell phone, and wallet. His iPhone screen was cracked and the brown leather wallet was stained with what looked like blood.

"Mrs. Lassiter, if I could have a word." Detective Ottilo took her by the arm and steered her back into the hall.

Jill pulled free. "What is it? Can't you leave us alone for five minutes?" She looked away from his probing eyes back into the room, but the attention of the guard and other police officers was on her, and the nurses standing at their station several feet away were also watching, and she could see the suspicion in their eyes and something else—excitement?

"Where were you this morning?"

"Out." Jill looked back at the detective who continued to stand there, his calm just increasing her frustration. She added, "Visiting friends."

"Did you see your husband this morning?"

"No." Didn't he know that David wasn't living at home? Of course, he must. They had to have seen David carting his clothes out of the house. Jill wondered if there were police officers taking turns patrolling her in-laws' house.

"So you didn't make an arrangement with your husband to hide the knife?"

The question took her completely by surprise. "Knife? What knife? What are you talking about?"

"Mrs. Lassiter, your husband was hit by a car in

366

the parking garage next to Adams Kendrick. He was seen hiding something in the trunk of his car. That something turned out to be a knife."

"What knife? I don't understand."

"It had your fingerprints on it," Ottilo continued. "As well as traces of blood."

"This is crazy. I don't know anything about a knife."

"Analysis indicates that the blood type matches your daughter's."

She gaped at him. "Sophia's blood? Are you sure?"

"Jill Lassiter, at this time I'm arresting you for the murder of Sophia Lassiter," Ottilo said, and as if he'd been waiting for this moment, the uniformed cop on the chair behind him stood up, producing handcuffs.

"This is crazy." Jill looked from one to the other. "I don't know anything about a knife."

The patrolman reached for her arm and she stepped back just as an alarm began shrieking in David's room and a woman's calm, disembodied voice came over the paging system: "Code Blue, five, two eleven. Code Blue, five, two eleven."

Medical personnel came racing down the hall, one of them pushing a crash cart. Jill stepped to one side, Ottilo and the patrolman to the other. Jill couldn't see past the crowd around David's bed. A doctor barked orders that Jill couldn't understand. Someone shifted and she thought she caught a glimpse of a flat line across the heart-rate monitor.

"What's going on? Is it his heart?" Jill yelled at the nurse, but she didn't answer. Ottilo and the patrolman's focus had shifted to what was happening in the room, not Jill. In a split second, several thoughts raced rapid-fire through her mind: David could die, she would be arrested, and if those two things happened Sophia would never be found. At the same moment she saw a red exit sign glowing above the door to the stairwell at the end of the hall. Jill hadn't fully processed the final thought before she took off running.

Chapter Thirty-six
Day Twenty-Three

The dog didn't bark his usual greeting when Bea got home. No sound came from the child's room and Bea went straight upstairs, grateful for a reprieve. She poured a glass of wine, wishing she had something stronger, and collapsed on the couch, taking a healthy slug. It was cold inside. She rubbed her arms and pulled a blanket down around her. Was David Lassiter alive? Had they arrested him yet? The remote sat on top of the TV, but she was too tired to stand up and get it. She wanted nothing more than to sleep, but Avery would wake up soon and Bea would have to feed her and the dog. Why hadn't he barked? He should have been barking by now, scratching and pawing at the door to be let out.

Bea forced herself up from the couch and went back down to the basement. The bolt wasn't drawn across the door. Bea cursed. In her hurry to leave she'd obviously forgotten to lock it, but the child was still drugged, she couldn't have gotten out. She pushed the door open, silence rushing at her instead of the dog. Bea cried out when she saw the empty room.

She ran to the bed, running her hands over the

sheets as if she'd find the child hidden in the bedclothes, but what she felt was stickiness and she remembered the drug shooting from the needle, spilling out when Avery bumped her arm. She checked under the bed just in case, but the child was well and truly gone. And so was the dog.

Bea grabbed her coat and ran back upstairs. She spotted a chair pushed against the kitchen counter and an empty package of cookies left on the table, with crumbs smattering the surface and the floor. Maybe they were in the backyard. She opened the door and looked out, but she couldn't see anything except falling snow. And then she thought of how cold the house had felt and ran to the front door. It stood ajar.

Bea shuddered from the cold, staring down at the front steps and beyond to the driveway disappearing beneath the canopy of trees. How far could the child have gotten? She couldn't have been on the driveway when Bea came home or she would have seen her. Could she have gotten all the way down the dead-end street and on to the main road? "Avery?" she called as she hurried down the steps—called not screamed, nothing loud enough to make any inquisitive neighbor call the police.

Snow fell in small, hard flakes that blew in stinging bursts against Bea's face. Already it coated the steps and gravel driveway and clung to the dead grass and dry leaves. There were no footprints, no sign that the child had come this way, but Bea started down the driveway anyway, diverting periodically into the woods on either side to search, stumbling over tree roots as she lost most of the light coming from the gray, cloud-heavy sky. Her pulse was erratic—pounding one moment, fluttering the next.

"Avery?" she called again, but the wind stifled her cries. Light sifting through the trees created shadows. She thought she saw the child up ahead and hurried down the hill toward her, but there was no one there. What if a car had stopped to pick the child up, or worse, hadn't seen her in time to stop? Bea's mind tormented her with images of the child's bloody body lying on the road.

As she reached the end of the driveway, she saw something through the trees ahead. The yellow glow of a house light. The house down below, the one owned by the snowbird. No one was supposed to be there, but there was a light coming from an upstairs window. Had Avery seen the light, too?

Bea ran down the neighbor's road, which curved like hers through trees. It ended sooner, opening up to a big circular driveway, a grand entrance for a large brick colonial. Parked out front was a white sedan that looked dingy next to the purer white of the snow piling up on the hood. Lights were on all over the house, spilling from the windows onto the snow-covered yard. As Bea watched, a man passed by a front window and paused to stare out at the driveway. It was the old man she'd seen out walking, the one she suspected of calling the police. She ducked back into the woods and that's when she heard it. A bark. A single, short yip, but it was enough. She knew that sound. She stood still, listening hard. Another yip.

She scanned the property and spotted a shed tucked left of the house. Bea moved stealthily along the perimeter of the yard, staying close to the trees. The shed was large, but old, graying boards with traces of moss and algae around the rusted closure on the double doors. It wasn't locked; one door stood slightly ajar. Bea pushed it open and the dog rushed her, barking a warning.

"Cosmo! Stop it, Cosmo, it's me!" She hissed as she stepped inside, fending off the dog with her foot. The shed smelled of motor oil and fertilizer, the walls hung with garden tools surrounding a large riding lawn mower. Dim light poured through a cracked and rotting window frame that had long since lost its glass. Bea peered through the gloom. "Avery, where are you?" she called in a hushed singsong. Something moved in a corner and she spotted the child huddled near some bags of grass seed.

"There you are! Come here." Bea took a step forward, but the child shrank back, shivering so hard that Bea could hear her teeth chattering. She wasn't wearing a coat, but at least she'd managed to put on shoes. "Come on, now," Bea urged, moving farther into the shed. "We need to get you home."

She tried to smile, stretching out a hand, encouraged as Avery finally inched toward her. Just as Bea was about to grab her, the child darted left, clambering over the fat tire on the lawn mower to get out the other side of the shed's double door. It burst open at her push and Bea sprang after her, but the dog was faster, darting between her legs to follow at the child's heels, while wheeling back to bark at Bea.

She hissed, "Shush, Cosmo, stop barking!" But the dog wouldn't cooperate, baring its teeth and barking like crazy as the child slipped on the frost-slicked ground, and Bea made a wild lunge for her, managing to catch the back of her sweater.

"No, no, no!" the child screamed. Bea wrapped a hand around the child's mouth, but Avery bit her and she cursed, dropping her hand long enough for the child to scream again. Bea stifled her a second time, pulling her coat sleeve into the child's mouth to block her teeth.

Cosmo barked frantically and Bea kicked out at him, trying to silence the damn dog.

A sudden loud noise came from the house, a whoosh of a well-insulated door opening, and she heard a male voice call, "Who's out there?"

Bea ducked back inside the shed, pulling the child with her. "Who's there?" the voice called again. "You're trespassing!" The sound of gravel crunching. Bea brushed against a pair of wicked-looking pruning shears and caught them by the closed straight blades before they fell, still holding the child pressed tight against her chest. She could feel the small body convulsing, the tiny nostrils flaring, as the girl struggled to breathe. Bea held her own breath as the foot-steps moved even closer.

"What the hell?" The door creaked. He'd found the open shed; he was right outside. Bea breathed shallowly. "If you're in there, you'd better come out! I've got a gun!"

She pressed her back against the cold boards, heart thudding in her ears. What should she do? What *could* she do? She pictured Frank shaking his head, urging her to give up. Years of resent-ment spurred her on. There had to be another move. She set Avery on her feet, releasing her. The little girl ran forward, Cosmo running out after her.

"What on earth?" the man exclaimed.

"I wanna go home!" Avery cried.

"Where did you two come from?"

Bea crept to the edge of the door gripping the handle of the shears. She was less than five feet from him, close enough to see the stooped posture of old age, the liver spots on his bare, bald head. He didn't notice her there in the shadows to his left; his focus was entirely on the child and the dog. He was quite old, with a tremor in his voice that suggested Parkinson's, and the shuffling gait of someone worried about breaking a hip. She could see a glint of silver in his hand—the muzzle of a gun. "It's okay," he said to Avery, beckoning with his other hand, "I won't hurt you." But when Avery took his hand, Cosmo ran at the old man, barking aggressively.

Startled, he stepped sideways too fast and lost his balance. As he fell backward, the old man put his hands out to catch himself and the gun went off, a boom loud enough to make everyone flinch and stop the dog barking.

"Stop!" Ottilo's surprised shout came as Jill reached the stairwell door. She pushed through it and hurtled down the stairs. She raced down three levels and burst through the door onto the second floor. Fortunately, nobody was in the corridor at that end. She walked quickly but quietly down the hall, smoothing her hair and trying to still her harsh breathing. The only thing she had with her was the bag with David's things. She tucked it under her arm and tried to look as if she knew where she was going. Monitors chirped and she heard the quiet chatter of television. The sterile rooms seemed populated only by the elderly. She walked past a room where a nurse was checking a patient's vital signs. The young woman looked up and her eyes narrowed. Jill quickly ducked around a corner just as the stairwell door banged open behind her.

"What is this?" a female voice demanded and Jill knew a doctor or nurse had stopped the police. Her heart raced. There was no time to get to the opposite stairwell and the police were probably already there. She passed a room where a tiny, ancient woman slept, seemingly swallowed up by the bed, an oxygen mask covering half her face. On impulse, Jill ducked inside and then into the bathroom, pulling the door until it was open just a crack. She stood there in the dark, heart racing, as heavy feet ran down the hall. "I'm sure she exited on this floor," a male voice said. She couldn't hear the reply.

Silence again. She pushed open the door a crack. Nothing. She slipped out and crept toward the door.

"Who are you?" A querulous voice from the bed. Jill whirled around to see enormous cloudy eyes open in a tiny prune-like face.

"Volunteer." She pointed at a withering bouquet on the windowsill. "I brought you flowers."

There was no sign of police in the corridor. Jill saw a nurses' station up ahead, but there were women and men milling about. How was she going to get out of there?

She ducked back into the room and pulled

the string, to set off the alarm. "Don't tell," she whispered to the elderly woman who solemnly nodded her head.

Jill dashed into the vacant room across the hall as nurses came at a run. She waited until they were occupied to hurry down the corridor. Only one nurse remained at the station, her back to Jill, engrossed in a large slice of the sheet cake splayed across a table. Someone named Nicki was having a birthday. A spare lab coat had been tossed over the back of a chair. Jill swiped it, slipping it on without stopping. She shoved the plastic bag in a pocket and lifted a chart off a patient's door while heading rapidly toward the elevators. A middle-aged man and his teary wife stood waiting, their backs to her. The down button had already been pushed. The man had hold of the woman's hand, patting it ineffectually. "She'll be okay," he said in a low voice, glancing at Jill. She flipped open the chart and pretended to be absorbed by it, really only reading the same sentence over and over again: "Prognosis poor; palliative care recommended." She tried not to think of it as a bad omen.

The elevator pinged and the doors slid open. "After you, doctor," the man said, and it took Jill a second to realize he was talking to her. She gave him a terse smile and stepped on ahead of the couple. The woman's sniffles increased during the short ride down. The doors slid back and Jill felt like crying herself when she saw the lobby filled with police. Through the large plate-glass windows beyond them she could see patrol cars, top lights spinning, parked around the perimeter of the building. There was no way out. Her pulse increased when she spotted Ottilo standing near the main doors. He glanced her way and Jill turned left, bent over the chart, heading down a hallway that led back into the maze of hospital corridors. A police officer and a hospital security guard came walking down the hall toward her. Jill kept her eyes on the chart, feeling their eyes come to rest on her. She wanted to run, but there was nowhere else to go. Closer, closer; they were going to pass one another. She flipped a paper on the chart as she passed them, pursing her lips to keep them from trembling. They passed by without saying a word and nobody shouted after her.

The hallway divided, splitting into left and right corridors. Jill picked the left one, hoping that this led to the back of the building. She needed to get out of there, but how? She kept moving, clutching the metal patient's chart as if it were a winning lottery ticket.

Three more turns in the labyrinth and it suddenly felt steamy; even the walls seemed to be sweating. An overpowering smell of bleach assaulted the air just before she saw double doors with laundry stenciled in white across them.

Jill stepped to the side as one door swung open to let out a man in coveralls pushing a rolling plastic bin overflowing with bed linens. He gave her a curious glance, but she barely noticed, fixed instead on what she'd spotted at the end of the hall. Another exit, and this one led outside.

She pushed through the stairwell doors and had just taken a step down to the door that led outside when a voice barked, "Stop! Police!" Jill froze, scared more by the unmistakable click that followed than by the command. The metal patient's file dropped from her hand, clattering down the steps.

"Hands in the air where I can see them!"

Jill raised her arms, trying not to shake. The bark again: "Turn around!" She started to pivot and the male voice yelled, "Slowly! And keep your hands up!"

She swung around on the step, trying not to lose her balance. The first and only thing she could focus on was the barrel of the handgun pointing straight at her. Then it lowered. She blinked in surprise as she recognized the young officer staring back at her.

"Tom Dilby?"

The man nodded, somewhat sheepishly. "I didn't realize you were the one they're looking for."

She'd never seen him in uniform. When she'd photographed him with his wife and stillborn son he'd been wearing street clothes. Hard to believe that had been barely over a month ago. It felt like another century. He said, "I've got to arrest you."

"It's a mistake," she said. "I didn't hurt my daughter."

"It's my job." He'd reached behind him for the cuffs on his belt.

"You offered to help me, do you remember?"

Clearly he did, he was already shaking his head. "That was different."

"You said if I ever needed anything—I need something now."

"This isn't a traffic ticket—you're wanted for murder."

"I didn't do it. I couldn't. You know me. You and your wife, both. Do you really think I'd hurt a child? After the pain of losing one?"

He had the handcuffs in one hand, the gun in the other, but he stood there, obviously wavering. "It's not up to me to determine whether you're telling the truth—I've got a job to do."

"I have to find my daughter. If I'm locked up, I can't find her."

"I'm sorry." He took a step toward her, holding out the cuffs. She took a small step back.

"Please. I'm begging you to let me go. You said if I ever needed anything. Anything at all."

There was a long moment where they stood there simply staring at each other. Then he sighed and his arm dropped to his side. He jerked his head toward the door. "Go. I never saw you."

"Thank you, thank you so much."

But he'd already turned, pushing through the doors back the way she'd come. Jill ran down the steps and out of the hospital before he changed his mind.

Chapter Thirty-seven
Day Twenty-Three

The old man groaned loudly, writhing on the ground, clearly unable to get up. Bea dropped the shears and stepped out from behind the shed door. Avery stared dumbstruck at the blood gushing from the old man's leg. The bullet had hit an artery; it would be over very quickly.

The old man's rheumy eyes widened as he looked up at Bea standing over him. "Help me!" It sounded like a gargle. She examined him dispassionately; she'd seen plenty of gunshot wounds in Florida, though most of the victims had been younger. She bent down and reached toward his leg, pulling the gun out from underneath him and cleaning it off in the snow before slipping it in her coat pocket. The man tried to touch her, but Bea stepped out of reach. There was nothing she could do to stanch the bleeding in time to save him.

Avery looked from the man to Bea, eyes round and wide with shock. "If you'd been good and stayed home you wouldn't have had to see that," Bea said. She took the child's hand and dragged her away, back through the woods up the hill. The child resisted her pull, digging her heels into the snowy ground and crying. "C'mon," Bea said, jerking her along. "You shouldn't be out here; it's too cold to be out here without a coat." When the child still dragged, she hauled her into her arms, ignoring the pain in her chest and the child's wriggling, hiking as fast as she could up the hillside with Cosmo running after her.

They would have to leave even sooner than she'd planned. Someone had to have heard the gunshot. They'd find the man and the police would come swarming over the hillside like ants. They would find her and the child and everything she'd worked for would be lost. Avery was a dead weight in her arms. As they reached the beginning of their own driveway, Bea put the child down for a moment. Avery promptly ran, scrambling back down the way they'd come. Bea's temper flared. "Get back here!"

She ran after the child, stumbling in the snow, her hand reaching out as she fell, hard, but managing to grab the child's ankle and drag her back. The girl cried, but Bea slapped a hand over her mouth to muffle her. "It's okay," she crooned, trying to hold the struggling child against her chest. "Everything will be okay."

She'd said the same thing to her daughter when she was little, soothing her when someone had said something mean or she'd gotten a bad grade on a test. Just one of the many lies that parents told kids. Because it wasn't going to be okay, it was going to go on being miserable most of the time. The most you could hope for were the occasional glimmers of happiness.

Avery bent her head and bit Bea on the finger. She shrieked. This child was nothing like her daughter—Annie would never have acted this way. Bea pried the girl's mouth off her hand. "Stop it, you little brat!" Her finger was bleeding and she felt in her jacket pocket for a tissue to wrap it in, but her hand closed on the gun instead. She realized she shouldn't have taken it. All she'd thought was it might be useful, but if she'd left it lying there beside the man then the police would assume it was all just an unfortunate accident. She had to go back down and leave it by him, but not now, not with the child. She had to get her home, fast, before anyone saw them.

Still searching for a tissue, Bea reached into her other pocket and felt something hard and cylindrical. A spare syringe. Frank would have called it dumb luck, but it was nothing of the kind. She'd been prepared for any eventuality, just like she'd told him. She had no time to wonder at the dosage, no time to do this right. She jammed the needle through the sweater into the child's arm, covering her yowl of pain. She held fast, staggering a bit, when the child went slack in her arms.

Bea trudged up the snow-covered gravel, so desperate to see the house that she didn't notice the tire tracks. When she spotted the roofline the relief flooded her with energy. Until she reached the clearing and saw a familiar-looking SUV parked on the driveway.

There was no way out; police cars surrounded the hospital. Jill ducked behind a row of huge metal Dumpsters and fumbled through her pocket for David's cell phone. Was it still working? The signal was faint, but there. She called Tania.

"Hello?" Tania sounded distracted, as if she'd been interrupted in the middle of something.

"It's me, please don't hang up."

"Jill? I'm watching you on TV! They're saying you escaped from police custody. Where are you? Whose phone is this?"

"It's David's. I'm in trouble—I need help."

"No shit."

"Please, Tania, I really need your help."

"I'm not even talking to you, remember?"

"I know. I'm sorry, but I couldn't think of who else to call."

There was silence on the other end, but Jill could hear her breathing. "Please, I'm begging you. I'm outside, in the cold without a coat, hiding behind a Dumpster."

A sigh and then finally, blessedly, Tania said, "I'm listening."

"I need you to come get me."

The great thing about Tania was that she didn't

insist on asking all the questions first. All she said was, "Where?"

Despite the cold, the trash bins still smelled. Jill switched hands, covering her nose with one and sticking the other in a lab-coat pocket, raising as high as a crouch every few minutes to stomp her feet in snow that seemed to turn gray as soon as it hit the ground.

Her life had definitely hit its lowest ebb: Hiding from the police, Sophia gone, maybe forever, and David. Was he dead? She kept seeing his bruised and waxy skin, kept hearing the sound of the monitor flatlining. Had he really hidden a knife in his car? Could he have hurt Sophia? But no, it was crazy, he couldn't have hurt her like that, he loved their daughter as much as she did even if he was a lying son of a bitch. It must be some kind of police setup. Maybe they were trying to force a confession because they were already so con-vinced that she or David had killed their own child. Were they even considering any other suspects? What about Lyn Galpin?

That reminded Jill of what she'd been doing before she heard about David. She scrolled through the contacts on David's phone, looking for anything that might lead her to Sophia. Jill had spent her life trying to live by the straight and narrow, always doing the right thing and playing by the rules when everybody else around her didn't. Not anymore. She knew her daughter was alive. She knew it even if the police didn't. If she'd followed the law, if she'd allowed them to handcuff and haul her off to jail, then no one would find Sophia.

There was no Lyn Galpin, no Lyn of any kind in David's contacts. Damn, it was cold out. Where was Tania? It felt like Jill had been waiting forever. She tapped open David's photos; maybe he took pictures of these women. The last photo he'd taken was a blurry shot of some woman taken through a window. Or was that a car door? Jill stood up and tried to get a better look at it.

The sound of a motor made her duck back down and shove the phone back in her pocket. Peering between two Dumpsters, eager to spot Tania's ancient Honda Accord, she saw a motorcycle instead. Big and black, it came slowly down the asphalt, the driver completely obscured by black leather and a black-visored helmet. Jill held her breath as the bike stopped moving and the driver sat back and up in the seat, resting large gloved hands on his lap. Was he police? Jill breathed shallowly, trying not to inhale the fetid scents around her. Suddenly the guy pulled off his helmet and Jill could see that it wasn't a cop at all, but a bearded man with a skull and crossbones tattooed on his neck: Leo.

She stepped out from between the Dumpsters and Leo rolled the bike her way. He grinned at her. "The cavalry's here."

"Where's Tania?"

"She says cops are watching her place, so she gave me a call. She figures they won't get to me for a while. Hop on."

Jill didn't want to go anywhere with him, but she didn't really have a choice. She'd started down this road and there was no going back. She swung a leg over the bike, trying not to touch Leo, but lost her balance and ended up forced to catch hold of his jacket, cold-numbed fingers slipping over thick leather. He reached a hand back to steady her and then lifted the flap of a saddlebag behind her, producing a sheepskin jacket. "Here, put this on."

"Thanks." It was too large and smelled like must and cigarettes, but it was warm.

"Nothing I like more than fucking with the police. You're my old lady if we get stopped— that's how I got past the fuckers. Said I was picking you up from work." Leo grinned again at her and she managed a sickly smile in return, trying not to cough when he lit a cigarette pulled from an inside pocket. The lighter's orange-blue flame quivered in the wind before he snapped it shut. He puffed away for a moment, glancing back at her through narrowed eyes with an irritating smirk before tossing the cigarette to the side. It sizzled as it hit the snow.

"Just one more thing," he said, and leaned

toward her. She reared back—she hadn't seen him since she'd given his name to the police; was this offer of help really about getting revenge? But he only reached into the opposite saddlebag, his jacket raising as he did so and she caught a glimpse of blue and green, a tattooed snake that disappeared into his pants. "Gotta wear this, too." *This* was a matching helmet, heavy on her head. "Okay, visors down while we get out of here. And you'd better hold on; we might have to outrun the cops—that's why I brought the bike."

For God's sake, did the guy think he was starring in an action film? The motorcycle jerked to life, forcing Jill to lean against Leo, arms clasped around his waist as he sped back out the way he'd come. There were patrol cars blocking all traffic in and out of the hospital and two police officers stopping vehicles. Jill knew the visor blocked her face, but she felt exposed all the same. She clung to Leo, trying to look like she wanted to be touching him. The cop barely glanced at the motorcycle before waving it through.

Leo maintained a sedate speed until they'd gotten out of sight, and then he sped up. She pushed up her visor, shouting to be heard above the noise, "I need to go to the studio."

He shook his head, pushing up his own visor. "No can do, the cops are there."

It startled her to think of being tracked that

way. She was officially a fugitive. She imagined her face on wanted posters. "Where are we headed, then?"

"My place." He must have caught her expression in the side mirror because he grinned again. "Hey, no worries, it's not like I live in a meth lab."

Not exactly reassuring; Jill let her visor drop and held on.

It might not have been a meth lab, but Jill suspected that Leo's house wasn't exactly drug free. A row house on the border of Bloomfield and Garfield, it was a run-down brick building with metal awnings over the windows and a worn kitchen chair holding onto a parking spot on a congested backstreet rapidly filling with snow. A faded BEWARE OF DOG sign sat propped in the front window. Leo jerked to a stop and flicked back his visor. He saw Jill eyeing the sign and said, "The dog's dead, we kept the sign to scare people."

The dark front hall was narrow and smelled of pot and body odor. Leo kicked boots and a snowboard out of the path, calling, "Hey, asshole, get your shit out of the doorway." He locked the door behind her, shutting out the snow, but there was no discernible difference between the temperature inside and out. Jill hugged the jacket around her and trailed after him. A sagging floral couch filled the cramped living room and another heavily tattooed young guy, impossibly skinny, sat in the middle of it completely engrossed in a game playing on the enormous flat screen wedged in front of a decorative fireplace. The couch appeared to be swallowing him.

"String, this is Jill, Jill this is String, a.k.a. the inconsiderate asshole who dumps all his shit around the house." Leo waved his hand and the other guy made a grunting sound, his fingers moving on the controller. "He's in sales," Leo said and Jill wondered what *that* guy could possibly be selling. Leo led the way down the hall into a kitchen.

Every available surface appeared covered in something. Piles of books and unopened mail lay scattered across a small table and dirty dishes filled the sink. There was a heavy smell of grease, probably related to the open pizza box with two decaying slices sitting on top of the stove, or the two other empty boxes poking out of an open trash can.

Jill tried to focus on what to do next; she couldn't stop shaking. She was officially on the lam; if she didn't find Sophia she would be charged with murdering her own child. It was only a matter of time until the police found her, and with the evidence they'd trumped up there was no way that she and David wouldn't be convicted. The court of public opinion and the media had already found them guilty.

Just like they'd vilified Lyn Galpin. Jill pulled

out David's phone and looked again at the last photo he'd taken, the shot of an older woman taken through a car window. Who was that person? Why had he taken her photo? The only other photos on his phone were family shots—his father's birthday party, Jill holding Sophia up to see the elephants at the zoo. Everyone smiling. It was like looking at a world that she'd lost. There were no shots of other women, not Leslie Monroe, not Lyn Galpin. Disappointment followed fast on the heels of the relief Jill felt at not having to look at David's other women. She was no closer to finding Sophia. "I need a computer."

"What you need is a drink." Leo reached into a dingy cupboard above the ancient gas range and pulled down an expensive bottle of whiskey. Good to know that his money was going somewhere. Failing to find a glass in a cupboard, he plucked one from the sink and gave it a cursory wash. Jill took David's phone to call Tania, but stopped, realizing that at that very minute Ottilo might be holding Tania's phone and waiting for Jill to call so they could track her.

As if he could read her thoughts, Leo said, "Tania's going to come over later if she can." He pushed the pile of mail aside to put down the glass. "Got to sort that shit at some point." He poured a healthy slug of whiskey into the glass and pushed it toward her. "Here, have a seat."

Jill didn't want a drink, she didn't want to sit down, she had to keep moving, but now she was in Leo's house and she was indebted to him. She shifted a pile of newspapers off a kitchen chair and onto the floor and sat down. "Thanks," she said, eyeing the dirty glass before lifting it in a small salute and taking a sip. She'd heard that no human pathogens could live in alcohol; she hoped it was true. The whiskey burned going down, but took away some of the chill. Leo moved more junk off the other chair and sat down across from her, watching her with frank curiosity.

"I thought you lived with your mother?" she said, wondering if Leo's mother could possibly be somewhere in this rat hole.

"I moved out; this is my own place." He looked at her over the coffee mug he'd filled to the brim with liquor. "Kind of ironic, don't you think?"

"What's that?"

"You turned me in to the cops, and now I'm harboring you." He grinned, but his eyes were hard.

"Yeah, I'm sorry about that."

"I didn't take your kid."

"Then help me find out who did."

He stared up at her for a long minute and she met his gaze, trying to project a calm she didn't feel. After a second he got to his feet. "The computers are upstairs."

Chapter Thirty-eight
Day Twenty-Three

Bea looked from Patsy Duckworth's SUV up to the house and thought she saw a shadow behind the curtain in her bedroom. She could leave right now, just load the child into the car and go, except she couldn't—her exit from the garage was blocked by the other vehicle. Bea tugged on the SUV's driver door and it opened. Cosmo jumped up onto the driver's seat, always happy to take a ride, but the keys weren't in the ignition. Bea left the dog in the car. The garage hadn't closed fully again; she'd never been so happy to see that five-inch gap. She slid the child under the door and crawled in after her.

The smell hit Bea as soon as she stepped in the basement. She tensed in the doorway, sniffing the faint, unmistakable odor of nicotine and ash. Patsy's cigarettes. Light shone under the base of the door at the top of the stairs.

Moving soundlessly, Bea carried the child back to the hidden room and left her on the bed, quietly bolting the door. She crept up the stairs, slowly and soundlessly. No one in the kitchen, but the lights were blazing. She heard a familiar, annoying voice whispering somewhere inside the house. She crept through the living room, following the noise down the hallway, pulse racing when she saw the door to the second bedroom standing open. Wearing a full-length white wool coat, Patsy Duckworth stood with her back to the door examining the far wall. It was too late to stop her. She was looking at what Bea had spread on the worktable and pinned to the wall. The woman's head bobbed up and down as she examined everything, muttering, "Oh dear Lord, I knew it, I just knew it."

Bea crept back around the corner closest to the front door and waited. A minute passed, then Patsy came clicking down the hall, struggling to hold on to her enormous leather handbag and text at the same time. Bea stepped out in front of her and Patsy leapt back, dropping the phone. "Jesus H. Christ!" she exclaimed, one manicured hand flapping against her chest.

"What the hell are you doing in my house?" Bea said.

Patsy tried her trademark Cheshire grin, but it faltered. "My, but you surprised me, Bea! Sorry to just drop in on you like this, but I told you the buyer and I were going to stop by. He should be here soon—I was just trying to call him." She squatted to retrieve her phone, but Bea put the tip of her shoe on it and pulled it back, bending to pick it up herself without taking her eyes off the other woman. Patsy stood slowly upright, swallowing like a bird with something caught in its gullet.

"Thank you," she tried, holding out her hand for the phone, but Bea didn't oblige.

"How did you get in here?"

"Well, I have the extra set of keys." The woman fumbled in her enormous purse and pulled out a jangling ring. "But I didn't have to use them—the front door was open." Her trademark nervous cackle. She even resembled a chicken, between the thrust of her massive chest and the shiny auburn coxcomb of a hairdo.

"You can't just come in here," Bea said. "This is private property."

"You're right, of course," the agent said, smile stretched so thin that her eyes were mere creases. "So rude of me, I'm so sorry. It was just so cold out, and I didn't think you'd mind." Her voice trailed off when Bea didn't say anything. She clutched her bag a little more tightly and stepped forward. "Look, today obviously isn't a good day. I'll come back another time when it's more convenient—"

Bea didn't move. "Don't you want to ask me?"

Patsy's head tilted sideways as she cackled again. "Ask you what?" Her gaze flitted to Bea and away.

"About what's in the second bedroom. I saw you looking at the photos."

Patsy locked eyes with Bea. In a strangled,

completely unconvincing voice she said, "What photos?"

"Now, Patsy, weren't you the one who told me I could always expect honesty if I chose you as my real-estate agent?" Bea moved slowly toward her and Patsy cracked, stumbling back, pointing a nicotine-stained finger at Bea.

"Stay away! Your grandson—he isn't a boy at all, is he? I didn't realize it when he—she—said the name, but I saw those pictures. That's Sophia Lassiter. You abducted Sophia Lassiter!" Her voice was high-pitched and hoarse, hysterical.

"Her name's not Sophia; it's Avery."

"Where is she? What have you done with her? She doesn't belong with you."

Bea shook her head. "You're wrong."

"I'm calling the police!" The agent leapt forward and snatched the phone from Bea, frantically pressing 911 and holding it to her ear.

"Don't bother," Bea said. "There's terrible coverage out here." She reached out and pried the phone from the agent.

The slightest quiver of the woman's face gave away her fear, but the begging Bea anticipated didn't transpire. Instead, Patsy turned and skittered down the hall on her high heels. Bea followed her, hearing the basement door open and Patsy clattering down the steps. "Sophia?" Patsy called. "Sophia? Where are you?" She hesitated at the bottom of the steps, flinching as Bea appeared in the doorway above her. "Where is she?" she demanded, but her voice quavered. Bea didn't answer, just reached in her pocket, the metal cold to the touch. She heard a gasp and knew that Patsy had remembered the hidden room. Bea went after her and found the real-estate agent with a hand on the bolt. She flinched as Bea approached, giving her a baleful look. "You can't keep a child locked in the basement. I'm taking her home."

"No," Bea said. "You're not." She stepped forward, arm raised, but the agent screeched, flinging out a hand to block her, and Bea missed, the gun firing with a deafening bang, the bullet sinking into Patsy's neck instead of her head.

A cramped bedroom on Leo's second floor had been converted into a crowded office. Two recycled doors resting on sawhorses served as desks and on them were four desktops of various sizes, two laser printers, a scanner, and dozens of wires and other equipment that Jill couldn't begin to name. A high-tech paradise in a low-rent house. "What exactly do you do?" she asked. Leo smiled. "We're consultants." Purposely vague; she decided she didn't really need to know. He pointed at a desktop. "You can use this one."

She googled Lyn Galpin again, hoping to find out where she'd gone after the accident. The woman had been pilloried by the media, all the worst details of her life exposed—the local bar where she'd become a regular, the empty wine bottles piled high in a recycling bin outside her cheap apartment. There were professional photos, too, headshots from a law journal and from Adams Kendrick's newsletter, but also gruesome shots of the crash scene and a few of a bloodied and unconscious Galpin being carted off on a stretcher.

Her family had been caught on camera, too; there were photos of her parents arriving at the hospital soon after the accident, caught off guard and unable to shield themselves from the media. Jill stopped scrolling, went back. The mother. She looked familiar. She zoomed in on the shot, but the grainy news photo dissolved into individual pixels. She zoomed back out and grabbed David's iPhone, bringing up the blurry photo and comparing it to the one on the desktop. "What the hell?"

"Holy shit," Leo said over her shoulder. "That's the same woman."

David didn't have a picture of Lyn Galpin on his phone, he had a picture of her mother. Why? "When was this taken?"

"That's easy." Leo plucked the phone from her hand and connected it by cable to the desktop. "You just connect a USB cable so you can download this and access the time stamp."

He quickly downloaded the iPhone's photos, his hands racing over the keyboard with the grace of a concert pianist. Larger versions of David's photos showed up in a separate window. Underneath the blurry shot of Lyn Galpin's mother was a single line of text that gave Jill an even greater shock.

The photo had been taken today. No more than an hour before Jill had been told about David's accident.

"You trying to find her?" Leo jabbed a thumb at the blurry image, a silver skull ring bobbing on his knuckle.

"Yeah. Or her." Jill pointed at a photo of Lyn Galpin on the other window. "They're mother and daughter."

"You think they took your kid?"

"Maybe. My husband had an affair with that one." She tapped Lyn's picture.

"Whoa!" Leo said. "He fucked her, so she took your kid? As payback or something?"

"Maybe. I don't know."

"That is some heavy shit, if it's true." He shook his head.

Where had David seen Lyn Galpin's mother? At the hospital they said he'd been hit by a car in the garage next to Adams Kendrick. Had he seen her in the garage?

Jill kept searching online, trying to find either woman. She opened a YouTube link to another longer, soundless segment of Lyn Galpin's accident footage. It had been taken from a short distance away; she could clearly see a car driving erratically, weaving in and out of the oncoming lane to pass the cars in front of it. As Jill watched, the car failed to calculate the distance properly and couldn't get back into its lane in time. It crashed head-on into a car coming in the opposite direction. Then a tractor-trailer, braking hard, slid sideways, jackknifing in an unsuccessful attempt not to crash into the other two vehicles. Another car slid into the tractor-trailer, and then the screen stopped and the footage began again: Weaving car, first crash, second crash, a moment's black-ness as the third car hit. Jill watched it again, then a third time. She realized that Lyn Galpin had been trying to catch another car moving ahead of her on the parkway. That car was speeding, too, faster and tighter in traffic, moving with a precision that Lyn Galpin didn't have. The other car shot ahead through a yellow-to-red light literally seconds before the crash.

Jill stared at the screen. She forgot about Lyn Galpin's mother, forgot about everything except that faster car. She played the footage a fourth time and paused when the other sedan was in the frame, staring with horrified recognition. She knew that car. It was David's.

Chapter Thirty-nine
Day Twenty-Three

Patsy Duckworth fell backward screaming, blood spurting like a geyser from the side of her neck, spattering her white coat, spraying everywhere.

"Damn it! You should have held still!" Bea panicked. She dropped the gun and bent down to grab one of Patsy's slim ankles, dragging the woman toward the utility area and the drain. It was slow work. Even with the size difference, it was not easy to drag Patsy. She struggled to kick free, screaming and clawing at her throat.

"Stop it! Just stop struggling!" Bea begged. She heard a strange noise and realized it was the sound of the other woman's fake nails popping off as she transferred her clawing to the floor.

"You shouldn't have moved!" she screamed, cursing as the high heel on Patsy's freely kicking foot grazed her forearm. She dropped her and ran for the gun, flashing back to years ago when she'd gone deep-sea fishing with Frank and he'd landed a massive tuna after a long fight, using all his energy to reel it up, out of that crystalline water and onto the boat, where it had flopped, untouchable, on the fiberglass deck until he had finally and mercifully clubbed it.

Frank wasn't there to do it; he was never around when Bea needed him most. She took the gun to Patsy in the same way he had, smashing it against the woman's head, until Patsy stopped moving, just like the fish, and merely twitched. Bea let the gun drop, panting. She waited for her heart rate to fall a little before she dragged the body the rest of the way to the gentle slope near the drain, kneeling to angle her so the blood dripped down it.

Sudden singing made Bea jump. For one awful minute, she thought *The Sound of Music* came from the bloodied cavern that had been the other woman's mouth. Then it stopped and started again and she realized it was a cell phone. She scrambled in the pockets and found it just as it stopped ringing and went to voice mail. A man's voice, "Hey, Patsy, Mike Reynolds here. I got held up in a meeting, but I can meet you at the property in a half hour if that's still okay?"

Bea texted a reply, her fingers leaving blood-stains on the keys. "Sorry, must cancel. Emergency. Next week?" She hit send, but it began to ring again almost immediately. "Shut up! Just shut up!" Bea smashed the phone again and again against the floor until it shattered.

In the silence that followed she could hear the sound of her own ragged breathing. Bea's vision cleared, and she stared down at the blood freckling her hands. She stood up on shaky legs

403

and stripped off all her clothes, but there was still blood on her skin. She staggered to the laundry tub and grabbed the bar of soap, scrubbing at her arms and face, running wet hands through her hair, desperate to get rid of it. Only she couldn't get rid of the smell. The metallic odor permeated the basement, the smell of raw meat and the slaughterhouse, the smell of death. She tried not to inhale, breathing only through her mouth, but it was no use, the odor filled the air like a mist; it caught in her throat threatening to choke her.

She stumbled upstairs to her bedroom, pulling a suitcase from the closet and throwing clothes blindly into it. They had to leave. Now. Tonight. They would find the old man down the hill first, and then someone would report Patsy Duckworth missing. It was only a matter of time. She thought she heard a noise and ran to the window, terrified that Patsy's buyer hadn't gotten her text. There was nothing out there except Patsy's bright and shiny SUV dusted with snow. What if the guy showed up? She had to dump the car to buy herself some time.

Bea threw on clean clothes and found a red wig in her collection, fixing it quickly over her hair. It wasn't a match for Patsy's, but it would do. She hustled back downstairs and into the laundry area, finding the agent's enormous purse and carrying it out the garage, rummaging for the keys as she walked. Cosmo, perched against the passenger window, barked a greeting, tail wagging. She ran back in the house to get his leash. "I'd forgotten about you," she said, sliding onto the driver's seat. She ran a hand over the leather. What a luxury. The only downside was the smoke smell, but some air freshener would fix that. For a moment, as she started the car and before racing down the driveway, Bea contemplated keeping the SUV and ditching the old sedan. Grand theft auto—the surest way to attract police attention. Someone out there might miss Patsy, but the car they'd truly mourn.

Snow was barely sticking to the salted main road, but it was falling steadily enough to cancel the roadwork. No police in sight and she sped away from Fernwood and toward the playing fields surrounding a private school less than a mile away. She'd passed by the property multiple times, attention pulled by girls running across the emerald lawn waving field hockey sticks. There was no one out today, snow like a shroud over the grass. She pulled into a small, deserted parking lot alongside one of the fields and parked the car. Of course Patsy had a box of wet wipes in her glove compartment—appearances mattered. Bea wiped down anything she'd touched on the interior, including Patsy's purse, and fixed Cosmo's leash to his collar. She saved one wet wipe for the outside handle and set the doors to lock, leaving Patsy's purse on the seat and the keys visible in the ignition. If she'd had more time, she could have dumped this car in some urban neighborhood where it would be sure to be spotted by a teen joy rider or stolen for a chop shop, and she could have guaranteed someone else's DNA as a distraction. Someone would find it here, but that someone would probably be a suburban cop. She just hoped they didn't immediately make the connection to Fernwood Road.

Cosmo hopped out of the car after her. She had to hold him back as she wiped down the outside handle, but then she let him take the lead, trotting back the way they'd come along the snowy road.

Jill stared at the screen, stunned. Lyn Galpin had been following David. Had it been some sort of insane drag race or had she been chasing after him and he sped ahead to avoid her? He hadn't caused the crash, her drinking had done that, but he'd certainly helped provoke it. Dear God, there was motivation enough right there to exact some revenge.

But where was the woman now? Jill unplugged David's iPhone to call the small law firm where Lyn Galpin last worked, but a monotone voice informed her that the number was no longer in service. They'd either changed location or closed shop. She continued doggedly scrolling through all of the links to Lyn Galpin until she found a small *Post-Gazette* article, DRIVER

RESPONSIBLE FOR CHRISTMAS CRASH TRANSFERRED TO LONG TERM CARE. There was another photo of the parents caught off guard outside a building, but this time they'd turned toward the camera, not away, and she could see their faces clearly. The man was unfamiliar, but the woman—Jill's pulse jumped as she stared at the woman's eyes, her drooping right eyelid. Jill had definitely seen her before, but she just couldn't place *where* she'd seen her. She stared hard at the photo, trying to picture the woman in different settings—the law firm, her studio, Sophia's preschool. A memory flitted through her mind like a fish swimming too fast to grab. Jill pushed at her forehead with the heel of her hand, groaning in frustration.

The article said that Lyn Galpin had never regained consciousness; she'd been in a coma since the accident. Then Jill noticed the background of the photo. The parents were standing in front of a building with ANGEL'S WINGS REHABILITATION CENTER emblazoned on a sign. She pulled up another search window and typed in that name. In less than five seconds an address had popped up. Jill turned back to look at Leo. "Can I borrow your car?"

Forty minutes later, Jill parked Leo's Chevy Impala in the lot at the Angel's Wings Rehabilitation Center. Docked would have been a more appropriate word. The car was circa 1975 and a boat. "Be careful with her," Leo had instructed, parting reluctantly with the keys. "This baby's a classic." Yeah, if classic meant gas guzzling, and cracked vinyl seats. The heating was on the fritz; she could see her breath inside the car. At least it had a good turning radius. She struggled to lock up, though she couldn't imagine anyone bothering to steal it, and ran through the falling snow into the building. The name Angel's Wings suggested something airy and comforting, but the rehab center was squat, painted cinderblock situated uncomfortably close to an on-ramp to the Pennsylvania Turnpike as well as a strip mall. The quiet inside was surprising, given the location. It felt like the hush of a church or a library, deliberate and somber, Jill's footsteps deadened by carpet. The lobby had the look of a low-rent hotel trying to masquerade as something fancier, an illusion fostered by the brass chandelier and ambient lighting and the young man in a suit and tie standing at a faux wood reception desk. She slipped off the sheepskin jacket, trying to look less shabby, and realized she was still wearing the lab coat. Might as well use it to her advantage. She pulled it more tightly around her and walked briskly to the counter, adopting the slightly superior mien of a busy medical professional.

"I'm looking for one of your patients, Lyn Galpin."

"Of course, doctor." The young man turned to a desktop computer, fingers moving nimbly over the keyboard, squinting at the screen. He had a little gold pin engraved with BRISK attached to his lapel. She didn't know if it was his name or a description. He scanned the screen, hit a few more keys, and made a faint "hmm" sound under his breath.

He looked back up at Jill. "I can't seem to find her. Can you spell the last name?"

"Yes. G-A-L-P-I-N. Lyn with one N."

A few more taps, a little more squinting at the screen. Brisk should get his eyes checked. Jill glanced around while she waited, feeling nervous when she spotted the security cameras mounted in strategic corners. What if the police had put out an APB on her and mentioned she could be masquerading as a doctor?

"Aah," the young man said with satisfaction just as the computer pinged its own triumph. "Here it is. A Lyn Galpin *was* a patient with us, but that was back in the summer."

"Did she come out of the coma?"

"Not exactly."

"So she moved to another care facility?"

"You could call it that, I suppose." He grimaced.

"Do you have the name of that place?"

"The afterlife. Ms. Galpin died in June."

Chapter Forty

Day Twenty-Three

Blindsided, Jill said, "She's dead?"

The man nodded, adopting a mournful look that seemed practiced. "I'm afraid so."

"What about her parents. I know they visited her here. Do you have their contact information?"

But he was shaking his head before she finished. "No and I really couldn't give that to you even if I did. That's not Angel's Wings' policy."

Jill turned away, stymied. Where did she go from there? Then she thought of something. "Is there anyone here who I can talk to about Lyn Galpin and her parents? I mean, anybody who took care of her while she was here?"

"I'm sure there are plenty of people," Brisk said in a distinctly un-brisk style. "We have a full staff and most of the nurses rotate, but I really can't—"

"Please, it's very important."

He frowned. "Which hospital did you say you work for, doctor?"

"Mercy." At least that was true of the lab coat. "I'm doing a study of coma patients and really hoped to include Lyn Galpin."

The young receptionist sighed and turned to the

computer again, clicking and moving the mouse for a minute until he found what he was looking for. "Okay, you're in luck. One of the nurses is here today. Valerie Docimo. If you have a seat, I'll page her."

The nurse who came to meet Jill in the lobby was fiftysomething years old and wearing bright pink scrubs emblazoned with smiling cherub faces, a look strangely at odds with the stocky, muscular body crammed into them and the glower on the square, makeup-free face. "Yeah?"

"Did you care for a patient named Lyn Galpin?"

"Yeah. So?" Was it possible to look any more surly and guarded?

"I need to know anything you can tell me about her and her parents."

"It's for a study of coma patients," Brisk helpfully interjected from the front desk.

The nurse glanced at the clock on the wall and put her hands on her hips. "I'm taking my break— you can talk to me while I have my snack." The snack turned out to be a large sweetened coffee and an enormous cinnamon bun. Jill took a seat across from Valerie Docimo in the cafeteria and waited as patiently as she could for the other woman to slowly chew and swallow a bite of the pastry before she began talking.

"I do my job, but I didn't like caring for her."

"Because of the accident?"

The nurse nodded. "Why does a selfish bitch like her deserve medical care? She shouldn't have been on the road at all, not when she'd had that much to drink."

"Did you meet her parents?"

"Oh, yeah, they were here every day. Or at least her mother was. Every single day. Made my life a living hell."

"How so?"

But the nurse had taken another bite of cinnamon bun, chewing with obvious relish. Valerie Docimo might have been a dieter for the number of times she chewed before actually swallowing a bite.

"She didn't think we did enough to bring her out of the coma. Always demanding we talk to her, stimulate her more. I told her that her daughter was in a persistent vegetative state. She was a nurse, she knew what that meant."

"Her mother is a nurse?"

"Was. She quit her job to sit by her kid's bedside twenty-four seven. Stupid if you ask me. Like her daughter would know the difference. Anyway, she gave me grief over not doing more. I told her that even if I had the time to read to her daughter, which I most certainly did not, it would be a total waste of time. Like reading to a stalk of celery. Nothing there, you know?" She tapped the side of her head with a meaty forefinger. She frowned for a moment at the memory, and then her face relaxed as she speared another bite of pastry.

"How did she die?"

Chew, chew, chew—it was like watching a cow grazing. Finally she swallowed. "Doctors pulled the plug."

"And her mother okayed this?"

Valerie Docimo snorted. "No way. Not at first. But the doctors were pushing to take her off life support and the drunk's father wanted it. He said it was time for her to be at peace—though I hope she's rotting in hell for what she did to those people."

"Do you know where the parents lived?"

"They were from out of town, I know that much. Florida, I think. The father left after a week, but then he'd come back to visit on weekends. The mother stayed here the entire time." She paused and wiped her mouth on a napkin. "I didn't like her, but I'll give the woman credit for that—she really was a devoted mother. She came every day to sit with her daughter. I think she only went home to sleep and shower."

"Do you know where she was staying?"

Valerie nodded. "Sure. Her daughter's apartment. Some crappy place near the Allegheny River. I remember because the bills were sent there—you know insurance doesn't begin to cover everything and the coverage always runs out eventually. She was always bringing the bills in and complaining about the charges. Left her crap all over the room, and I saw those damn envelopes often enough—Riverview Estates, apartment 7B." She snorted. "Can't believe I remember crap like that, but I do."

"Do you remember her name?"

"Yeah. Bea something. Wayne? Walters? No, that's not it—wait, I've got it. Walsh. Bea Walsh." She actually smiled for a second, transforming her face, but then it settled back down into frown lines. "She had a different last name than her daughter—second marriage, I think. Sad woman. You know, a lot of people blamed the parents for what their daughter did, but I wasn't one of them. You're not responsible for your kids' behavior once they're grown. They'll do what they want to do no matter what you say. They'll break your heart. You got any kids?"

Jill tried not to react. "Yes. A daughter."

"Then you know—they all go their own way when they're teens. But some mothers, they just can't believe that their little precious would ever do anything bad. Bea Walsh was one of those. She acted all surprised about her daughter's drinking, like she didn't know, but she was even more surprised by the pregnancy."

Stunned, Jill said, "Pregnancy? What pregnancy?"

Valerie Docimo stood up and finished her coffee in three large gulps. "It was right there in her medical records—Lyn Galpin had a kid."

Chapter Forty-one

Journal—December 2011

You won't take my calls or answer my emails. Do you think I'm going to just give up? The firm never hired weak-willed people. I'm not going anywhere until I get our child back. My child back—she has nothing to do with you. You were just a sperm donor.

I tried to go up to see you the other day, but the security guard in the lobby stopped me. Did he tell you about it? I'm sure you told him I'm just some disgruntled former employee. I tried to explain, I tried to tell him that I just needed to talk to you for a minute, but he wouldn't listen. Fucking fake cop. I wouldn't leave, not until a real police officer came into the lobby and escorted me out. I told him I was there to see the man who'd stolen my child, but I slurred my words a little, and the officer walked me over to a Starbucks and suggested I drink some coffee and sober up before he had to arrest me. I'd had one drink, maybe two with lunch. I was not drunk.

The adoption agency is no help. The woman they ushered me in to see, some social worker, listened sympathetically and then told me that unfortunately it was a closed adoption and there was nothing she could do. It's such bullshit, but I know how to play the legal system. I told her that the father hadn't given consent to the adoption. That got her interest for a minute, but then she said that if that were the case then the father had to be the one to contest the adoption. Even then, she said, it might take years for the courts to sort it out.

I don't want to wait years. I want our child now. "Do you really want to take her away from the only parents she's ever known?" you said during the one and only meeting we've had since that day on the street. We met at a bar just as seedy as the hotel you probably still frequent. You told me I was beautiful and I'd fall in love with someone better and have his child. I'm so proud of how I replied: "Children aren't interchangeable, asshole."

You've blocked my calls and I have no one else I can turn to. I can't sleep, I can't concentrate. The head of the penny-ante law firm in Butler actually put me on probation for taking too much time off. I told that toad-faced fucker he'd been lucky to have me for as long as he did. I hoped to provoke a reaction, but all he said was, "Have you been drinking, Ms. Galpin?"

I'm going to follow you home one day, D., and confront you in front of your precious wife. Maybe then you'll help me get my little girl back.

Chapter Forty-two

Day Twenty-Three

"What happened to the baby?" Jill asked, an icy finger trailing down her spine.

The nurse shrugged. "Who knows? Lyn Galpin didn't keep it, that's all I know." She trudged out of the cafeteria, clearly done with the conversation, but Jill hurried after her.

"Could she have had an abortion?"

"No, definitely not."

"How can you be so sure?"

Valerie Docimo smirked. "Basic pelvic exam. Your cervix doesn't lie." She must have seen the confusion on Jill's face because she snorted and said, "Guess you're not a ob-gyn are you, doc? When you give birth your cervix changes—less round, more oval—it's very obvious. Bea Walsh just didn't want to believe the truth about her precious daughter, she was sure there'd been a mistake in the transcript. After a couple of the docs spoke with her she finally stopped talking about it." She pushed open a door that said STAFF ONLY on it, but Jill grabbed her arm.

"But the baby," she said. "Did she try to find out what happened to it? Did Lyn Galpin give it up for adoption?" She thought of David broaching adoption after being so adamantly against it, of David arguing against tracking down the birth mother, of David seeming unaffected upon learning that the birth mother had died.

The nurse shook her loose. "All I know is that if the bitch gave away her baby then that child is way better off. Imagine having *that* as your mother. Still, I did feel a little sorry for Bea Walsh. Can you imagine finding out you're a grand-mother, but you never even got to see your own grandkid?"

Jill walked slowly back to the lobby, struggling to accept that Lyn Galpin could be Sophia's birth mother. A man in scrubs wheeled a patient through the sliding doors, bringing in a gust of freezing air, tracking snow onto the carpet.

"You find what you were looking for?" Brisk called from the front desk. Jill pulled the fleece jacket back on, buttoning it with hands that already felt numb.

"Not yet."

Back in the Impala, she dialed Andrew's number. He picked it up on the first ring. "Jill? Where in the hell are you?"

"What was the name of Sophia's birth mother?"

"What? Where are you?"

"The birth mother's name—what was it?"

"What does this have to do with anything? She's dead, Jill."

"Was it Lyn Galpin?"

Silence for a long moment. Throat clearing. "Yes, but Jill, listen—"

She hung up.

Whoever named Riverview Estates had delusions of grandeur. Even the snowfall couldn't mask the sheer ugliness of the place—rigid rows of identical townhouses, each clad in industrial gray siding with dingy white trim. The front doors were the same shade of dirty white, and the seasonal wreaths hung on some of the doors seemed like desperate attempts at individuality. The gates surrounding the complex might have been to keep people in, not out.

Jill tried to turn the Impala's windshield wipers up a notch so she could see the sign more clearly. Was this really it? But there was the name in large, fading gilt letters: ESTATES. What a joke. Listing in the snow next to the large sign was a smaller metal realty sign with APARTMENTS FOR RENT. It was faded, too. Jill pulled slowly through the front gates. A small guardhouse sat like an afterthought in the median dividing entrance and exit. Jill caught a glimpse of a portly, balding man in a security uniform leaning back in a chair, playing something on a tablet. He glanced over at the sound of the Impala lurching past, but made no move to stop her.

She had to circle twice before finding the

townhouse marked with a flaking brass 7B. Jill got out and knocked on the door, moving from one foot to another, trying to stave off the cold.

Nobody answered. She knocked again, more loudly, and jammed both hands in the pockets of her sheepskin coat. Snow settled on her hair, her shoulders. She knocked a third time before trying to peer in the windows, but there was only a slit visible through drawn plastic blinds and she couldn't see anything. "Sophia?" she called at the glass, but her words were swallowed up by the wind.

She drove back to the guard booth and kept the motor running as she hopped out and rapped on the dirty glass window. The man looked up from his tablet as if it cost him a great effort and reached up to slide the window open just enough so that she could hear him. "Yeah?"

"I'm trying to find Bea Walsh."

"Yeah? Get in line." He laughed at his own joke, revealing crooked, tobacco-stained teeth. "Like I've been telling every other collection agent—she ain't here no more."

"Do you know where she went?"

"If I did d'ya think they'd still be bothering me?" He slid the window shut and looked back down at his screen. Jill tapped on the glass again. He gave her an incredulous look before getting up and sliding the window fully open.

"Look, I really need to get in that apartment."

"I told you already—she's gone and she ain't coming back." He tried to slide the window closed again, but Jill stopped it with her hand.

"This is urgent—she has my daughter."

He didn't seem impressed. "The only daughter she had was a no-good drunk. Do you know how many vacancies we got 'cause of her? People don't want to live next door to no murderer, not to mention them reporters snooping around day and night. Months they was here! All them news vans blocking the drive—who wants to put up with that? And when that drunk bitch finally dies her parents up and leaves in the middle of the night. No forwarding address, nothing. Place stinks, too—management can't get anyone to rent it."

Jill latched on to that. "I'm interested in an apartment—show me that one."

That stopped his rant, but the man looked scornful. "If you really wanted to see an apartment you'd ask to see one of them bigger end units."

"I want to see apartment 7B."

The townhouse was empty, just as the security guard had said. He stood in the doorway, keys dangling from one hand, tablet from the other. "You can't trust no one these days," he said when she glanced at it.

His voice echoed in the empty space. Jill stood

in the living room, feeling disappointment dragging her down like a weight. There was nothing here. She'd been sure she'd find Bea Walsh with Sophia, but it was clear from the funky, musty smell: no one had been in the place for months. Thick dust coated the ceiling-fan blades and window blinds. Cobwebs crisscrossed doorways and even the kitchen faucet. If she'd brought Sophia here, it wasn't recently. The guard closed the front door behind them, shutting out the cold, as Jill tried to think. "When did she leave?"

The security guard kept looking from her to his tablet as if he were anxious to get back to his game. "I don't know—May, June? I think it was June."

Jill scrubbed a hand over her face, trying not to despair, but to think of something, anything, that could be useful. "Did she say where she was going?"

The guard shook his head, sniffing the air. There was a peculiar smell in the place, an odd sickly odor that had grown worse since he'd shut the door. There had to be something here, something that would tell Jill where this woman had gone. She started opening cupboards in the kitchen and sliding back drawers, hoping that she'd find an answer. They were empty, except for discarded scraps—twist ties, a paper clip, greasy takeout menus, a scribbled-on flyer for a local realty company. Jill left them piled on the counter, starting to feel pity for the woman who'd lived in this depressing space.

"She probably let her dog crap all over the carpet," the guard muttered, sniffing the air. The smell was really bad. He set up his tablet on the kitchen counter and started his game again, turning up the volume as if that would somehow cover the odor.

"She had a dog?" Jill had to repeat the question to get his attention.

"Little furry mutt—it was against the rules, but she didn't care." Something about the dog—it pinged Jill's memory, but it was just an odd sensation, nothing tangible. She opened the refrigerator, but it was as empty as the rest of the place. A lone box of Arm & Hammer sitting on the shelf. Clearly the smell wasn't from here. She headed down the hall, feeling increasingly desperate. The smell was stronger; she held her hand against her nose.

There had to be something, some clue. The first bedroom had a metal bed frame with a stained mattress on it. Jill went through every drawer in the cheap dresser standing against the wall. She got down on her hands and knees and searched under the bed. Nothing but an old sock and several dust balls.

"Management needs to fumigate again," the guard said, blocking the bedroom door. He had one arm covering his nose. Jill pushed past him and into the bathroom, hitting the light switch, but of course the electricity was off. Dim light shone through a tiny window set high on the wall above a cramped shower and tub combination. She pulled back the shower curtain, which had mildew creeping along the edge, and felt the shower head. Dry. The drain was dry, too. The vanity was dingy white, foil-pressed covers peeling back from particleboard drawers. She pulled open the drawers one by one. A ponytail holder with a strand of hair twisted in it. A cheap emery board. A plastic ring.

Jill shut the drawer, then immediately jerked it back open. She stared at the ring for a second before reaching in with trembling fingers to pick it up. "What's that you got there?" the guard said, straining to see what she was holding. "If you find anything of value it belongs to management."

This was Sophia's ring, the pink plastic ring with the pink glass gem that she'd lost that day at the park. Jill was sure of it. Sophia hadn't wandered off that day at the park; she'd been taken by Bea Walsh. "Oh my God."

"What is it?" The guard deflated when he saw what she was holding. "Oh, it's just a piece of junk."

She ignored him, clasping the ring and pushing past him. The second bedroom was exactly like the first, except for a bigger closet. Jill opened the folding doors, and metal hangers pinged against one another. A man's large blue windbreaker hung in a far corner. She searched the pockets, but there was nothing in it.

There was only one door left. "That's just a utility closet," the guard said, retreating back down the hall with his tablet. She opened the door anyway. The smell poured out at them, an overwhelming scent, sickeningly sweet and rancid, reminding her of a childhood trip to a farm, where the odor of cow manure had mixed unappetizingly with that of apples rotting in the orchard next door. "Jesus, Mary, and Joseph!" The guard's voice came out muffled through the hand he'd flung over his nose. "What the hell is that?"

Jill flung the door closed, breathing hard, then clamped a hand over her nose and opened it again. Water heater, furnace, and a stackable washer and dryer unit all crammed together in a tight space. Brownish liquid puddled on the floor near the front of the washer/dryer. She caught a glimpse of something white behind it.

Please no, please no, please no. Please let it not be what she thought it was. A prayer repeating inside her as she pulled and pushed against the unit in a frenzy, finally shifting it far enough that she could see a cylindrical looking package wrapped in white sheeting and lots of duct tape. It was too tall, too big. She sagged with relief, just before it fell toward her. Jill jumped to the side, crying out as the package brushed against her before landing with a thud.

"What the hell?" the guard repeated, coming closer.

Holding her sleeve against her nose, Jill crouched down next to the bundle. The liquid had come from here; it stained the sheeting, puddling near the bottom in a sickening way. She could hear the guard breathing through his mouth, loud and labored, and she had to swallow down the bile that rose in her own throat as she struggled to pull back the sheeting at the top of the package. She knew what it was before she saw the thatch of iron gray, knew what it was even as she kept pulling the sheet, stopping only when the whole head appeared.

Gagging, she dropped the sheet and reared up, bumping into the guard who'd come forward to look.

"Well, I'll be damned," he said. "That's Frank, the husband."

Chapter Forty-three

Day Twenty-Three

Even expecting it, Jill couldn't help crying out and stumbling back, her hands pressed against her mouth, but the vomit came anyway, spilling from her onto the cheap carpeting.

"Now that's something more to clean," the guard complained.

"She killed him." Jill's legs folded, and she dropped to the floor. "She killed her own husband." If she could kill her husband, this woman was capable of anything. Jill thought of Sophia's bloody nightgown and retched again, head down and eyes watering, her stomach feeling as if it were being pulled inside out.

The security guard muttered an oath and retreated back down the hall, complaining about the mess. Jill staggered after him, away from the body. She couldn't think, she couldn't breathe. The guard was in the kitchen talking on a cell phone.

"Riverview Estates, off Allegheny River Boulevard in Verona." He paused, listening. "No, I didn't do CPR." Another pause. " 'Cause he's dead."

Jill had to go before the police got there; she had

to leave. She reached in her pocket for the keys and found the ring. She could show the police the ring! The ring tied this woman to Sophia. But why would the police believe her? Ottilo would listen to her story with his usual impassive expression, and then he'd arrest her.

She shoved the ring back in her pocket and ran to the front door but not before the guard stepped in front of it, blocking her path. "You're not going anywhere!" he snapped. Over his shoulder Jill could see fresh snow covering the windshield and hood of Leo's car. The guard narrowed his eyes at her. "I don't know how you knew about that body, but you can explain it to the police. They're on the way."

And they were. The promise of a dead body had gotten the police moving; already she could hear sirens. The guard turned to look out the front door, eager to flag them down.

Jill scanned the apartment wildly, searching for another way out. She had to leave. She saw a sliding door hidden by cheap sheers and ran to it, fiddling with the lock before it finally gave and the door slid back with a squeal. "Hey! Stop right there!" The guard lumbered after her.

She dashed out only to stop short on a small square of concrete patio completely encased by a wooden privacy fence. Jill hesitated for a split second before shoving a rickety metal table—the only thing on the patio—against the fence and scrambling on top. The guard made a grab for her, hand on ankle, but she shook him loose, getting over the fence and dropping onto the snow-covered ground on the other side. It looked soft, but wasn't.

Sharp pain flashed in both her knees, but she had no time to linger. Jill struggled to her feet and did a wide loop around the building, searching for her keys in the pocket of the jacket as she ran. The Impala's door locks were snow-covered. She swiped it off, shoved the key in, and yanked open the long, wide driver's door just as the security guard came huffing out the front door of 7B.

"You can't leave!" he shouted as she threw herself into the car. She slammed the door, pushed down the lock button, and thrust the key in the ignition. The Impala stalled as the security guard ran toward her, arms waving. "C'mon, c'mon," Jill muttered, trying again. The guard reached for the car door, but slipped as he stepped off the curb. The Impala started, roaring to life. The guard scrambled backward on his hands and feet, like a large crab. He was still shouting, but she couldn't hear him over the noise of the motor.

She pulled out with tires slipping and squealing in the snow. A trio of police cars, lights flashing, turned into the complex. Jill yanked up the collar of the jacket, hunching a little as she sped toward the exit. The Impala passed one side of the guardhouse as the first of the police cars passed the other. She caught a glimpse of a police officer's face turned toward hers, mouth agape, and then she was gone, racing back up the side road that she'd taken down to the river, getting back on Allegheny River Boulevard.

She didn't know what to do, where to go. This madwoman had Sophia, she had to have her, but where had she gone? Jill tried to slow her breathing, to calm down enough to think rationally. She didn't know what to do, where to search next. All she had to prove a connection between this woman and Sophia was a cheap plastic ring. Her mouth tasted sour from throwing up, her stomach sore and roaring its emptiness. She couldn't remember the last time she'd eaten. She pulled into a Sheetz station and went inside. A pimply-faced teen manned the cash register, paying more attention to the wall-mounted TV than to his customers. Jill hunched her shoulders and ducked into one of the aisles, trying to focus on the row after row of chips and other crappy snacks, but her ears were tuned to the news broadcast. "Snow, snow, and more snow in the forecast," a bubbly announcer chirped, "but first the roundup of today's top stories." Jill picked up a protein bar and stepped to the freezer case that ran the length of the back wall to find bottled water.

"Hey!"

Her head jerked up at the shout. She looked back, fully expecting to see the teen staring at her, but he was addressing an older woman carrying a small poodle. "You can't bring that dog in here," the teenager said, hand rising to pick worriedly at one of his boils.

"She'll freeze if I leave her in the car in this weather," the woman protested.

The dog yipped as if to confirm her story. *Little furry mutt—it was against the rules, but she didn't care.* The security guard telling her about Bea Walsh's dog. And all at once Jill realized—the woman with the dog at the park on the day Sophia disappeared—it had to have been Bea Walsh.

Jill brought her purchases to the counter, head down as she handed over the money. The teen rang her up, too focused on arguing with the old woman to do more than glance at her. Meanwhile the announcer was still talking. Jill looked up when she heard, "The search continues"—expecting to see a photo of Sophia, but it was a crash scene—"for the cause of the deadly bus accident in West Virginia."

"Do you need a bag?" The teen handed over her change.

Jill shook her head, grabbing her bar and water and ducking out the door. Back in the Impala, she pulled out before tearing open the wrapper on the protein bar and wolfing it down. Her stomach pain eased a little. She gulped the water, trying to steer the boat of a car with one hand while she got the cap off. It was relief to wash away the sour taste.

Jill tried to think logically, order all the facts. She thought of David and the way he'd talk about facts and supposition, and the conclusions one could reasonably expect a jury to reach. Fact: David had an affair with Lyn Galpin. Fact: Lyn Galpin had given birth. Fact: their adoption attorney provided a death certificate for Sophia's birth mother. Fact: Lyn Galpin was dead. Fact: Lyn Galpin was Sophia's birth mother. Supposition: If Lyn Galpin was Sophia's birth mother then David was the birth father.

Jill felt another wave of nausea; how could he have fathered a child with someone else while he was with her? It would explain his sudden about-face on adoption. He'd never been interested, not before what happened to Ethan, even when they'd spent all those agonizing months trying and failing to conceive. She'd always been open to it, had known she'd have no trouble loving any child, but David hadn't wanted to discuss it, had gotten annoyed when she brought it up. Back then she'd concluded that the mere suggestion of adoption somehow called into question his masculinity.

And later, after Ethan? Jill's eyes filled remembering those first awful weeks after his death. They hadn't talked about another child then; it would have been obscene, as if they were trying to replace their son. The truth was that they'd barely talked at all, both of them moving as if in a trance, arranging the funeral, the burial, the return to an apartment both empty and tainted. They'd lived under the same roof and slept in the same bed, but Ethan's death had separated them as effectively as if he'd been the glue holding them together.

Until that day seven months later, Jill remembered it vividly, when David came home from work one evening and asked if *she* would consider adoption. "We could get a newborn," he'd said. "A new baby." She'd shaken her head at first, an automatic no to the thought of anyone in Ethan's place. They'd been sitting in their dining room, a place rarely used. They'd always eaten in the kitchen with Ethan pulled up next to them at the small, round table, first in a bouncy seat and then a high chair. She hadn't been able to eat at that table after his death. Too many shared meals, too much laughter. It hurt to remember him, the pain coming at odd moments, stinging and sudden, like being grazed by a jellyfish. The surprise of how things so small, so seemingly harmless—a stuffed toy they'd missed when they packed everything away, a little hat lying on a closet shelf—could cause so much pain. She'd become avoidant because of it, staying away from anything that reminded her of Ethan.

She remembered David reaching his hand across their dining room table and grasping hers. "We need to do this, Jill. We need someone to love again." And she'd burst into tears because she'd known it was true—the loss of Ethan had been like having her heart torn away and she needed another child to fill that awful, gaping hole. Neither of them mentioned going through the hell of trying again on their own. When he said that he'd heard about a young woman who wanted to give up her child, that Andrew could arrange a private adoption, Jill had never stopped to question the convenience of it all. How could she have failed to recognize that the similarities between Sophia and David were more than just a happy coincidence?

Jill gulped the rest of the water, crushing the bottle in her hand, feeling another surge of anger at David—the elaborate lies he'd told! What would he have done if she'd refused to consider adoption? If Lyn Galpin was Sophia's birth mother, then Bea Walsh was her grandmother. That was motivation enough to take her. But Bea wouldn't hurt her, would she? Except she'd killed her own husband.

Jill watched the streets pass outside, trying not to think about Ottilo unfolding that bloody nightgown. Bea Walsh hadn't left Pittsburgh when she vacated the Riverview Estates. She stayed so she could abduct Sophia. But where? Jill

434

passed a small strip mall with a grocery store on one end and a savings and loan on the other. An accounting firm, a yoga studio, a bakery. It was all a blur until a billboard caught her eye. She braked hard, pulling off the road, and the car directly behind her blared its horn in protest. She stared up at the billboard. It was an ad for a local real-estate firm. The same real-estate firm that had been on the flyer she'd found in the kitchen at the townhouse.

Chapter Forty-four

Day Twenty-Three

Top Ridge Realty sat, incongruously, on flat ground, boxed in by a Chinese restaurant and a tanning salon. The middle-aged woman behind the front desk stood up with a smile that faded when Jill asked her question.

"Bea Walsh? She's not my client, but I can check our database and see what comes up." She plopped back down with a resigned expression and pulled on the pair of reading glasses dangling from a chain around her neck.

It was a long shot, but Jill had nothing else to go on. She bounced on the balls of her feet while the woman clicked away at the keyboard. Even with the glasses the woman squinted at the computer screen. "Walsh, you said? No, I'm not showing any Walsh."

"You're sure?" Jill leaned over the counter trying unsuccessfully to see the screen. "Maybe it's under the first name, Bea."

"Bea Walsh, Bea Walsh . . . yep, here it is." Her lips pursed as if she'd bitten a lemon. "Apparently she's one of Patsy Duckworth's clients."

"Can I talk to Patsy?"

The woman scowled, taking off her glasses. "Sure, if you can find her."

"She's not here?"

"Nope. Just because she's a top producer, she thinks that she doesn't have to show up—"

Jill interrupted, "Do you know when she'll be back?"

"Your guess is as good as mine. She's supposed to be here now. I got called in to man the phones when she didn't show up. So, of course, I came. Because I don't like to let people down—"

"Did Bea Walsh buy property from Patsy Duckworth?"

The woman's eyes narrowed, but she slipped back on her glasses and looked at the monitor. "No. She didn't purchase a home."

The sense of defeat drained Jill's energy. She leaned against the desk, but the woman wasn't done looking at the screen. "She's not a buyer," she repeated. "She's a renter. In one of Patsy's listings."

Jill looked up. "Do you have that address?"

"I can't give out personal information," the woman said primly. She looked Jill over, her gaze lingering on the ratty jacket. "How do you know Bea Walsh?"

Jill said the first thing that came to her mind. "I'm her daughter."

"Really?" The woman didn't bother to hide her skepticism. "Then how come you don't *have* her address?"

"Um, I've been away. She emailed it to me, but my computer crashed."

"Hmm." The woman stood back up. "I'll have to check with our manager. She's actually in the midst of a closing right now. Why don't you call the office tomorrow, and I'll let you know what she said."

"It's urgent that I reach her today," Jill said. "Please."

The woman gave her another once-over before relenting. "Okay, I'll head back to the boardroom and see if I can interrupt her for a minute. Just wait here, miss—?"

"Walsh. Jill Walsh."

The woman bustled down the hallway. The minute her back was turned Jill ducked behind the desk and scrolled down the screen. There it was: 115 Fernwood Road. She grabbed a pen and scribbled the address on her hand, heading out the door just as the woman came back. "Hey, wait!"

Jill floored the Impala out of the parking lot. She mapped Fernwood Road on David's iPhone, shocked when she recognized some of the street names. This house couldn't be that far from hers—ten miles away at most. But they were hilly miles, and a few hills later she'd lost reception. Jill had to stop once and ask for directions and then double back to find the street, the sign partially obscured by an overhanging pine

438

branch. Underneath FERNWOOD the sign said PRIVATE ROAD. It ran almost straight up the hillside, roughly paved, as if the cheapest skim coats of asphalt had been laid over it year after year, only to rub away in patches, the potholes never properly filled, so the tires dipped down in spots and the entire car rocked.

Jill drove slowly, peering out the window through a lace curtain of snow, trying to scan house numbers on the mailboxes posted on either side of the road. This area was filled with private homes, but they were back far from the road, at the end of driveways that snaked off into trees so thick that the most she could see were houselights winking in the distance.

She didn't think this could be right, but it said Fernwood Road and she had nothing else to go on. Finally, halfway up the hillside on the right, she spotted a mailbox marked 115.

She turned sharply onto the driveway, which was really just another, albeit narrower, road paved with pea gravel, which sprayed noisily against the underbelly of the car. The Impala barely fit. The road snaked deeper and deeper up into the woods, and just as she'd convinced herself that the numbers were wrong, that there was no house at the end of this at all, the road suddenly widened, the canopy of trees parting like a curtain, and through the veil of snow, Jill could see a small stone house. There was a light on somewhere inside; it glowed faintly, but Jill could see no movement.

The snow out here had already covered the woods, and roads would be impassable soon. How would she even get this boat of a car back out of here? Jill pulled up and turned off the engine. She was so nervous she was panting, little white clouds hanging in the air in front of her.

David's cell phone was on the seat beside her, but there was no signal this deep in the woods. She slipped it in her coat pocket anyway. She thought back to fleeing the townhouse and decided to leave the keys in the ignition. Better to have them ready if she needed to make a quick exit.

She decided to go around the side of the house instead of to the front door, but when she stood on tiptoe to peer in a window all she could see in the dim light was an empty, innocuous bedroom. What if the real-estate agent had been wrong and this wasn't where Bea Walsh lived? Jill crept along the side of the house, but the next window was blocked with a curtain. She kept going. Around the back of the house, treading carefully across a snow-covered stone patio, only to stop short when she saw a door. Through the inset glass panel, she spied an empty kitchen. She tried the doorknob. To her surprise, it opened.

Jill ducked back around the corner, fully expecting the noise to alert someone, but nothing happened. She came back, stepped inside. The kitchen was deserted, but only just. Cupboard doors stood open. Dishes sat in the sink. An empty wine bottle and a dirty glass sat on the table, a full bottle on the counter nearby. Jill crept across the hardwood floor, waiting for someone to appear, but the house was eerily still. The small rooms were sparsely furnished with what looked like cast-off furniture—a scarred table with mismatched chairs in the dining room, an old velvet couch and even older box TV in the living room. The house was a circle; she came around to the front bedroom, the one she'd caught a glimpse of through a side window. When she turned on the light she saw a suitcase open on the bed with clothes tossed inside. Someone was packing to go.

Jill continued down the hall, trying to walk softly on the old wooden floors and pausing to listen outside another door before slowly turning the knob. It opened with a slight creak and she could see candles flickering faintly in the darkness, but nothing else. She felt along the wall for a light switch and the room came to life. Jill bit back a cry. There, taped to the wall, were photos of Sophia. Of Jill. Of David, too. But dozens of Sophia—at preschool, in the backyard, at the park. Jill felt as if every hair on her body stood at attention. There was a topographical map of Fox Chapel and a scribbled timeline for Jill and David's daily lives, along with what were obviously surveillance photos of the three of them and of their house and in their house. Jill's skin crawled. In every photo of Jill or David their faces had been scribbled over with black marker or scratched out.

There was another display to the right of that one, with a headshot of Sophia pinned next to a photo of another little girl. They looked similar, but the other photo was older, and the little girl in it had slightly darker hair and a dusting of freckles. The eyes and the smiles were alike; they could have been sisters. It was only when Jill looked over at a small, lace-covered table in the corner that she realized who it was.

Framed photos lit by votive candles had been arranged on either side of a portable DVD player that was open and quietly whirring. In the first framed photo, a woman sat on a beach chair laughing out loud, smile wide, blonde hair falling forward, her face beautiful and relaxed. The matching frame told a different story: A thin, wan patient in a hospital bed, wires and IV lines running from slack arms to monitors and drips, face puffy and purple-lidded eyes closed. Without the blonde hair, Jill wouldn't have known they were the same person. Lyn Galpin.

But it was the silent montage playing on the DVD that mesmerized Jill. Footage of Lyn Galpin filled the screen, photos and home movies— Lyn blowing out birthday candles, Lyn learning to ride a bike, Lyn walking across the stage at her high school graduation. Footage of the accident had been spliced together with video taken in the hospital, the camera zooming in on an emaciated Lyn lying there dead to the world. Jill startled as Bea Walsh stepped into the frame, moving to sit beside her daughter and lovingly brush the comatose woman's hair. It ended with that scene and then started all over again, the footage looped together for Bea Walsh to sit and watch.

For a moment Jill felt the squeeze of sympathy for another mother's pain. There was love and grief in this shrine, and a fierce longing to go back in time. Jill knew what that felt like, could empathize with the other woman, until she turned and saw the worktable that held wigs on stands, a bowl with familiar-looking keys, a box of latex gloves, and Ziploc bags holding what looked like human hair. Bea Walsh had been watching them for months. All those times when Jill thought she'd heard noises, or thought someone was in her space, in her things—it had been Bea. She'd infiltrated their lives and their house waiting for just the right moment to snatch their child.

And it hadn't been enough to take their only child—Bea's biological grandchild. She hadn't been content with that alone. There was a pile of news clippings on the worktable, too, articles from papers and magazines, all of the ones that questioned whether the Lassiters were murderers.

Bea Walsh had planned it all—every single move had been orchestrated to make sure that Jill and David were accused of killing their own child. Jill felt as if she'd stepped in something unbearably slimy. She yanked the cell phone from her pocket and dialed 911 as she fled the room, but she couldn't get a signal.

There was no one in the house. Jill made it back around to the kitchen and found a door to the basement. She crept down the stairs, listening for something more than the hum of a fluorescent light hanging from the low ceiling. She followed a narrow hallway lined with metal storage shelves that rattled slightly as she crept past. At the end of the hall a door stood ajar. She tiptoed across to it, peering around the corner, but it was only a dingy bathroom. There was a door to the left and a trail of something dark and sticky across the concrete floor that led from that door to another door on the far right, a door partially hidden behind a steel support pillar. Mounted to the top of that door-frame was a large, sliding bolt.

Jill forgot the need to be quiet; she forgot everything except her daughter. She ran to the door calling, "Sophia! Sophia, I'm coming!" The lock stuck; she struggled to open it, desperate to free her child who had to be waiting on the other side. Just as the bolt shot back, in the split second before her fingers fully turned the doorknob, something slammed against Jill's head.

The blow knocked her sideways. She cried out, clutching the side of her head. A woman with a drooping eyelid stepped back, panting, holding a handgun. "You shouldn't be here." Bea Walsh sounded strangely calm, or maybe that was an effect of being hit so hard. The room spun like a carnival ride. Jill dropped to the floor as Bea hefted the gun in her hand.

Jill couldn't get the room to stop moving. She tried to sit up. "Where's my daughter?"

"She's not yours," Bea said with an edge. "She doesn't belong to you, she belongs to Annie."

"Who's Annie?" Jill tried to say, but the name slurred.

"Lynanne was her full name. She started going by Lyn in college. Thought it sounded more sophisticated." The woman bent down next to her and started searching for something in Jill's pockets. "But she was always Annie to me." Jill tried to move. She pushed up on her hands and knees, lifting her face to look up at Bea Walsh.

"Please," she said, trying not to slur her words, "please don't hurt Sophia."

"There is no Sophia," the woman said and she swung the gun again.

Chapter Forty-five

Day Twenty-Three

Bea loaded the suitcase into the wide trunk of the Impala and got behind the wheel. Her arms were sore from dealing with both the real-estate agent and Jill Lassiter, and her chest ached. She reached automatically toward the glove compartment, only to remember that this wasn't her car and she'd forgotten to grab the pills. They were on the kitchen table, but she had to leave, there was no time to go back to get them. She'd have to pick up more on the road. Bea glanced in the rearview mirror as she pulled out, catching a last glimpse of the house lit up by the taillights. She'd grabbed what she'd could, taken what was important, but there hadn't been time to do everything. She'd left evidence behind including the old car, but there hadn't been time to move this one and come back for the other. Sloppy, Frank would have said, but she'd left him behind, too.

She glanced again in the rearview mirror and saw Annie fast asleep in the backseat covered with a blanket, the dog curled up beside her. "I'm here," she assured her. "I'll never leave you, Annie." She blinked, and it wasn't Annie, but Avery. "I'm here," she repeated.

The driveway was treacherous in the snow. The car was too large, too wide. Bea had to concentrate to keep on the curving, narrow path. She thought they could make it to Florida in two days, maybe less if she drove straight through. They would go back home, the two of them, and everything could be the way it once had been.

"We can make your room just like it was," she said to Annie. "I'll find that same furniture." Annie didn't stir, but Cosmo lifted his head at her voice. Bea had always said no to having dogs in the house. Too messy, she'd insisted when Annie tried to bring a stray home. Too much work. But this dog was different; he could stay with them. "You always wanted a dog," she said, but the child didn't answer.

The pain in her chest became deeper. It bore a hole through her, spreading along the lines of Bea's back like wings. Her hands gripped the steering wheel. In the seat next to her, Annie said, "It's okay, Mom, it's going to be okay now." The fire burning inside her chest roared through her and the car drifted left, finding a gap between the trees. Her body convulsed with a massive heart attack, forcing her foot down on the accelerator. The car surged forward, scraping over a boulder before crashing into something immovable. The windshield shattered, glass spraying across Bea's face as she slumped against the steering wheel. Horn blaring, dog frantically yipping—Bea dimly heard the cacophony of noise through her dying. Annie reached for her hand and she smiled at her daughter, reaching up to touch her face. "I've missed you so much."

A thud woke Jill. She opened her eyes, an effort, head throbbing. Darkness. A musty smell overlaid by something sharp and sour, metallic. Dampness, something wet and sticky against her back, her hand. She pressed and felt cold, hard floor. She was lying on her side, something pushed up against her back. She lifted her head and her eyes exploded in red and white starbursts. Her body warred with the pain, but her head landed back on the floor with a faint clunk. It hurt. It hurt like the worst headache she'd ever had. Her chest felt sore, like she'd been punched hard, every breath an ache. Her arm ached, too. She squeezed her eyes shut and that hurt. One hand tapped the sticky wet. She brought it to her face and gave it a cautious sniff. Blood.

Memory rushed back in, overwhelming her. "Sophia!" she screamed, but it came out gravelly, barely louder than a whisper. She had to get up, had to find Sophia. She moved to sit up and something dropped hard from her other hand as whatever was behind her moved. Jill reached out, hunting, and cried out as she touched someone. She scooted away, scrambling to her feet and staggering blindly, arms outstretched, searching for a light. She screamed again as something brushed lightly against her face. A string. She pulled it and light flooded the room, blinding her. A naked incandescent bulb swung back and forth above her. Squinting, she saw sloping concrete floor, a body lying next to the drain. It was a woman with a bloody, mangled faced, one eye barely visible, staring unblinking up at the light, her mouth a frightened *O*. Jill bent over her, trembling hands searching for a pulse, but the skin felt rubbery, inhuman. A gun was lying beside the body; that was what had fallen from Jill's hand.

She grabbed it, stumbling out into a hallway, struggling to hold the gun out in front of her. "Sophia?" She found the exit out to the garage, balancing against the old sedan while waiting for the garage door to slowly whir its way up and against the ceiling. Even with fading light, the contrast from the dark house to snow was blinding. She could hear a horn blaring somewhere in the distance. Jill blinked, head throbbing. Leo's car was gone; the woman had taken Leo's car. "Sophia!" Jill ran out into the snow, crying her daughter's name. She reached for David's cell phone, forgetting that there wasn't reception, but there wasn't any phone either—it must have fallen out in the house. The car in the garage. Jill ran back to it, yanking open the driver's door, but there were no keys in the ignition. She had to find the keys, she had to go after them. But she couldn't drive like this even if she found the keys. She had to find help. Desperate and disoriented, she took off running down the driveway.

Dusk in winter. Under the canopy of trees the world reduced to black and white—dark spires of trees and the snow-covered road that cut through them. She ran along the tire tracks left by the car, slipping and sliding, falling once into the cold, wet mess before scrambling to her feet and running on. She saw the glow from the car before the wreck itself, taillights casting red shadows across the snow like wine spilling across a white tablecloth. The Impala had gone off the road as if Bea intended to take a shortcut through the surrounding woods, but the front of the car had rolled across a boulder before crumpling against a solid tree trunk, smoke billowing from the engine. "Sophia!" Jill screamed, but it was impossible to hear over the noise of the horn. She ran to the wreckage, holding the gun up for protection, yanking at the closest passenger door, but it was locked. It smelled acrid, like burning plastic, and there was the faintest odor of something else. Gasoline? The dog startled her, leaping against the window with teeth bared, barking like crazy. Jill tried to see past him, to peer through the tinted windows, but he kept blocking her view. She could dimly see something or someone in the backseat, but it wasn't moving. "Sophia! Sophia!" Her throat felt hoarse from cold and screaming.

She ran around to the driver's side, slipping the gun in her pocket when she saw Bea slumped over the wheel. The driver's door was unlocked, but stuck from the crash. Jill fought to pull it open, gagging on smoke.

It finally gave and she shoved Bea's body off the horn, Jill's ears ringing in the sudden silence. The body fell against the passenger seat, blood smeared across her forehead, eyes blank and glazing over. Jill reached around to unlock the rear door to get in the backseat, the dog growling and yipping. The only other sound she could hear was her own keening. She could see a still, small form wrapped in a blanket on the backseat.

In that moment four years fell away, and she was opening the door at the end of the shadowed hallway, approaching the crib where the still, small body of her son lay. It couldn't happen again, she couldn't lose Sophia, too. Gasping, Jill yanked open the passenger door and a small white dog raced down the blanketed body, barking furiously, teeth bared.

"Sophia!" Jill reached toward the blanket, pulling at an edge, but the dog leapt, catching Jill's coat sleeve in its jaws, unable to get through the thick fabric to skin. She shook it off, stumbling back, her breaths coming shorter and louder as she saw fine blonde hair. "Please no, please no, please no," she repeated over and over, an increasingly desperate mantra as the child didn't move. She was afraid to touch Sophia, afraid to face the worst, but she had to know.

She found a branch on the ground and threatened the dog with it. "Move! Get away!" He bared his teeth, ears back, but cowering, and when she reached again toward Sophia he ran from her, huddling near the child's feet, yipping frantically. Jill's hand shook as she peeled back the blanket and touched Sophia's face. Her skin was warm. Afraid to hope, Jill pushed the blanket away and pressed a hand against her daughter's small abdomen to see if she was breathing.

Chapter Forty-six

Day Twenty-Three

Two seconds of agony. Three. And then, the slightest rise of Jill's hand. Sophia was alive. Sobbing with relief, Jill rapidly ran her hands over her daughter, checking for any visible injuries before gathering her into her arms and carrying her away from the smoking wreck. She had to get help, get both of them to a hospital, but David's phone was in the house. She carried Sophia back up the winding driveway, keeping the blanket wrapped protectively around her daughter while snow lashed her own face. Jill's arms ached, and the headache had gotten stronger. She was probably concussed. Even if she could find the keys, it probably wasn't safe for her to drive. As she reached the open garage, motion-sensor security lights came on, startling her. She didn't stop until she'd carried Sophia into the living room, where she laid her on the sofa and tried to bring her around, rubbing her hands and tapping at her cheeks. "Sophia, wake up. Wake up, baby." She gently pushed back her eyelids; Sophia's eyes were disoriented, rolling in their sockets. She'd obviously been drugged. "C'mon, Sophie, c'mon, wake up."

Finally, Sophia stirred, her eyes fluttering open and shut. "Wha-a-at?" she slurred, and then her gaze found Jill's face and she seemed to focus clearly for a second. A trace of a smile as she said in a faint, hoarse voice, "Mommy?"

"Yes, it's Mommy, I'm here," Jill said, laughing with relief as she wiped away fresh tears.

"Thirsty," Sophia said next, one small hand rising to her throat. She licked dry, chapped lips.

"I'll get you a drink. Just stay here, okay?"

The little girl moved her head in what might have been a nod, and Jill raced to the kitchen, filling a coffee mug at the sink. She carried it back to the living room with shaking hands, water slopping over the sides, to find Sophia sitting up, the blanket falling around her shoulders. Jill noticed the shorn hair, the boy's clothing. "Where's Cosmo?" Sophia asked.

"Who?" Jill held the mug to her lips and Sophia drank greedily, her own small hands rising to hold the cup along with her mother. She wiped at her mouth and said again, "Cosmo."

"Who's Cosmo?"

"My doggie."

"He's outside," Jill said.

"I needs him," Sophia said. "He's a good doggie."

Jill took her gingerly on her lap. "Does anything hurt?"

"No, just my head is knocking." She pointed at

her head with a small index finger, and Jill kissed it, then her hand and her face.

"Stop it, Mommy," Sophia protested, trying to push her away, and Jill laughed tearily.

"I've missed you so much, my one and only ever Sophia," she said, rocking her daughter gently.

"I missed you, too, Mommy. Why didn't you come for me? I wanted you to come get me."

Jill squeezed her hard. "I wanted to, baby, I wanted to so much, but I didn't know where you were."

"I'm not a baby."

"I know," Jill said, smiling through fresh tears. "You're a big girl. Can my big girl wait here while Mommy finds her phone?"

Jill hunted through the house, but either she'd dropped David's iPhone outside or Bea had taken it with her. She'd taken almost everything else. The photos of the Lassiters had been hastily stripped from the walls, the worktable wiped clean. Gone were the map of Fox Chapel and the layout of Jill's house. Strips of tape were all that remained, some with the corners of paper still stuck to them. The shrine had been hastily dismantled, the DVD player and framed photos taken, the lace cloth left, hanging askew. Something had been left behind on the shelf underneath the table. She picked up a small book with journal embossed on its leather cover. Jill flipped through the pages long enough to see that it was a record of the affair between Lyn Galpin and David. Jill didn't want to read the sordid details; she left it on the table and continued searching for her phone.

Jill came back through the kitchen and noticed a door standing open. The basement. The phone could have fallen out when she was down there. Jill hesitated. She didn't want to go back down there, but she had to. "I'll be right back," she called to Sophia before finding the light switch and starting down the wooden steps.

The lights she'd left on cast yellow pools, creating shadows in the dark space. Jill crept around the body in the laundry area, and spotted the phone near the drain. She tried not to look at the poor woman as she grabbed it off the concrete floor. As she left, she remembered another, almost hidden door and went to look inside. A windowless room of concrete block. So this was where Bea had kept Sophia. It was monstrous and yet the woman had obviously cared about her, too—the pink walls, the children's furniture and toys. Jill spotted Blinky on the bed. She grabbed the toy and a child's brown coat discarded on the floor, and ran back upstairs.

Sophia sat on the couch where she'd left her. She smiled and held out her arms for Blinky. She didn't smile at the coat. "It'll keep you warm," Jill said.

Sophia shook her head. "No. It's ugly."

Jill smiled; whatever had happened in this house, it hadn't crushed her daughter's spirit. "Just put it on for now, okay? I promise you don't have to wear it anymore after today."

She paced the room with the phone held high, searching for reception. She hit 911, but quickly pushed the end button. What would the police think when they found Bea dead and Jill there with Sophia? Would they believe her story? She dialed Andrew's number instead. He answered on the first ring.

"Jill? Where are you? The police have issued an APB; everyone is looking for you. You have got to turn yourself in."

"I've found Sophia."

"What? What do you mean you've found her? Where? Is she okay?"

"She's fine, she's fine." Jill laughed shakily. "But we need to get to the hospital." She tried to explain what had happened—Lyn Galpin, her mother, the dead woman in the basement, and the gun Jill had been left holding. Andrew interrupted her.

"Have you called the police?"

"No, not yet—"

"Okay, that's okay, I'll call them now. You just wait with Sophia. And she's okay?"

"Yes, yes, she's okay, a little groggy. She's been drugged, but she seems okay."

"Good, just sit tight. I'll be there right away."

"Okay."

Jill pulled the blanket around Sophia and held her close. It was almost as cold inside as out. Bea Walsh must have stopped paying the gas bill. Jill just hoped that the electricity wouldn't give out before the police and Andrew arrived.

"Is Daddy coming to get us?" Sophia asked.

Jill swallowed hard, giving her daughter an extra squeeze. She'd forgotten to ask about David. "No, Daddy can't come, but Uncle Andrew is coming instead."

"Mommy, I want Cosmo," Sophia begged. "What if he's cold outside?"

Jill gave in and opened the front door, but the dog didn't appear even when Sophia called for him. "He has fur, honey," she tried to reassure Sophia, carrying her on her hip as she paced the front of the house. Sophia dozed off against her shoulder. Jill was so tired, but she couldn't stop moving or she might fall asleep, and she knew she shouldn't fall asleep with a concussion.

At last she heard the crunch of gravel, and Jill zipped the coat on Sophia and carried her down the front steps as headlights emerged from the dark woods. The motion-sensor security lights came on again as Andrew's black BMW pulled into view. Jill blinked against the glare, surprised that he'd made it there before the police.

"Amazing, I can't believe you found her," he said, striding over to them, with arms outstretched. "Come give Uncle Andrew a hug, sweetheart."

Sophia didn't object, giving him a sleepy smile, so Jill handed her over. "Did you see the crash?"

He nodded, holding Sophia close. "This driveway is terrible. I think branches scratched off some paint."

The lights from the garage illuminated his car, snow beginning to cover the windshield. Jill stared at the side of the car, head starting to throb again. She saw a scratch along the side and a crack in one alloy wheel.

"I'll call 911 now. I didn't want some SWAT team beating me out here and jumping to the wrong conclusion," Andrew said, looking around at the house and the woods. "You're sure that woman in the car was Lyn Galpin's mother?"

Jill nodded, yawning. She had to stay awake, but the desire for sleep was overpowering. In a daze, her eyes kept being drawn back to the wheel.

"We need to get you two to the hospital," Andrew said, handing Sophia back to her. "Go ahead and get in the car, and I'll just do a quick run-through of the house while I call the cops. Where's the other b-o-d-y?"

"Basement."

"Oh, and what about the g-u-n? Is that in the basement, too?"

Jill shook her head, shifted Sophia to one arm so she could pull it out of her coat pocket.

"Jesus, careful." Andrew shook out a hand-kerchief and took the gun from her, tucking it in his own coat. "Sit down before you drop. I'll be quick." He took off up the front steps, while Jill carried Sophia over to Andrew's car. She opened the passenger door and realized there wasn't a car seat. "Just sit here for a minute," she murmured to Sophia, stooping to put her down in the backseat. She stood back up and looked again at the side of the car. Something about it was bothering her. Maybe it was David rubbing off on her. He hated having any marks on his car. David's car was pristine.

And suddenly Jill understood. She'd seen that cracked wheel on the accident footage playing on the looping video. The same cracked wheel was on the car that Lyn Galpin had been pursuing.

David's car.

Except it wasn't. It wasn't David's . . . it was Andrew's.

"Okay!" Andrew's voice made her jump. Jill turned too fast, dazedly watching as he came running down the front steps. "I tried to call the police, but I couldn't get through. You two wait in the house and I'll find reception down the hill. Here, I'll carry Sophia." He stepped toward the car door, but Jill blocked his path. Andrew's smile wavered. "Jill? What's wrong?"

"It was *you*."

"What was me? C'mon, it's too cold to stand out

here." He smiled again, the confident smile of a man used to getting his way. So much like David. David, who admired Andrew enough to take his advice on so many things, including purchasing the same model BMW.

"*You* were the one Lyn Galpin was trying to catch."

Andrew laughed. A hollow sound. "You're not making any sense, Jill. We need to get you to an ER pronto."

"I saw the footage. It's *your* car she was pursuing, not David's."

"I don't know what you're talking about—" Andrew started, but Jill cut him off.

"That's the same crack," she said, jabbing a finger at his wheel. "That crack is on the car Lyn Galpin chased. It's in the police footage. It wasn't David, it was you! *You* were the one she was chasing when she crashed."

Andrew barely glanced at his car, already shaking his head, dismissing her. "No, that damage came from the trees crowding this driveway."

"Stop bullshitting me, Andrew! I know it's the same!"

"Okay, Jill, you need to take a breath and calm down," he said, putting a hand on her arm.

She knocked it off. "Don't tell me to calm down! You're the 'D' in her journal. 'D' stood for Drew, not David! You're the reason we've been going through this hell!"

"I don't even know the crazy woman who lived here," Andrew protested.

"You knew her daughter—"

"It wasn't like that—"

"You got her pregnant. It was you. And then you decided to give that child to us!"

"Let's go in the house—we can talk, I can explain."

"Was this adoption even legal?" Jill's throat was hoarse from shouting.

"Of course it was legal!" Andrew snapped. For a moment there was no expression on his face, the light outlining his aquiline nose and perfect cheekbones. He might have been a statue in a museum, but then his lips curved again, this time into a tight, nasty little smile. "What do you want me to say, Jill, that I had sex outside my marriage? Okay, fine, I cheated. Just like your husband. Just like plenty of other men—"

"Don't try to pretend this is the same!"

"But the girl wouldn't get an abortion. I would have paid for it—she didn't have to arrange anything—but she insisted on having the child. At least I convinced her that she should give it up for adoption. She couldn't keep the baby—it would ruin us both! You needed a baby and she had a baby to give. Everyone wins."

"Don't pretend that you thought about anyone except yourself!"

"And you wouldn't have?" Andrew said. He

snorted, a mirthless sound. "The stupid girl was deluded. She thought we could be a happy little family. As if I'd jeopardize everything I worked for, everything my father's worked for, to set up house with some piece of tail?"

"God, it wasn't just a Halloween mask," Jill said with amazement. "You really are a monster."

"Don't look at me like that." Andrew grabbed her by the shoulders and gave her a firm shake. "C'mon, Jill—don't be like this. It wasn't just about me—it was you and David, too. I was protecting you."

"Let go of me!" Jill struggled to break free, but he only held on tighter, trying to make her look at him.

"You need to listen to me! *She* signed the adoption papers—I didn't force her. Then six months later she went crazy and wanted the baby back. Wanted me to contest the adoption! I couldn't do that to you—I couldn't let you and David lose another child."

"This had nothing to do with us—you were protecting yourself!"

"Would you stop saying that?" He shook her again, much harder this time, and Jill screamed at the blinding pain in her head.

"Be quiet!" Andrew said, voice and eyes panicked. "Just shut up and listen to me and you'll understand!" He smashed his hand against Jill's mouth to silence her, but then Sophia began wailing. She slid out of the car and ran to her mother's defense, flailing at Andrew.

"Let go of Mommy! Don't hurt Mommy!"

At her screams, something small and white shot from the garage and sank its teeth into Andrew's ankle. He yelled, jerking his hands off Jill. She grabbed Sophia and took off running down the driveway, away from the house. Behind her, she could hear Andrew cursing as he tried to shake Cosmo off his leg. A muffled thud and then the dog whined, a pitiful sound.

"Jill, come back, I didn't mean to hurt you," Andrew called, a hint of the old charm on top of desperation. She looked back and the lights from the garage illuminated him standing at the edge of the woods—hair lifting, top coat flapping around his legs.

Jill ran into the cover of the trees, stumbling through the darkness with Sophia's sobs rising. "Ssh, baby, it's okay, ssh," she crooned, doing her best to soothe her. Jill didn't turn back to see if Andrew was following on foot; she didn't have to. She could feel him coming after them. She passed the steaming wreckage of Bea's car, the smell of the gasoline strong now, and kept going. Hadn't anyone been woken by the crash? Surely it had to have drawn attention, but most of the other houses were far away and no one had their windows open in this weather.

Over Sophia's whimpering she could hear cracking as frozen twigs and branches snapped under her feet. A louder, whooshing sound and Jill turned in time to see the car wreck go up in flames.

Jill scrambled away, stumbling in her haste. She fell to the ground, landing hard on her shoulder to keep from crushing Sophia. Jill struggled to her feet and hoisted her daughter back up. Sophia was crying, but otherwise seemed okay. Jill's left shoulder felt sore; she saw a trail of dark spots in the snow and realized she must have cut herself on something. Fear kept the pain at bay, spurred her on. "It's okay, honey, just a little longer."

She ran downhill as fast as she could, but it felt like lumbering between the snow and the weight of Sophia. Jill could hear Andrew struggling, cursing as his flat-soled wing tips slipped in the snow, but he wasn't carrying a child. She could hear him gaining. Jill swallowed hard, tasting smoke. She hoped that she'd make it to the main road in time to flag down a car before he caught up.

Her mouth tasted like blood; her arms screamed for release. She couldn't go any further; she paused to rest behind the wide trunk of an old tree. Sophia struggled to get down, but Jill wouldn't let her go.

"Jill?" Andrew called; his warm voice seemed to echo through the trees. "Jill, wait for me. You and Sophia need help. You know I'd never hurt you."

465

She didn't know that. She didn't know anything anymore. Not after the way he shook her. Her head was throbbing. She could hear the sound of Andrew's footsteps crunching through the snow as he came closer, searching for them.

"Sophia, don't you want to go see Daddy?" Andrew called.

"Let me go—" Sophia said, but Jill clapped a hand over her mouth, pressing both of them back against the trunk of the tree, her feet slipping in the thick carpet of snow-covered pine needles. She couldn't put Sophia down, she wouldn't. She could feel her daughter's breath hot against her hand, then the warmth of tears. Maybe Jill was wrong. But she'd been so scared at the way he put his hand across her mouth.

She moved ever so slightly to see around the trunk of the tree. In the light from the flames, she could see Andrew standing about twenty feet away, looking for them. For a moment, before he spotted her, she saw Andrew's face contorted by rage, the face of a powerful man angry at being thwarted. He shifted, and looked right at them, his face morphing back into its friendly mask, but something glinted in his hand. The gun.

Terrified, Jill ran, holding Sophia tight as she raced down the hill. She hoped the startled cry behind her meant that Andrew had slipped, but she couldn't stop to look back. A pinprick of light pierced the dark woods. Was she imagining it?

No, there it was again. Light shining through the trees. She could see the roofline of another house. Jill sobbed with relief. Surely someone would help them.

The house came into view as Jill got closer, a large brick colonial sitting at the middle of a circular driveway, lights blazing in multiple windows. She ran to the front door, setting Sophia down in front of her as she banged the brass knocker repeatedly against the wooden door. "Help! We need help!"

"The man got a boo-boo and he's went to sleep," Sophia said.

"Don't worry, honey," Jill said. "He'll wake up." But there was no answer. No sign of movement through the curtained windows. She looked behind her and thought she caught a glimpse of a figure moving through the trees. "For God's sake, open the door!" she shouted, slamming the knocker so hard it chipped the paint.

"Mommy, he's here," Sophia whispered, peering around Jill's legs. Jill looked over her shoulder and saw Andrew stepping onto the driveway. There was nowhere to go; they were trapped. Jill rattled the doorknob and the door suddenly opened. She fell inside, dragging Sophia with her and slammed the door behind them, locking it.

"Hello?" She called, but no one answered. The

lights were on in the living room; there was a fire burning low in the hearth and a book face-down on a table as if someone had been sitting there, but the chair was empty. "Is anyone home? Please—I need help! Call the police!" Her voice seemed to echo through the house.

"The man's went to sleep," Sophia repeated, tugging on Jill's jacket. "He no wakes up."

Jill looked at her. "What do you mean? Where did he go to sleep?"

"Out there." Sophia pointed toward the door. Jill looked in that direction and thought she saw a shadow at the window.

"Let's check upstairs, okay?" she said, scooping Sophia back up with one arm and grabbing the brass poker from the set of fireplace tools with her free hand. She hustled up the stairs, calling out as she ran. "Hello? Is someone here?"

She held onto Sophia's hand, dragging her down a hall decorated with old-fashioned floral-and-vine wallpaper. Empty room after empty room. Where had the owners gone? Jill could hear Andrew back at the front door, rattling the knob. One bedroom had an old phone sitting on a nightstand, but when Jill yanked up the receiver there was no dial tone. She remembered David's iPhone and pulled it from her pocket. Still no reception. Jesus Christ. She opened a closet. It was dark and smelled of dust and mothballs, but it was stuffed with bagged clothes and there were

468

shoe boxes piled high on the floor. She shifted the pile and pushed aside clothes in the back to make a spot. "We're playing a game with Uncle Andrew," she said. "You're going to hide in here and be very, very quiet, okay?"

Sophia grabbed her around the legs. "But I want to stay with you!"

"You have to stay here now. Mommy's going to come back and get you, but you have to stay here for now." Jill tried to peel off Sophia's hands, one at a time, but as soon as she freed one, Sophia latched on with the other.

"No, Mommy! Don't let go!"

Jill knelt and hugged her hard. "I'm never letting you go. I'll be right back. You hold onto Blinky and be very, very quiet or we won't win the game, okay?"

Sophia nodded, clutching Blinky, but her lip trembled. Jill lifted her into the spot and tucked the bags and boxes around her. Sophia whimpered as Jill pulled the closet door, leaving it open just a crack. She fled along the hall checking other bedrooms, but couldn't find another phone. She tried the cell phone again, but this time there was too much static and the 911 operator couldn't understand her.

She heard glass shattering downstairs. He'd found a way inside. It was just a matter of time until he found them. Jill gripped the poker. It crossed her mind that she hoped Sophia wouldn't see Andrew killing her. She ducked into yet another uninhabited room, still clutching David's iPhone as if somehow, miraculously, it could save her. And then she had an idea.

Chapter Forty-seven
Day Twenty-Three

The sound of floorboards creaking. Andrew was searching downstairs; she could hear doors being opened. The desire to run was overwhelming. Jill grabbed hold of the doorknob to stop herself. She shrank back, slowing her breathing, willing herself to become invisible. She tried not to think about Sophia. A distinct footstep, then another. He was coming upstairs; he would find them.

"Mommy? Daddy? I need you! Where are you?" Sophia's voice carried in the silence of the house.

Jill's eyes teared at the sound, but she stayed where she was. It was too late to come out. Too late to do anything but stay where she'd hidden, hoping that if he found Sophia, Andrew wouldn't try to kill her, too.

"Daddy, Mommy, I need you! Mommy!"

Footfalls pounded up the stairs and down the hall into a bedroom. They stopped abruptly. Andrew's voice exclaimed, "What the fuck?" Jill stepped out from behind the bedroom door with the poker raised just as he stood from picking up David's cell phone. She'd left it on the center of the floor playing an old recording of Sophia's voice.

The poker missed his head, landing against his shoulder instead, but it was hard enough to make him drop the gun. It skittered across the wooden floor and for a split second Andrew and Jill stared after it. She lunged first, throwing the poker like a spear at him as she dove for the gun. He cried out and she knew the poker had hit him, but then he landed on top of her, his weight like a hammer nailing her to the floor, his arm reaching alongside hers, each of them with a hand splayed wide, skin taut and white, desperate to reach the gun. His hand was larger, fingers longer. His fingertips brushed the metal. He would kill her.

Adrenaline surging, Jill reached her other hand up and around her head to claw at his face. Andrew shrieked in pain. "Shit!" He reared up, grasping her hair with his free hand and shoved her face into the ground, but he'd shifted his weight off just enough that she managed to slide forward. She searched blindly, keening, her hand tearing at the floor until it closed around cold metal. Andrew yanked her back by the leg, but she twisted around in his grip, grasping the handgun in both hands and aiming it straight at his face.

"Get the fuck off me!"

He dropped her leg, rearing back. Jill scrambled up, holding the gun outstretched. It felt heavier than she would have expected, a substantial weight. Andrew got slowly to his feet, hands held up, palms out.

"Be careful," he said. "That could go off." He sounded surprisingly calm, sliding back into his usual charm even if his appearance belied his tone. Dead twigs and leaves were caught in his once beautiful coat, a pocket ripped, the high sheen wing tips coated with debris. The camera-ready hair now fell in limp strands; angry red gouges from her fingernails tore down one side of his face from eyelid to jaw. "I'm sorry I scared you, Jill. This has all been a big misunderstanding. Let's put the gun away, and we can sit down and talk."

"Give me your phone," Jill demanded. As Andrew started to lower his hands, she shouted, "No! Just one hand. Slowly!"

He raised an eyebrow at her, but reached into the breast pocket of his coat and took out his phone. "I wasn't going to hurt you, Jill. I'd never hurt you. You've got to believe me." He held the phone out to her, but she shook her head.

"Place it on the ground, then kick it toward me."

"C'mon, Jill, this isn't the movies." He smiled and there was something both desperate and mocking in it. "I'm not a bad guy."

"Just do it!"

Andrew sighed, giving her wounded little-boy eyes as he slowly placed the phone on the ground and slid it across to her. It landed near her feet. Jill kept her eyes on him as she stooped to pick it up with one hand, the gun still raised in the other.

Andrew's phone always had connectivity. She dialed with her left hand, listening to a sporadic ringing, and then finally, blessedly, a voice: "911, what is your emergency?"

"There's been a car crash, I need help—"

"Are you injured?"

"Yes. I need the police to come to—"

"What is your location, ma'am?"

"Fernwood—" The phone died. "Hello? Hello?" Jill pressed redial, but she couldn't get reception. "Damn it all!"

Andrew's hands lowered. "Keep them up!" Jill shouted, shoving the phone in her pocket and gripping the gun again with both hands. He smiled, taking a small step toward the door.

"They're not coming, Jill."

"Stand still!" The wound on her shoulder—or was it fear—had weakened her grip; the gun shook in her hands. Sweat, or was it blood, dripped into her eyes. She blinked rapidly, trying to hold the gun steady.

"You're not going to shoot me," Andrew said, taking another step back toward the door. "It's not in you to shoot anyone."

"Stop moving!"

"Mommy?" A tiny, trembling voice. Sophia stood in the doorway.

Jill's gaze shifted from Andrew to her daughter. "Get back, Sophia!"

But her moment's inattention allowed Andrew

474

enough time to step to the door and catch the child. She screamed as he grabbed her, holding her high against his chest like a human shield, one hand clasping her small neck.

"Let her go!"

"Drop the gun or I'll hurt her!"

Jill stared into her daughter's wide, frightened eyes, watching her dangling helplessly in Andrew's grip. She slowly lowered the gun.

"That's it," Andrew said, "drop it—"

The gunshot to his knee cut him off mid-sentence. He shrieked, an inhuman, high-pitched sound, releasing his grip on Sophia as he collapsed backward on the floor. Jill ran forward, holding the gun on him as she grabbed Sophia, trying to shield her from seeing the blood pouring onto the floor.

"You bitch!" Andrew pulled at Jill, trying to climb up her, and Sophia screamed, flailing at him with tiny fists.

"Let go of my mommy!"

Jill kicked him off, carrying Sophia out into the hall. She headed for the stairs, looking back as Andrew crawled into the hallway after them.

"You can't leave me here, you stupid bitch! I'll bleed out!"

She only moved faster, helping Sophia climb down the stairs and walk back toward the front of the house. Andrew's cries followed them out the door.

Jill dropped the gun in one of the stone planters flanking the front walk. Up the hill the night sky was lit by fire. Flames from the wreck had caught the dry branches of nearby trees, traveling from one to the next like birthday candles being lit on a cake. She hurried down the driveway holding Sophia's hand. Neither of them had boots on, and Sophia's legs were so much shorter than Jill's. After a minute, her mother hoisted her up once again in her arms, trudging down the driveway toward the road while the canopy above them burned.

"It's going to be okay," she told Sophia when they got to the road, but Jill was losing her grip. "Wrap your arms around me." She felt her daughter's small hands lock around her neck.

They were clinging to each other, staggering down the snow-covered road, when Jill finally heard the wail of approaching sirens.

Epilogue

October 2014

In what had become a weekly ritual, Jill dropped David off for physical therapy before taking their daughter, as promised, to the park.

"Have a good time, you know I won't," David said, groaning in an exaggerated way to make Sophia giggle, before he got out of the car with his cane and limped into the building. The park was only a ten-minute drive from the medical center.

It was a hot afternoon and Jill held Sophia's hand as they crossed the road to the playground, clutching the dog's leash in the other. "C'mon, Mommy, c'mon!" Sophia pulled free and ran toward the slide, outwardly unscathed despite what happened in this same spot little more than a year ago.

"Children are surprisingly resilient," the therapist said.

Cosmo pulled against the leash, straining to follow Sophia. The dog was a constant reminder of what had happened to her, to all of them. But after the police found him half-dead in the snow, Jill couldn't deny him a home. Cosmo had saved their lives. Some mornings, Jill would find him curled up in bed next to Sophia and she'd say that he'd comforted her when she had a bad dream. The nightmares were becoming less frequent, fading away along with the memories. Given her young age, it was likely that Sophia wouldn't remember much of what happened as she grew up, if she remembered anything at all.

Adults weren't so lucky. What had happened had imprinted itself on Jill in ways that could never be erased. "You'll probably always feel the pain," the therapist had told her, "but it will hurt less over time."

She and David still moved around each other tentatively, like guests in each other's lives. Jill supposed it would be like that for a long time while they found their way to a new normal. So far, there had been no big discussion about the future of their marriage. At first because David had been physically unable to, and later because having all three of them back together under one roof had seemed like too big a miracle to mess with.

"Slow down!" Jill hurried after Sophia, careful to keep her in sight. The sun beat down, just like last week, and the park was crowded. A nice day so late in the fall meant everyone was out enjoying the sunshine. Sophia clambered up and around the plastic fort and slid down the slide with other children while Jill stood to one side with other parents, watching. A slightly older boy ran up the slide the wrong way, catching her eye. Something about him seemed familiar, but it wasn't until she saw Sophia playing with him that Jill made the connection. She moved closer to get a better look. "Andy?"

The boy looked up from his play, giving Jill a jolt because Andrew Graham's namesake looked like a miniature version of his father. Just then, a familiar voice called, "Andy, let's go!"

Jill turned to see Paige Graham standing across the field by her SUV flanked by her two other children, the oldest in a little league uniform. Her middle son took off running toward the car and before Jill could stop her, Sophia bolted with him. "Paige!" she called, running fast across the field, her blonde hair flowing behind her like a kite.

"Sophia, come back!" Jill ran after her, Cosmo bulleting along at her side. When Paige Graham spotted them, her immediate reaction was to turn her back, opening the SUV's rear door and ushering her kids inside.

Jill hadn't seen her since that awful day last November when she'd confronted Paige on the soccer field. She had no desire to see her now. Paige's husband hadn't bled out in the empty house; the police rescued him in time. Andrew had done his best to deny his part in the whole sordid mess, but the police had plenty of evidence that corroborated Jill's story, including Liz

Galpin's own journal entries. They were soon leaked to a tabloid. Senator Graham hired a top civil defense team, but even he couldn't stop the stream of women who came forward to detail for the media the full extent of his son's sexual aggression.

Jill ran faster to catch Sophia, grabbing her just before she got to Paige, but it was too late to turn back, too late to pretend she hadn't seen her.

"How are you?" Jill said as Andy climbed into the backseat to join his brothers.

Paige closed the door on them. "We're fine," she said, Southern charm kicking in automatically, but the smile was small and tight, her eyes cold. She looked unchanged—the same beautifully coiffed hair and perfectly applied makeup, the same attention to detail in clothing that she'd always shown.

"I got a dog," Sophia announced, reaching for the leash that Jill held. "His name's Cosmo."

Paige stared down at her for a moment, face expressionless, before shifting her gaze to Jill. There had been a change—Paige was thinner, her face harder. "What do you want, Jill?" she said, her perfect exterior cracking. "Haven't you done enough damage to my family?"

"I didn't do anything to you—your husband did that damage all by himself." Facing disbarment and a slew of sexual harassment lawsuits, Andrew had taken down a favorite gun from his own collection and ended his humiliation, though not his family's.

His widow's face turned white, then red. She glanced around, afraid that someone had overheard, before leaning closer to Jill, hands twisting the wedding ring set she still wore. "You're no better than I am, so don't think you are. Standing here all smug with your *bastard*." She hissed the word, voice shaking with barely repressed rage. Jill stepped back, pulling Sophia with her, but Paige followed. "You think I didn't know?" She gave a harsh laugh. "Of course I knew. I knew about every single whore he bedded."

Revulsion rose in Jill. She couldn't believe she'd ever felt inferior to this woman. "I feel sorry for you."

Paige kept talking as if she couldn't hear her. "None of them mattered. I had the home and the children and the money. He came home to *me*."

Jill turned her back, pulling her daughter and the dog away. Sophia glanced back over her shoulder and then up at Jill. "Why is she mad, Mommy?"

"Life didn't turn out the way she wanted," Jill said, struggling to keep her voice even. She felt an odd sort of pity for Paige. Her high expectations hadn't been met, but then when were anybody's? Jill thought of the album that Detective Ottilo had returned, of how she'd wept over the pages of Ethan's short life, of how many other parents she knew turning the pages of the albums that she'd made for them. She'd wept again as she wrote a letter to her son, saying good-bye before tucking it in the album's final pages.

When Jill was younger she'd believed that if she worked hard and planned with care that life would proceed in a sensible, orderly fashion, that she'd be guaranteed the family that she'd wanted complete with a matching set of perfect photos to celebrate every milestone. Except life didn't work that way. Life was more often about what happened outside of the frame, on the margins. But love happened in the margins, too, and in the end love was the only infinite thing.

Jill clasped Sophia's hand in hers and started back across the field, their little dog running ahead.

Dear Ethan,

I have tormented myself with asking why you had to go. Why, when so many children are born and thrive did you have to die? Why, when other people abuse their children and take them for granted, did you, who were so longed for and so adored, have to slip away like a forgotten guest at a party?

But "why" is the wrong question. The right question, I've come to see, is not why you had to die, but how you ever came to be in the first place. Life is so fragile and such a great mystery. It is beautiful and terrible and more often than not both of these things at once. I don't know why you had to go, but however brief your life it did have meaning. You were wanted and cherished and I treasured every day I had with you. I will never forget you.

Your spirit will live on in me, your dad, and most of all your sister. I see you in her every day, but she has her own life to live and I can't tether her to yours. I have your album on a place of honor on a shelf, but please don't judge me a bad mother if it gathers some dust. I need to let you go, just a little, so I can live. I know that we will meet again some day and when that day comes, you'll have to forgive me if I want to spend all of eternity holding you.

Love forever,
Mommy

Acknowledgments

Thank you to Leslie Williams, whose love and devotion to her children helped inspire this book. Thank you, also, to Abby Leviss, who writes so poignantly about loss on her blog, Missing Maxie. And thank you to the Now I Lay Me Down to Sleep (NILMDTS) organization and the work of all bereavement photographers, whose generous service to grieving families also inspired this novel.

Thank you to the Fox Chapel Police Department and especially Sgt. Mike J. Stevens and Officer Richard Klein for patiently talking me through police investigative techniques and the particulars of major crimes investigation in Allegheny County. Any mistakes are entirely my own.

Thank you to Pittsburgh readers for indulging my creativity with the geography of my adopted hometown: I've added street names and places that don't exist in the 'Burgh.

Thanks to my lovely and talented agent, Rachel Ekstrom, and all the wonderful people at the Irene Goodman Literary Agency (IGLA). Thank you to my two editors extraordinaire, Jaime Levine and Anne Brewer, and the incredible team at Thomas Dunne/St. Martin's Press; I'm privileged to be one of your authors.

A special thank you for the support of my writing pals, especially Nicole Peeler, Annette Dashofy, Meredith Mileti, Shelly Culbertson, Kathryn Miller Haines, Lila Shaara, Meryl Neiman, Nancy Martin, Kathleen George, and Heather Terrell who read early drafts, brainstormed plot complications, helped me navigate social media, and in general served as sounding boards for this book. You're some of the smartest, funniest women I know.

And for their encouragement, thank you to my friends and walking buddies, Lisa Lundy, Mary Lou Linton-Morningstar, Marilyn Fitzgerald, Sharon Wolpert, and especially Donna Wallace, who was an early reader and champion of this novel.

Finally, the most heartfelt thanks to my husband, Joe Mertz, and our children, Joe and Maggie, for your constant love and support.

Center Point Large Print
600 Brooks Road / PO Box 1
Thorndike, ME 04986-0001 USA

(207) 568-3717

US & Canada:
1 800 929-9108
www.centerpointlargeprint.com